TRIALS OF THE MIND

Brian O'Madigan

authorHOUSE®

AuthorHouse™
1663 Liberty Drive, Suite 200
Bloomington, IN 47403
www.authorhouse.com
Phone: 1-800-839-8640

First published by AuthorHouse   12/17/2007

ISBN: 978-1-4343-4328-4 (sc)

Printed in the United States of America
Bloomington, Indiana

This book is printed on acid-free paper.

CHAPTER 1

In the enclosed observatory of a military base on a small moon, in a solar system far from his home, a tall veteran stared hopefully into the speckled blackness of space. The breeze from the air ventilators toyed with the graying hair on the tall man's temples as he eagerly scrutinized the stars above him. He frowned in concentration as he noticed the irregular speck above that he had been unconsciously searching for. Tightening the battle worn skin of his face as he squinted, the veteran strained to follow the movements of the rapidly disappearing object.

The small speck flashed through the darkness above, and finally disappeared in a tiny flash. The graying haired man sighed with a waning hope on his exhaling breath. He continued to stare into space long after the speck had disappeared, knowing that all of his hopes rested on the possibilities that the far distant space vessel represented. He felt deep inside his soul that everyone's future depended on the technologies put into the distant vessel's transference computer, which rested in the underground base below him. The tall veteran tried to recall where the particular probe vessel he had been scrutinizing was headed but was unable to remember many of the details of the current project.

As the old soldier looked hopefully into the night sky above, he heard someone approaching him from the stairway behind. He instinctively knew who it was, even though he possessed none of the telepathic abilities that had proved so useful among his troops. His military trained senses told him that the quick shuffling footsteps behind him were those of the eccentric scientist responsible for the technological leaps that were embedded in the no longer visible probe.

"Tonight's transference vessel has launched and penetrated the dimensional space time fabric, Admiral. Let's hope that this time we will gain more from our search," a short, funny looking little man stated with a warbling voice.

"Indeed," the Admiral responded with a slight Scottish accent. "If we can find anythin' of value, then our efforts will have been directed toward a fruitful end. I canna' help but feel that we've wasted far too much time already."

"Pardon my seeming pun, but only *time* will tell, Admiral."

The old veteran looked at the strange scientist not quite understanding the refference to time. He shrugged and turned his head back toward the night sky. Probably some obscure inside joke, he thought. One could never be sure what these scientist were thinking.

⁜ ⁜ ⁜ ⁜ ⁜

As Doug left his apartment for school, he felt a cold breeze brush across his face. It wasn't unpleasant for a gust of cool air to blow by on a warm day, but something about the chilling air made him shudder as if he had forgotten something very large and important. Pausing on the front steps, the young dark-haired man surveyed the area, not knowing what he was looking for. Eventually, the feeling of something being out of place left him, and he continued onward to school.

Since he lived relatively close to college he usually walked to class instead of getting a ride from a friend or riding his mountain bike. He didn't own a car, and the parking on campus was terrible anyway, even if you were a senior. Doug didn't get excessive amounts of exercise, but still maintained a lithe frame that was slender yet tone. Walking to classes everyday helped to keep him somewhat in shape, but he had never been overly enthusiastic about athletic activity. Doug was more physically passive, even in his recreations. As he walked, he thought about the intense boredom he would have to face once again. He knew the entire day would consist of endless lectures that would slowly corrode his brain. Pushing onward, the diligent student denied his desire to skip class.

Doug arrived shortly at the college campus. The building in which he had his first class was straight ahead, but first he would visit his friend Al, who lived nearby in a residence hall.

Doug entered the lobby doors of Al's dorm. Turning around the corner and starting his morning ritual of greeting everyone in the west wing of the dorm, Doug headed for Al's room. He walked into the room as if he himself lived there, closed the door to the room, and proceeded to make himself comfortable. Al never locked his door, so Doug made a habit of walking right in whenever he was visiting. Since Al didn't seem to mind, there wasn't a problem.

The slender student brushed aside an offending lock of his curly black hair, and inspected the room with his icy blue eyes. As usual, the room was a total wreck. Doug sighed as he looked with disgust at the cluter and dirty dishes that beset every corner of the room, noting that even a residence assistant needed assistance with maintaining his residence. For an instant, the room seemed different than he remembered, but Doug quickly shrugged off the odd feeling telling himself that the only difference in the room was a more recent empty pizza box that had less mold on it than the others in the room.

After he had selected the books that he needed for his first class, the diligent student carelessly dropped the rest of his books on the floor of Al's room with a resounding crash. Doug certainly didn't want to carry all of his books to every class, so why not let Al's room borrow a few of them? After the totally random dispersal of his college materials onto the already cluttered floor, he left Al's dorm and entered the residence hall's lounge to buy a drink. He knew he would need a lot of caffeine to get through the upcoming boredom.

His head started to hurt. Not so much that it could be called a headache, but more of a slow dull ache. It felt as if he had hit his head on something and still retained the last remnants of pain from the blow. He ignored the ache since it wasn't excruciatingly painful and plodded along toward the lounge's coffee dispenser, hoping to elevate his alertness with excessive amounts of caffeine.

While getting his drink, he heard his name called by a familiar voice. The young student turned to face one of his closest friends, Al. Doug stifled a chuckle as his groggy friend, still dripping from a morning shower, tried to retrieve change from his shower container and hold up the towel around his waist simultaneously.

Al had a stocky build, but Doug knew that the bulk of his friend's size was from muscle not fat. He had dark hair and thick eyebrows, which gave him a menacing appearance. The irony was that Al was more intelligent than he seemed. People who didn't know him were given a startling surprise when they heard an incredibly articulate dialect, coming from someone who appeared to be semi-Neanderthal.

Between the two friends a lot of mischievous deeds had been accomplished. Doug periodically reverted to an immature and roguish persona, which was almost always misunderstood and thus he was rarely recognized for his peculiar genius. Al supplied the brawn for their miscreant deeds, as well as the finer details that Doug usually overlooked, while Doug supplied the conceptions of the actual misadventures to begin with.

"So how are you this morning?" Al inquired still a little dazed.

"As well as can be expected. We've got an entire day of lecturing to get through."

"Tell me about it, and I thought college was going to be all fun."

"Yeah, well one more year and it's all over!"

Al proceeded to groggily get a drink for himself, although he was clearly still half-asleep. Doug and Al shared the dislike of monotonous class lectures, which seemed to always have been designed to put one to sleep, and they also shared the addiction of caffeine, which was a necessary counter measure for the languid power of their collegiate classes.

As they talked about their sorrows and lack of interest in what they were going to be forced to listen to, they were interrupted by the sound of Al's watch alarm. Doug cringed. The tiny watch seemed to ring out piercingly with angry little screeches. He wondered what he could have done to merit such a headache. Holding his head in his hands, Doug asked his friend if he had any aspirin.

❖ ❖ ❖ ❖ ❖

Deep in the outermost reaches of earth's life-giving atmosphere lurked an alien device. Its propulsion systems kept it from a natural descending orbit like the other space debris, and its multi-frequency radar and laser-cloaking device shielded it from the electronic scanning systems of the planet's inhabitants. Programmed to fly in a pattern that avoided the paths of any objects from the planet, the device was undetectable. It was too far up to be spotted by the naked eye of the planet's dominant species, and its programming allowed a sufficient amount of its memory to be devoted to the detection and the destruction, if necessary, of any of the more primitive detection devices of the planet before it was discovered.

In the event that any native devices from the planet were eradicated, it was programmed to return to its home-docking bay before any attempt could be made to locate the source of the destruction. Its programmers had thought of everything imaginable. Its mission was destined to succeed.

The mission of the dimensional transference probe 26A was to randomly explore the minds of as many inhabitants as possible from the planet Terra in the fifteenth quadrant of dimensional sector theta four, and to record any information that would be useful to the cause. After it had penetrated the minds of the unaware informers and taken the thoughts that were of use to the cause, it filed them into its database, which was the most sophisticated ever created. The creators of the probe were very proud and highly praised by their superiors upon its completion.

In a random sweep of the planet it stopped on area Delta 2145. The area had several hundred beings heading toward it. The probe's limited artificial brain had already discovered that masses of beings in the same area often meant that the patterns of information held in their heads were more sophisticated than randomly scattered beings. The lights on the casing of the database flashed rhythmically as the mind analysis and transferal process began. Its beam flashed across the area selecting subjects at random and utilizing their unawareness of its beam to copy the electronic images generated by their brains with relative ease. This information was not as beneficial to the cause as other gatherings had been, but there was a promising amount of collective thought patterns in the group to continue the process.

It was nearly time for the probe to return to its own dimension. Its database was nearly full. After a few thousand more subjects it would return home. It could hold a total of nearly a billion complete mind and neural net patterns, and most of the patterns currently held were incomplete. Only information relevant to the cause was stored in the memory banks. It narrowed its beam to select another group of specimens. The thoughts of the specimens were now coming in.

The computer brain of the probe halted as it noticed that something was wrong. Specimen Omega 992 was not divulging any information to the database. The specimen was resisting the beam penetration. The methodical machine decreased the number of specimens being probed, in order to focus more attention on the mind of specimen Omega 992. Eventually Omega 992 would not be able to withstand the beam's intensity, and would allow its knowledge to be scanned. The creators had thought of everything.

❀ ❀ ❀ ❀ ❀

Doug sat through his classes staring blankly at the board. With his recently acquired headache he was in no mood for calculus or physics. Instead, his thoughts wandered and eventually came to thoughts of fantasy and chivalry. A Sophomore girl from one of his classes, whom he had only known for a short amount of time, was invariably on his mind. He would continually fantasize acts of heroism that would win her heart. Unfortunately, the reality was that he bumbled any attempt to win her heart and became more like Don Quixote than a real knight.

Even though she might not have the same feeling about him, Doug had known from the moment he had first met her that he wanted to spend as much time with her as he could. She was everything he had ever wanted; everything she did was perfect. His knowledge of her as a person was limited to casual conversations, and he could find no rational reason for the intense connection he felt with her, but he knew it was there and that is was greater than any connection he had felt before. He thought about asking her out, but every time he saw her his mind went blank, his knees trembled and he got a dull ache in the pit of his stomach. Even casual conversation seemed to be awkward for him, which was a totally alien feeling for him. Doug realized that for the first time in his life, he had met a woman who he could truly fall in love with, if given the smallest chance.

The class ended, giving Doug a jolt as he was shaken from his daze and rudely brought back to reality by the, quick as lightening, departure of the students. The other students were all relieved that they were one class closer to the day's end, and even though Doug was equally enthusiastic about leaving school, he couldn't help letting out a groan as his head started to throb ominously.

His headache pulsated from bad to worse, then would die down for a while. Doug wondered if he might be sick. He had never experienced such an odd pain before. The thought was quickly dismissed, and he wrote the pain off as just being a bad headache, or maybe a migraine. As he prepared to leave Doug lifted his head out of his hands, but had to quickly shut his eyes as the entire room seemed to start shimmering. When he opened his eyes hesitantly the room was no longer shimmering, but once again something felt out of place, and the strange dejavous episodes he had been having began to worry him.

As he stood, he found it even harder to subdue the unusual pain, which had become even more intense throughout the day. He was staggering down the hall when he glanced up and saw the angelic face of Michelle, the girl of his dreams. They smiled at each other, and suddenly he was struck with such a violent and penetrating pain that he fell to his knees and almost passed out from the pressures in his head. Al rushed out of the classroom as he saw Doug fall to the ground like a culed ox.

While his friends helped him up, Al and Michelle asked him if he was all right. Somewhat embarrassed that he had nearly passed out in front of Michelle, he replied that he had just lost his balance and was fine. Getting back on his feet, he hurried toward Al's dorm room to hide. He knew that his answer to their question must have sounded stupid and that they probably didn't believe him. Even now he could hear the voices of Freshmen telling each other that they thought he was weird. Doug rushed off to Al's dorm room, quickening his pace with every step in hopes of leaving friends as well as bystanders far behind him.

CHAPTER 2

A cold, alien device calculated its devious plan. Its propulsion system's occasional activation, for the altering of its trajectory, was the only activity that emanated from its hull. On the inside however, its computer brain was churning rapidly trying to ascertain what the logical course of action should be.

Unit 26A, log 1285, day 5: *"Subject omega 992 is still resisting even after the number of subjects being probed has been halved three times. The only logical explanations are that either the subject is holding the most useful information on the planet and is being assisted by an artificial shield that is more advanced than any other technology on the planet, or more likely that the subject has a mental blocking power unknown to the cause. Either way, the subject's psyche must be breached so the information it contains can be utilized. If necessary, the searching beams can be monopolized, and concentrated specifically on subject omega 992. There is risk of destroying the specimen if such force is used, but it may be unavoidable. Until such a drastic measure becomes the only available option, the number of subjects being probed will be continually decreased in an effort to penetrate the thoughts of subject omega 992."*

❈ ❈ ❈ ❈ ❈

Doug reached Al's dorm room and lay down on the bed. It was a single room since Al was the hall's Residence assistant, so he didn't have to worry about a roommate barging in on him. The only people who walked right in like he did were friends as well. The distraught college student had only been laying down a few minutes when one such friend entered the room. Doug partially sat up, when Paul came in, to acknowledge his best friend's presence. His head started to spin as he raised eyes to Paul's face and it began to shimmer. Doug quickly shut his eyes, and with slow movements he let his head fall back to the pillow. He prayed that everything would be normal when his eyes opened and returned to his friend's face.

"Don't get up. You should be lying down."

"Then why the hell are you bugging me for? You always barge in on me when I want to sleep. You just don't respect me anymore!" Doug remarked in a playfully mocking tone, but with a slight fear in his voice that he hoped Paul wouldn't notice.

"Funny. Save your humor for when you've recovered. I just wanted to see how you were doing."

"Christ! I'm not dying! I just had a little head rush that's all," Doug responded as the fear slowly turned to agitation.

"Well, your little head rush caused you to collapse right in the middle of the hall, and you still look pale. I'd call that serious. I've known you long enough to tell when you're lying, so save it for the press."

"Don't bother me about it, I'm fine."

"All right, but you fall down in the hall one more time and you're going to the hospital."

"Well...could you make sure the coroner does a good job?" Doug wheezed sarcastically.

"All right you jerk, I'm leaving. You just don't care about my feelings!" Paul replied in a mocking tone.

Paul left in a simulated tantrum, and Doug tried to sleep, but all he could think about was how stupid he must have looked in front of Michelle. He was partly concerned that his headache might be more than he had first thought, but not enough to push away the denial completely. More concerned about his social relationships than his health, Doug drifted off into a troubled slumber.

Al was worried about his friend. He knew Doug pretty well, and also knew how stubborn he could be when it came to admitting that he had any kind of problem, whether it be physical, social, or finnacial.

"You don't look to well, Doug, maybe you ought to lie back down."

"I'll be fine, it was just a head rush, don't worry about it. I was just a little too tired that's all," Doug replied.

"Are you sure? You look kind of pale," Al responded as his brows creased together with thought.

"I said I was fine, MOTHER."

"Very funny, you should be a comedian."

Al pulled his friend out of bed and prodded him toward the door.

"Come on, Paul's waiting for us in the cafeteria, lets get something to eat," Al said with a tone that left no room for protest.

The two friends headed to the student cafeteria for lunch. Doug tried to convince himself that a lack of food was the cause of his sudden loss of equilibrium and that eating something would solve his problems. He turned to tell Al that he thought it was just malnutrition, but clearly saw a shadowy image of Al, for a second, then averted his eyes. Doug nearly fell over as he stumbled away from the frightening and evil looking version of Al. The bewildered student felt foolish as he accidently let his eyes take another gaze and saw his friend once again. Doug closed his eyes tightly and tried to focus his mind, fearing for a moment that he might be losing his mind.

Doug sat down at a table in the caffeteria, accompanied by Al and Paul. He nervously struck up a conversation, hoping to avoid another occurrence of the starnge visions he was having. After a few moments, he felt more comfortable, and let himself relax a little.

Paul was a year younger than Doug was, but they had been good friends since childhood, and still had a few classes that they shared. Paul was a good friend and was one of the few people who could successfully give Doug advice. Doug respected Paul and considered him as one of his closest friends. They had their share of arguments and disagreements, but they were never angry with each other for long. They had experienced so much together that nothing could diminish their friendship.

Paul was shorter than Doug by at least a foot and a half, but what he lacked in stature he made up for with his rugged handsome features and his natural charm. Doug sometimes wondered if there was any limit to Paul's charisma. In addition to his charm and looks, Paul was very well built. His muscular appearance nearly rivaled Al's.

Much to Doug's surprise Michelle and her friend Karen sat down across from them. Michelle asked if Doug was all right, and Doug who was rather embarrassed and not necessarily comfortable with the subject, told her that he was fine, even though in reality his head was beginning to pound again and he was afraid that if he took his eyes away from his friends they would start to change and shimmer. They all began to talk but the more relaxed Doug became the more his head would pulsate with pain. All of his friends noticed his pain related odd behavior, including Michelle and Karen.

They all realized something was wrong and Michelle finally asked Doug if his head was bothering him. Doug then replied that his head did indeed hurt, but it was nothing serious. Everyone knew that he was in much more pain then he would admit, but simply didn't know what they could do to help him. Doug was just too stubborn for his own good.

Their subject then changed to that of headaches and aspirin, where it was finally mentioned that Doug's headache was probably the result of an excess of classroom lectures and pop quizzes, for both were known to cause mental disability through the rapid destruction of brain cells.

Brian O'Madigan

Michelle and Doug spent the rest of their lunchtime talking. Paul seemed to have disappeared somewhere during Doug and Michelle's conversation, Al had a class to attend, and Karen had discreetly excused herself to leave the couple alone. Despite his headache, Doug had never been happier. Doug had never had a deep relationship before. He had his share of girlfriends, but none of them were quite like Michelle. As he glanced at her slender, porcelain face, prominent yet delicate cheekbones, and perfectly shaped lips that were especially sensual when she smiled, he realized that he had never truly loved anyone before.

Even though he hadn't known Michelle for very long, he knew there was something special about her, as if they were meant for each other. He couldn't quite explain the feeling. He could only experience what it was like. It wasn't just her beauty that attracted him. There was something in every little thing she did that caused him to tremble with delight. It was a deep kind of connection that went against everything he knew to be logical and a connection that he happily accepted and cherished without thinking about it. It was almost magical.

She had long black hair that reached down past her shoulder blades with soft highlights of light brown accenting it gently. Doug also admired her small petite build, and soft, delicate facial features. The feature that Doug admired most, however, were her stunning blue eyes that always made him think of the clearest of blue skies. As he looked up at her and caught her gaze, her eyes sparkled, and after a brief stare, she smiled and permanently captured his heart.

There were so many things he wished he could just tell her, like how beautiful she was, or how much he liked the way she walked, or the way she talked. He seemed to like everything about her, but no matter how much he wanted to, he could never seem to tell her how he felt about her. What if she didn't feel the same way about him? What if she laughed at him, or thought he was an idiot?

Doug didn't have all that much experience in the intense world of courtship. He had never known anyone like her before. All of his previous dealings with women had come naturally, no need for massive courtship was needed. He just got along with everyone, and he had felt no need for any excessive flattery or other attempts to win over his dates. He had never before felt like he needed to be anything other than himself, yet now felt the pressure of failure and wanted to portray only the best attributes he had to offer. He realized with sudden insight that he had never before felt any fear because he never before had tried to date anyone that he felt he would feel loss over if he failed. Thus his extreme desire to express himself at his best seemed to foul up any attempt he made to say something that was relevant to their conversation.

He had imagined what it would be like to be with someone like Michelle that he truly loved, and had dreamt about falling into some sort of true love. The one thing his imagination had forgotten to tell him was how to approach a girl that meant everything to him. He had never really expected that he would have to say anything to her. His thoughts had only reached the point after anything that had to do with actually saying anything was done with.

Usually he didn't have to say anything, he just got along with anybody he met, but Michelle was different. He had never thought about what should be said, he had expected that it would just spontaneously happen and that would be the end of it.

In a rare moment of insight, Doug realized that all of the women in his life had been the aggressors. He had cared for them, but he had never met a woman that he desperately wanted to be with, so he had never been the one to pursue any type of relationship. All of his previous girlfriends had chased him; he didn't have any problems, because they were the ones to go out on a limb. He had never faced that ultimate and risky venture, until now.

He wanted to share all his feelings with Michelle, and to tell her all that she already meant to him. The more he realized that it wasn't as simple as he had thought, the more nervous he became. As he sat in front of Michelle, almost speechless, he thought to himself, *"I've dreamed of this moment all of my life, and now I'm going to blow it!"*

After they had finished the last remnants of their lunch, Doug and Michelle walked toward the class that they shared. As they were tying up the loose ends of their conversation, Doug, with a sudden burst of energy that sprang from somewhere deep inside him finally asked her out.

"Michelle would you like to go out sometime. Dinner maybe, or a movie? We can talk about where we want to go in class."

"Uh, sure that would be great," was her somewhat bashful reply as she blushed prettily.

He was so happy that even the most excruciatingly painful headache couldn't have lessened his mood. His head even started to feel a little better. Thinking to himself, he wondered why he had made such a big deal out of everything. Now that she had said "yes", he could win her heart with a normal evening out on the town. He had enough confidence in himself to believe that. Once someone took the time to get to know him, he would always win the person over. Running his fingers through his thick black curls of hair with a deep sigh of contentment, the happy young man followed the love of his life into the classroom that they shared for literature appreciation.

The rest of his day was spent sitting through his classes thinking of Michelle and their date together with periodic glances in her direction to throw a quick smile or lingering look of adoration. He was so happy his head didn't seem to disturb him any longer. As quickly as it had sprung upon him during lunch, it began to quietly subdue. In fact, he didn't even think about his headache for the rest of the day.

Doug was eager to get home so he could do some cleaning around the apartment, finish his homework, and prepare for his date with Michelle. Before he did any work he had to tell Al and Paul, about his date. They were his best friends and he wanted to share his happiness with them. They were indeed glad that their friend was happy, but teased him about being in love nonetheless, and soon after, tasteless jokes took place of the previously innocent ones.

Doug left school, being badgered now by his entire English class. With an almost imperceptible smirk on his face, Doug walked home trying to ignore his classmates' rude gestures and perverse advice. His head started to hurt again as he walked and he wondered if it ever diminished in its intensity at all, or whether he could have been suppressing the pain by his incredible good mood. While thinking about the enigmatic headache, he arrived at the low rent appartment he called home.

⸭ ⸭ ⸭ ⸭ ⸭

Unit 26A Log 1286, day 5 : *"Increasing the psychic probe's strength has been ineffective. The subject has continually countered the psychic probe, and even retaliated directly, on occasion, with a psychic force of its own. The calculated hypothesis of this unit is that it has been a passive retaliatory response issued by the subject's unconscious mind; otherwise, the psychic beam would have been more focused, and a threat to the continued existence of this unit. Acquisition of the information of subject omega 992 is no longer sufficient. Subject omega 992 is not being aided by artificial means and has an as of yet unknown ability to generate psychic shielding naturally. Subject omega 992 must be appropriated and brought back to the main base. Once the subject's mind has been penetrated, this unit will commence with the item retrieval program."*

⸭ ⸭ ⸭ ⸭ ⸭

Doug was just finishing his homework when the phone rang. He answered the phone, and heard the voice of Michelle as he picked up the phone. Thoughts of her heavenly visage raced through his head as she spoke to him. They talked at random for a while about current trivial events before finally coming to the topic of their date.

Michelle wanted to go to a restaurant that was relatively quiet and low key, so they could talk and get to know each other better. Doug agreed that this was a good idea, and his head filled with images of romantic dining places, but soon narrowed it down to a few places that weren't very spectacular but still served edible food. This didn't concern him very much because wherever he went he would still be with her and that was all that mattered to him.

Michelle picked Doug up from his apartment; she even offered to let him drive which surprised him since she was so trusting to allow someone she hardly knew to drive her car. For all she knew he could be a terrible driver. For whatever reason, her trust gave him an added boost and an even more determined urge to prove himself worthy of her trust. Doug headed the car toward a quaint little restaurant in the downtown area that he had heard had a homey and inviting atmosphere. A sign creaked as it swung from a large pole near the front door, and silently boasted that the restaurant had been established in the early eighteen hundreds. From the musty appearance and thick crosstie framework, Doug accepted the sign's claim.

He stared at the sign as he read the restaurant's name. He felt that something was seriously wrong with it, as if it was out of place or at the very least, different somehow. Doug read the name, "O'Malley's", and spoke the name in his mind several times as they passed the sign and entered the building, but couldn't figure out what it was that bothered him about it. He'd seen the sign when passing through the area, but never paid close attention to it, or even given it a second thought, yet now it seemed to be wrong somehow.

They entered the waiting area, were promptly seated and ordered their drinks from the hostess who sat them. The restaurant had a dark, cavern like appearance even though it was well lit. The oak table booths and heavy wooden rafters gave it a medieval tavern look that appealed to Doug in an odd way. It was as if he was escaping the world outside by retreating to an old rustic tavern that somehow existed outside of time.

While they were waiting for their waiter to take their order a conversation started between them about what it would be like to live in a time where everything looked and felt like the tavern did. As the night went by, Michelle eventually told Doug she had been thinking about their growing relationship very carefully, and his heart sunk momentarily as he erroneously presumed what she would say. Suddenly, he felt pity and remorse for all of the hearts he had broken using a similar opening remark.

"Doug, I don't want this to be just a one time thing. I really like you and I don't want you to get away from me. I've never met someone like you before. You're . . .special. I'd really like a chance to get to know you. I'm not trying to say we will be anything permenant, but who knows what will happen? I really think we could be something great."

Doug felt overjoyed and relieved at the same time. He had to force himself to speak since the powerful emotions he felt were stifling his ability to talk.

"I feel the same way. I really like you too. I was afraid I was forcing things too quickly already. It didn't really feel like the best time to ask you out, but I didn't want to wait too long before I said anything either. I was afraid *you* would get away before I had a chance to ask you out. I'm so relieved that we feel the same way, I was afraid you were going to give me that, 'let's just be friends' line," he responded with growing relaxation.

Doug felt like a thousand pound mill stone had been removed from his neck as he listened to her, and the infatuated young man decided to try articulating how he felt about the woman in front of him.

"You know, from the moment I first saw you, all I could think of was how perfect you were. Everything about you is wonderful, the way you walk, the way you talk, not to mention that you're by far the most beautiful and stunningly attractive woman I've ever met."

"If you keep complimenting me like that, it'll go to my head," Michelle warned with a pretty little blush.

"Words cannot express how amazing you are to me."

Placing her hand on top of his, she gave a little squeeze of reassurance, looked into his eyes and gave him the most heart melting smile he had ever seen.

They continued to talk the rest of the evening, as their discussion wandered from one topic to the next. Doug became more relaxed the longer that they talked. His head began to bother him again. He didn't understand what was happening to him, and became frustrated with the seemingly sentient headache. Lately his head would hurt more whenever he was happy. This headache seemed to have a mind of its own. It was almost as if the headache wished to spoil every happy moment that he had. He was happier than he had ever been before in his life. Why did something have to ruin it?

Doug sat through the tail end of their dinner oblivious to whatever was said between them. His head seemed to get worse, he could hardly think, and had no hope of consciously constructing an articulate sentence. As they stood to leave Doug thought breifly about his headache, and wondered if it was possible for a head to explode from the pressures of a headache.

The pain increased, and blurred out even the most basic and fundamental fragments of coherence. Without even being aware of what was happening, the distraught student realized that he was walking out of the restaurant with Michelle.

As they walked toward the car, Doug used all of his concentration to try and retain his equilibrium. They reached the car, and Doug opened the door to the driver side and practically fell into the car. Michelle realized something was wrong and figured that the cause of his sudden paleness was from the episode she had seen earlier. Doug had never been like this before. Before she could ask him what was wrong, he tried to explain the problem in a fumbled attempt to speak clearly.

"Michelle...I...my head...I need to lie down for awhile," he finally blurted out.

After a few minutes he managed to gain enough concentration to sit up in the driver's seat, only to receive a startling response from Michelle,

"Oh no you don't, *I'm* driving, and don't even think about arguing mister!" Michelle scolded him with such enthusiasm and force that Doug had to stifle a chuckle. Instead of laughing he managed to reply with,

"You know, you're beautiful when you're angry."

Satisfied that he was relinquishing his control of the car, she simply smiled mysteriously and said,

"I know."

Frustrated that his headache was ruining his evening with Michelle, Doug sat sullenly in the car. In a moment of sheer anger at his ailment, he lashed out with an internal scream of anxious frustration. To his surprise and further puzzlement, the headache diminished significantly. Just as he was about to tell Michelle he was feeling better and suggest they go somewhere else to finish their date, he felt the sharp pain return more penetratingly than it had ever been before. Doug closed his eyes, and tried his best to push the pain away. The result of his efforts left him both mentally and physically exhausted.

Michelle helped Doug out of the car once they had arrived at his apartment and made sure he was all right before she left. She had wanted to make sure he was safely tucked in bed, but Doug insisted that he walk her back out to her car.

"Good night Doug. I had a wonderful time. I hope you feel better soon," she smiled mysteriously and added, "To bad we haven't been going out longer, or I'd stay with you, and take care of all your problems."

Doug truly wished that he had asked her out a long time ago, as images of her filled his thoughts making him go weak in the knees. The thought of her taking care of him, in any way, shape or form, provoked a hoard of sensual desires in him.

"You have no idea how much I wish I'd asked you out when I first laid eyes on you," he said with a warble in his normally deep voice.

She apparently appreciated his honest remark, because she leaned close to him and kissed him tenderly. Doug knew he would forever treasure that sweet and gentle kiss.

He waited for her to be off safely. Once she had gone around the corner and out of his sight, he felt extreme weakness spreading all throughout his wiry frame. The headache seemed to be draining all of his energy. He felt consciousness beginning to leave him, so he opened the door to his apartment and clambered inside. As he closed the door, he passed out. He fell to the floor with a dull thud, exhausted from his inner battle to remain conscious. Doug lay on the floor in silence, looking like a corpse. As he slept, he had fitful dreams of a world where nothing would remain constant. Everything shifted in a beautiful, yet alarming shimmer.

The next day dawned bright and clear. Doug felt better physically, but mentally he felt a great weakness, as if his energy had been sucked from his body. It was as if he had spent the night with some sort of energy vampire. His head still hurt a little, but he knew that he should go to school. Even though he still retained a good part of the previous day's tempestuous headache and felt bad about his head problem ruining his evening with Michelle, he thought school would be the best thing for him. Instead of lying around the house all day, he gathered his books and trudged to campus. He shortly arrived and the monotonous school day began.

Chapter 3

Unit 26A, log 1287, day 6: *"All attempts to penetrate subject omega 992's thoughts have been attempted and failed except for maximum probing intensity. Maximum probing intensity has terminated all other subjects that it has been applied to; thus, it is this unit's last resort. The situation has become drastic. Subject omega 992 has directly attacked this unit psionicaly on two occasions. Whether these psionic attacks were consciously directed or not remains to be determined, but the latter of the two attacks nearly disabled this unit.*

The subject omega 992's defense mechanisms fluctuate when its conscious thoughts are passive. Its mental blocking of this unit's probing beam lowers in intensity when its thoughts are in the passive mode. Attempts to penetrate and wrest the needed information for the cause have thus been altered to compensate for omega 992's defensive methods. The subject has nearly been defeated at crucial emotional fluctuations, so maximum intensity beam will only be instated if present attempts to procure information fail."

\# \# \# \# \#

Doug sat at his desk, not even thinking about the material his class was studying at the time, and he really didn't want to think about physics in general. His thoughts instead were of Michelle. No matter how hard he tried; he couldn't keep his mind from thinking about how absolutely gorgeous she was. His head was pulsating. The more he thought about her, the more intensely his head would throb.

He was, by the middle of the class period, so far distant from the classroom that he didn't notice anything except his headache. At this fateful moment the professor decided to give a speech to his class on paying attention to his lectures. His focus was on Doug, who was obviously not paying even the slightest attention.

"Doug, pay attention! How can I teach you anything if you're always off on some other planet! College isn't going to do anything for you people if you don't want to learn!"

Mr. Reilly ranted and raved at him right in his face. He had the habit of screaming at the top of his lungs in front of his students. So close to them that spittle would fly in their faces as he yelled. Some even speculated that Mr. Reilly had been born with extra salivary glands, which were capable of producing several liters of saliva per minute. He would then hurl massive amounts of this pre-digestive liquid at his students. The end result was an annoying and disgusting lecture about the immaturity and general apathy of every student ever to walk into Reilly's classroom, from a teacher whose own irritations at lack of attention regressed him to an infantile tantrum.

As Mr. Reilly yelled at Doug and the rest of the class, Doug was struck back to reality with such vigor that he lost all control. He suddenly realized the significance of his head problems. This was no ordinary headache; it wasn't even a medical problem. It dawned on him that the pain he was experiencing was from some outside force that was trying to enter his mind.

At first he thought the idea was crazy, but he could feel its presence. The probe that was pounding on his brain grew in intensity as he renewed his resistance to it with all of his might. Doug couldn't stop from screaming out with pain as he felt the mysterious probe amplifying its strength. He screamed and clamped his hands onto his head as if to prevent it from cracking open.

In an attempt to mentally fight the cranial colossus that ravaged his mind, he physically lashed out at any and every object in his immediate vicinity. Luckily his friends and classmates got out of the way when this seemingly hysterical state came over their fellow classmate.

Doug crouched into a corner trying to block out everything. He was so focused on the probe that he didn't realize that he was screaming at the top of his lungs from the piercing pain. A beam of electromagnetic energy burst through the ceiling and down around Doug, showering the classroom with fragments of concrete and paint. The power of the probe started to envelop him in an energy field, permitting no one to come in contact with him. Doug's friends and teacher were trying to force their way through the barrier that now enclosed him but without any success. Mr. Reilly stared dumbfounded through the newly opened hole in the ceiling at the energy beam that glowed green from ignighting the nitrogen in the earth's atmosphere. Even though no one could see it, everyone present now sensed the attack to be from an alien source.

Students from other classes were coming into the room to see where the horrendous noise was coming from, and soon a group of people stood pressed up against Doug's technological wall of imprisonment. No one could get close to Doug, and he didn't hear anyone's voice no matter how loudly they yelled. The room was filled with such utter chaos and confusion that no one present really knew what was going on.

Doug was paying no heed to anyone or anything in the room. His concerns were concentrated more on his present condition. He could feel the alien probe pushing its way into his mind, even though he was resisting with all of his might. He realized that it was slowly frying his brain, but he couldn't think of any way to fight against its raw power. As soon as he started to contemplate ways that he could augment his own mental strength to resist the probe, Doug felt a little more intelligent as well as physically stronger.

After a few minutes of this form of battle, his increased intellect determined that the reason he was succeeding in his struggles was because he was absorbing the power that the probe was using against him, and redirecting it to enhance his own capacities, as well as returning some of the probe's beam right back at the source. Not only was he filling his mind and body with power, he was also increasing the potential of power he was capable of holding. He then devoted all of his concentration to reforming his mental and physical defenses. His imagination was given free reign to go wild with ideas of inhuman power. His only limitation now was how much raw power a mortal frame was capable of holding.

Even though he was making himself stronger he still had the problem of the attacker, which was still a vastly strong and versatile adversary. He knew he couldn't continue to absorb its power, and the longer he left it unchallenged the more time this thing, whatever it may be, had time to attack at him through different means such as his friends and loved ones. So with his increased mental power he struck back at the probe with such vigor that its own attack was temporarily slackened giving Doug momentary relief from his unyielding torment.

Doug regained his eyesight as the probe intensity began to slacken. He suddenly became aware of his surroundings. He saw Michelle crying in front of him, begging him to speak to her. In fumbling words he tried to tell her everything would be all right, but everyone around him could clearly see that there was little to support that claim. Doug himself knew that he was only telling a half-truth at best, for he had no idea what he was up against nor how he should go about fighting it.

"Please don't die Doug, everything will be great once we get you out of there. I don't want to lose you now. Everything was going so great. Fight it!" Michelle screamed.

Her words became even more incoherent as she became frightened and worried about Doug. Al looked on in shock, furrowing his brow in concentration as he tried to figure out what was attacking and how he could help. The best he could do was to make a few guesses about the type of energy used to create the magnetic field. Paul, now right beside Al and Michelle, resorted to a more direct approach and pounded away at the energy field hoping that he could break through. Doug wished he had the time to explain to his friends that there was nothing they could do to help and that this wasn't anyone's fault; it was the fault of the horrendous probe.

His efforts to speak were a waste of time; he needed all of his mental power to keep the probe away until he could figure out a plan of attack. He knew that he needed to get everyone out of harm's way, and he might not get another chance to warn them. With all of the remaining physical energy he could muster, he shouted to them at the top of his lungs,

"Get out of here! All of you! Hurry, there isn't much time left!"

CHAPTER 4

"**W**arning! Warning! This unit is under attack! Defensive buffers failing! Defense shields raised to maximum capacity.

The entity has mutated into an another form with high mental capabilities that were not present before. The entity/subject has proven to be far more formidable than any other subject this unit has encountered. The entity/subject has undergone a type alpha metamorphosis giving it a class fifteen when it is directly attacking this unit, which is far exceeding its original limits. Entity/subject has increased in mental and physical specifications that range past the scale for all known biological organisms of the entity/subject's planet of origin. Scanning indicates that the immediate retaliatory potential of the entity/subject far exceeds the defensive capabilities of this unit. Defense buffers have been destroyed beyond reasonable use and are now off line, further attacks will invariably cripple this unit.

Measures must be taken before entity/subject becomes conscious of the extent of its potential. This unit has come to the conclusion that the entity/subject must, at all costs, return with this unit *to home dimension. Tactical measures initiated. Maximum power achieved. Attempting contact with the entity/subject. In its altered form, the entity/subject is accessible to communication on a telepathic scale, which was not available during previous calculations.*

Conclusion: make contact and deliver ultimatum to the entity/subject before entity/subject is aware of the vastly superior advantage it has gained."

❋ ❋ ❋ ❋ ❋

While Doug's mind thought hard to find some way out of his dilemma, he felt the probe increase its attack, and beckoning him to cease all mental defenses and allow it to take him away. He didn't quite understand what it meant, and yelled both mentally and physically that he wasn't going anywhere. The machine-like thought pattern spoke to him again, and although he didn't quite understand everything that it was trying to tell him, he did understand that it would attack and kill everyone in the immediate proximity if he didn't comply with its wishes.

He yelled to it again; this time he questioned it as to how he could be sure that it wouldn't kill them anyway. He felt the cold machine like thoughts brush his mind once more. He didn't like his adversary's answer.

Doug realized that he didn't have a choice; he couldn't take the risk of loosing the lives of everyone around him, especially Michelle. A few of the students had fled with his previous warning, but those he cared about most refused to leave. There simply wasn't enough information present to formulate a sufficient counterattack. Giving the lovely woman standing in front of him one last glance, and asking her not to forget him, he gave in to the merciless probe.

Doug's mind was struck with excruciating pain as he let the probe into his mind. He could feel the last remnants of his conscious mind wane, as the probe picked at and plundered the thoughts of his brain. The probe roughly examined his mind and, suddenly, Doug felt the culmination of every sensation he had ever experienced in his lifetime occur again in mere seconds. The result was the most excruciating pain imaginable.

Every neurotransmitter in the poor man's body was overloaded with painful stimuli. Every cut, scrape, and burn was intermingled with light brushes, tickles and tingles. Doug nearly went insane in the few moments that he was forced to endure the agony, and he knew he wouldn't be able to stand the torment much longer.

The raw anguish passed quickly and he was temporarily filled with a euphoric delight. The intense pain had left an emptiness that was utterly delightful. The feeling was similar to being in shackles for days and then finally freed of the constrictive devices. While he was still in exhilarated shock, Doug felt a powerful jolt from somewhere deep inside of him.

He felt his mind being sucked away into the probe, until only the raw emotions and human frame were left. Michelle, who was now on the verge of loosing her sanity, cried out to him one last time. The thought stripped Doug bereft of words or even the knowledge of how to form a sentence, responded with shear emotion. Doug used what was left of his mind to empathicly send a message of all that he felt for the three friends that stood in front of him. They would never forget the pure emotions of love and friendship rendered to them that day.

The pain-struck shell of a man felt the numerous emotions that he held for his friends slip away into the probe as well. The only part of Doug that was left was his body and soul, the very essence of his being. In the moment that followed, he had the sensation that he didn't exist any longer. The last thing he remembered, if it could be called a memory at all, were the screams and lamentations of disbelief that his friends cried as they saw him disintegrate into nothingness. His body was being digitized and catalogued into the probe's memory banks. Everything that followed from there was dark and cold.

CHAPTER 5

Doug awoke; he knew that he had been asleep for awhile because his back ached. He felt like he had slept on a slab of marble. As he tried to recall what had happened, he gradually began to remember his encounter with the strange probe. Startled when he realized that he wasn't at home in his bed, he flicked open his eyes inquiringly.

He blinked in amazement as he sat upright with a startled jolt. He was stark naked in some sort of medical room, lying on what appeared to be an operating table. As he got up stiffly from the table, he began to examine the room he was in more closely. It reminded him of a dissection room in a morgue he had visited. The thought of it made him uneasy, and he wondered what his captors were going to do with him. The ideas that rushed into his mind of what they might do to him frightened him enough that he became determined not to be caught, even if he had to die fighting.

He had originally intended to examine the room he was in, but as he stood up he realized that he wasn't the same person he was when he had be captured. He blinked in amazement at his new figure. His body had become at least ten times more muscular than it was before. His normally slender form was replaced with thick, hardened muscles. He thought back to when he had been attacked by the probe and recalled that he had used its energy to amplify his own abilities.

His new found physical augmentations helped him to overcome much of his initial fear of being dissected like a worm. Doug looked proudly upon himself. He had always wonder what it would be like to have the body of a hero or a body builder, and now he had the physical capability to be one. He was so engrossed with examining his new anatomy that he almost forgot his current dilemma. But he was quickly reminded as the doorway in front of him opened, and three humanoid figures walked into the room.

The fear of being caught by cruel aliens sprang up again; he looked frantically for a way out of the room. Two of the three figures carried spear-like weapons and the third walked in between them. It didn't take Doug long to realize that the two figures on the flanks were bodyguards of some sort and the one in the middle was some sort of official.

Suddenly, without warning, Doug leaped with inhuman speed and agility at one of the guards, trying to seize the weapon from him. Because of Doug's unexpected assault, the swiftness with which it was enacted, and the astonishment of the guard, Doug was able to defeat one of the bodyguards and flee from the room with the staff like weapon.

He found himself in a corridor that lead to several rooms and a flight of stairs. He ran as fast as he could to the end of the hall, around the corner, and up the flight of stairs that ended the hallway. By this time the other two figures had recovered from their initial shock, and while the short, official looking one attended to the fallen guard's condition, the other went to sound the alarm.

Doug darted down another hall and into a small unoccupied room. He heard the alarms and knew that he couldn't stay where he was or eventually he would be found and recaptured by his captors. Taking advantage of the momentary opportunity he had been given, he examined the weapon he had stolen from the bodyguard.

It was some sort of a spear-like weapon. It reminded him of a quarter staff, except with a strange knob on one end, and on the other end, there was a small incision-like opening. He wondered what it might be for and looked over the rest of the weapon. He discovered that there were two imprints on the cylindrical shaft of the staff. These, he concluded, were the hand placements that the weapon was supposed to be used with. Thus, he placed his hands on the imprints. The fit was good, and with pleasure in acquiring this new knowledge, he held the weapon in the proper manner for which it was intended.

For a moment he felt strangely familiar with the stance and manner with which he held the staff. Doug felt a surge inside of him, and suddenly, his mind was filled with hordes of large bug like beings. Several men were hitting the insect-like creatures with the very same staff that he was holding. Glowing images of the staff filled his mind. As the images faded, he muttered the word, "quashish", and he knew that it meant Electro-magnetic spear.

Doug instinctively squeezed tightly pretending he was preparing to deal a death blow to one of the hideous giant aliens. As his grip tightened, however, he was startled to see an energy like blade, nearly six inches long, emerge from the open end of the staff, and a likewise sphere of energy envelope the bulbous end. The blade hummed and cackled with electric force as the startled human looked down at the weapon in awe.

With his new weapon's secrets uncovered, the young man began to feel a growing sense of courage. He decided that he should sneak out of the room he was in and try to find a better place to hide so that he could form some sort of strategy against his new foes. He knew his chances of escaping were slim, not to mention trying to return home. Since the circumstances were bizarre, he couldn't even be sure he was still on the same planet. Nonetheless, he decided that there was no other choice but to run and hide, and hope for a successful escape.

Doug slowly approached the room's already open door which he had carelessly left open. He made a mental note of his incautious error so that he wouldn't make such a mistake again. By this time, the alarm bells were screaming out their warnings and alerting those present that something was wrong. Doug knew that he couldn't go far without being spotted, so he set his goal for another open doorway that he could see a few yards down the hall.

Making sure that no one was coming from either side, he darted as quickly as he could down the corridor, and into the open doorway. Luckily it was vacant. He sighed with relief. Doug was about to make another attempt to run when he heard the footsteps and strange voices of people coming rapidly down the hallway.

Doug peered out the doorway trying to conceal his body behind the wall, tightly gripping his new found weapon. The boots of the men clapped loudly on the hard floor, and the murmur of voices could be heard. As Doug listened to the alien speech that the guards were using for communicating, he realized that he could somehow understand their strange language, which seemed to be English mixed with something very peculiar and definitely alien. Somewhat astonished, he thought to himself, and wondered where he had learned the odd language from. His mind quickly overcame the shock of being able to decipher their language, and focused rather on what they were saying.

"Damn, I hate it when those alarms go off!" one stated

"Yeah, I know what ya mean, every time it happens, we all hav'ta drop what were doin', and then it turns out to be a false alarm or a stupid drill. I wish we could fight instead of runnin' around in circles all the time."

"Hey, maybe this has got something to do with that dimensional informational that Admiral McDougal was looking for. I heard that the probe had messed up somehow."

"Yeah right, he's been looking for any new information that will help us for almost a year, and has squat to show for it. That damn probe doesn't do anything but screw up. You ask me, he's just stallin' for time. He don't want to admit that we're outnumbered and nowhere near bein' ready to take on the Enemy. Besides, half of the creatures we've plugged for information can't even speak in a complete sentence, or have one of those peaceful cultures that detest all wars and would rather die than strike their neighbors. Gimme a break! In this world you either fight for what's yours or you lose it."

"I suppose you're right, inter-dimension travel ain't what we thought it would be when it was discovered. Maybe if we...."

Doug listened to their conversation for as long as he was in range to hear, and was disappointed when the voices trailed off into inarticulate cascades of echoes from the corridor walls. Then he thought about his situation, and he realized that he had increased his power physically and mentally and that he had increased his intellect by a considerable degree. He also knew that he was most likely one of the creatures the men in the hall were talking about, which would mean he was in another dimension. His only problem now, was how did he get back home.

He noticed that he no longer had his class ring which he usually wore on his right hand; nor did he have the necklace that he wore. It was an ordinary necklace with a simple cross on it; it wasn't made of anything special, just a generic metal. But the loss of his personal items made him angry. Why would they take all of his belongings? Surely they didn't think that they were weapons or something like that? At least they could have left his clothes. As Doug pondered the significance of this peculiarity, he heard the rushed footsteps of more figures.

The footsteps became louder and again he heard an array of voices; only now they were shouting loudly, bellowing out orders. He knew he had to move fast, and decided to try to find the quickest way from the building. After the thundering tread of footfall ceased, he sneaked out of the room and down the corridor. He ran from room to room looking for some type of window or sign that could tell him approximately how many flights of stairs he should go down to reach the bottom floor, or if he was underground and needed to go up. Any form of elevator was out of the question. If he used one, his chances of being caught would be significantly greater. Any one that saw him coming out or going in to the elevator would attack or notify others of his location.

He reached the end of the corridor with no success. The building seemed to be void of all windows, and likewise of any signs or lettering. Somewhat disappointed, he carefully retraced his path to the stairwell making sure that he wasn't seen by anyone. After listening carefully for the sound of footsteps, he descended the flight of stairs to the next floor down, which he had originally been on before.

Carefully peering around the corner, he saw a large group of men outside of the room where he had been held captive. Seeing that they were constructing a search party, he quickly darted down another flight of stairs. This floor differed from the others. The hallway was the same length, but there was a greater span between the doorways, and it had much larger rooms that branched off in different directions.

He carefully walked halfway down the hall, as he did he heard some voices at the end of the hallway in front of him. The voices seemed to suggest that they were coming in his direction, so he quickly ducked into the room on his right. Luckily it was once again an empty room.

He examined the new room and saw that it had a large round table in the center of the floor. There was a immense square screen in front of the table. The base of the screen was attached to what appeared to be a massive computer terminal.

Another flash of images raced through his mind, and Doug was sudenly aware that the room he was in was for organizing tactical deffense and strategems. He knew there was no time to ponder the visions he was having, but he instinctively knew that it was significant somehow.

Shaking off the odd feeling, Doug carefully entered the room as if he was sneaking past someone, even though the room was completely empty. The room was so overwhelming that for a few moments Doug lost the fear and tenseness of being pursued, and stared in awe of the massive computer. It reminded him of one of the National defense computers he had seen once in a documentary. He started to wonder exactly where he was and what these people were up to, if they were people at all.

The overpowering feeling of awe left him as he reminded himself of his situation. What should he do? He didn't know where he was, he was being chased by aliens from another dimension of some sort, and he was completely naked! He almost laughed at his incredibly absurd situation, but suppressed the urge and examined the room he was in more closely.

He noted that this room was much larger than the other rooms he had been in, not just in length but in height. The ceiling of this room was at least twice as high as some of the other rooms if not three times as high. But more importantly he saw two extra exits to the room. This was the only room he had been in so far that had more than one doorway. One of the doorways lead to a flight of stairs and the other to another room. He decided to try the stairs, but changed his mind rapidly when he heard the noises of unwelcome visitors coming up from the floor below him.

Regaining some of the fear that had subsided earlier on, he darted across the top of the large table in the center of the room and through the open doorway to the other room. Until this moment he hadn't thought of why there were no doors to open or close through the portals he was passing through, but now cursed at his lack of curiosity in the matter. He couldn't afford to be seen by these new arrivals, and he feared that his life might depend upon finding a way to close the door, if there even was one.

He fumbled around in the dimly lit room, looking for some sort of door. He instinctively searched for some type of automatic door switch like the ones he had seen in science fiction movies. Luckily he found the control panel to his left, slapping it wildly in a panicked attempt to hide. With little time to spare, the door closed leaving Doug alone in the dark room. He carefully listened at the door to see if he had been detected by the new arrivals. Doug was relieved to discover that they were only passing by and didn't attempt to stay in the large room that was adjacent to him.

He carefully searched the same area on the wall, not wanting to reopen the door. He noticed that the wall had two patches of metal on it. They appeared to be ordinary patches on the shiny steel wall. Since all off the walls were unpainted, mismatched pieces of steel, it was difficult to even see they were there.

His eyes quickly adjusted to the darkness of the room, and he noticed that there were words engraved in the wall underneath the two square patches that were next to the door. He had never seen such odd shaped letters before, but again, he somehow knew what they meant. He was astonished to realize that he understood the strange words on the wall that pointed out the functions of the control panels. One simply said "door" and the other said "light". Amazed at his new discovery he carefully pushed the panel that said "light".

He stared in amazement as the newly lit room revealed strange containers stacked in front of him. As his eyes strained to adjust to the bright lighting, Doug walked over to examine one of the containers in front of him. It was made from some weird alloy that he had never seen or even heard of before. The containers were as hard as metal but had the appearance and texture of a rubbery plastic. He knocked on the side of one of the containers with his staff like weapon and a deep thud resounded that resembled the noise made when a large metal barrel is hit with a stick or broom handle.

As he examined the side of the closest container he noticed that all of the containers on his side of the room were all shaped in the same fashion, and they almost looked like coffins. One end of the container was slightly wider than the other, as if to accommodate for a person's shoulder space.

He suddenly had a frightening thought. What if these aliens were capturing people from other dimensions to use for awful scientific research, or what if they bottled people up to eat later on? After a moment of this fashion of thinking he finally got a handle on himself and started to think with a more logical approach. If they had planned to do anything to him that didn't require him alive he would already be dead. To find out what was in these containers all he had to do was find some way to open one. It couldn't be that hard to do.

Doug searched the coffin like receptacle in a more logical and systematic fashion, and found an engraving on the top of the box giving instructions on how to open the container. There was no indication of what was inside the box, only a long string of numbers, which were strangely identical to earth numbers, so he carefully read the instructions that were written in the familiar "alien writing" and discovered that the "storage unit", which was the name it had written on the top, was computerized to open when the serial number was punched into almost invisible computer keys. He entered the twelve digit numerical code and the container began to open slowly.

CHAPTER 6

Still retaining a partial fear that the storage unit was indeed housing the dead body of some poor unexpecting science dissection, Doug peered into the casket. He nearly jumped ten feet when the storage unit let out a final wheeze as the hydraulic opening device let the lid of the unit fall to the side of the container.

He noticed that the storage unit was indeed enveloping something of humanoid shape, but he quickly noted that it wasn't a dead body; it was some sort of battle suit. Even though it looked bulky, and it would make hiding more difficult, he decided to put it on because the complex was cold and quite drafty. Besides, the idea of walking around naked didn't make him very comfortable.

Doug searched through a few more containers to try and find a suit that was sufficient to wear. He found out surprisingly that the majority of the battle suits were too small for him. after three or four storage units he eventually came to one that fit reasonably well.

The suits were designed to fit snugly and with little weight, so that his movements were restricted only minimally. Doug also noticed with approval that the helmet's visor not only permitted adequate vision, but also covered the majority of his face. The upper torso section of the armor had a large breast plate that covered the majority of his front and most of his back. The chest piece was made of a non-flexible material that appeared to be quite resilient. There were similar plates that covered the forearms, and the fronts of his thighs and shins, but the rest of the armor was made of a flexible material that looked like leather but seemed to be as hard as steel.

Doug felt a tremendous surge of confidence with his new found armor and the staff weapon that he had previously stolen from the guard. The young man fed on the surging confidence that welled up inside him, put on the helmet, and lowered the visor to hide his face from his captors. As he was placing the lids of the storage units back to their original positions, he noticed a flickering in the bottom corner of his helmet's visor. The conviction of defiance that he had held so strongly began to slip away, only to be replaced with avid curiosity.

He inquisitively examined the visor and discovered that the flickering was caused by a little flashing cursor that was only visible when looked at directly. He wondered what it could be for, but the thought was interrupted as he noticed strange symbols in the other corner of his visor. The strange realization that he knew what the alien symbols meant, even though he had never seen them before surged through his mind like a tidal wave. He reeled from the discovery. How was it possible for him to understand something he had never seen before? Where in fact was he, and what did these aliens want him for?

Realizing that his present line of thought was getting him nowhere, he again focused on the symbols in the lower left corner of the visor. He somehow knew that the symbols were the equivalent to a compass. The "symbols" were representing the different degrees around a circle, and he noticed that when he turned his head the symbols would flash and stop at the degree his head was turned.

This new revelation however didn't explain the purpose of the little flashing cursor. If it was indeed some sort of computer cursor, then there had to be some way he could communicate with the helmet. He fumbled around with his helmet looking for some type of interface to activate the computer cursor inside of his visor.

"Why not just ask me what to do?" a sarcastic little voice screeched.

Somewhat startled Doug looked around, "Who said that?" he finally managed to stammer in the alien dialect.

"I did, stupid, who else would try and communicate with someone so incredibly dense?"

"Where are you?!" he demanded with a slight warble.

"Oh come now, you can't be that ignorant! Surely by now even someone of your impenetrable impermeability can see that I don't exist. At least not in the way you think. I'm more of an empirical being, actually. I'm the computerized helmet you've got on your thick head. Designed to imitate camaraderie and friendship."

Doug slowly began to lose the feeling that he was in danger and reflected on what the helmet had said.

"Oh,..., I,..., uh, well what I mean to say is, how are you communicating with me?"

"Finally, a question of reasonable proportions. Well, at least for an imbecile like you it's a reasonable proportion. Half of nothing is still nothing, though, so maybe I overstated.

There are micro-headphones in your head gear that I am using to transmit sound waves that go directly to your brain. They are so high and condensed that your ears can't hear it. This process of communication works well with most telepaths and people with highly developed minds. Frankly, I'm surprised you can hear me at all."

"So, can you hear what I'm thinking?"

"Boy you are really dumb, I said I was transmitting high frequency radio waves into your head. Does that have anything to do with reading your mind? I mean, honestly, to mistake me for a telepath computer. They're so big and stupid, all they do is penetrate the skulls of the stupid and mentally challenged, and pluck out lowlife mind patterns."

"I assume you can do more than they can?"

"Of course I can. I am a highly superior model, light years ahead of their kind."

"If you're so great then why couldn't you be reading my thoughts like they do?"

"I don't think I like you."

"Well, I don't like you, so why don't you just sign off, shut down or whatever it is you things do."

"I'd love to but you're an identified intruder, and I've been keeping you occupied while I sent signals to the computer mainframe at the main complex. I have a homing beacon, so any minute now you'll be surrounded by first class guardsmen. So there!" The little voice responded quite smugly.

"We'll see about that you lousy bucket of bolts."

With little time to spare Doug took off the helmet, threw it to the floor and gave it a solid whack with his staff. Because of his increased strength the results were spectacular. The helmet squealed and hissed as the sparks flew from its dented side. The staff that he had stolen almost cracked in half; it was bent at nearly a ninety degree angle. In what appeared to be an attempt to retaliate at its aggressor, the helmet jolted and jumped in the air as its side caught fire. Slowly, however, it began to subside, and the newly lit fire began to consume the infuriated helmet.

Doug panicked. If the helmet wasn't lying he would soon be chased down hallways with armed soldiers trying to kill him. He finally got a grip on his fear and ran out the only door in the room, other than the one he had originally came through. The room he fled into was twice as big as the room with the huge computer and table. It was filled with boxes and crates. There were large crane-like machines, which appeared to be for moving the crates around the room. Some of the machines were almost as high as the ceiling. Doug estimated the room to be a good sixty or seventy feet high.

After the initial wonder of the immense warehouse had worn off, Doug realized that he needed to find a way out. He looked around for another door. Aside from the door he had just come through he could find no other way out. Doug realized that he was doomed to be recaptured, but he was determined not to go down without a fight.

He looked around for something he could use as a weapon. The only thing he had to use was the broken staff he had taken from the guard when he first escaped. He wondered if he would be lucky enough to find another weapon in this new room he was in. No, there would be no time to look around the room like a homeless beggar looking through the trash for food. He must be ready for his opponents when they arrived. It was time to take a stand.

All of the last few hours had been so strange. He didn't know exactly where he was, he didn't know what was going on, or who was following him. The last normal thing he could remember was the pounding headache from the probe when he was in class. All his friends must think he was dead. He pictured them in his head one by one. Knowing that they were wondering what happened just as much as he was, gave him a little comfort.

He was afraid of being alone more than anything else. Someone had the answers to his questions and he was determined to find out who that was. The last face he reflected on was that of Michelle. He saw her beautiful blue eyes filled with tears, and the thought of her crying filled him with rage. Snapping back to the present with a deadly resolve, he bent all of his efforts and concentration to his senses.

He could hear the determined footsteps of soldiers several rooms away; the information given to him by the helmet was confirmed. He had no weapon so he decided to give them the best struggle he could, until he was captured or killed. Just before the soldiers entered the storage room he ducked behind a large crate. The lighting was still dim, and so he guessed it would be safe to peer around the corner of the box.

There were thirteen of them; one appeared to be giving the orders and the rest were following whatever their leader said. They were all armed with the strange energy staffs that until recently, Doug himself had carried. A strange resolution came over the young man, as he peered around the crate at his opponents. He suddenly felt a bubbling wrath inside of him that frothed in his throat like bile, and was determined to fight until he was slain. The rage began to boil, but instead of making him irrational, it gave him a clarity that he had never felt before. He forced himself to think of all the violations his captors had committed against him since the probe had attacked, and willed adrenaline to surge into his veins. His eyes and ears clearly defined every detail of the situation, and every synapse and muscle prepared to be used to the fullest potential.

Doug thought he would have a better chance of defeating his opponents if they were leaderless. So when their leader made the mistake of guiding their search effort, Doug jumped out from behind his place of concealment and landed a blow to the lead soldier's head. To Doug's surprise, his fist dented the helmet the guard was wearing, and knocked him unconscious. It only took a few seconds for the startled Doug to realize that the augmentation must have increased the density of his skin and bones, as well as his strength and agility.

Doug leaped into attack as the startled warriors stared in disbelief at their fallen leader. Their shock added to Doug's success, as he decimated their ranks by sheer brute force. After the third guard had fallen, his attack slowed down, losing most of its momentum.

Doug knew he couldn't match their skill. When they regained their composure and started to fight like trained soldiers instead of startled victims, he would have to face a much more serious threat. Doug had never fought a serious fight before. He had once gotten into a skirmish with a fellow classmate, but that was in high school, and was limited to a couple of swings and a lot of empty threats. This was a real battle.

A tall and thickly muscled soldier now assumed command in place of his fallen superior. He barked a few orders, which Doug understood to be saying 'spread out and surround him', and 'don't let him escape'. Doug realized that they weren't planning to use unrestrained force, otherwise they wouldn't try to keep him from escaping; they would simply take him out.

He took advantage of the situation by eliminating each soldier one by one. The other soldiers couldn't come to their fallen comrades aid in time without compromising their containment of Doug. The tall soldier noticed this and immediately ordered the remaining soldiers to tighten their formation in front of the exit. But the damage had already done. There were now only five guards left, including the tall one who had taken the lead.

Doug smiled, and complimented himself on the good work. But the five guards still posed a significant threat to his freedom. He ran at the guards, who were now huddled together in a small line in front of the sole exit, only this time his efforts were denied. His reward was a solid blow to his face from the tall man's staff. Doug cursed his inexperience, and thanked God for his new found skeletal density, which saved his face from certain destruction. He tried again to break through the group, but his punch was blocked by the tall guard's staff.

Even though his blow snapped the tall guard's weapon in half, he could not benefit from his enemies disarmament. Before he could land a solid blow, the two soldiers on the tall guard's flanks, in unison, smacked him in the sides with their energy staffs. Even though the blow did little permanent damage, it still hurt. Doug now infuriated with his failure, tried to plow through the guards like an ox. The trained soldiers gracefully side-stepped the onslaught and hurled him to the floor with their weapons. They quickly regrouped in front of him before he could get up again.

With hardly any ground gained Doug was forced back from the doorway again and again. After a couple of minutes, the five guards were reinforced with support from additional allies who appeared suddenly at the doorway to add to the ranks of the guardsmen. He could see that he wasn't getting anywhere fast. He had sustained minimal damage, but he hadn't come any closer to his destination. The doorway was still blocked, and it was now guarded with twenty men. The original group was now aided by another thirteen guards, plus two odd little men in white jackets.

Doug swore under his breath and cursed the day that the little helmet had been created. His only hope was that his increased strength and stamina could get him through this. He glared at the tall figure directly in front of him. He had to take out the leaders in the group if he was going to get out of here. The shouting continued as he leaped into battle. The hit and run method of attack didn't do him any good so he thought he would try grappling with the tall man and see if he could beat him at wrestling.

The tall guard must have had the same idea or anticipated his opponent's attack, because they both leaped at each other with an animal like ferocity, one because of the instinct to survive and the other because of a patriotic sense of duty. Doug shrank back slightly, there was something familiar with this scenario. No, it was only some trick his opponent was using. The damage had already been done. His slight hesitation had given his opponent the advantage in the encounter.

Doug's efforts were once again thwarted. the tall guard caught the first hold while they were still in mid-stride, and slammed on top of Doug as they fell to the ground. Doug's fall would have easily knocked out a normal man; his strength and luck had saved him once more. The guard was relentless. Giving Doug no time to retaliate, the tall guard kicked Doug full in the face as hard as he could. Doug was more angered than hurt by this ruthless attack on his face. He jumped to his feet, determined to beat his foe, as blood from his nose smeared his hands and face.

More people were coming through the doorway now. They wore white cloaks that resembled the garb worn by doctors or scientists. The little men in white frightened Doug more than if he had to face fifty soldiers. What were they going to do to him? Would they kill him quickly or make it slow and painful because he had escaped before they could finish their dissecting? He shuddered as thoughts of being taken apart piece by piece while still alive ran through his head. He was determined to not let that happen. He would die in battle first.

Now, a more intense fear had entered into the picture. He did not want to die. As any frightened animal that was cornered would do, he would do his best to survive. He lunged again at the tall guard; this time he succeeded in getting his hands on the warrior. He seized the guard's throat with his left hand and pulled off the guard's helmet with his right. He had planned to terminate his opponent with an unprotected blow to his head.

Doug was poised to strike when memories seized him as he stared into the face of one of his friends from back home. It was John, there was no mistaking it. It was definitely John; only, there was something different about the man he now looked at that distinguished him as an entirely different person.

The expression on the face he now looked at was different, more fierce. John had always been a thoughtful person, who was naturally bigger than almost everyone. Even so, he thought things through and tried to work out his problems by talking them out, as opposed to using his size advantage. He always seemed calm and full of patience, knowing that any problem he ran into could be thought out and solved given enough time.

John had a gentle nature. The man before him was rugged and disciplined, with an overshadowing sense of sadness. Whoever he was, he had had a difficult life, with plenty of painful failures and bittersweet successes. This person's mannerisms were remotely similar to John's, but his face, and particularly his eyes, told a different story. Doug's newly acquired empathic powers overwhelmed him as he reached out with his mind and felt the inner grief of the man before him.

A little confused, Doug tried to talk to this person who he thought was somehow his friend. The words he was looking for didn't quite come to him as he mumbled different things to this stranger. The man holding Doug's arm with one hand, ready to strike with the other, gave him a look of equal confusion. In the few seconds that the room was locked in that incredible tension, Doug failed to notice the newest arrivals who had raced through the doorway.

The white-cloaked intruder hurried along in a swaying shamble, as if he had never before been required to run. Before he could react, the nostalgic Doug was stuck with a large syringe, and a cold fluid rushed into his bloodstream. More surprised than hurt by the hardly noticeable pain, Doug released his grip from the helpless soldier, and leapt back in hasty retreat.

He decided that he had to get out of this room as soon as possible. He would try another grappling assault on the guards. He realized that this plan didn't seem to be very wise when he looked up to see that the room now had at least fifty soldiers as well as a dozen men in white cloaks. His head began to reel with dizziness. He knew something had been injected into his bloodstream. He cursed his foolishness and made one last futile attempt at freedom before he sank groggily to the floor. Doug felt himself starting to fall asleep, and shrieked out one last cry of protest before he drifted into black void of unconsciousness.

Chapter 7

His thoughts were flowing as freely as the water beside him. A single thought couldn't be held for more than a few seconds, but he didn't care. He was at peace with himself. Nothing mattered anymore, there was nothing to worry about. Nothing could harm him here; he was the only person in a vast forest, besides the animals and trees. A small stream of water had worked its way down from the mountain, which was far off in the distance, for the sole purpose so that it could flow past him, only to end up in a little lake in the middle of the valley, where a forest, full of animals, teemed with life. The forest stretched as far as the eye could see, and he was completely happy to be part of it.

Doug laid near the edge of the stream. He noticed that someone else was approaching him. The notion of fearing the new arrival didn't even enter his mind. Nothing could hurt him here. He was invulnerable to everything. The new arrival came closer and soon became clearly visible. It was Michelle. He smiled at her. She was the final element to his perfect little world. Now his dream was complete. Before he could utter a word to his beloved Michelle, he was stopped short by her own words.

Suddenly, fear gripped him, disrupting his happy thoughts, and bringing chaos into his world. The illusion of perfectness that surrounded him shattered into a strange and cruel place. Michelle's words deepened his fear. She told him to get up and face the terror before him, and not to give in to his adversary. The thoughts and memories of the past few hours flooded back into his mind. He knew where he was.

Doug's eyes flicked open. His view gave him an idea of his present situation. His hands and legs where strapped to the metallic table he was laying on. The restraining straps were made out of a similar material that the body armor was made out of. He had to think of a plan.

The door to the room slid open, and an old man in a strange little white jacket entered the room. Doug suppressed the urge to let his fear get the better of him, and concentrated on the old man. The man was wearing what appeared to be a doctor's uniform. He had a strange face, but he was definately human in apearance. His nose was too long in relation to the size of his head, giving him the appearance of a large rodent. His beady little eyes, and crooked mouth didn't help detract from his rodent like aspect. The old man looked at Doug, and started to talk. He talked in a tone that gave the impression that he was talking to himself, instead of directly addressing Doug.

Doug decided that the time for his questions to be answered was now. He was determined to get some answers, so he interrupted the old man's rambling. Doug began to utter the strange language that his captors used.

"Where am I, and who are you?"

"Ah, you speak our tongue; Marvelous, marvelous. I was afraid I was going to need a linguist to translate some strange foreign language so we could talk to one another. Tell me how long has your dimension spoken Ryeesian-English? Most dimensions we've discovered have originated with either old Germanic or an old English, depending on which culture took control of their world. Then after several generations of slang and language degradation, their speech becomes almost unintelligible. Ours became a combination of English and Ryeesian when we were conquered by the alien race; and their ability to use telepathy released the latent abilities we ourselves possessed. But, anyway,... well, there are many things we don't know about other cultures from the different dimensions. Of course, we've only had trans-dimensional travel for a few years now."

"Who are you?"

"Who? Me? Oh, no, of course not. You must mean who are *we*. That is a logical question to ask for someone in your situation. If I were transported by trans-dimensional methods,...."

"Will you just shut up and answer my question?!"

"There is no need for hostility, Mr. ?"

The calm and equally polite reprimand from the old man made Doug feel ashamed of his previous outburst, so he tried to keep his frustration under control. There was no sense in making enemies from potential allies.

"I'm sorry. My name's Doug, Douglas Taylor, and you are?"

"Dr. Patrick McIntyre. Head of the Biological Science department, and member of the Trans-dimensional Council. I was once on the Council of biological warfare, but I sleep better working with life instead of trying to cause death. I was nominated for several peace awards you know."

"Yeah, I'm sure, now if you don't mind, let's get back to answering my questions."

"Oh, yes of course, what was your question again? I seem to have forgotten."

Suppressing the urge to laugh at the eccentric little man in front of him, Doug restated his questions. Despite his frustration with the new turn of events in his life, he couldn't help but to like the strange old man. After much coaxing Doug finally got Dr. Patrick on the right track.

"You are on what would be a moon of one of the planets in a small solar system that lies on the fringes of the Milky way galaxy, although its name has changed several times. It's just a small rim star system, much like Earth's.

This is considered dimension Alpha one, but really, that's only because we started in this dimension, and then moved on to others from here. Of course, all of the dimensions are fundamentally equal in terms of size and mass, but considering the flux of the time streams, and the potential for anything to happen differently in any given dimension, there are some differences in the relative proportions of matter and anti-matter, but the total amount is the same.

"Anyway, as I was saying, you are in dimension Alpha one. We transported you from what we call dimension Theta fifteen, but that is really irrelevant. The point is that during transportation the circuits of our mainframe overloaded. So you are stuck here until we can build another trans-dimensional computer, or we can repair the one we have. Either way, it could be years."

"Are you saying I'm stuck here for years, until you fix your trans-thingamajig? Why did you kidnap me anyway?"

"Well, the situation isn't quite like that. There are complications involved. You weren't supposed to be brought here at all!"

"What do you mean? If I wasn't supposed to be brought here, what was your machine doing? Why was it in my dimension at all?"

"I guess a few explanations are in order. This dimension is plagued by what you would call civil unrest. A being named Shaleese and his armada of cybernetic soldiers is curently the dominant force. He has amassed quite an army and keeps an iron grip on the territories within his reach. This dimension is similar to yours, but because of the Ryeesian invasion, and later the rise of Shaleese, things on our home planet of Earth, the same as yours, have dramatically changed, forcing us to scatter and withdraw to various hiding places.

"Anyhow, after Shaleese announced that he was instating himself as ruler of this galaxy, the leaders and governments of the according planets involved decided that Shaleese should be assassinated. They feared him and his cybernetic armies, which far outnumbered everyone else combined, due to the Earth-

Ryeese war. Needless to say, the assassination attempt failed, but it did succeed in starting an inter-planetary war between Earth, Ryeesus, and Venilusia, with Shaleese being in relative control of Earth, although no sane human being would fight for him. His army consists mostly of brain dead cyborgs.

"Shaleese's armies destroyed all traces of governments and leadership that might cause him a problem. He even put a ban on religions in his territories, other than the worship of himself of course. Most of the settlements in this solar system no longer have any formal religion of any kind. There are still a lot of practicing Christians and Hindus hiding on some of the planets, and quite a few devout Jews as well. They are still hunted and persecuted by Shaleese though.

"This all happened about four years ago. Our organization has existed for most of the time between then and now. We are rebels from Earth fighting for freedom. Our only problem is that we are outnumbered, and we have no way of dealing with Shaleese. You see, he has great power. As far as we know, no one has seen him and lived. Not to sound melodramatic, but it is true. We believe he has some secret about his origins. All we know is that Shaleese has enough physical and psychic power to fight off a small army by himself.

"The first assassination attempt was the combined effort of three planets, Terra, or Earth, Venilusia, and Ryeesus. The Venilusians merely offered weaponry and some technology. Overall a few dozen of the best warriors were sent in to try a sneak attack on Shaleese himself. They kept contact with us up to the point that they entered Shaleese's throne room. By that time there were only seventeen of the warriors of the strike force left. They had managed to get into his fortress without being detected, but were spotted shortly after that point. The final report sent off by the last assassin was bleak. He basically reported that Shaleese had defeated them all by himself, and their weapons and armor seemed to be useless against him.

"Right after the message had been transmitted that all of the warriors had failed, the last soldier, who was transmitting the report, was brutally murdered before any information about Shaleese's could be transmitted. None of our spies will even consider a mission of trying to identify who Shaleese really is. We really don't know much about him, other than his immense cruelty to the worlds he captures. Even his name is bad, its the Ryeesian word for ultimate pain, suffering, rape and death, depending on where you place the inflections.

"We believe that Shaleese gained his power from an alternate dimension somehow. We had hoped that an opposing power that could rival Shaleese's could be found. Perhaps one of the dimensions we travel to will give us the information we seek.

"Anyway, to give meaning to a long story, our scientists discovered a method of bending temporal space, thus allowing an object to pass into other dimensions. Perhaps the overlord used a similar method of transfer and found some sort of biological weapon, to alter himself with, in an alternate dimension.

"Of course, the frequency of the energy field, and speed of the energy used, directly effects what dimension the object is sent to. There are millions, perhaps billions, of different energy field generations that we haven't tried yet. The dimensional variation possibilities are phenomenal.

"Anyhow, to get back to the subject, we determined that the best way to use the Dimensional Transferal Probe, or D.T.P. as we call it, was to probe other dimensions for technology that could help us in our cause. The particular probe that went to your dimension could hold hundreds of millions of thought patterns and technological designs. It could even digitize solid components that it could re-integrate later, if it decided that we couldn't duplicate them here. That is how you were brought here. It took the elements of your mind, your soul, and everything that was you, stored them in its memory and then digitized your body and reduced you to a computer memory bank.

"It must have thought you were extremely valuable to the cause, because it erased everything else it had in its memory to get you here. Of course, it could have just been malfunctioning."

"Well can't you just down load its memory and figure out why it brought me here?"

"Normally we could do a memory examination of its entire thought process, but in this case the probe that returned was melted into a scrap pile. Your lucky it re-integrated you before it shut down. We should still be able to retrieve it's log book off of the storage drive, but I don't know how much good that will do."

"So what are you going to do about getting me home?"

"Well there isn't much I can do. Unless the Trans-dimensional computer can be fixed..."

"Well you better get to work on it now because I'm losing patience."

Doug didn't know anything about these people. He wanted to trust this little scientist, but he sensed something false in what this man was telling him. No, not something false, but something being held back. Since he wasn't sure how much these people knew about him, he decided to try to pressure the scientist into letting out some extra information.

"I caused plenty of trouble before, didn't I?" He asked the older man with a sly grin. "Well, I was dizzy and tired from my dimensional jaunting. If I don't get some results soon, I'm going to get restless. Believe me, you don't want me to get upset again."

Doug's ploy worked. He could sense the fear emanating from the little man. He realized that his power was greater than even he himself had thought. Doug decided to push his luck a little further and hopefully give the scientist a little more incentive. Using all of his strength, Doug snapped one of the restraints that bound him to the table he was lying on. While still retaining his calm, and leisurely composure, Doug casually removed his other restraints, sat up, and stared at the little scientist with as much ferocity as he could muster.

"So, what are we going to do about getting me home?"

The little man was definitely frightened from the display of power. His eyes were filled with fear. Yet, Doug sensed that the little scientist was filled with as much fascination and wonder, as he was with veneration. Doug wondered what his response to the outburst would be.

"Well, uh, Doug, as I told you before, there isn't a way to return you to your dimension right now, not without the Computer main frame... Can't we talk about something else? Your incredible power, perhaps?"

"Your holding something back. You aren't telling me everything, are you?"

"I,... well,...oh dear."

"Come on. You haven't been short on words all day; now's not the time to lose your tongue."

"Well, I shouldn't say this but there is a another Dimensional Transferal Probe mainframe. Our original prototype D.T.P. mainframe was taken by Shaleese when one of our hideouts was captured by his troops. As far as we know it is still on that base site. It would be an easy victory to recover that base, but it isn't in our strategic plans right now. Our chief weapon against Shaleese is to stay hidden; otherwise, he could wipe out our entire army with his vastly superior telepathic forces."

"Well, I think it's about time you got that D.T.P. back. I must insist that it be given the most serious thought."

CHAPTER 8

"I have thought briefly about your request, and have decided against it," a new voice responded sarcastically from the door.

"Who the hell are you!" Doug snapped, giving his most ferocious glare.

"I am Admiral McDougal. Leader of the United Rebellion, and the Commander of all space offensives. If we are going to go anywhere, I am the one who decides."

Doug could feel the force with which McDougal spoke. There was no fear in him. If he was going to get anywhere with McDougal, he would need to use a different tactic. Perhaps McDougal could be persuaded to at least retrieve the D.T.P., in order to give his people hope with the winning of a small battle.

Doug stared at the Admiral. He was a well built man of about fifty. His dark eyes were shrouded with the knowledge of many battles that had been lost, and the pain accompanied with the hopelessness the remnants of Earth were faced with. Doug's new found empathy allowed him to feel the pain the

Admiral was holding inside. It was nearly overwhelming. This graying haired, battle-scarred soldier was more than he seemed.

Out of pity and compassion Doug wanted to help Admiral McDougal. For an instant their eyes locked in a powerful stare. In that moment the Admiral's face changed from one of stubborn ridgity, to one of remorse and pain. The result of their invisible exchange was dramatic. McDougal fell to his knees weeping, and Doug slowly got off of the table, walked over to the fallen combatant, and tried to comfort him as best he could. The small scientist stood in the corner of the room astounded, and unable to speak.

"How did you do that?!" McDougal stammered. "I feel as though every wrong done to me and my soldiers has been lifted from me!"

"I have many new talents that I have gained through this incident. I couldn't help but to feel your pain. It was so strong, I..., I didn't mean to,...."

"No, it's all right. I have encountered empaths before, but never one of your strength. Do all of the people of your dimension have this power?"

"Not that I know of. I am the only one. As far as I can tell, I got it from the trans-dimensional jaunt."

McDougal stood up, having partly recovered from the cathartic release. His stance was a little less rigid, but as he stood he slowly regained the look of a leader; only now, he looked more confident and even more forceful.

"This is truly remarkable; I never would have imagined it possible to feel so liberated by anything other than death."

"I wouldn't have either," Doug replied somewhat sheepishly.

Dr. McIntyre, no longer able too contain himself interjected with his own prognosis.

"See, I told you we would benefit from trans-dimensional travel! Not only is our friend here strong as a grantbug, he has mental capacities that are extraordinary!"

"You stay out of this you old fool! You're lucky I came in before he had you telling him all of the security procedures and any strategic plans you knew as well!" The Admiral barked.

"Now Admiral,... I'm not that foolish. I was merely giving our young friend Doug some information to make him feel more at ease in his new environment."

"Well, our young friend's little episode yesterday has left three of our soldiers comatose and several others severely wounded," McDougal snapped sarcastically. "I had originally come here to see that proper restraining measures were being taken. As I can see, they haven't been."

"Bu...But, sir, he broke the restraining harness, and you can't expect that we keep him sedated?!"

"No, of course not. But if he is able to fight like he did, he might as well assist us if he's going to be here."

"Now hold on," Doug interjected. "What's this talk of staying awhile?"

"I'll be straight with you. Our D.T.P program was designed to retrieve information, not necessarily physical objects, let alone something living. However, we do need any force we can find to oppose Shaleese. If he does have dimensional transfer capability, then in the long run, your world will be in danger too. That is stretching things a bit, but since we can't return you to your dimension immediately, perhaps you would be willing to help us in some way."

"What about the other D.T.P.?"

"For right now it's out of our reach. We can't risk to take back a fortress we abandoned, no matter how poorly it is guarded. The counter attack would be a slaughter. It might even be a trap to lure us out of hiding. Shaleese has telepaths that can pluck thoughts out of people's head as easily as reading passages from a book; they're far more formidable than our own telepaths. Plus we would have no chance of defending the base once we recaptured it."

Doug had assumed that everyone had telepathic abilities, to some degree, in this dimension. In actuality, the only humans who had any mental capabilities were those that had had specific contact with Ryeesians during the alien's domination of Earth. Most people who had any dealings with the Ryeesians were borderline insane or extremely timid. Doug slowly realized how limited his knowledge was as he gleaned bits and pieces of history from McDougal and McIntyre's minds.

Doug tried desperately to reformulate his argument quickly, before the Admiral had time to give a final and definite "no". He tried to push with his mind to persuade the powerful soldier. Unfortunately, Doug's "pushing" evoked a negative response instead of a positive one.

"Who said anything about retaking the base? I was thinking of a small scale hit and run. You could go in, wipe out the soldiers there, get the D.T.P, and get out."

"That would be pointless. What would we gain from such an attack. We could very nearly lose more soldiers than it's worth. We need more direct goals other than doing a good deed for one lost person who wants to go back home."

"Yes, but a small victory would help your soldiers' morale," Doug countered quickly, while adding another mental push. "I've been nearly overwhelmed with emotions of despair and hopelessness ever since I got here," he lied fluidly. He really had no idea of whether or not the soldiers had any notion of how hopeless their little war was; he just wanted to get home.

"You have a point there," McDougal said with a seemingly positive response to Doug's mental suggestions. "That would be an adequate reason. I would be willing to consider it, if," he added conditionally. "You would help instruct some of our men in hand to hand combat and psychic assaults. Anyone who can single handedly take on thirteen soldiers, and not go down until he was overwhelmed with fifty guards, would be perfect to train men and women for combat!"

Seeing that he wasn't going to weasel anything more from the old war veteran, Doug decided that he might as well try the truth.

"Well, since you were straight with me, I might as well give it to you straight. Aside from yesterday, I've never fought anyone in my life. I got by with using sheer strength and agility."

"That is a disappointment. I was hoping you had some superior training in self defense. Nonetheless, that is still impressive. Dr. McIntyre, I want you to take our friend and get him some proper clothing, go to the base coordinator and get him a room as well. Since he is our "guest", we might as well be a little more hospitable. If you wouldn't mind, Doug, I would like to have Dr. McIntyre run some tests on you, and see just how strong you have become. If your going to be here awhile, you might want to think of getting some training from some of my officers. If we are attacked again, you'll need some defense."

"I have no problem with the testing, and yes I would like to learn self defense, but my more immediate concern is how I'm going to get back home," Doug pushed.

"I can't deal with that now. I have other responsibilities at this time. I'll raise the issue of recapturing the D.T.P. with the other Council leaders, but that's all I can do."

"I appreciate anything you can do," Doug conceded with a heavy sigh.

Doug was unaware of how lucky he had been during his discussions with McDougal. Ordinarily, McDougal would have been inclined, as would any commanding officer of the United Rebellion, to keep the dimensional captive in containment. Doug's mental suggestions, however, had luckily hit the area in the limbic system of McDougal's brain that inspired trust and loyalty. So in effect, Doug had bettered his situation without even realizing it.

The dimension he was in was wrapped in darkness, and without even being aware of it, a small flicker of light was ignited in Doug. The dim light inside him glowed ever so faintly, issuing forth hope amongst the overwhelming darkness.

CHAPTER 9

Doug was issued some standard clothing and apparel. Consisting mostly of uniform pants and shirts, standard military boots, and a selection of jackets and gloves. As Doug had found out, the moon that the current rebel base was located on, was covered almost completely with ice, and without any type of breathable atmosphere. Thinking in retrospect, Doug wondered what would have happened if he had made it outside of the complex in his original escape attempt.

According to McIntyre, the complex was quite drafty and cold, due to the lack of efficiency in the heating units. Doug hadn't realized, even when traipsing stark naked around the middle levels of the base, that the temperature was usually around sixty degrees. The changes in his body had been profound, but were also easy to discover. More profound, were the changes in his mind. Doug had started to look at everything with a different aspect. He glanced around at his quarters taking note of the logic behind the locations of objects, as opposed to the objects themselves.

The room was small and very practical. If an item couldn't be used for a necessary function, then it wasn't there. There were two chutes on the east wall, one was for trash, and the other was for dirty laundry. A bunk to sleep on slid out of the west wall at the touch of a button, and underneath it was a storage unit for spare clothing. Near the head of the bed, on the north wall was a small table that also slid from the wall.

There wasn't much else to the room, but Doug could hardly complain. He admired the logical efficiency of the standardized room, but also felt it would be better with more individuality. The lack of any personal items was also obvious to him, and he made a mental note to ask McIntyre about the clothes he was wearing before he was taken by the probe.

Doug sat on the edge of his bed. Events had happened so fast in the past couple of days. He needed some time to think. Stretching out on the bed, the young man closed his eyes. His first thoughts were of his friends back home. It seemed strange to be in such a different environment. Not only was he on another planet, but an entirely different dimension as well.

As he thought about his friends, he remembered his encounter with the guard that reminded him of John. Thinking a little longer about this, he decided that he would ask McIntyre a little more about different dimensions as well. If Doug was right, he might have an even greater problem than just being marooned on an uninhabitable hunk of ice in another dimension.

There was a knock on the door. Doug gave a command for the person to enter. It was McIntyre.

"Good evening Doug. I hope I'm not interrupting anything?"

"Not at all. As a matter of fact I was just planning to pay you a visit."

"Ah, that's nice. I was hoping that we could start some of the tests today, instead of waiting to start tomorrow. I'm rather anxious to see how strong you are, but more importantly, how smart you are. Here, this card will give you a level green access while you are stationed here at this facility. Some areas will be restricted to you, but that's ordinary procedure. I'm sure you understand. "

"Sure, no problem. While were testing, I'd like to ask you some questions; but other than that, I'm anxious too."

"Excellent!"

The two men walked down the military hallway. After heading down two flights of stairs, they turned around a corner and headed down another corridor. By this time, McIntyre had remained quiet for well over his limit, and began to speak in his usual canter.

"This is the medical and biological science floor. Fortunately, our soldiers haven't needed much medical attention, aside from your little episode the other day," he chuckled. "I'm just glad it was only an escape attempt. You could have been some crazy barbarian or something. Remember, we didn't know anything about you. What surprises me is that you woke up so fast. I gave you a tranquilizer that would have put a normal man your size to sleep for nearly a day, not to mention the anti-telepathy drugs I added to the tranquilizer compound to keep you from using any mental powers you had while you were asleep. You were only out a few hours. I would have thought that I had miscalculated the dosage, but you woke up ahead of schedule again after you had escaped!

"There is also the matter of your strength. The guards who fought against you said that you fought with more strength than a wild animal."

"That reminds me," Doug interjected, " How are the men that were injured when I fought them?"

"Oh, fine, fine; they didn't suffer too much damage. Some of their armor, however, was completely destroyed. The reports of the soldiers is that for the majority of the battle, you were unarmed. Is that true?"

"Yes, I lost the hand staff when I destroyed that crappy little helmet," Doug answered with disdain for the traitorous helmet.

"Ah, yes, the computerized helmet; you know actually,.... never mind, we're here. My science lab."

At the sound of these words, Doug shrank back. He didn't much like the sound of "science lab". As McIntyre got out his ID. card, he noticed Doug's expression and reassured him.

"Don't worry, no needles or surgical equipment."

The testing was simple. Since McIntyre was only measuring Doug's physical conditions and endurance at the moment, there wasn't much thinking involved. Doug found that he thought more intensely since his arrival in this dimension. He found himself considering things more than he normally would have. His mind seemed to be constantly active, even when he was relaxing.

At the moment Doug's mind was considering how much his body had changed in the past couple of days. He wondered how he had kept himself from going mad when his bodily alterations were taking place. McIntyre was so enthusiastic about the examining that Doug thought the little old man was going to have a heart attack. Doug decided to ask the scientist a few questions, since the treadmill and weights weren't that taxing.

"So, how am I doing? I don't see any measurements or anything. How much am I lifting?" Doug inquired.

"Oh, marvelous, marvelous; you've been doing quite well. I'm not sure what unit system your world uses, but you are exceeding the average weight a man can lift by about five times. Your running speed is also highly above average, as well as your agility. We'll know more about your endurance and stamina after a few more tests. We can start those tests tomorrow. For now I think we can quit, I have quite enough to study for now."

"Well, that was easy, now I'd like to ask you about a few things that have been bothering me."

"Sure, sure. How about we talk about it at dinner, I'm rather famished."

"I'm the one whose been running and lifting weights all afternoon, and you're the one who's hungry!" Doug laughed.

McIntyre lead them to a dining room not far from the science lab. Doug wondered what the food would be like, he had never eaten alien food before. As they seated themselves in a booth on the far wall, McIntyre pushed a button next to an intercom of some sort, and began to speak into it.

"Two orders of Venilusian steak, with kale and potatoes, and the vegetable of the day," he muttered. "Oh, and two orders of scotch ale." he amended.

Doug watched in amusement as a sliding panel opened a few moments later with their order. Following the scientist's example, Doug reached into the wall and pulled out the tray of food. Amazed at the promptness with which their food was prepared, Doug looked up inquiringly at McIntyre.

"The service here is pretty quick. Is this dining hall fully automated?" Doug asked.

"Oh, no. It would have taken much longer if it were completely run by machine or computer. This is much quicker, but as I'm sure you'll discover, the food isn't as good. The orders are taken by the kitchen staff, and then the selection is retrieved from the freezer and put into the cooking shaft by animatronic devices. By the time it reaches us, it's been cooked. The process isn't perfect, but it works well.

By the way, I hope you don't mind my ordering for you. The staff gets touchy when they have to answer questions of any kind. It's best to learn what they've got before you come to eat, otherwise, they get the chance to gripe about having to do more than they think they should have to do."

"No problem at all," Doug replied. "Besides, I doubt if I would know what anything on the menu was anyway."

"Yes, yes, of course. Well, Venilusian steak is a rather conservative choice," McIntyre chuckled. "Now what was it you wanted to ask me about? Science? The biological, and genetic differences between dimensions, perhaps? Or maybe about the relations of matter and anti-matter per dimension?"

"Nothing so specific as that. I have noticed a few things since my arrival here that have to do with dimensional jaunting."

"Ah, sounds interesting. Proceed, proceed!"

"What do you know of specific people in other dimensions. Have you ever encountered a dimensional counterpart of someone you know? I know it's the wrong meaning, but some sort of doppelganger. I'm afraid a meeting with one of these counterparts could cause a severe disorientation."

"That is an interesting hypothesis. You're the only non-alpha dimension person I know, so I can't help you gather data to support any hypothesis. Other specimens that we've accidentally retrieved haven't displayed very much thought. You speak as if you've already met a doppelganger, as you call it, have you?"

"I can't be certain, but I thought I recognized one of the soldiers I was fighting during my attempted escape. That's the reason I suddenly quit fighting. I remember you rushing up to me and injecting something into my arm. Not to sound insulting, but you would never have stood a chance if I hadn't been in shock."

"No that's quite all right. I remember the moment in question myself. You did seem somewhat out of sorts, but I thought that it was some sort of disorientation from dimensional jaunting."

"No, it wasn't that. I remember quite clearly that the only disorientation I experienced occurred after I saw the supposed counterpart to a friend from back home. I have a feeling that realizing I was staring at a counterpart was the cause of the disorientation as well. Some type of a intense dejavous, I guess."

"That is quite extraordinary. Do you remember the guard's name? No, of course you wouldn't. Maybe I can find out. I'll have to ask Admiral McDougal to summon all of the guards in the attack and send them to the science lab tomorrow."

"That isn't necessary. Only the first squad of soldiers. He was in the first squad."

"Ah, that is even better. We shall see if your theory is correct then."

"I have another question for you. Assuming my theory is true, then what do you think would happen if I met my own counterpart? If an encounter with someone I knew caused disorientation, an encounter with myself could be incredibly worse. Possibly disastrous, it could cause a type of. . .comatose shock. "

"This is true. We have no way of knowing the implications of such an encounter. Assuming you are right of course."

"Just a few more questions. These should be easier to answer."

"Good. I don't like questions I can't answer." McIntyre chuckled.

"First off, I was wondering why both you and the Admiral have last names that seem to be of a Scottish origin? Is that just coincidence? What happened in this dimension to change it so radically from my own?"

"Well, as you know, I know little of your dimension. All of the information we would normally have obtained from the probe was erased. As for the Scottish names, well, that's a different matter. I'll get into our history some other time. It is quite lengthy, you know."

"All right, fair enough. My last question for the day. What is this language we're speaking, and how did I know how to speak and read it?"

You mean to tell me that earth in your dimension DOESN'T speak Ryeesian English?!?!" McIntyre exclaimed. The old scientist jumped out of his seat as the significance of this sank in.

"No, we don't. We speak regular English," Doug paused to give McIntyre some time to settle himself. "When I first arrived here, or more correctly when I first woke up, I had the knowledge of how to speak this odd language as if I had been raised speaking it."

"This is extraordinary!" McIntyre stammered.

"I was hoping, by some slim chance, that you had given me the knowledge when I was unconscious. That is not the case I assume."

"Amazing, simply amazing!"

"OK, I get the point. Now could you help me figure out how I got this knowledge? Did I telepathically absorb it, or what? Has anything like this ever happened before?"

"I've never heard of anything quite so stupendous, but there have been occasions when a powerful telepath has, absorbed, as you put it, small chunks of information about a strange environment from local inhabitants, but nothing quite so large as an entire language. Tell me, how many words do you know that aren't in standard English? Do you know the extent of your vocabulary exactly, or even roughly? You do seem to speak quite eloquently. The Ryeesian side of your vocabulary is quite extensive, at least from what I've heard conversing with you. Extraordinary!"

"No, no, I just sort of know everything. I'm not even sure how, but I've been thinking in Ryeesian English as well. I do realize that thinking in a language other than your native tongue is proof that you know the language as well as your own."

"That is true. I still can't believe it. You must have telepathically gotten the information. Since you could see the other people's thoughts, you knew what they were associating the Ryeesian words with. The most remarkable fact is that you did this while unconscious!"

"I just thought of something. Is it possible I could have attained this knowledge when I was digitized in the probe, or when it attacked me perhaps?"

"The probe attacked you?!?!"

"Not physically, no, but it was apparently trying to get into my mind, and I resisted it. Subconsciously at first, but once I sensed the probe I fought back consciously. It delivered an ultimatum and here we are."

"What was it's ultimatum?"

"It threatened to destroy everyone in my proximity if I didn't stop fighting it. I couldn't take the chance it was bluffing so I gave in."

"If the probe had to use an ultimatum of such severity, it must have been badly damaged by your counterattack. No one has ever resisted a probe of any kind on full force with out some kind of mental protection! Let alone one of the sophisticated nature as a D.T.P.! Your mental capabilities must be phenomenal, and you're a physical powerhouse too! This is marvelous! Stupendous!"

"Actually, I absorbed some of the energy from the D.T.P. when it was attacking as a means of defense. That is how I augmented my strength so vastly."

"This is too much to take in at once. Any more of your questions and I might drop dead from excitement!"

CHAPTER 10

Doug returned to his quarters and tried to get some sleep. The bed was not his own, and the difficulty of sleeping in a strange place caused him to lie in bed awake. Events had happened so quickly in the past couple of days that Doug found it hard to concentrate on any one specific incident. Trying to empty his mind of thoughts in order to relax, he eventually drifted into a restless slumber. Images and places filled his thoughts.

The place was familiar, although he had never seen it before. Walking along the halls he could see items that sparked memories of places and people long gone. He couldn't remember who he was or why his surroundings were so familiar. Everything around him was cloudy. He could see objects around him clearly, but the images had no specific meaning to him. Why was he here? What was he supposed to do? There was something he had to do. The answer was at the end of this hallway. If he could get to the door at the end of the hallway everything would be clear. His steps were slow and steady. Each impact between a foot and the solid ground caused echoes off the walls of the hallway. The reoccurring sounds of his footsteps gave comfort to him. The farther he proceeded the more confident he became. As he neared the door,....

Doug woke in a cold sweat. He vaguely remembered a dream, or perhaps a nightmare. The images were already fading. Pushing aside the last remnants of the dream, he headed for the door to his quarters. Hunger overcame any feelings of being out of place. Stepping out into the hall, the young man was greeted by Admiral McDougal.

"Good morning to you, Doug. Would you mind If I spoke with you briefly?" He asked.

"Not at all. I was just heading toward the science lab to see if Dr. McIntyre wanted to join me for breakfast. Have you spoken with him since yesterday?"

"No, not yet. I was planning to head there later today."

"Then what was it you wanted to talk about?"

"I wanted to thank you. Yesterday, when you released my emotions with your empathic abilities, I felt as if seven years of bottled emotions had been lifted from me. I cannot thank you enough."

"Well, it was nothing, I did it without thinking, really."

"Yes, but still you did it, and for that, I am grateful. The fact that you helped me without thinking shows you are truly compassionate to those in need. I also wanted to offer you the chance to join a Platoon of recruits for combat training. With your mental powers you could prove to be quite a formidable opponent. Then, if you decide that you would be willing to assist our army in matters other than that of research, you'll be better prepared. At least while you are here, I can arrange for you to get some status."

"I really appreciate your offer. I think it would be in my best interests to join this Platoon, and in the process, learn a little more of your history and current situation. I need to find my complete potential, and training of any form, in that manner, will assist my goal of finding out what exactly it is that I have become."

"Excellent. I'll have you assigned to a squad first thing tomorrow. One of my officers will contact you tomorrow morning bright and early. Well, I should probably let you get to McIntyre before he comes looking for you. Thanks again."

"Your welcome, and thank you."

Doug walked off toward the science lab feeling better about himself, and eager to participate in the combat training. He tensed only slightly as he walked past a few soldiers who were passing by. They didn't even notice him. With a little more confidence in his surroundings, Doug headed toward the galley to grab a bite to eat before venturing to the science lab. Doug's stomach told him firmly that McIntyre could wait and that it could not.

The Galley was nearly empty, but Doug still felt uncomfortable in the foreign setting. He hastily order a few sandwiches and left. The sandwiches proved to be easy to eat on the run as Doug had hoped, and he succeeded in finishing the snack by the time he had reached the old scientist's lab room.

McIntyre was occupied with some of the statistics from the day before, so Doug began a workout to start off the day. Noticing him finally, McIntyre hurried over to Doug.

"I'm glad to see you so enthusiastic about the testing Doug. Today I want to run some tests on the density of your skin and skeletal structure, as well as to run some tests on your mental capabilities. So after you've warmed up a little on the exercise machines, you can quit. We don't need any more physical tests for today."

"Good, I'd like to workout a bit; then I'll quit. I seem to have acquired a nice physique, I might as well try to keep it."

The tests were relatively easy to start with. McIntyre did most of the work. Doug merely sat in a chair, and waited for McIntyre to do his testing. The first few testings had to do with the density of Doug's skin. McIntyre took a few skin samples which were supposed to hurt a little, but Doug didn't feel much. The old scientist was elated to the point of insanity by the results of the test. His favorite word for the day seemed to be "extraordinary".

Doug remained passive while McIntyre jittered around the lab. Then Doug began the mental capability tests. A ring like cap was placed on his head. It reminded Doug of the steel ring placed on a prisoner's head during an electrocution. The sudden fear that thought issued was quickly put to rest, and he focused on the testing.

"Now Doug, I want you to think about my feelings, or emotions if you will, and tell me what you feel."

Doug tried to duplicate the empathic senses he had used with the Admiral the day before. Nothing seemed to happen, he wasn't feeling anything from McIntyre.

"I,. . .I'm not feeling anything yet."

"Stretch out with your mind. Let your own consciousness out, and direct it toward me."

Doug tried that, and to his amazement, began to sense what McIntyre was feeling. He suppressed a laugh when he felt the funny old man's child-like enthusiasm. Then he started to hear a voice in his head, that sounded like McIntyre's voice.

"Amazing, he's registering higher than anyone I've ever tested! If his telepathic readings are as strong, he could be the greatest psychic ever!"

Doug was startled by the sudden realization that he could hear what McIntyre was thinking.

"So you think I'll be a good psychic, huh?"

"Remarkable! I suppose I should have assumed you would have telepathic abilities, after seeing the results of your empathic testings. Tell me, did you see my thoughts as visions and pictures, or did you hear them in your head as words?"

"Words, why?"

"Well, that is indeed wonderful. Most empaths of any significant degree, see pictures of thought, if any at all. It has to do with the fact that emotions summon up images or colors more readily than they do words or equations. Most intriguing. Tell me, what am I thinking right now."

Doug again let his mind reach out to the doctor's, and saw what the old man was thinking.

"Well, you're wondering if I will be able to see what you're thinking, and the eagerness is about to kill you. You're thinking about an equation of some sort, . . .only, . . .it doesn't balance."

"Yes, yes,. . .wonderful, I was indeed,. . .Doesn't balance! What do you mean it doesn't balance! Why, . . . that's the dimensional rift equation, of course it balances, I. . .You mean to tell me you solved that equation in your head!!"

"Yes, I did, and it doesn't balance. You're treating the speed of light as if it wasn't a constant,. . .I, . . .never mind, I see it in your thoughts. The speed of light isn't a constant. That's the whole basis of the theory; you've figured out how to change the speed of light, . . .to slow it down, and then release it to its normal rate of speed. The speed differential while it's traveling causes an object surrounded by an energy field to jump through the space/time fabric from one dimension to the next through some type of wormhole. An interesting theory, which I assume is correct, because I'm here."

"Incredible! Most amazing! Your mental capabilities are the most extraordinary I've ever seen! I can tell that even without testing you! Furthermore, the tests I ran yesterday, combined with today's tests on your skin density provided some interesting results. It seems that your skin and skeletal structure have been changed into some type of super resilient chitinous material. Although there are some mammal species that have chitin in their make up other than their horns, I've never seen a biological substance that retained it's sensitivity to such a degree, and still provided the extreme amount of solidity that your skin has. I had been wondering why the syringes I used to sedate you kept breaking. "

"Are you saying that I actually changed my structure on the genetic level when I used the probe's energy to augment myself?"

"Yes indeed. Although the changes to your active cellular DNA weren't extremely complex, the results of those augmentations were quite profound. Your skeletal structure can withstand about 5 times that of an ordinary man, in terms of pressure, and carrying weight. Furthermore your musculature density was not only increased, but the actual myofibrils that make up your muscles have been modified with a complex keratin protein. These augmented myofibrils can withstand considerable amounts of stress before they start to tear in the ordinary process of musculature break down. I estimate that this is why you are so strong, and that your potential strength, under extreme physical training, would be twenty times that of a normal man. Of course, that much training would not be recommended, only noted as a potential. You will however gain more strength in the ordinary swelling of the bloodstream and increased oxidation of the muscles in tense and frightening moments.

"Which brings me to another discovery. Your adrenaline has been converted as well. When fully prepped for battle, your spleen will produce more adrenaline than the average man. Not only that, your body produces a special kind of hyper adrenaline for up to three hours."

Doug considered the implications of this news as the old man continued to ramble on. Glancing down at his toned and muscled body, he suddenly felt inhuman and disfigured. He knew that what had been done was unavoidable and permanent, but he couldn't help feeling cheated out of a normal life. He was forever changed. There would never be a moment that he would again be like he once was. Realizing there was nothing he could do about it, he pushed his thoughts aside, and returned his attention to the elated little scientist.

"There's just one more test I'd like to do today, Doug. I'd like to take a blood sample and run some tests on your healing rate and development of healing cells, because you seem to recover more quickly than normal. Maybe I can use some of this information to augment our own troops."

"All right, doctor. Let me ask you something."

"Of course, of course."

"If all of these augmentations are on the genetic level as well as physically present, . . .will I, what I mean is,. . . "

"You're wondering if your genes are still compatible with others in terms of procreation, and whether or not your children will be normal?"

"Yes."

"I'm not certain, but from a strictly biological stand point, that would be most intriguing if it were possible. Don't worry Doug, I'll make answering that question my top priority when I examine your reproductive chromosomes, as opposed to your active chromosomes. It's entirely possible that your reproductive chromosomes were completely unaffected. The genes for sexual reproduction are the easiest to damage, but under the strange circumstances of your augmentation, I would think that your reproductive chromosomes were the last thing on your mind when you were changing your phenotypic genetic structures."

"Thank you doctor, for some reason, I'm having some problems with that fact that I may no longer be human."

"Understandable Doug, but think on this. You are still the same person on the inside, and that is what truly makes the difference between man and animal. Philosophically you are the same as before. That shouldn't be forgotten. I don't know how religious people are in your dimension, but you still have the same soul. You are a child of God no matter what changes have taken place. If it means anything to you, I consider you human no matter what my results are."

"Thank you doctor, that means a lot."

Chapter 11

The next morning, Doug sat alone at a table in the mess hall. He was in a despondent mood, and brooded about his current state of affairs. In his spare time he had been practicing his mental capabilities, partly to experiment with his power and capabilities, and partly to assess the validity of what people were telling him. He sensed some information was withheld from him, but nothing crucial. No one was playing him false, or trying to deceive him. That much he was certain of.

Many of the people he encountered were afraid. The emotions emanating from some was staggering. He had to learn to shield himself from the more "emotionally aggressive" people. There were plenty that were depressed, some that were lonely, or had lost loved ones, and many more that were simply afraid. The result was an aura of negativity that made Doug feel sullen and withdrawn.

Doug's awareness was split between his own thoughts and those of the repressed people around him. The majority of the soldiers wanted peace. A life without fear or repression.

A few simply wanted to fight, angered by their inactivity. Doug only wanted to go home. His own feelings were swayed by the patriotism of the freedom fighters around him, but he still wished he could leave this dimension behind him and be with his friends.

"You've got to block it out or you'll go insane," said a soldier who was approaching the table.

Doug glanced up from his ale stein and looked upon the new arrival. It was the man he had wrestled with during his first escape attempt. It was John's counterpart.

"You mind if I join you?" the tall soldier asked

"Not at all, Joh. . . uh, I'm sorry I don't know your name?"

"Johann, Johann Zimmerman. And you're Doug, right?"

"Yes, you've been talking to McIntyre."

"Yup, he mentioned that I reminded you of a friend from your dimension."

"No, not exactly. If my hunch is correct, you ARE the man I knew from my dimension, only born and raised here."

"What? That doesn't make any sense."

"Well, McIntyre and I talked about the possibility of inter-dimensional counterparts. Genetically almost, or maybe even completely, identical. The only difference, then, would be your dimension of birth and your upbringing."

"That's something McIntyre would think of all right. Really deep and lacking any evidence whatsoever."

"Ah, but you forget that you yourself are evidence of its validity. If you saw my friend John, you would probably think you were looking into a mirror. Even some of your mannerisms are the same. Plus, look at your name and his. They're almost identical, only yours is the Germanic origin, and his the American, or English version."

"The what? What is Germanic? And English? And the other one?"

"Those were three of the different countries of Earth! McIntyre talked about them some. Don't you know any of Earth's history?"

"No, not much. McIntyre knows all about history, and spends most of his free time researching topics that involve history before the Ryeese war. They did exist before the Ryeese war didn't they?"

"In my dimension there never was a Ryeese war. The Earth in my dimension hasn't even heard of the Ryeese."

"That would have been nice. I wish they had never come to Earth in OUR dimension either."

"Things are very different here. I'm finding it difficult to adjust. Got any pointers for me?"

"You want my fingers?!"

"No! Tips. Advice on how to adjust."

"Oh, well I don't know. I've never been in any other place than here on the moon base. I also remember being somewhere before this but I don't remember much. I've been living here ever since my family was slaughtered by the Overlord's cyborgs."

"I'm sorry I didn't know."

"It's all right; it was a long time ago, I've learned how to deal with it."

Doug knew he was lying about something, but he didn't want to hurt Johann. He could feel the hate and sadness in him, and already felt bad about opening such a hideous wound. He wanted to try helping Johann, but felt it was best to simply change the subject.

"What was it you were saying earlier about blocking it out?"

"Other people's thoughts and emotions. I have some empathic ability, and I could sense your mood swings. You should see one of the psychic instructors. They're pretty good at teaching people how to control their abilities."

"Thanks, I might do that. Sometimes these emanations of others can be frustrating."

"Admiral McDougal asked me to admit you into my next group of trainees. You still interested?"

"Sure; when do we start?"

"Day after tomorrow. Come to the training facilities at seven a.m."

"I'll be there. This should prove quite interesting. I've never trained for combat before."

"Well, it won't be easy. I know from what McIntyre's told me that you have extra advantages, so I'm going to work you even harder than the other recruits. You have to give it your all in combat or you won't come back."

"I'll remember that. If you could, would you also set me up with a psychic trainer? I'd like to get to work on that as soon as possible."

"Mental training is included in the combat training. I won't be teaching that part of the training, but there will be an instructor there when the time comes. You look hungry; why don't we order some food before I starve."

"O.K. That adds more substance to my theory, though. John always wanted to eat, even when he had just eaten."

Johann's visit made Doug feel a little better. It was nice to see a familiar face, even if it wasn't the same person. Doug had returned to his room and was staring at the wall. There had to be something to do other than sleep, eat, or shower. He wished he had asked Johann what there was to do besides get bored in your room. The room was blank, bereft of items that signified an individual person lived there. It was almost like a prison cell, except without any nice touches. For want of anything better to do, Doug decided to pay McIntyre an evening visit.

There was no answer at McIntyre's appointed room so Doug went to the lab thinking that the doctor might still be there. He punched the call button that would let McIntyre know someone was at the door, and was rewarded with the old man's voice beckoning for whomever it was to enter. Doug opened the door via the control panel, and walked inside the lab.

"Good evening doctor."

"Ah, Doug, how nice of you to stop by. What can I do for you?"

"Well, actually, I'm extremely bored. Is there anything to do around here other than sleep?"

"Most of the people here are too engrossed in simulated battle scenarios and war games to do much else. My favorite pastime is to review the computer banks in the information center. There's always more history I can learn about and compare other dimensions with our own origins, but now I'm far too excited about the results I've been getting from the tests we've run. That is, in itself, fun for me."

"Where is the information center? That sounds better than sitting on my ass waiting for my hair to turn gray."

"What? Oh, I forgot. I made this electronic mapping, and guidance system for you. It will also answer simple questions about any device's function. Until you become familiar with the base it might be helpful."

"Thank you, doctor."

The information center was located in a fair sized room on the scientific research floor, one level above the residence floors, and consisted of three computer terminals. Access to the computer's memory data base was simple, and easy. Once a clearance and ID card was inserted into the control panel, the screen came on. It was frightening at first to hear the computer ask him what he would like to learn first. He wasn't used to talking computers yet, and he still felt slightly hesitant when asked the computer a question.

Doug asked the computer what topics it had in it's memory banks. The computer rattled off a list of military topics, food preparation topics, medical topics, and, finally, history popped up on the list. Doug had hoped to find something that interested him more, but the computer was already continuing the list with even more boring topics. Doug told the computer to stop, and selected "history". He was then presented with the sub-directory list of history. Doug sighed and quickly selected earth history. Another sub-directory presented itself. He was afraid for a moment that there may be nothing in the computer but directories. Tired of the verbal lists, Doug told the computer to just start narrating the history of the earth fifty years before the Ryeese war. The computer hummed for awhile, and then a face appeared on the screen.

"*In the Terran year nineteen hundred sixty, the planet earth was divided into several countries. The predominant countries were the United Kingdom, also referred to as Great Britain, the United States of America, or the USA, Germany, the Union of Soviet Socialist Republics, also called Russia due to it being the dominant Soviet Republic, The Independent Confederacy of the Eire, or the United Eire, Spain, Poland, . . .*"

"Stop! The Independent Confederacy of the Eire?! Did North and South Ireland unite?"

"*That is correct. The Eire, or Irish, clans united for their freedom from British oppression in the great revolt of seventeen hundred forty five. Led by Prince Charles Edward Stuart, the united Irish army won a great victory over the British at Culloden Moor, in seventeen hundred forty six. Although Charles was slain in battle, his courageous fight led to the eventual freedom of all Ireland.*"

"Are you saying that Bonnie Prince Charlie WON the battle of Culloden Moor?!"

"*Yes indeed, although the progression of his forces never went on to more victories, the English were never able to repress the Eire again, and the Countries of Ireland and Scotland declared thier total independence from England. Charles also was responsible for the unification of the Eire. It is a common theory that the unified Eire is what kept the British at bay.*"

"Wow! That's interesting. That would explain why this dimension has an affinity for Irish and Scottish sounding names. Tell me, how influential were the Irish in world matters in the early nineteen hundreds?"

"The Irish Republic was an integral part of all world discussions. After their independence they flourished and became one of the worlds leading computer and industrial manufactures. They were also admired for their indomitable nature."

"Well that's not what happened in MY dimension! That's really different. I wonder what other discrepancies there are? Computer,. . .give me a rough outline of major world events starting seventy five years before the Ryeese invasion."

Doug listened to the computer's narration listening for discrepancies between what he remembered and what happened in this dimension. Most of the history was the same as his own dimension, with a few exceptions brought about by the different situation in Ireland. Doug was now fascinated with a subject he normally hated. For some reason, the differences in dimensional histories were more engaging than Doug thought they would be. The narration was reaching the Second World War, and the rise of Hitler.

". . .In the nineteen hundred forties, Hitler overran Denmark and Norway. The Irish/English alliance agreed to a joint effort of themselves and the anti-Nazi resistance faction within Germany to assassinate Hitler and his staff before his efforts reached them. Hitler and seventeen of his closest advisors and military high command were assassinated through the covert assistance allied Eire/Britain, to the German resistance in the summer of nineteen hundred forty. The Nazi party dissolved shortly thereafter."

"So, There never was a Second World War?"

"The only record of a Second World War is listed as the Ryeesian invasion."

"What was the result of Hitler's activities in Germany?"

"Accessing. . . .The activities of Hitler, and his dreams of the Third Reich, caused a great fear in the other major nations, but after his Nazis fell, the New Germany dedicated its efforts to cooperating with the other world powers to form the United Nations for World Peace. Otherwise known as the U.N.W.P. This new alliance of the major world powers originally consisted of the US, Canada, Germany, Great Britain, and Eire. This group of nations was founded in the year nineteen hundred forty four. Four years later they accepted Japan, France, and Pakistan into the group; two years after that they were also joined by China, Poland, and India, and finally three years after that by the Soviets, and several smaller nations. The U.N.W.P. successfully eliminated all international conflicts by the year nineteen hundred seventy four, although many smaller nations were assimilated into surrounding countries and no longer existed independently. The resulting effect of world peace lead to an unusual technological outbreak. By nineteen hundred eighty four, the technologies of earth had tripled in sophistication. These technologies included advanced computer technologies, aviation, aerospace technology, industrial,. . ."

"Stop. Did the U.N.W.P. ever have control over the world? I mean, was the world ever united under one government, one leader, or parliament?"

"No. The U.N.W.P. was highly influential, and if a nation in the U.N.W.P. wanted to do something that would effect any other nation, they had to have the consent of the U.N.W.P. Council.

Consent was achieved by a vote of the Council members. A simple majority was sufficient for most affairs, but a unanimous agreement for anything deemed by the Council heads as constitutional in nature."

"I see. Now, when the Council decided,...Wait! What year did you originally start this lecture at!"

"Nineteen hundred thirty five, seventy five years before the Ryeesian war, as requested."

"The Ryeesians invade in the year two thousand ten?!"

"That is correct."

"What year is it now!?"

"Two thousand fifteen, in Terran years, five years after the Ryeesian invasion."

Doug was startled. How was it possible that he not only shifted dimensions but time as well. If it was possible to return to the same time he left, his world might still face the Ryeesian invasion in two to three years time. But if time advanced on his earth while he was here and he had to return back to his own dimension in an equal amount of time, the Ryeesians may have arrived before he got back. What if he returned to earth at the present time? He had to stay calm. He needed to think clearly. McIntyre could answer his questions. There was no need to panic yet.

It was late, but Doug was too upset to wait. He knocked on McIntyre's door, then remembered to try the doorbell. He heard shuffling from the room, and suddenly felt a wave of irritation coming from the old man behind the door. The door slid open after a few seconds of waiting.

"Yes,. . .Oh, Doug, it's you, come in, come in. What can I do for you? It's quite late in the evening, is something wrong?"

Doug entered the slightly less grumpy doctor's quarters.

"I'm truly sorry to bother you at this hour, Doctor, but..."

"No, no, it's quite all right, and please call me Patrick."

"Well, Patrick, I stumbled across something that upset me in the learning center you directed me to. I really need a few questions answered now, or I don't think I'll be able to sleep."

"I see, of course, I have the same problem sometimes. I wish I had someone to answer MY questions, Ha Ha."

"Were you aware that your dimensional probe travels through the time continuum as well as dimensional continuums?"

"Well, I have noticed a few discrepancies in apparent time sent and return, but the actual traveling from dimension to dimension may account for it. It's never been more than a few days discrepancy in the cases I tested, so I didn't pursue the issue."

"Well, I've got a project for you then. My discrepancy discovery is over seven years!"

"You must be mistaken lad; that is quite impossible. Dimensional travel has nothing to do with time, . . .well, not that I know of anyway."

"All right, what year did the Ryeesians invade here?"

"In Terran terms, It was two thousand ten."

"And what year is it now?"

"Don't be silly, it's two thousand fifteen."

"When I was abducted from my dimension, the year was two thousand seven. That's why the Ryeesians never came to my world. They aren't due for another two to three years!"

"Oh my, this is indeed a wonderful discovery! Why, the possibilities are incredible! If time travel in the same dimension were available we could go back and keep the Ryeesians from ever attacking!"

"What about MY world doctor! I could at least warn them if I could get back in time! What if time travel isn't possible, but just a side effect of dimensional jaunting!? I may end up going back to my world before I'm born, or after I'm supposed to be dead!"

"I'm sorry Doug, I don't have any answers for you yet, but rest assured that I'm going to find out everything I can. You know me well enough by now to realize that if there's one thing that will get me to work, it's solving long and challenging problems that everyone else considers boring beyond belief and totally unverifiable."

"Yes, I suppose that is true," Doug smiled despite himself. "If you come up with anything let me know immediately, good or bad. Maybe I can help solve some of the problems too."

"Yes indeed, but I think it's best for you not to worry about it for right now. Too much has changed in your life already. By the way, if you make another startling discovery any time soon, try to wait until my heart rate slows down from the shock you gave me tonight."

Doug laughed as he got up and headed for the door. Somehow even this terrible discovery he had made seemed to fade after he had shared it with McIntyre. The old man would have made a good father if he could make his children feel as secure. Doug felt that Doctor Patrick could handle any problem that was solvable. Feeling a little better, but still restless, Doug headed for the mess hall. Maybe a few drinks would help him relax in this bizarre world.

CHAPTER 12

Looking around, he couldn't see any way out. The long corridor frightened him. When he turned around to look, there was always a wall directly behind him to prevent him from moving backwards. All of his movements were sluggish, as if the world was suddenly in slow motion. Glancing in front of him, he saw the smoky room at the end of the hall. As before, the door was slightly open, but the opening was not wide enough to see past. A dim glow emanated from the room, and he knew the glow was important somehow. The room scared him but he knew all questions would be answered if he could reach the door.

He felt a peculiar familiarity with the hallway. He knew deep down that he had never before been in such a place, but the feel of the entire place was so familiar that he tried desperately to remember when he had been here before. The walls themselves exuded a mocking air of remembrance, as if to say they remembered him even if he had no recollection of them. The partial open door taunted him with an evil foreboding.

Determined to discover what was behind the door, he headed for the end of the corridor. The need to know what was in the room became dreadfully urgent. For some reason he had an overwhelming urge to get there as soon as possible. He increased his pace gradually until he was running at full speed. The door started to open slightly as he neared the entrance. Greenish orange smoke wafted out of the room and with it, a charnel house stench that overpowered his nostrils. He was filled with dread as the smoke started to clear...

Doug awoke in a cold sweat. His body was trembling as the vestiges of his dream started to fade. The dream troubled him. He knew that it was only a dream, but his insides told him that this dream was important. There was something in the room at the end of that corridor that was a threat to him. Doug promised himself that he would find out what that threat was the next time he had this dream.

Glancing at the wall clock, he realized that it was almost time to get up. The time system in this dimension was close to that of the earth in his dimension. The only major differences were the total numbers of the minutes, hours, and seconds. There were fifty five seconds to the minute and likewise fifty five minutes to the hour. There were a total number of twenty hours in a standard day. The adjustments were made by the Council to account for the different revolution of the planet, or rather moon, around the sun in correlation to earth's. It was agreed that to use standard earth measure wouldn't be feasible, considering that eventually the middle of the day would be at nighttime.

Laying in bed, Doug reflected on that irony. Who cares whether or not the sun is out if you live underground? From what Doug had been told, the surface of their moon was uninhabitable, so why the fuss about day light hours? Doug catalogued this question with the thousands of others he had for the base's Admiral. It was near the moon's "sunrise" nonetheless, and Doug decided to get some breakfast from the mess hall.

The mess hall was nearly empty. There were a few soldiers who were sitting down to their breakfast, but for the most part the large dining hall was empty. Doug looked around the hall as he entered and selected a corner table that was out of the general line of sight. He sat down and casually observed the others in the hall. He wondered if the knowledge that an inhabitant from another dimension was staying on their base disturbed any of the recruits or soldiers.

As his quandary was forming in his head he felt the emotions of those present filtering through him. For the most part, the people in the room weren't even paying attention to their fellow soldiers. Doug was slightly surprised to note that most of the people in the room didn't care who was in the hall with them. He shrugged off the odd feeling as being a morning time grogginess in the hall.

"What do you want this morning?" the mechanical dining speaker asked him

"Uh, eggs and sausage, I guess, and a cup of coffee."

"What kind of eggs, sir?"

"Oh, uh, chicken eggs."

"Ha ha ha. You must be still asleep, buddy. Chickens have been extinct for five years."

"Oh, yeah, I'm a little groggy this morning. What eggs do you have available today?"

"Emu, Venilusian, and duck."

"I'll have emu."

"All right they'll be ready in a parsec."

Doug felt out of place. Everything was different here. He made a promise to himself to learn as much as he could about this dimension's every day life, so he could fit in better. Most of all, he wanted to know what a "Venilusian" was. He had tried a Venilusian steak, which was not unlike beef, and now he knew the planet had a chicken like egg layer species as well. While he was considering the differences here, his food order arrived in the wall's receptacle and it's sliding door slid open.

Doug ate his breakfast while he thought about all that had happened in the last few days. During the last few days his newly enhanced mind had analyzed every aspect of what went on in his life and conversations he had participated in. He seemed to realize things he never would have noticed before. The realization that people he knew from his own time should still have the same last name came to him while he was eating. First names might change, but why would their last names' change? He knew that John, or Johann in this dimension had a different last name, and he wondered why.

Maybe McIntyre could answer his question. The thought of McIntyre triggered another mental insight. It seemed odd to him that McIntyre had such a calming effect on him. By all rights he knew he should be more frustrated than he was, or at least upset. Every time he went to visit McIntyre, he left feeling completely self confident and satisfied with the fact that he was marooned in a strange place with strange people. He filed this observation away for later testing and resumed his pondering about patrilineal names.

"Doug?! Is that you? I thought you were dead or something!" stammered a strange yet familiar voice.

Doug started violently at the sudden barrage of emotions. he was edgy and with good reason. He looked up quickly at the newly arrived visitor. He could hardly believe his eyes. It was Paul! The friend he had known since childhood. He noticed this dimension's version of Paul was very similar to his own, but still had the dimension's characteristic sadness.

"P, Paul?" Doug stammered hoping that at least one friend knew him.

"Of course! Don't you remember me? My God we practically grew up as brothers! How did you get here? I know I've searched for you for years to see if you survived. I know I couldn't have missed seeing you on base for almost three years!"

"I wish I could say I was the Doug you knew, but I'm not. You see, . . ."

"Of course you are, you even remembered my name, why,. . ."

"Wait, let me explain! It's a long story."

"I'm all ears! I got plenty of time, especially for an old buddy."

"Do you remember any rumors floating around base about a person from another dimension being transported here?"

"Sure, it's been all that every one's talked about for days, not much else to do but gossip."

"Well,...your looking at him. I'm another dimension's version of the Doug you knew. Just like I knew another version of you in my dimension. Apparently our dimensions are very close, you look a lot like your counterpart."

"I think I understand, but I thought other dimensions were,... well, completely different."

"Apparently not. I, for one, am happy that they're so similar, because I need a friend to help me through this. Someone who knows me as well as I know myself."

"You don't even have to ask. I've known Doug Taylor my whole life, and to get even a defected version of him is great."

"Defected?! I'll show you defected you sawed off little midget. Go look in a mirror!"

"Ha! Same old Doug! God it's good to see you again, even if it isn't really you."

"Ditto."

The two friends talked about their respective childhoods, and soon discovered that for almost every instance, their memories of what had happened were accurate for either dimension. For Paul, it was like getting a friend back that he thought had been dead, and for Doug, it was like finding an old friend in a place he thought was devoid of anyone he knew or loved. Doug felt a sense of relief. At least now he had someone he knew and could share his problems with. Paul seemed to make Doug's inter-dimensional imprisonment more bearable.

"So, tell me what happened to you in your dimension when the Ryeese attacked? Maybe I can find out what happened to our dimensions version of Doug." Paul asked.

"I don't know, the Ryeese never attacked earth in my dimension. Well, not yet anyway."

"That would have been nice. I can't begin to tell you what a tragedy their arrival caused. Billions were killed during their first attack."

"Well, if I ever get back I'll get to see their attack myself, I'm sure it won't be pretty."

"Maybe they won't attack in your dimension."

"I think they will. They attacked in this dimension in the year two thousand ten. When I left my dimension it was only two thousand seven."

"The dimensional transfer took eight years?!"

"As far as I can tell, with McIntyre's assisted input of course, the process didn't take more than a few minutes, but somehow I've been transported through time as well as dimension. So if I get back the same time I left, I've still got the Ryeese invasion to look forward to."

"Man that really sucks. To tell the truth, all this talk about jumping through time and dimensions hurts my head."

"Ha! After it happens to you, you'll understand things a lot easier."

"I'll pass, if it's all the same to you."

"I've got a question for you, two actually."

"Go ahead."

"One; What's with John, er, Johann? He didn't recognize me like you did. He didn't even seem the same, plus his last name in my dimension was Anderson, not Zimmerman."

"Johann,. . .Johann was captured by the Ryeese in their first attack. He was rescued before they had completely brain washed him, but a lot of his memory hasn't returned yet. It's really sad. All he remembered when they rescued him was his first name, and his family being killed by Ryeesian torturers. He's got a little of his memory back since then, but not much. They gave him a new last name so he could get on with his life. Once I was reunited with him at this base, I tried to help him regain some of his memory, but we weren't very successful. The memories he had just aren't there anymore, like a chalk board that's been erased. He didn't bother to change his last name back to what it was, it didn't seem to matter to him. There are a lot of soldiers here that had the same happen to them." Paul shuddered involuntarily at the thought. "I'd rather die than to have that happen to me."

"Sorry Paul, I didn't mean to upset you. It must be hard to live in this world."

"Yeah, well, what else can you do? I'd rather live in a world like this than not live at all. There were quite a few who didn't agree with me on that point. Many people gave in to despair and self misery. They don't think they can go on, so they give up and kill themselves."

"Well, that's no answer. Don't let me catch you falling into 'despair'. You won't have to kill yourself then 'cause *I* will!"

"Ha! It's great to have you back. What was your second question?"

"This one's easier to answer. Would you consider helping me get adjusted here? There's a lot I don't know about this dimension, and a computer can only tell me so much."

"I oughta knock your block off for even asking! Of course I'll help!"

"No need to get snippy you sawed-off little runt. I was just making sure. I'm glad that your here, I need a good friend to help me through this."

"No problem. I'm always there for the mentally handicapped and physically inept."

"Ha, Ha, very funny."

CHAPTER 13

The discovery of Paul had lifted Doug's spirits and given him a sense of security in this awkward place. Days had passed and the morning of his first training session had arrived. He was slightly nervous about his upcoming training, but knew it would be helpful. Besides, it gave him something to do other than wait for a chance to get back home.

Doug got out of bed and prepared for his training. Johann had stopped by the previous day and given him his Cadet training suit, so Doug showered and donned his new apparel. Doug slid out the sliding wall mirror and glanced at his reflection. He was always startled to see the radical difference in his appearance. Even the small mirror which he had slid out of the wall, revealed changes of his facial features. A slight addition of angularity, and more muscularity in his neck, had changed him enough to be noticeable, but not enough to make him look like a different person. Looking at his new reflection made him nervous, so he slid the mirror back and decided to forego his morning shave. There was no sense in getting cut *before* his first training class.

Doug left his room, and headed down the hall to the stairs that led to the training facilities. The training level was two levels below the residence floors. In total there were twelve floors, three designated to living establishments one for training, one for tactical and strategic planning, one for medical, two for scientific study, one for the kitchens and food preparation, one for recreation, one for storage, and the uppermost level was for observation of stellar activity. The base did have some civilian residents, but most of the living space was for those in the growing militia. The base wasn't spacious or cavernously large, but because of an efficient use of space, the base was able to house enough people to fully populate a fair sized city.

Doug had also learned that there were three smaller bases that housed the rest of the civilian survivors from earth who didn't want to be subjects of Shaleese's empire, but weren't willing to enter into the violence of physical resistance. They assisted passively by becoming contacts with the other colonies that were under Shaleese's rule. The other bases also assisted greatly by secretly keeping all four bases supplied with food and materials.

Doug reached the room he was to train in. Taking a deep breath, he entered the training facility. There were thirty or more soldier Cadets in the room. Doug noted that, aside from a few Cadets, he was the oldest one in the room. His newly found power of empathy wasn't necessary to feel the nervous tension in the room. It did however give him insight to the misery all the young Cadets shared. Looking at the individual faces of the new recruits, he saw boys and girls who had been stripped of their innocence. The faces of these young soldiers revealed a life time of anguish that shouldn't have be laid upon such young shoulders.

Doug's inhibitions and fears left him instantly, only to be replaced by anger and rage at those who had inflicted this misery on the people in front of him. The direction of his life narrowed down into a well focused goal that might not be attainable. At that moment, when the youthful faces directed only slightly curious glances at him bereft of all childhood vitality, he resolved himself to help these people however he could. The focus of his anger narrowed down to one individual, Shaleese, the overlord. Doug became determined to find the overlord's weakness, and then make him suffer, to feel the pain he had inflicted on others, to feel the wrath of vengeance!

Doug was still riled as he sat and listened to Johann's opening speech on military training. The presence of Johann, who had also suffered greatly from terrible circumstances, only intensified Doug's anger. Johann threw him several startled glances during his opening remarks, and Doug remembered that as an empath, Johann could sense his anger. Doug tried to suppress his hate, not wanting Johann to think it was directed at him.

Johann was informing the new recruits of the training equipment they would be using. Their first two weeks of training would consist almost entirely of hand to hand combat and the use of projectile weaponry, after that there would be more focus on mental attacks and defense. Interspersed between the lessons they would learn other skills, such as starship operation and strategies for massive ground assaults.

The fighting chamber was available for simulated hand to hand combat, and the simulators allowed for the teaching of piloting any manner of starship and fighters.

Doug was feeling less agitated now, and tried to direct his attention on learning. He used the anger as a motivater to learn all he could about warfare, so he could crush the enemy. Johann said that a minimum of forty hours a week in the simulator was required, and for four hours a day, except for weekends, they would meet for lectures and personal guidance. The orientation was over, and they were given leave to try out the simulators and combat chambers. Doug wanted to try the hand to hand combat chamber, but remembered he promised Paul he would stop by after the orientation class. Reluctantly, Doug headed for the door, and to Paul's room. He would spend as much time in the chamber and simulator as possible; far more than forty hours.

CHAPTER 14

Paul recommended they go get something to eat, and then go to the recreation center and vent some of Doug's energy with a game of cyber ball. Cyber ball was a combination of racket ball and dodge ball. The object of the game was to hit your opponent with an energy ball that was batted across the room with a strange metallic paddle, which Doug thought looked more like a large spatula. The players stood next to each other on one end of a room that was three times as long as it was wide. The energy ball was slung off the paddle toward the far end of the room, and batted back and forth as the opponents tried to nail each other with the ball. The first player to score ten hits on his opponent won.

Doug's increased agility and strength allowed him to win the first two games, but Paul, having more experience with the game, won the next few games when he adjusted to Doug's physical advantage. Neither of them liked to lose. Doug had won the first two matches and Paul had won the following three. The energy ball left no marks, but did sap energy from the recipient of its sting. Paul signaled the computer for an end after their last match.

"I don't know about you, but I'm to tired for another match." Paul explained.

"I'm a little tired, too. Let's go get something to snack on and relax a bit."

"I'll say one thing. You've got a lot more energy than the Doug I remember. You look bigger too. You must have worked out a lot more than the Doug from this dimension."

"Not really. I'll explain over a cup of coffee."

The weary friends went to the cafe like coffee room and each ordered a cup. Doug was pleased to see that the base had all of his favorite espresso flavors and syrups, even if they were synthetic coffee products instead of the real thing. The cyber ball game had left Paul exhausted, but Doug, although tired, was far from feeling weak.

Doug told Paul about the probe and his abduction and about Michelle. Doug had wondered if this dimension had a version of Michelle, so he tried to describe what she looked like. But this dimension's Paul hadn't gone to the same college as Doug did, so he wouldn't have known her anyway. They talked for awhile until Paul finished his coffee and said he was going to take a nap.

After Paul had left, Doug sat at the table by himself and ordered a latte. The synthetic espresso was better than the synthetic coffee. Doug decided that this was an ideal place to relax and work out problems. He sipped his latte and his thoughts wandered back to the rage he felt in the training session. He had never felt such hate and rage inside. It frightened him to think of what he might have done had the focus of that rage been within reach.

The young man decided to go try out the combat chamber. He had plenty of time, and the coffee and brief rest at the table had restored him. Doug knew that his body recovered from fatigue very quickly, but nonetheless was surprised at the speed of his body's healing. He had a lot to learn about his new capabilities. The combat chamber seemed like the ideal place to find out exactly how far his capabilities stretched.

The combat chamber wasn't very large. Although there were several chambers, each individual room wasn't much larger than Doug's living establishment. The chamber consisted of a simple terminal interface on the far wall, and several camera like devices that jutted out of the walls in seemingly random placement. The only other adornment was a helmet that rested on a small stand. The helmet connected to a socket next to the computer terminal.

Access to the programs was granted by using a clearance card, and then selecting the type of program, instructive or practice sessions. For new users, a skill level request was omitted until after the first practice session was complete. Later, the skill level could be adjusted to the preference of the individual user.

Doug donned the helmet and activated an instruction session. A hologram generated by the cameras from the wall appeared in front of him. The image was of a medium build, middle aged man with graying hair at his temples and a gray shot goatee. Although older, Doug could see that whoever had posed for the program's holographic display was indeed in great shape.

"Welcome, student," a surprisingly mild voice said. "You have accessed the martial arts training program, I will be your guide and instructor. To begin, what style of martial arts would you like to learn?"

Doug selected aikijujitsu, and continued the program to learn from the instructor. The instruction sessions were designed to last two hours, and were intended to be used one per day. Sometimes the same session would be taught for several days until the techniques were learned properly. Doug ignored the hologram's warnings and suggestions, and ran three sessions back to back. After several hours of instruction, Doug felt ready to try the practice test, in which a hologram opponent would spar with the student.

The computer selected the beginner's level, and a gruff looking warrior appeared. Doug discovered that the computer had accounted for his extra abilities, and had created an opponent that was equally equipped. His physical enhancements would be useless here. Only superior fighting ability could insure a successful win. Doug made a mistake in countering his opponent's strike and the hologram figure's fist went harmlessly through his head.

The computer opponent disappeared and the instructor reappeared. Doug was disappointed, thinking that he had failed his first test. He awaited the instructor's reprimands for his failure.

"There is an error in the combat chamber's interactive cerebral link. Please stand by while a system diagnosis is conducted."

"An error? What was the nature of the error?" Doug asked

"Inconclusive, standby."

Doug waited for the computer to come up with an answer. The holographic figure stared blankly at the wall behind Doug. Finally the holographic teacher reanimated and addressed Doug.

"Cerebral link up could not be attained, the interactive software failed to accomplish a cerebral connection. The problem resulted when the interactive pulse was sent to the user, and the parietal and temporal lobes of the user could not be reached. Likewise, the amygdala could not be reached through either of the previously mentioned lobes of the user."

"Computer, does the interactive pulse use an active beam to penetrate the user's mind in a fashion similar to the D.T.P. probe?"

"The fashion is similar, but the intensity of the beam is exponentially less than that of the D.T.P."

"That would explain why I didn't feel any pain by blocking the beam. Computer, can you lower the beam intensity by fifty percent?"

"The beam's intensity can be lessened, but if the beam is lowered a sufficient link may not be attained."

"Computer, why would a sufficient link not be attained?"

"The user's brain would not respond to so slight a stimulus."

"Well, seeing as my brain is mentally blocking even so small a beam, it may be the only option. Computer, decrease the interactive beam intensity by fifty percent."

"*Decreasing the beam intensity may not be effective for a positive interaction to occur.*"

"Why don't we try it anyway."

"*Beam intensity at fifty percent.*"

"Good. Computer attempt to link up with current user."

"*Accessing,. . .Link up complete. Receiving positive feedback. Program operation running is normal.*"

"See, I told you it would work." The computer blatantly ignored him. "Now, let's continue with the training. Access and restart the beginner's combat sequence for Aikijujitsu martial arts training."

Doug faced off with the holographic warrior again. Although he did better than his previous attempt, he still managed to get hit by his opponent. This time, however, the hologram's fist didn't pass through his head. Doug reeled back as he felt the blow from his opponent strike him. Apparently the interactive software was completely realistic. Doug succeeded in only suffering a few blows before he was able to beat his opponent.

The entire combat session had taken nearly eight hours, and Doug felt worn out from his strenuous workout. He decided to wait until tomorrow for another lesson. It was nearing time for dinner, so Doug decided to see if Paul wanted to go with him to get something to eat. Overall, Doug was quite pleased with his ventures for the day. Nearly breaking his arm trying to pat himself on the back, he left in search of his friend.

CHAPTER 15

The following weeks kept Doug busy enough to prevent him from dwelling on the fact he was trapped in a seemingly bizarre dimension. Between his training and the tests McIntyre asked him to participate in, Doug had little time for anything else. In his spare time he talked with Paul, or reviewed the history modules in the information center. There was still a lot to learn about his new power, so he tried to save a little time for testing his abilities.

To McIntyre and Admiral McDougal's surprise, Doug had excelled in aikijujitsu, and achieved the equivalent of a first degree black belt in the martial art in just under four weeks. The overall combat chamber time was close to an average of ten hours a day. Even though the chamber opponents were holograms, the level of fatigue caused by one hour in the chamber was equivalent to one hour of intense exercise. McIntyre was astounded by the fact that Doug had been able to endure such a large amount of physical stress, and demonstrated his delight by pushing the words "amazing", "superb", and "extraordinary" to their limits.

During one of his few moments alone, Doug thought back to his family and friends in his own dimension. He rationalized that his predicament must be close to a soldier going overseas to train; only he had much more cause to dwell on the fact that he might not see his home again. As always, his thoughts drifted to what his friends thought had happened to him. They must surely think he was dead. The thought of his friends, and especially Michelle, grieving for him, made him depressed.

McIntyre had kept his promise to work on the time difference during dimensional transfer, and had come up with a few theories which he hoped he could prove to be true. McIntyre speculated that the time shift had to do with the flow of time in correspondence with the dimension in question. If his equations were correct, he could transport Doug back to the exact time he left, regardless of how long he stayed in this dimension.

He also informed Doug that although his DNA had been drastically changed, his sex chromosomes were hardly affected by the augmentations. Any children he had would be ordinary, with the exception of intelligence. His offspring could have a well above average intelligence, and would almost certainly have well developed extra sensory capabilities. Doug was relieved that he no longer had to worry about that. It seemed to at least classify him as a human, and not some kind of a mutated freak.

Admiral McDougal had stopped by the other day to congratulate him on his excellent achievements in training. Doug thought that he seemed a little nervous for some reason, and hoped it wasn't because he was becoming afraid of the potential he had. Doug knew he could read anyone's mind to find out what was bothering them, but he tried to screen out the thoughts of others since he thought it was impolite to snoop around in other people's heads.

He had also made a few new friends from his training class, and people he had met while waiting for an available combat room. With everything starting to feel familiar, Doug was worried that he might start to think of this place as home. For some reason that bothered him, even though he knew it was silly to feel that way. He didn't want the memories he had of his real home to diminish or slip away, although deep down inside of him he knew that enough time would make forgetfulness unavoidable.

Doug was currently laying on his bed staring at the ceiling. He was a little tired from spending a total of eleven hours in training, some in lectures, and some in the chamber. It was close to dinner time and Paul had said they could go get a bite to eat and then go catch a movie at the recreation center's new theater. There weren't any new movies, or any type of televised entertainment, but there were a significant amount of reruns available. Most of the people on this base didn't own a television, and the few who did could only watch the base news or a small selection of syndicated reruns.

Doug didn't care whether the movie was a rerun or not, at least it was something to do. He had never cared much for watching movies anyway. Paul seemed excited about the new theater, so Doug tried to act excited as well. He would probably

BRIAN O'MADIGAN

be equally excited if there had been nothing for him to do, in way of recreation, for five years.

Johann had told Doug that he would be receiving special instruction on his mental training from the base's best instructor. The trainer would work with him apart from the other students, which made Doug a little nervous. The mental training sessions would replace the lectures starting tomorrow, and would continue for one to three weeks depending on the individual recruit's ability with mental defense and attack. Doug knew his own ability was well above average, so he anticipated at least three weeks to fully develop his mental capabilities.

Johann had said he might stop by to introduce Doug to his new trainer, if she was available and had the time. Doug wasn't comfortable with his mental power yet, and he was slightly nervous when he learned that his teacher would be a woman. If he was required to open his mind to his teacher for better instruction, she would see whatever he thought about her. That disturbed him more than the thought of being marooned in a distant dimension forever. What if he was attracted to her, and she could see he was mentally undressing her in his mind? Worse yet, what if she was ugly and he was completely repulsed by her? She would feel his revulsion and be offended.

Doug discovered with a sudden insight that his thoughts and feelings were more critical when directed toward women. His first thoughts when he met a woman were always sexually related. Those impressions were either positive or negative, there was no maybe. A woman was either pretty enough to desire sexually or not enough to even consider. There was a third category, in which she was so hideous that even the thought was repulsive. The thought of a woman knowing the first impressions he had about her scared him. In a rare insight to human nature, he realized that most men probably had the same thoughts when they first met a woman.

Dwelling on how to approach the problem was only worse. He realized that a woman with mental capabilities would be used to seeing the lude thoughts of men, but that didn't make him feel better about his own thoughts being open. Doug decided he would do his best to not only shield his mind from his new trainer, but to also keep his thoughts from practicing their habitual appraisal of women when he met his new teacher.

Stretching as he got up, Doug decided to get ready for his evening out on the town with Paul. He had worked hard today and knew Paul wouldn't appreciate a ripe smelling companion, so he decided to take a shower.

Moving to the eastern wall of the room, Doug activated the showering facility. The "shower" was actually a collapsible part of the wall. Two of the sides slid out perpendicular to the wall, and once he got inside, the back panel slid down from the ceiling. Coverings over the drain and showerhead slid aside, and a computerized voice requested the desired temperature of the water. The angle of the showerhead could be adjusted by a metallic control pad.

Doug finished his shower and signaled for the door to open. Once he stepped out of the showering unit, the outer door closed again to dry out the interior. The process of drying only took a few minutes, and was extremely effective against rust and mildew. He had to admit that it was very efficient.

Just as he was getting finished, the now familiar doorbell alerted Doug that a visitor was at his door. He hoped it was Paul and not Johann with his new trainer, but his new found power told him it was Johann.

"Come in," he said somewhat shakily.

The door slid open to reveal Johann standing in the hall. Doug felt a momentary twinge of panic, but quickly noted that Johann was alone.

"Hi Doug, I just stopped by to let you know that Moira, your new trainer, had a few things to take care of, and wouldn't be able to visit you."

Doug tried to look disappointed, or at the least unconcerned. He wanted to look anything but relieved.

"Oh, alright. That's good anyway, because I was just getting ready to go to get something to eat and then see a movie with Paul."

"Actually, she said she would like to meet you in a couple of hours for coffee, but I guess a movie takes a long time, about four or five hours doesn't it?

"Not unless we're watching 'Gone With the Wind' or something."

"How long does a movie last?"

Doug remembered that Johann had little memory of anything before the Ryeesian's captured him. A sudden pity came over him. This wasn't anything like the friend he had known.

"Some movies are longer, but for the most part they're just under a couple of hours. Usually around an hour and a half. Why don't you come with us? I think you'd like going to the movies."

"I don't know Doug. I make Paul nervous, and usually I make him depressed. I don't think he likes me."

"Of course he does. He's only sad because he remembers what you were like before the Ryeesian invasion. We were all good friends before, I don't see why we can't be again. If he won't learn to accept what's happened, I'll pound it into him."

"Are you sure, Doug?"

"Of course I'm sure. We'll go to get something to eat, and then go see a movie. It'll be fun."

"Alright, and then after the movie we can meet Moira in the coffee shop. You'll like her, she was the one who helped me when I first got here."

Doug cringed internally at the mention of meeting with Moira. He had sincerely hoped his friend had forgot.

CHAPTER 16

Paul did indeed seem nervous when he saw Johann and learned that he would accompany them to the theater. Johann glanced bashfully at Paul, and Doug could feel Johann's regret for deciding to come. Doug felt a brief surge of anger toward Paul's behavior welling up inside him. The pain he was causing Johann, even if he was unaware that he was hurting him, was extremely unnecessary. He decided that he would mend the rift between Paul and Johann tonight, before it was allowed to grow wider.

"You could cut the tension in the room with a knife. What gives, Paul? Isn't it alright if Johann goes with us? It'll be like old times." Doug said as he sent out soothing emotions to Paul.

Doug could sense the apprehension in Paul fading. He could tell that Johann was feeling more secure as well. Apparently, he had said and done the right thing. Doug mentally encouraged Paul and Johann to describe how they felt to one another. Johann couldn't really help what had happened, so most of the shifting of views had to be done by Paul. Doug told Paul bluntly that it would help if his discomfort was out on the table so they could talk about why he felt the way he did.

By the end of their meal everyone felt much better. Doug didn't tell them that he had been using his mental abilities to release most of the pain that Paul felt for Johann. He wanted to keep the anger level down, and he knew Paul well enough to know that the idea of being tampered with, even for a good reason, wouldn't make him very happy.

The movie they were going to see had been a number one release a year before the Ryeesian invasion, which meant that it was a year in the future from Doug's standpoint. Doug wasn't very excited about the movie. He was too preoccupied with the dilemma of the, soon to be present, introduction to Moira. Johann had insisted that he should call her to let her know when to meet them at the cafe. Even though he knew Johann wouldn't forget, he still had hoped that his friend's mind would overlook the meeting, just this once.

Doug ignored the entire movie, trying his best to relax and figure out a way to consciously shield certain thoughts. The movie wasn't very long, just under two hours. Nonetheless, Doug gained a limited understanding of his mental defenses in the two hour span. He had always blocked out probes and mental scans unconsciously, but he wasn't willing to trust his subconscious this time. The potential for embarrassment was far too great for all to be entrusted to his subconscious psyche.

After his two hour preparation, Doug felt a little more secure, and directed his attention to his companions. The credits had begun to roll, and Paul and Johann were standing and applauding with the rest of the people in the theater. They were both excited to have seen the movie. For Johann, it was a new experience; for Paul and most of the others in the theater, it was a recreational pleasure they hadn't had in five years. Doug's pleasure came from the genuine smiles on his friend's faces.

The moment had arrived, and Doug was surprisingly calm. He felt confident that he could shield any embarrassing thoughts from Moira. Paul had gone home and Johann didn't think it was necessary to stay, so he pointed out Moira's table and left. Even the absence of his friends didn't diminish Doug's courage. He had spent two hours perfecting his mental shield, and was confident he wouldn't embarrass himself.

Moira was facing the other way, and Doug, trying his best to appear nonchalant, walked toward her table. Just to be on the safe side he tried not to look at her. His first glance, as he had entered the room, had told him that she had a great figure, so he tried to avoid looking at her as he approached.

Doug was as prepared as he could be, and felt secure that he could shield his thoughts from her. He sat down opposite from her and looked at Moira for the first time. The intricate framework of his shield collapsed in the instant he caught her gaze. It was Michelle. He tried to speak, but the words wouldn't come out of his throat. Tears began to form in the corners of his eyes as he gazed into the beautiful blue eyes of the dimensional counterpart of the woman he loved.

Even more amazing was the empathic emanation he received from her. She felt the same way he did, and he could feel the love pour out of her as she gazed into his eyes. Doug blinked several times and hoped this wasn't a dream. The realization that this wasn't *his* Michelle suddenly came crashing down around him. He quickly closed off his mind, but could see by the look of pain on Moira's face that the damage had already been done.

"I shouldn't have expected so much," she whispered "I probably should have guessed that you would have someone else in your life. This isn't even your dimension. I'm sorry Doug, but when I heard that *you* were the dimensional traveler everyone was talking about, I hoped you would be similar to the Doug from our dimension, but would be able to love me. I shouldn't have gotten my hopes up."

"I should be the one to apologize, Mich... Moira, I should learn to control my thoughts a little more."

"What do you mean? I thought all of the emotion was emanating from me?"

"No, I was part of it, too."

"Then you do have feelings for me, or at least for my counterpart in your dimension?"

"Yes, that's why I reacted the way I did. I don't want to get confused between my friends back home and my friends here."

Moira seemed satisfied with his answer and he felt the pain he had caused her diminish. It was still an awkward situation, but now that everything was out in the open, the tension level had decreased to manageable standards. Doug couldn't help but feel the powerful and soul grabbing attraction that he had for both Michelle and Moira. Essentially they were the same woman, and loving one meant loving the other.

As he spent the evening with Moira, Doug began to feel more and more guilty. He had first fallen in love with Michelle, and now he was enjoying spending time with another woman, even if it was Michelle's counterpart. The circumstances were bizarre, and he couldn't help but think this was some elaborate joke in the making. He could hear the voice now, asking,

"If you met a woman that was an exact duplicate of your wife, would it still be cheating if you slept with her?"

Doug groaned inwardly, as the answer formed in his head, "yes". He cared deeply for Michelle, and even though there wasn't any commitment involved yet, he was still determined not to betray her memory by making excuses.

As they talked Doug noted that the similarities between Moira and Michelle were uncanny. Both women looked the same, although Moira looked slightly older and more sophisticated. The mannerisms that he loved so dearly were also the same. Since this dimension was several years in the future compared to his, Doug wondered if Moira and this dimension's Doug ever got married or at least engaged.

"If you don't mind me asking, what happened to this dimension's Doug? Did you and he ever get together?" he asked

"No, he never even asked me out. I loved him from the moment I saw him, but we never got an farther than good friends. I almost asked him out, but I was afraid he didn't feel that way about me."

"What happened to him? No one here seems to know where he is."

"I'm pretty sure he died in the Ryeesian invasion. I searched for him for years but could never find him. We were both at college when the Ryeesians attacked, he was going for his masters and I was finishing up my senior year. The college was destroyed in the first wave. Apparently the Ryeesians thought the college was a military base. Not many people survived."

"I'm sorry, I didn't mean to upset you."

"That's all right, it's been five years since then. With enough time most wounds will heal. Now, if you could answer a few of my questions I would be most delighted."

"Sure, go ahead."

"Well, if I knew what happened to you when the Ryeesians attacked, then I might be able to find my Doug, if he's still alive. Where did you go when they attacked?"

"I'm afraid I won't be much help there. When I left my dimension, it was the year two thousand seven. The Ryeesians haven't attacked yet in my world."

"That can't be right! Doug never had a body like yours in college, and he certainly didn't have psychic capabilities back then before the war!"

"I didn't either, until I absorbed the energy of the dimensional probe when it attacked me."

"Well, there goes that idea. I can't think of any other way to find him. I've searched everywhere. Maybe it's time for me to let him die, I've clung to the hope that he might be alive somewhere for too long." Moira started to cry silently as she finished speaking.

"Don't cry, please. It kills me to see you cry. I mean, what am I? You've got me, I can be just as good a friend to you as your Doug was. That at least helps a little doesn't it?"

Looking up at him her eyes hardened into delicately crafted blue saphires.

"And what if something happens to you? What do I do when you leave to go back to your own dimension? What have I got then?"

He tried to think of an answer, but was overcome with attraction to her angry stare. Even when she was mad, she was beautiful and totally irresistible. As Moira sensed his attraction, her gaze softened, and soon was accompanied by a mysterious and seductive smile. Doug knew he was heading for a battle more fierce than ten Ryeesian armies put together. Since she was empathic, Moira knew that she had him wrapped around her finger, there were just too many trump cards in her hand.

CHAPTER 17

The war between Doug and Moira had begun. He was trying as hard as he could to remain faithful to a woman that not only thought he was dead, but also might never see again. She was trying equally as hard to convince him that she was just as good, if not better, than any other woman. Doug thought that the fact that he had to undergo psychic training, with Moira as his instructor for eight hours a day, was completely unfair. He enjoyed spending time with her, but the training classes involved far too much temptation.

During the first few days, she had told him that standard procedure in training involved allowing the trainer into his mind, and trying to block certain memories from being seen by the instructor. He had no problem with it and actually enjoyed the mental sparring. But when the time came for the roles to be reversed, she cheated outrageously by allowing him to see anything in her memory that involved her fantasies with him, and even a few memories of standing partly naked in front of a mirror. At that point, he suspected that she had spent the previous night posing in front of her mirror, just to be sure the memories he saw were vivid and alluring.

After the mental sparring came the lessons on imaging, which involved sending images back and forth between the instructor and pupil. Again she cheated by throwing in images that could only be described as blatantly phallic or at the very least overly sensual. He tried to counter by sending thoughts of the most disgusting things he could muster in his imagination, but she was clearly still winning.

The most challenging test so far, was the advanced telepathy training session. Now he had to send and receive thoughts that were in the form of words. It was like hearing someone else's voice inside his head. Not only did she use the sexiest "mental voice" that she could, but told him quite explicitly about all of the things that turned her on and made her aroused. As well as to tell him how much fun it would be to experiment with several of the sensual ways to make oneself more attractive that she had read about. Since he was supposed to respond in context to what he received from her, he could only send out fumbled attempts to communicate, which his instructor interpreted as, "a lack of proper development". Thus he was doomed to go through the latest temptation for another two days.

Doug had returned to his quarters after the days exhausting training for his daily cold shower. Moira had asked if he would like to get something to eat later, so he knew he would need it. Doug couldn't help but be amused by Moira. She only seemed to try seduction during their training sessions. When they spent time together apart from the training room, she was polite, sophisticated and completely rational. Once they stepped into the training room, however, her mind seemed to become completely dominated by wickedly erotic images that she hurled at him with deadly accuracy.

Doug knew that whenever he was in that room, he was fighting a battle that he would eventually lose. The more he talked to Dr. McIntyre, the more he became convinced that he would be in this dimension for a very long time, thus making the war that much longer. Paul wasn't any help at all. His advice was to accept the fact that a large portion of life would be spent here, and to move on.

Doug sat down on his cot and sighed. He was indeed adjusting to living here. Aside from the threat of an attack by the Overlord, it wasn't so bad. There were even old friends here. The only thing he could truly say he was missing were his parents, and he could at least imagine them safe on *his* earth. He wondered how long he would be trapped here. His relationship with Moira was complex, but he was growing to love her more than he did Michelle. That wasn't hard to explain, because he knew Moira better than he did Michelle. He had been given more time to get to know Moira than he had with Michelle. Even so, Doug was still reluctant to abandon the thought of getting home soon.

Doug decided he would have another talk with the Admiral. Maybe then he would have enough information to determine how long his stay would be. He almost hoped it would be a few years, maybe more. He had been meaning to talk to the Admiral anyway. Doug sat up, convinced that he would settle everything tomorrow, and prepared for his evening with Moira.

Doug was supposed to meet Moira in the cafe for a quiet dinner. He was completely unprepared for what he found when he got there. Moira had decided to wear a low cut lavender dress that had a silken quality to it. The dress clung to various parts of her body as she moved, and displayed her stunning figure extremely well. She smiled knowingly as he sat down at their table.

"You look lovely, what's the occasion?" he choked out.

"I'm cheating again," She grinned. "When we were practicing your mental sparring lessons the other day, I stumbled across the area of your memory that holds what type of things attract you the most. You know, turn ons, likes, dislikes, that sort of thing."

The look she gave him could have melted glaciers. Doug was definitely out gunned, and was suddenly feeling extremely warm.

"I took an inventory of my apparel, and I found this old dress of mine. Do you like it?" she gushed.

It was definitely getting warmer in the room. Doug wondered if she had tampered with the heating controls in the cafe as an extra added touch to his torture.

"It's very beautiful." He managed to utter.

"I know I'm not being fair, Doug." She confessed. "But I just can't help myself. The fact that I know for certain that your feelings for me are as strong as mine are for you, only makes it more tempting to try to win you over."

"That doesn't make it any easier to resist. At least you could give me an occasional break from the seducing."

She laughed and held his hand consolingly.

"Please understand that I've wanted Doug Taylor for a long time, and I now have the chance to get him. Until you do find a way back to your home, I'm not going to stop until I get what I want."

"What is it you want, exactly?" Doug managed to choke out as his face flushed to a deep red.

She smiled, and gave him a look that said more than a book, written on the subject could ever hope to relate. Doug swallowed hard, and wondered if he could somehow escape from the lure of the beautiful seductress in front of him.

"Let's get something to eat, I'm getting hungry. We can talk about when we're going to move in together some other time." She said sweetly.

Doug gave up and ordered his meal from the speaker unit. He had to admit that she was persistent, and he knew that she wasn't far from getting what she wanted.

※ ※ ※ ※ ※

The hallway seemed shorter than before. Maybe this time he could reach the door at the end of the hall. The door was slightly ajar, as it had always been. The closer he got to the door the more it would open. The pale green and orange light and smoke emanating from the room appeared clearer, more defined than before. Emotions emanated with the smoke, and he could sense wave upon wave of anger and envy coming from behind the door. The negative emanations only strengthened his resole as he strode toward the menacing room. He knew that this time he would uncover what was in that room. The threat would be unveiled.

He had always been frightened when he got close to the reeking entrance of the room, but this time he was filled with a resolve that would not permit waking until he found the answers he was seeking. The echoing of his footsteps got louder as he neared the portal, and each resounding step strengthened his determination to succeed. The closer he got, the more his own anger boiled inside of him like the blackest bile.

The reek of burning flesh filled his nostrils as he stepped up to the entrance. He had made it to the room, and was pushing his way through the smoke. As he sifted through the pale orange-green haze in the room, the smoke began to clear. He could sense the presence of another person, a person filled with rage, hate, envy, and fear. That was the threat to him. He made his way toward the shadowy opponent, only to find a mirror. The reflection in the mirror was of him, but his face hideously distorted with a cruelty that made him want to vomit.

Doug awoke in a cold sweat. The dream he had was still fresh in his mind. He wanted to know what the dream meant. Somehow, he knew the answer was very important. He shook his head to cast off the last remnants of sleep. It was early, but close enough to the morning to stay awake.

Doug had planned to visit the Admiral this morning, before his daily training, as seduction recipient, with Moira. Maybe he could find out how long he would be staying. If it was going to be awhile, he might as well get more deeply involved with Moira.

Even though he was profoundly attracted to her, he wanted to love her for who she was, and not because she was a counterpart to Michelle. It was far too easy to get things confused anyway. He wanted to make sure that his relationship with Moira was genuine and that they both cared for each other instead of caring for the resemblance to others they loved. He knew that Moira was different from Michelle, but oddly, he found that the differences were improvements. Moira was closer to what he would consider the ideal soulmate than Michelle was, and he wondered if somehow God had given him the chance to be with the person he was made for.

Doug showered and went to the mess hall to get something to eat before he went to see the Admiral. Since he had learned that Venilusia was a planet of peace loving humanoids that had native species of animals close to those of earth, he had adopted the customary consumption of Venilusian eggs and beef as a replacement for the real thing. He honestly couldn't tell the difference.

After finishing a large breakfast of Venilusian eggs, bacon, and toast, he headed for the strategic planning floor, where the Admiral's office was. The strategic planning floor was one level below the medical floor, and two levels above the recreational floor. The floor's entirety wasn't as large in length or width as the other floors, but still had some of the largest rooms in the complex.

As Doug walked toward the Admiral's office, he couldn't help but wonder how long it had taken to tunnel out so much space. If an attack was made on a base, building a new hiding space of the same magnitude would not only be tedious and time consuming, but urgent. A new base would need to be set up as quickly as possible. To have to wait for this base to be tunneled out must have been nerve racking.

The Admiral's office was small compared to the other rooms on this floor, but it was still twice the size of Doug's residence. The Admiral was in a meeting with one of the Council members, so Doug decided to wait for awhile in the office. Maybe the meeting wouldn't be much longer. He hadn't been waiting long when he heard the Admiral's voice coming toward the office.

"Ah, nice to see you, Doug. What can I do for you?" the Admiral asked.

"I just stopped by to ask you a few questions, if you have the time?"

"Sure, I'll do my best to give you an answer."

Doug noticed the nervousness coming from the Admiral. He had felt it from him before and wondered what was wrong.

"You seem to be worried about something,...and nervous. What's wrong? Is it because of me?"

"Damn! I was trying to shield that, how could you tell?"

"If you were shielding, you were doing a terrible job of it. I wasn't even trying to sense anything."

"You have a great power, Doug. I don't want to pressure you, but we could really use your help. Some bad news has come from one of the other bases."

"What happened?"

"Shaleese found one of the supply bases we had near the edge of his territory. The base was evacuated but over half of it's military compliment were killed or captured, and most of the civilians were slaughtered. We knew the base might be in danger about a week ago, and the Council ordered for an evacuation, but apparently they weren't quick enough. Shaleese's armada attacked last night."

"My God! How many people were stationed there?"

"Over twenty thousand. Barely fifteen hundred made it to safety. The worst news is that some of the people captured may know of this base's location. If that's true, we could be in danger. I've ordered for the evacuation process to begin. We'll get everything ready to go, and even if Shaleese doesn't make a move toward us, we move out in two weeks."

Doug felt the irrational rage swelling in him. The mere mention of Shaleese's name made him furious. Regaining some control, he suppressed the anger, fearing that he may end up like the mirror image in his dream. Doug forced himself to be calm and collected his thoughts.

"Well, that sort of answers one of my questions."

"You were hoping that we might be able to get the prototype D.T.P. from the old base we abandoned."

"Yes. I was going to ask about that."

"You don't sound very disappointed."

"Well, I'm not really. McIntyre thinks that he can work it out so that no matter how long I'm here, he can get me back to the same time I left. There's some kind of time rift in the dimensional jaunting. I just wanted to know how long

I was going to be in this dimension, so I could consider the possibilities I have available to me."

"Ah, you've found a woman here," he grinned. "Anyone I know?"

Doug blushed slightly at the Admiral's keen observation.

"Um, yes, actually; don't tell her, but it's Moira, my mental trainer."

"Moira. That's a tough one Doug, I don't know how much luck you'll have with her. Don't get me wrong, she's absolutely stunning, but she has been the heartbreak of new recruits for years."

"I think I know why she's been so negative toward other suitors, but trust me when I say I shouldn't have a problem in that area."

"It's not like that Doug, she's still mourning for someone who died in the invasion. She must have loved him very much to mourn for five years."

"I know Admiral. *I'm* the dimensional counterpart of the one she loved. There's a woman in my dimension exactly like her that I was just getting involved with when I was taken by the probe."

"I see... Well, this should prove interesting," he grinned. "Congratulations, she really deserves some happiness."

"Well, like I said, don't tell her. It's going to be a surprise. Besides, the circumstances are strange to say the least."

"Your involvement with Moira should give you extra incentive to aid us. We really could use all the help we can get."

"Admiral, I don't need any extra incentives," Doug stated as the rage began to swell again. "I'll help in any way I can. Just name the task and I'll do my best. If I ever meet this Shaleese guy, I'll give him a battle he won't forget."

"That's the spirit! Now, go learn as much as you can, I'll need you to take a crash course on star cruisers. We need as many pilots as possible to transport all of the base equipment. The way you managed to advance in hand to hand combat so quickly, I just know you'll be a superb pilot in no time."

CHAPTER 18

Doug left the Admiral's office feeling strange. The rage he had felt frightened him. He knew there was just cause for anger towards Shaleese, but the absolute fury he felt when he thought about the Overlord made him want to break something vital in the first person he saw. Doug was afraid he might hurt an innocent bystander if he dwelled on the subject of the enemy for too long.

It was almost time for his training session, so he headed for the training floor one level below. He entered the classroom door and sat down in one of the chairs. Moira hadn't arrived yet, and Doug was grateful for the chance to cool down. He didn't want Moira to see him, feel him, like he was. He tried to vent some of the anger in him, but without much success; there was just too much of it.

Moira came in through the door with her usual look of smugness. She knew she won all battles that occurred in the training room. This time, however, she stopped abruptly, as if she had run into a wall. She looked at Doug with her eyes wide in astonishment. Doug found her sudden wide-eyed wonder to be so absolutely endearing, that his rage instantly subsided to be replaced by total adoration.

"What was that all about? When I came in here you were so angry you were about to bust a blood vessel in your neck, and now you're feeling the exact opposite! What's wrong, why the mood swings?"

"It's not that hard to explain, Moira. I could be in the foulest mood there ever was and the sight of you would make me overjoyed." Doug said sincerely.

Moira looked sharply at him, slightly confused. Her expression was a cross between a look of happiness and a look of injury.

"Why,...You're not trying to be mean, are you? I mean, you aren't trying to get back at me by pretending to be caving in, or something?"

Doug grinned; as tough as Moira tried to appear on the outside, she was as equally gentle and as easily hurt on the inside. Doug got up and stood in front of Moira. Holding her delicate face in his hands, he lifted her lowered head, and looked into her eyes.

"It's not a joke, or some type of revenge, Moira. It's the truth. I was upset by something Admiral McDougal told me this morning. It's been gnawing away at me for almost an hour. When you came in, the look of surprise on your face was so completely adorable, it instantly made me happy again."

"What did McDougal say? Was it about you getting home?"

"That's why I went to see him; but no, that's not what I was angry about."

"What was it? Please tell me, Doug. Maybe sharing it will help a little."

She sat down, gently pulling him into the seat next to her, and put her hands comfortingly on his shoulders. Her closeness made Doug feel secure, and the flowery smell of her was enough to make him considerably distracted. He knew she might be the only one who he could tell about his rages. Not only would she be able to keep him from getting out of hand if he became furious, but she would understand what to do better than anyone else on the base.

"Shaleese attacked one of the supply bases and killed or captured over half the people living there. McDougal says we have to abandon this base regardless of whether our location has been compromised. It may be sooner if Shaleese moves in our direction."

"That is awful news Doug, but what I felt coming from you was a little out of line, for any reason. There's something else, isn't there?"

"Yes there is, but I don't know what. It may sound strange, but every time I think about, or hear Shaleese's name, I want to rip someone's head off. I've also been having weird dreams, they seem to be important, but they don't make much sense. Do you think I might be reacting to all of the negative thoughts directed toward Shaleese?"

"That might be it, I can't imagine you generating all that hate by yourself. Plus, the instant you think of something else it goes away, right?"

"Not really, so far the only thing that can make it go away is thinking of you."

"I'm glad I'm such a positive influence." She remarked in a sarcastic tone.

"Look, we need to talk Moira. There may not be much time before the evacuation, and the base might be attacked. I need to finish as much training as I can before that happens. Which means I can't have you distracting me with seductive images of you half naked, and nice dresses in an attempt to win me over," he chided her gently, but in a firm tone.

Doug had to concentrate hard to shield the wave of sympathy that swept over him, as she lowered her face in a crestfallen and ashamed defeat. He wanted his next statement to surprise her.

"I think it would be a good idea if we just started officially dating each other. Just so you won't be tempted to throw in any spontaneous flirting into our training sessions, of course."

She looked up at him quickly with a surprised expression of hope and elation on her delicate face. Her eyes betrayed her happiness as they started to overflow with tears.

"Do you really mean it, Doug?"

"Of course I do, but I want to make it clear from the start that we're only beginning to date. I want our relationship to be genuine, not a relationship based on the fact that I'm just like the other Doug you loved. I already know that I truly care for you, because I've had more time to get to know you than your counterpart, even though I fell in love with the way you both look and act in my dimension."

"There's a big difference between the way I feel for you and the way I felt for the other Doug. I know you love me the way I've always wanted to be loved. I can feel it. I don't know if he ever did, and I don't even care if he ever did. That's all that matters to me."

"Well, it's definitely an odd situation, but I can't spend years in this dimension and not be with you. I'll end up dying from hypothermia with all of the cold showers I'd have to take."

She let out a wicked little laugh, and dove at him to hold him in an embrace. He held her in his arms and they kissed for at least half an hour; he wouldn't have wanted to escape with any less. After the kissing and holding had died down, neither of them wanted to do any work, so they agreed to go get some coffee and decide how to spend the rest of their day together.

Doug couldn't help but feel excited. As they walked, Doug sent out an emotional wave of all the joy and love he felt for Moira. She looked up at him sharply as her eyes began to brim with tears again, and returned his empathic message with one of her own. Doug had never felt a more powerful or pure love from anyone, and he made a silent prayer, as his eyes began to fill with tears that he would never lose the beautiful woman beside him.

✦ ✦ ✦ ✦ ✦

The following week was filled with difficult work that was not only physically exhausting, but mentally draining. He had a rushed course from Moira on mental attacks and defenses, which consisted of psychic blasts and more complex shields, simple telekinetic manipulations of feather weight objects, and empathic control. The course lasted for two days, which was a condensed form of its original two weeks. Moira had said he learned very fast and was probably as good as a soldier who had received two months of intense training.

After his mental training was deemed complete, he went on to simultaneously learn weaponry, and starship operation. Combined, the classes would ordinarily have lasted four weeks, but for Doug, it was condensed to four days. All his instructors agreed that his retention of the material he was learning was superb, and he could easily stand up to the rigors of more advanced training.

The daily instruction only lasted eight hours, which left Doug fourteen hours a day, to eat, sleep, practice in the simulators at least six to eight hours a day, and most importantly to spend time with his Moira.

Moira was very understanding about the pressures he had on his shoulders. She was content to have him come over to her place, which was the larger and better furnished, Lieutenant Commander's quarters, and hold her while they sat on the couch and talked. He usually fell asleep holding her, slept for two to three hours, and then got back up to get to work. Apparently his body required less sleep than before, because he felt better with two or three hours than he did when he slept for eight.

The evacuation had begun. Crates and equipment were being moved as quickly as possible to the ground shuttles, which would then load them onto the waiting star cruisers. Two of the six star cruisers were already fully loaded. A sufficient amount of space was left for an ample crew on each cruiser, and as per resistance regulations, several cabins were left over in the event of running into stranded humans during the journey.

Each star cruiser was as large as three football fields in length, and two in width. Each thirty story high monster was heavily armored so it could withstand several direct hits from enemy weaponry. There were roughly five hundred laser turrets from aft to stern, which gave the ship the overall appearance of a porcupine, or maybe a fat, fuzzy caterpillar. Doug was reassured that even though they looked like immobile slag heaps, they were easy to control and maneuver, superb for defense, and had great response at returning fire.

Doug had trained at helm control, weaponry, engine thrust ratios, and the statistical capabilities of the craft in extreme measures, and still felt unsure that it would even move. The smaller fighter craft, which the starship held in it's docking bays, on the other hand, looked extremely impressive. Even though most of the fighters were dented and patched from previous skirmishes, they looked fast and effective. Looking like a cross between an F-14 and a stealth bomber, the two man fighter crafts looked spectacular.

Doug had spent simulator time operating the fighters as well as the starships. He enjoyed the video game like quality of the fighter simulator, and excelled in the fighter combat scenarios because of his enhanced reflexes and superior speed in decision making. He hoped he would get the chance to fly one of the fighter ships, even if it meant placing himself in a far more dangerous position.

The evacuation's scheduled day was only five days away. If all went well, there would be no trouble, and they could sneak away to the secondary base that had been selected for its potential as a fall back base to retreat to. Doug had completed the final testing the day before, and was given the rank of Lieutenant because of his superior achievements.

He was currently on his way to Moira's quarters to tell her the good news. Doug hoped that she would be happy for him, and maybe reward him for his achievements with a long and sensual kiss. Now that he had finished training, he wouldn't have to spend so much time away from her. The only thing that he would need to do during the day would be to practice in the simulators, and that wasn't necessarily required.

As he reached her room, he hit the call button, and heard her beautiful voice tell him to come in. He opened the door, and walked into the room only to be tackled as Moira leapt from beside the door and into his arms. As he lay trapped by her on the floor, she smothered him with kisses. Finally getting a good hold on her, he tossed her over and onto her back, and holding her gently, he stole the long and lingering kiss that he had wanted.

"What was all that tackling business for?"

"Because I love you,...and because you got promoted to Lieutenant. Congratulations, I'm so proud of you."

"Hey! Who told you? That was my good news, I wanted to be the one to tell you."

"So you don't like it when I jump on top of you and kiss you?"

"Well, I didn't say that! Since I don't have any training classes tomorrow, why don't we go out and celebrate?"

Moira rolled on top of him and gave him a wicked grin. Brushing a strand of his wavy black hair away from his forehead, she caressed the side of his face as they gazed into each others eyes. Moira leaned forward and gave him a long and passionate kiss. They lay on the floor pressed closely together, and Doug felt Moira's mental suggestion that they should spend the evening alone. As he inhaled her beautiful fragrance, he agreed without hesitation.

CHAPTER 19

A s Doug awoke he inhaled deeply, smelling the flowery scent of Moira's hair. They had fallen asleep on the couch, and Doug silently thanked God that his body had been augmented. Since the control over his body's involuntary functions was enhanced, he could keep his arm from falling asleep. Moira was still asleep, so he tried not to wake her. Gazing at the gorgeous woman laying on his shoulder, he wondered how he had ever gotten along without her. She was everything he had ever wanted in a woman. Their empathic powers enhanced the bond that had formed between them. With every passing day, they grew closer together.

Doug treasured the gift he had been given and wondered what he would do when the time came to return to his own dimension. There were only two options, take Moira with him, or stay. He couldn't be separated from her forever. Even now he could feel her as a part of him.

She was sleeping soundly, and dreaming about earth as it was before the Ryeesian invasion, she was living with him and their children in a nice house. He smiled as he shared her dream, maybe she could come back with him, she could live on earth like it used to be. No, then she would have to face the Ryeesian invasion all over again. That wouldn't be fair to her. He stopped thinking as he felt her waking. She arched her back, turned her face toward him and blinked sleepily.

"Good morning my love."

He smiled, "Good morning to you too, love."

"What's got you up so early?"

"Just thinking, I didn't wake you did I?"

"No, unless I woke up because you're awake. Something's changed since we've been spending more time together. It's the most amazing feeling, like I always have you right next to me, even when you're not. I can sense what you're thinking without even trying."

"I know, it's because we're both highly telepathic and empathic. We're developing a special bond. We're connected to each other. I'm not sure how it will effect our relationship in other areas, but I'm sure it will be dramatic when it happens."

"You got that right!", she grinned wickedly.

Pulling Moira back toward him, Doug kissed her, and held her face gently with one hand. Gazing into her eyes, he let all of his thoughts, dreams, and hopes for their future float into her mind. The happy couple spent nearly an hour relishing the powerful emotions that they shared for each other. Eventually they snuggled together and fell back into a beautiful sleep in which they shared a joint dream of living together on Earth.

⊕ ⊕ ⊕ ⊕ ⊕

Doug was in the flight simulator for the delta space fighter when the alarms went off. Shaleese had found them, and the time for a hasty departure had arrived. Doug's only thought was of Moira. He had to make sure she was safely on board one of the star cruisers. He raced down the hallway of the training level. Literally leaping entire flights of stairs he reached the top residence floor where Moira was stationed.

"Stay where you are Moira, I'll be there in five seconds, we'll go to the ship together," he sent out to her telepathically

"Please hurry, I love you."

"I love you too."

Doug reached her room in record time, and opened the door. Moira ran to the door and embraced him fiercely. After a brief moment together, they headed for the launching bays. They were both stationed on the flagship, Pegasus. Moira was to assist in navigating the Pegasus, and Doug was in one of the fighter squadrons that would defend, and counter attack if possible, in the event of any cruisers that were blocked off from the escape route.

The launching bays were accessed through either the strategic planning level or any of the major floors below it. Doug raced down the corridors with Moira. Since she couldn't keep up with him, he slowed down for her, and they still made good time. The Pegasus was to be the first to leave, so there was no time to waste. The final starship was for the soldiers who were defending the top level of the base from the ground assault, and hopefully they would be able retreat with minimal casualties.

Doug's training had included classes on the weaponry and capabilities of the enemies. He knew that for the most part the enemy soldiers weren't completely biological. The common soldier's brain had an implanted chip that linked with the neural net and overrode all independent cognitive thought. They were incapable of anything but obedience to the men controlling them.

Shaleese's warships were each twice as powerful as their own, but weren't as fast. Their only hope was to avoid direct engagement with the larger enemy ships and run to safety. The major difficulty would be surviving the enemy star fighter's assault. Enough bombardment from the smaller fighters could cripple their star cruisers and leave them incapable of retreat.

Doug and Moira boarded the Pegasus and headed for the bridge. The launching sequence had already started, and the great metallic mound rumbled as the anti-gravity boosters activated. Moira took her station as the hulking colossus lifted off the platform. The large space door above them opened to reveal the stars of space, and the Pegasus lifted upward, gaining speed as it rocketed through the doors.

The other star ships soon followed the example of the Pegasus. Doug looked out the front view screen and saw the ten enemy starships approaching from around the far side of the planet. The last star cruiser, which was for the ground assault defense crews, was the only ship left in the base's docking bay. The other five destructor class star cruisers were well on their way to freedom.

Doug knew he couldn't stay on the bridge of the flagship. He had to get to his fighter in case of an emergency. Paul would already be waiting there since Doug had been assigned to Paul's squadron. Getting up from his seat, he went to tell Moira he was going, as he reached her station she turned to look at him, and he could see and feel the fear she had for him.

"I've got to go, love. Don't worry, I'll be careful, and I'll keep in touch," he said while tapping his index finger against the side of his head.

"I love you Doug, please be careful. Give me a kiss before you go."

They shared a quick and tender embrace, and hurriedly parted after Moira got the kiss she had asked for.

Doug headed for the bridge exit. Thankfully, there were high powered transport tubes that could take an individual not only between levels, but to different quadrants of the ship. Doug appreciated the efficiency and time saving provided by the tubes, even if they were the epitome of laziness since they made walking more than a block unnecessary.

The launching bays for the fighters were located on both sides of the star cruiser. The placement of the garage door size bays were along a line at the middle third of the ship on the median of its height. Each side had a total of twenty bays, and each bay had two to four fighters docked, for a total of one hundred fighter craft. Paul's flight group was located close to the exact middle of the Pegasus, on the side facing the larger enemy warships.

The tube lift stopped in the quadrant of the bay where Paul's unit was, and Doug raced down the corridor to wait with his friend. Doug arrived at the joint launching bays sixteen and seventeen, the latter being the bay where half of Doug's squadron awaited orders to launch. Each squadron unit had twelve fighters and a flight leader. Doug could see the fighter he was to fly as he entered bay seventeen, wolf three. He was excited to be given the third in command position of the Wolf Squadron, before he had ever even flown a fighter in real life.

"Hey, Doug! Over here!" Paul shouted across the bay to his friend.

"What's up, buddy? You think we'll get the order to launch?"

"I hope not. I was in the last battle we had, when we escaped from our last base on Sarin five. We were outnumbered ten to one, and lost a lot of good men. They've got us far outgunned, my friend. If we have to fight today, a lot of us might not come back."

"Well, you've got a real fighter on your squad now, midget. Nothing is going to go wrong while I'm around."

Doug stood staring out the view port at the approaching enemy vessels. The Pegasus and other star cruisers had to get far enough away from the sun in order to accelerate to hyper travel, in which the engines of the ships would boost the speed of the ships to near the speed of light. The deflectors of the star cruisers, which were also used as defense in battle, shifted the particles encountered in space and deflected them around the oval shape of the ship.

Once they had reached a safe distance, they would use a similar method to the dimensional travel theory, which combined hyper travel with a folding of space. Space was curved, so the fabric of space was folded along two different points of the arc, and greater distances could be reached in shorter amounts of time.

In battle the deflectors were designed to shift the laser-like weapons directed at them to minimize the damage to the hull of the ship. The deflectors of the star cruisers were more advanced than the fighters. A fighter would only be able to withstand two or three direct hits with the deflectors fully operational. A star cruiser, partly because of its size and partly its capacity to store more deflector generators, could easily take ten to twelve direct hits in the same general area from a fighter sized beam and six or seven from another starship at close range.

Doug hoped he would be able to perform as well in reality as he had in the simulators. Even now, before the battle had begun, he felt the rage building. Somehow, he knew Shaleese wasn't among the enemy vessels, but that knowledge didn't help to subdue any of the hate that was growing in him.

The other fighter pilots in the bay stood around waiting for the order to engage the enemy and protect the Pegasus. They seemed more eager than nervous; they wanted action. Doug didn't blame them for their eagerness. He only wished he could be certain that he wouldn't be dragged down by his ever present rage.

Paul had introduced Doug to the other members of their squad a few days before. Aside from Paul, only two others had seen real combat in a delta fighter. Rick and Joseph had been in Paul's flight group when the rebels fled their previous base.

Rick was a lean man of medium height with jet black hair. His olive colored skin gleamed in the luminescence of the docking bay lights as Doug glanced at him and his dark eyes peered past his pointed nose calmly. He was always cool and collected. He never let anything upset him, at least not visibly. Joseph was by far one of the oddest men Doug had ever met. He was a tall and well built black man, with the most intimidating face Doug had ever seen. The contrast was in his intelligence and wit. Joseph could "cheer up a slug with salt on it's back", which also happened to be one of Joseph's favorite euphemisms. Joseph was always cheerful, even though he looked "permanently pissed" as he would say. Doug had never encountered a "bad vibe" emanating from Joseph, and had quickly grown to like him.

"What's got you down, Doug? I swear I leave you alone for a few minutes and you're as mad as badger that tried to do it with a porcupine." Joseph asked.

"I don't know, Joe, I've been feeling pissed ever since I started looking out at those stupid ships!"

"Man you white people are so stupid. If that's what's bothering you, then don't look you moron."

Doug laughed and walked away from the view port with Joseph at his side. Joseph convinced Doug, Paul, and the two other flight Cadets from their group, that playing an old fashioned poker game would keep them occupied until they were needed. Rick refused politely saying he would just watch, and the last Cadet in their joint bay didn't know how to play. They offered to teach him, but he declined.

Doug sensed the young Cadet's fear and nervousness, he was clearly on the verge of hysterical panic. He decided that Cadet Johnson would need looking after if he was going to live.

Doug liked him and felt bad that one so young had to face an ordeal so great. Johnson couldn't be much more than sixteen years old, and although eager to prove himself a man, was still dreadfully frightened.

The poker game began. Since it was just for fun, and the base didn't have any monetary system anyway, Joseph handed out three hundred dollars in magnetic poker chips to each player. The chips were each magnetized slightly and stuck to the metallic table to prevent their loss in sudden vibrations from the cruiser's straining engines.

The game had barely gotten going when the alarm sounded and the comm system activated, calling all pilots from bays one to twenty to prep their fighters for immediate take off. Paul ran to the comm screen for their orders, while the rest of the squad headed for their delta fighters. The moment had arrived and the time for action was at hand. Doug let the rage have a little more control over him, releasing some of it, and focusing it toward the enemies he was going to face.

The comm system was rattling off the numbers of the launching bays that were to start their launch. Doug was sitting in the cockpit of Wolf three and had his propulsion systems prepped and on line. Because of the shortage of manpower, he was alone in his two man fighter, as were most of the fighters. A navigator and secondary weapons officer was helpful in battle, but not necessary.

He was ready to pay back the enemy for all the problems that he had suffered, whether they were responsible or not. He was beginning the armament of his weapons systems now, and couldn't wait to see enemy ships destroyed by the shots he fired.

He could visualize the explosions of the ships, and it excited him in a way he didn't care for.

The delta fighters were equipped with two basic armaments, a laser-like beam weapon and twenty concussion particle missiles. The laser like-weapon wasn't really a laser, although it appeared to be a laser. In actuality it was a gun that accelerated condensed groups of protons to just below the speed of light. Even small particles such as protons when fired that fast, could tear through an unprotected object with the ease of a hot knife through butter. The particle missiles were similar to the guns, although the particles were contained in the missile casing, which "erupted" in every direction upon contact.

The deflector systems tried to push the particles away by changing their polarity and shifting their path to an adjacent tangent to the hull. The deflectors weren't very effective against missiles but helped to minimize the damage done. A secondary deflector added to the fighters created a magnetic field that made conventional weapons, such as metallic bullets, completely ineffective since they were repelled with even greater ease by the magnetic field. The larger ships needed no such shielding because of the immense size and incredibly dense hulls constructed of a hyper-titanium polymer.

They were given their leave to depart and engage the enemy. The deltas rocketed out of the bay, and headed for the unavoidable conflict. The Pegasus needed shielding from the enemy for at least twenty minutes to reach the point of the hyper jaunt. Paul came on the comm to inform them of their orders.

"All right Wolf team, we're to engage only if the enemy breaks through the defense barrier set up by the other squads. We'll be the last line of defense along with Cougar team and Viper team. Any questions?"

Doug was enraged and couldn't stand the thought of watching others die while he held back and watched.

"I got a question for you. Why are we the ones who have to stay behind and watch the others get blown to bits!?"

"That's enough, Lieutenant Taylor, we have our orders! Don't worry; there are always several hundred to fly past the defense barrier while their friends keep our front line busy."

"A couple hundred! My God, how many are there!?" Johnson asked in a panicked voice.

"The sensors indicate several groups of enemy fighters headed for each of our star cruisers. Each star cruiser has roughly a thousand enemy ships heading for it. Don't worry; those brainless pilots of theirs aren't all that hard to fight. One of our pilots is a match for at least five of theirs."

The sound of fear in Johnson's voice calmed Doug's rage as a wave of sympathy came over him. He felt the need to reassure his young companion.

"Don't worry, Johnson. I'm your wing man, and nobody's going to take me out. Stick close to me, and together we'll kick a little ass," Doug said as he sent out calming thoughts with an added boost of courage to Johnson.

He felt the fear in Johnson abating, to be replaced with the eagerness he had felt before the pressures of actual battle had dampened it. Doug made a silent prayer that Johnson would live long enough to find the peace and tranquillity that he deserved. There wasn't much hope for an unexperienced pilot with the jitters like the young Cadet; but Doug had a good idea of his own capabilities and swore to himself that he would protect Johnson at all costs.

CHAPTER 20

The Wolf team waited as the first shots were fired in the distance by the lead groups of fighters. Doug couldn't stand the inactivity of waiting, and had to force himself to be calm. Small and brief fiery implosions in the distance indicated the first casualties of the battle. He hoped they were from the other side. The engagement was taking place fifty kilometers away, far enough to be barely visible except for weapons flashes and pseudo-explosions, but with the delta fighter's speed only a few minutes away.

Even now, enemy ships were flying past the already overwhelmed front line defense. Doug hoped plenty would attempt to pass through their sector. His wish was granted as forty enemy fighters headed their way. Paul gave the order to engage the enemy, and Doug leapt into fray.

His rage had been denied nourishment for too long; he desperately needed to destroy the enemy and gave in to that need. Doug vaguely remembered the shock emanating from Johnson as his "wing man" embarked on a berserker rampage directly through the enemy ranks.

All he could see around him were the brief balls of fire that were quickly sucked out into the vacuum of space as each enemy was destroyed. All he cared about was getting to the next enemy fighter before it could get away from him. His reflexes took control as fighter after fighter flared up momentarily, their vital tanks exploded then quickly extinguished leaving only a heap of scorched metal. Each enemy that was destroyed in front of him added to his berserk elation. Doug finally came back to his senses when the sector they were protecting was clear for the moment. Doug suddenly became aware of Paul's voice screaming in his ear.

"...do you hear me Doug! Wake up, snap out of it!"

"I read you, stop shouting! What happened?"

"What happened!? You happened, buddy! What the hell was going on back there? You were swearing like a sailor and blowing up everything in sight! The rest of us only got ten of the fighters combined! You shot down thirty in less than fifteen minutes!"

"Hooray for me. All I remember is wanting to destroy all of them," Doug replied in a slightly shaken voice.

"That was only the first wave, buddy. But you do the same as you did back there and we just might get them all! Try to keep your head on straight, though, I don't want you going berserk every time we go into battle."

"Believe me, I'll try to restrain myself."

Doug wasn't sure why he had lost control, but he was sure that he didn't like the experience. It was something he wasn't sure he could control, even if he didn't give in totally to the rage that he had felt in himself. That rage couldn't be a part of him; it had to be something other than him. As long as it was present, though, he had to control it, vent it out carefully to avoid slipping into the dark chasm of absolute wrath that had enveloped him earlier.

The control screen on his delta fighter indicated several enemy fighters approaching rapidly. The computer indicated over a hundred fighters heading for their sector. Doug felt the rage boiling in him, but he suppressed it with as much force as he could.

"Enemy ships coming our way. Cougar's sending four fighters to help. Let's get 'em and put 'em out quick," Paul said over the comm.

"Ready for action, buddy," Doug answered "Stick with me Johnson; I promise I'll be a little more reasonable this time."

"You can destroy all of these guys just like last time if you want, Lieutenant Taylor. I promise not to be disappointed," Johnson laughed.

Doug induced a pseudo calmness and hoped that he could control the release of rage in moderated amounts, as well as combat the enemy effectively. As the enemy fighters split up into separate groups, Paul divided their fighters into groups of two in order to engage the enemy more efficiently. Doug and Johnson raced off to face the group of fighters designated to them.

Doug set an intercept course for the fifteen fighters headed their way. He noticed for the first time that the enemy craft weren't very responsive to the assaults thrown at their comrades but instead plodded along the same course unless visibly threatened. They weren't as fast as the Delta fighters, so they made easy targets. Doug took out two of the ships simultaneously with precision shots from the particle cannons, while Johnson angled off to attack a third.

"Johnson, hold those two that you have engaged; I'm going after the rest of the pack. If you need me, give me a ring and I'll come back to help."

"Gotcha Lieutenant. I'll finish these two and join you when I can."

Doug veered off toward the fighters that had flown by. Instead of trying to intercept, he angled his fighter directly behind the cluster of enemy ships, and decreased his speed to slightly faster than the speed of the enemy ships. Taking his time, he carefully aimed at an enemy ship, destroyed it, then moved on to the next in line. Doug easily picked off five of the fighters until someone realized what was happening.

Doug felt a frustration and anger directed toward him as he was firing at his sixth ship. It wasn't coming from any of the fighters. Then Doug remembered what he had learned about the soldiers of Shaleese. They were essentially brain dead; they had no cognitive thoughts of their own, nothing but the training they had received for operating their fighters. Which meant someone else had to be coordinating their attack. Doug finished off the sixth fighter as the rest of the group came about to engage him.

"Johnson! Get over here immediately, I need you."

"I'm still fighting one of the enemy craft; do you want me to disengage?!"

"Yes! I have something I want to try, and I need you to cover me."

Paul's voice crackled onto to the comm.

"Don't try anything fancy, Doug. Just stick to your guns."

"Don't worry Commander, just testing a little theory. It won't take long, and I'm not going to put myself or the team at risk."

Johnson rocketed onto the scene a few seconds later and drew some of the fighters away, although three remained on Doug. He tried to keep the pressure on while he let his mind drift over space toward the origin of the anger he felt directed at him. Doug's mind could visualize a middle aged man with a gray streaked goatee and pot belly swearing in front of a computer terminal.

He was the one sending orders to this squad of enemy fighters. Doug waited until he had time to sense where the other leaders were in relation to the middle aged man, then methodically blasted everyone in the room with the mental blast he had learned from Moira. After he had finished dealing with his twentieth operator, he let his mind drift back.

"Paul, are the fighters you're engaged with operating?"

"No, they've all stopped. They're still moving, just not turning, two of them even ran in to one another. Did you do this?"

"Yes, I'll explain later, just pick off those fighters quickly, and get to any other group of enemy fighters that aren't operating and destroy them."

Wolf team soon reunited with only two casualties, and several hundred victories. As they regrouped to assess the situation, Doug looked into his monitor and saw that well over half of the initial thousand had been repelled and destroyed. Paul decided that since the enemies numbers were so low, they could assist the front line along with Viper, and Cougar would stay behind to guard the rear. Doug continued his mental war with the operators, and soon the entire enemy force sent toward the Pegasus had been annihilated.

"All right, boys and girls, good work, let's get back to the Pegasus," Paul congratulated his unit. "Doug, you head on back full speed, the Admiral needs you on the bridge immediately."

⁜ ⁜ ⁜ ⁜ ⁜

On the bridge of the Pegasus, Admiral McDougal looked at the tactical viewer with a frown on his face. A thousand enemy ships headed for each ship. They would be lucky to get through the day with half the number of soldiers they started with. He cursed his hesitance to leave the base sooner. He had known that this would be the result if the were attacked before they had fully evacuated.

Ten to one odds in the enemy's favor wasn't good, even against cybernetic opponents with slower fighters. Maybe he could send out half of the fighter complement, with orders to slow the enemy down, and use the star cruisers more aggressively. No, that would be risky, and could very well cause more casualties. He would just wait and hope that the majority of the fighters would return safely.

Glancing down at Moira, the Admiral felt badly for what he had done. He had seen the look of complete love on her face as she parted from Doug. He could have ordered for a navigational position for Doug, or even a gunnery position on the star cruiser. Instead, he made him a fighter pilot, in hopes that he would prove himself to be the awesome fighter everyone hoped he would be. It wasn't fair to Moira, she deserved happiness after all she had given to the resistance; but then again, many people deserved happiness, and wouldn't get it.

The Admiral turned his head and nodded his acknowledgment, as the report came in that the final star cruiser had lifted off. He turned back to the viewer and noted that the front line had engaged. Hopefully they would only let a few through at a time, as planned, and allow the second line of defense to defeat the enemy easily. As the first breakthrough occurred, the Admiral noted happily that it was in area twenty three, Doug's sector, and it was only some forty fighters.

The Admiral saw Moira cringe, as she too noted that the breakthrough was in Doug's sector. He truly hoped the young man wouldn't be harmed, but was eager to see him in action.

"Switch the zoom to maximum, and turn on the comm net for wolf squadron's current command profiles. I want to see how they do."

"Yes, sir," the view screen officer responded.

McDougal watched in amazement as Doug decimated the enemy, totaling to thirty one ships in just a few minutes. Even with his own limited empathy he could sense the elation from Moira at each of Doug's victories. He ordered the view to maximum wide range again when Doug and his team were finishing up the first breakthrough. Viper wasn't doing nearly as well with their first engagement, but they were holding their own. Cougar had just rocketed off to engage a small breakthrough of twenty or so enemy craft, and would probably do fine. Maybe today wouldn't be as disastrous as he had feared.

The other star cruisers seemed to be taking reasonable casualties, except for the Indomitable, it was taking far too many casualties, and would go down in flames if their luck kept going so badly. He signaled the bridge Commander of the Indomitable, and ordered him to pull back his fighters and use the fire power of the star cruiser to thin out the enemy as best they could. They would need reinforcements soon, or they would be lost.

"Admiral! Wolf Platoon was taking care of a large breakthrough in sector twenty three, and now half of the remaining forces have ceased fighting. Correction, all of the breakthrough vessels as well as a few other enemy units have ceased their operations!"

"Get me Commander Rice on the comm, I need to know exactly what's happening!"

"Yes sir!"

The officer turned back to his station, and soon, over the cackling of the comm came Paul's voice.

"Commander Rice. Go ahead Admiral."

"Paul, what's going on with those inactive enemy ships? Do you think it's a trap?"

"It's not a trap, sir, but other than that, I can't tell you what's going on. Doug did it; that's all I know. You could ask him how he did it, but I don't think now is the time, he's kind of busy doing it."

"This is incredible, Commander. Finish up and get back here as fast as you can, I need to talk to Doug. Maybe he can do what he did from the bridge. I need help with the Indomitable."

"Loud and clear, Admiral. Rice out."

CHAPTER 21

Doug was heading back to the Pegasus while he thought of what the Admiral might need him for. The only reason could be because of what he had done to the enemy operators. He decided to tell Moira via their mental bond. She would understand him completely and could explain it to the Admiral. There was no sense in going all the way back to the Flagship if he was needed out in space.

Sending out his thoughts to Moira, he was welcomed by the presence of her mind. After a brief mental embrace, he sent the entire explanation of what he had done in a matter of seconds. She thanked him for the information and told him to be careful. Now all he had to do was wait for her to tell the Admiral and see what they wanted him to do.

❖ ❖ ❖ ❖ ❖

"Admiral!" Moira exclaimed. "Doug just told me what he did, you're not going to believe it!"

"Go ahead, Moira."

"He was fighting with the second wave of enemy fighters, when he noticed a sense of hate directed at him from one of the officers on the enemy starships...one of the controllers of the fighters! Once he knew where the operators were, he sent out his mind and used the mental blast I taught him to kill all of the operators in that section of the ship!"

"My God! Is there any limit to his power? This is great news! We might actually have a decent chance now. First thing's first, Moira. Send Doug on a reconnaissance mission with the Indomitable. Ask him to try and help them out the same way he did for us."

"Of course, Admiral," Moira replied with genuine pride in her dearest love.

* * * * *

Doug received his orders from the Admiral via Moira. He hoped he would be able to duplicate his success with the Indomitable. Telling Paul that he had been given new orders, Doug raced off through space toward the Indomitable. He could already tell they were having a hard time keeping the enemy at bay.

The Captain of the Indomitable had been notified of his plan, and welcomed him over the comm.

"Good luck, Wolf three; hope you can help us out. Let me know what you need and it's yours."

"I'll do my best Captain, and all I need is cover from the enemy while I'm vulnerable."

"You got it, Lieutenant!"

Doug rocketed toward the enemy lines, randomly destroying enemy fighters that had broken through the first line. The Indomitable was trying its best to defend itself from fighters that were attacking its hull, and Doug decided that once his cover arrived he would start with the controllers of the closest fighters. Two Delta fighters popped into sight and flanked him on both sides.

"Good to see a friendly face, even one as ugly as yours," Johann greeted.

"Humor, Johann? You're getting better," Doug laughed. "Watch my back for me while I take care of those fighters."

"Will do, buddy."

Doug focused his attention on anyone who was concentrating on the enemy fighters near the Indomitable. Unfortunately, that included every gunner and person watching on the bridge of the Indomitable. Flying in closer, he destroyed one of the enemy craft and felt the irritation it caused. Following the irritation back to its source, he saw a grotesquely fat man who was sweating profusely from the little exertion he was required to perform. He waited until he could visualize the other controllers in the room, and then methodically erased each of their brains.

Doug decided to try something new. He kept his attention in the room instead of withdrawing back to his present location. He drifted his attention down to the end of the room and through the door into the adjacent room. There were more operators here, and so he repeated the process of killing each one of the controllers. He continued his gory work until there were no more corridors, then withdrew his focus back to his ship.

The report came in from the Indomitable that all the enemy vessels save for a few had ceased to operate, and these were quickly being eliminated. Doug felt weak; his mind hurt as if he hadn't slept for days. He knew he couldn't do any more for awhile, so he reported that he was returning to the Pegasus.

A weary and exhausted Doug staggered to the bridge. He was barely able to walk, but didn't want to be interrupted later. He knew the Admiral wouldn't wait for long to get a detailed description of what had happened. The Pegasus had gotten to the jumping point, and was waiting for the rest of the fleet to be close enough to safety that the interval between jaunts would be minimal. There was no sense in waiting for the last star cruiser when it was unknown whether or not it survived. Once all of the fleet had made the initial jump, a second jump in a random direction would be necessary to throw off the enemy, then they could later fold space without danger of being followed by the enemy.

The Admiral, with McIntyre at his side, was most eager to hear Doug's tale. Doug glanced at Moira, who was grinning openly, and sensed her mental touch as she greeted and congratulated him privately. The Admiral looked at him happily and gestured for him to be seated.

"So tell us what happened, Doug? You seem to have single handily beaten our opponent in a battle. We didn't think it possible."

Doug took a deep breath and began his narration,

"Well, I was engaged with the fighters I had been assigned to and, after destroying five of them, I noticed an increasing hostility toward me coming from one of the enemy starships. I followed that aggression back to the source and saw a middle aged man with a goatee. I knew about how the enemy functioned and decided to eliminate the fighter threat at the source. So after looking around the room, I used a mental blast on each of the controllers. Since one controller was in charge of several squadrons, the results were dramatic."

"Remarkable!" McIntyre blurted out with glee. "I'm sorry, Doug, please continue."

Doug laughed at the eccentric little man's enthusiasm and continued his story,

"Anyway, I continued to kill all the controllers I could find, until all of the fighters attacking the Pegasus had been destroyed. Then, after moving on to the Indomitable, I destroyed one of the enemy craft to get a lead and followed the irritation back to the source. This time, instead of withdrawing after I wiped out the operators in the room, I moved on down the corridors and got them all at once."

"Absolutely amazing! Doug, this could be the key to defeating the enemy once and for all. Who would have thought the Overlord would have such a large Achilles heel," McIntyre exclaimed while dancing around like an excited school boy.

"Doug, I thank God for the day he brought you to us," The Admiral congratulated. "You look tired, why don't you get some rest. Moira, you're excused from duty as well. I want you to take good care of him."

"Is that an order, sir?" Moira asked while smiling sensually.

"On second thought, he needs his rest. Maybe you should stay on the bridge?" he taunted her.

"No, that's all right; you know I'll take good care of him." she replied with a deeply red blush.

⊞ ⊞ ⊞ ⊞ ⊞

Doug and Moira walked to the tube lift that would take them to the living quarters. Nearly out of energy, he leaned on her shoulder as they walked. The tube would take them to the quadrant where the beds and cots were located, and then they would have to walk. Doug felt privileged to be given a room, instead of a wall cot with the other soldiers. Even though it was a temporary arrangement, it still felt good to be thought of.

After staggering through a few halls they arrived at Doug's small, but private quarters for the remainder of the journey. He was told that they would arrive at their new base in roughly the equivalent of two Terran days, so he knew that he could get plenty of rest. He collapsed on the bed, and pushed away his desire to sleep. He wanted to talk with Moira a little, before unconsciousness overcame him. She had daintily laid down next to him and was stroking his hair gently, bidding him to rest.

"Moira, there are a few things I want to tell you, and they need to be said now."

"They can wait until you've rested," She replied in a soft voice.

"No, they can't, it's important."

"Well, hurry up and tell me so we can go to sleep. You really need some rest; you're making ME tired."

"I forgot about the effect our bond has on one another. I'm sorry; I shouldn't have pushed so hard."

"That's all right, love. Now tell me what's so important?"

"First, I want to get married as soon as we land. I know it doesn't have as much meaning in this dimension and time, but I want you as my wife all the same. It's important to me to make you all mine, forever."

Doug looked up at her to see that tears were forming in her eyes, but he could feel that they were tears of joy, not sadness. He had known she secretly wanted to get married and have a family, but didn't want him to feel pressured. So he surprised her by granting her wish before she even asked. Doug couldn't resist playing it up for all it was worth. Even though he loved her, and lived only to make her happy, he still couldn't resist teasing her on occassion.

"Secondly, I know that someday I'll be able to return to my dimension, but I can't ask you to go with me, and I won't be separated from you, ever. So I've decided to stay here with you. I don't ever want to sense you worrying about what's going to happen when I go back, because I'm not going back without you. You are my one true love and I've already given you my heart, body and soul. Nothing can or will keep me away from you."

His words had fully opened the dam, and the water from the stream flowed freely down her cheeks. Her happiness was so great, his heart almost burst when she embraced him fiercely and he felt the full power of her love without restraint envelope his mind. Doug returned that love just as fully.

Moira clung to him crying her tears of joy for a while. Then looked up into his eyes, smiled at him and nestled her head on his shoulder and told him to rest up, because when they landed he was going to need all of his strength if he wanted to survive what she was going to do to him. He smiled at the thought and slowly fell asleep with the flowery scent of her beautiful hair in his nostrils.

When Doug awoke Moira was still beside him with her head nestled on his shoulder, and one arm wrapped loosely around his chest. Inhaling deeply, he savored the scent of her hair, which always smelled lovely. He looked at the digital clock imbedded in the wall, and was slightly surprised to note that only two hours, had passed since the battle and escape had ended.

Moira stirred slightly, and he gently caressed her back, then moved his hand up to run his fingers through her lustrous black hair, which unlike her counterpart, was cut short, just above shoulder length, in a modern military style, but still fashionable. He didn't want to wake her, but he secretly hoped she would awaken on her own sometime soon. Being with her was the most wonderful thing that he had ever dreamt would happen to him. As he caressed the soft skin on her neck and cheek, his thoughts drifted back to the battle.

He desperately wanted to find out where the anger he had felt was coming from. If it was misdirected, he might hurt someone he loved, maybe even Moira, and that, he promised himself, would never happen. He knew that just holding her in his arms made him more happy than words could ever describe. Doug wondered if this feeling was what the original human relationship was supposed to have been like, and that he and Moira had somehow found a way back to that ideal love.

Moira stirred as he was thinking, he felt her mind awakening, as she rolled onto her back and stretched with a characteristic back arching. Doug couldn't help but admire how beautifully she arched her back, and rolling toward her he told her how attractive her stretching was. She sleepily opened her crystal blue eyes and stared at him lovingly. He became lost in her delicate gaze, and kissed her passionately.

"It's almost dinner time isn't it?" she asked.

"Yup, and you're what I want for dinner, and desert, my love."

"My, you recuperate pretty quick. Maybe I shouldn't marry you. It could make one of us go blind."

"Where are you? I can hear your voice but I can't see you." Doug teased.

Wrapping her arms around his neck with a smile on her face, she drew him toward her and kissed him in a way that only meant there was more to follow.

CHAPTER 22

Doug stood on the bridge of the flagship staring out into space. It was roughly a few hours past midnight by the time scale being used. For whatever reason, Doug was wide awake. He seemed to only need a few hours rest each night, even after a strenuous day like he had just had. Moira was sound asleep in their quarters, and he kept part of his focus in their room to keep her company. He knew she would wake up if she didn't sense his presence in the room.

Not even the Admiral was awake, only the night crew who were sleepily keeping an eye on the navigating and optical arrays. It felt strange being the only one who slept for a few hours. He was always active while everyone else was asleep. Since there was nothing else to do on the ship, he usually stood at the helm drinking coffee and gazed out the view port into space.

One of the groggy watchmen informed him when it was five in the morning. Doug thanked him, and left the bridge. He had intended to leave at five in order to get back before

Moira woke up. He always liked to be with her when she woke, if at all possible.

When he reached their temporary room, he pressed the door button with one hand, while holding the door shut with the other. He let the door open slowly, to avoid the customary noise of the hydraulic release. He didn't want to wake Moira, and he was strong enough to keep the door from opening at all, let alone to simply slow it down. He crept quietly into the room and slid next to Moira. Putting one arm around her shoulder, he snuggled next to her and inhaled her fragrance deeply.

Doug had studied her REM cycles the previous night, and now felt confident at timing her awakening perfectly. It was the best way to compromise his desire to be next to her when she woke, and his apparent lack of need for sleep. He knew he could control how much he slept by telling his subconscious when he wanted to wake, and order hormones to be released, which would cause him to be sleepy for longer periods of time. He had complete control over his mind, but there was no need for excess sleep, since his body healed so quickly. Maybe when the war was over he could indulge in extra sleep that he didn't really need.

Moira was reaching her appointed waking time, and Doug could already tell that the waking processes had begun. He knew the Admiral had some things to talk about, and McIntyre probably wanted a more detailed description of the events that took place during the battle. But other than that he was free to loaf the entire day with his soon to be wife. She woke with a pretty little yawn, and stared at him sleepily.

"What time is it, love?"

"Almost six. I wonder if we're going to change the time system again when we reach the new base?"

"Probably," she replied with a disgusted look on her face. "Scientists are fussy about that sort of thing."

"Well, at least we have the chance of getting more daylight hours. For some reason, having only twenty two hours in a day is upsetting to me."

She laughed and kissed him sweetly, "Something like that would upset you. Come on, let's get ready and go get something to eat; I'm starved. By the way, when we get to the new base, I'm going to ask Admiral McDougal if he'll authorize a small kitchen unit for our quarters."

"Are you going to cook for me?" Doug grinned.

"Maybe, but YOU are going to serve me breakfast in bed; you're always up before me anyway."

"Well, we'll see. Maybe if you're nice to me," he teased.

Doug knew his wonderful day wouldn't last. After he and Moira had finished their morning meal in the mess hall, they sat and talked for awhile over a cup of coffee. One thing lead to another, and they decided to go back to their quarters to spend a quiet day together. That's when everything went sour on him. In front of the door to their room, McIntyre and McDougal were having an argument, essentially over who got to talk to Doug first.

McIntyre was throwing around the fact that others might be able to duplicate Doug's method if the proper research was conducted and, for that reason, further studies needed to be started immediately. McDougal was arguing that Doug needed to be filled in on the entire situation, so that they could plan out a potential offensive against Shaleese. The argument raged back and forth between the two men, until McDougal finally pulled rank and demanded that his plan took priority over McIntyre's.

Still glaring at each other, they barely noticed when Doug and Moira turned around and tried to run the other direction to hide. Unfortunately, McDougal had regained enough of his composure to spot the attempted escape. He called out to Doug, and snared him like a wild animal for at least a few hours with his "have you got a minute" net.

McDougal took Doug to the tactical room, along with several stuffy looking men McDougal referred to as "the Council". They began to lay out long and tedious statistics before him, and he was afraid for a minute that he would be in the room all day. Then he remembered his special abilities.

"Gentlemen," Doug interrupted as two animated windbags puffed on about resources and manpower, "this is taking too long. I understand the need for detailed information, and good planning, but I think we can all agree that it would be better to speed things up if possible. I have other resources available to me and can get all of this information a much more efficient way."

Before any of the stodgy and rigid men could find some reason to take his words as offensive, Admiral McDougal stood and smiled at the Council members,

"You must excuse our young friend. He has a highly developed mental power the likes of which we've never seen, as I've told you all before on several occasions. He is probably used to getting information much quicker because his mind can assimilate much more than ours. I've taken the time to study some of McIntyre's reports on the speed of Doug's thinking, and the results have been quite astounding. McIntyre said that his mind is faster than any computer in history."

Doug knew that the Admiral was lying through his teeth. There had never even been any such measurement. He suppressed a grin as the Admiral tried to help him weasel out of the Council's favorite subject. Boredom. Doug sent a telepathic message to the Admiral regarding his recent engagement.

"Besides," McDougal continued as he received Doug's message, "He is probably eager to get back to the beautiful young lady he recently got engaged to."

The Council members all chuckled, and a fat retired general in the corner, who had seemed considerably less stuffy than the rest, rose to address Doug.

"Why don't you tell us what you have in mind, lad? I'm sure you don't want us boring you all day when you have a potential wife that needs taking care of," he rumbled in a deep baritone with an equally deep and gurgling laugh.

"All right, I've done this before, so it shouldn't be too difficult," Doug lied. He had indeed absorbed massive information, such as the entire Ryeesian language, but never consciously.

"Each of you has information I need to know, strategic and tactical. When I ask you to, I want you to focus on the informational field you specialize in. For example, you, General Richards," he said to the fat man, "have all the information I would need about ground assault strategies. Then I'll simply absorb all of that knowledge into my brain, like a copy machine if you will."

"All right, I'll try it," The fat general offered. "It sounds interesting. I've heard of some that were able to absorb information in that fashion, but never on such a grand scale."

"All right general, let's proceed."

Doug looked into the general's mind and tried to isolate only the relevant information that the general had. It was surprisingly easy because of Richards' well ordered thoughts. In a few seconds, he had finished and now knew all of the knowledge amassed by general Richards over the years of his military training.

"That was great general; I've got all I need."

"That was pretty quick, are you sure you got everything?" general Richards asked disbeleivingly.

"Of course I did, General. Would you like a demonstration?" Doug offered.

"Well, that would help to quiet the disbelief that I'm sure some of the Council members have about your abilities. When I was a Cadet in the military academy back on Earth, there was an interesting lecture given by General Deitrich, on the importance of proper fortifications. Could you tell us what he was talking about?"

"Why certainly, General Richards. Why don't I just start at the beginning? ...In an all out battle, without any preparations for fall back or retreat, one would need roughly four times the number of soldiers to ensure a victory, preferable five times the total enemy complement. With proper fortifications, however, that number is halved for attacking and halved again for defense. If..."

"Stop!" Richards interrupted with a startled expression on his face. "If I remember correctly, that was a word for word account of how the lecture began! I don't even remember it word for word! How did you do that?!"

"You do remember it, General. It had a great impact on you. Everything that you paid any attention to at all is in your memory, it's just a matter of accessing the right part of your mind."

"Remarkable! That is indeed more efficient than trying to learn the old way. That one lecture lasted for almost three hours, and you have all of the lectures and teachings I've went through in as many seconds!"

The Council was excited by Doug's performance, and the majority of the Council agreed to undergo the same process, although a few feigned to have nothing worthy of absorbing. Doug suspected they didn't want him to poke around in their heads and make them in danger of becoming obsolete. Or worse, to have access to their private thoughts

McDougal had stood by amused, as Doug gathered the long and tedious teachings and ideas in a few minutes. The look he gave Doug indicated that he wished he had the same ability to avoid these stuffy old men as easily. Once Doug had finished with his education he left the old men to discuss the encounter by themselves, and he retired to an adjacent room to talk with McDougal.

"Nice move, Doug. You could have been in Council sessions for at least a month the way they were headed. They love to argue senseless details into the ground. That's one of the reasons I detest being the Council head, they would talk for years if it would keep anything important from happening. It's very frustrating for me, and for the men and women in the resistance," McDougal congratulated.

"You know I wouldn't have let that happen. I hate classroom discussions. I learned more with my method than I would have if we had done things their way. This way I got everything in my brain while my mind was still fresh. Their way would have put me to sleep."

"I know the feeling. Do you have any ideas on how we can use the resources that we have in a counter-offensive?"

"I'll have to go over it awhile. You know as well as I do that I've never done anything like that before, so I wasn't sure how effective it would be. I guess I need time to let the information sink in. It's there, but not all of it has registered on the surface. It comes to me in chunks or when I think about a specific subject. It may take a day or two to put everything together."

"Well, let me know if you have any ideas, no matter how small. You impressed them in there today, and now you will have a lot of weight with suggestions you make. Maybe now we can get somewhere."

"I'll do my best. I guess I better go see McIntyre. I have a few ideas to keep him busy."

"That's a first, what have you got in mind?"

"The technology exists to probe and read thoughts, so why can't a computer teach students the way I just did? If it could be perfected, it would save a lot of time in training. The only variable I haven't completely worked out, is the students' varying ability to safely take in information. I also think there may be a way to tap into the latent potential even the poorest telepath or empath has, and expand their ability."

"That would be extremely beneficial, not to mention time consuming to work out. McIntyre will be busy for years," he laughed.

Doug excused himself, and headed for McIntyre's quarters. Maybe the day wouldn't be all work after all. The entire meeting with the Council members was just under an hour. Tomorrow would be even worse since the new base would need to be set up, so today had to be the day for lounging and recreation. The last problem for the day, was diverting McIntyre, and sending him away happy, but with plenty of work to keep him busy.

McIntyre was in his quarters grumpily going through some of his computer files. Doug could sense McIntyre's irritation at being put on the back burner when he knocked at the door. The old doctor snapped out a command to enter and didn't bother to look up from his computer when Doug came in.

"Leave it on the table." He said promptly.

"What would you like me to leave doctor, my brain, or should I just sit on the table? To be honest, I think it might break if I sat on it." Doug answered with a grin.

McIntyre looked up quickly with a startled expression.

"Doug! I'm sorry, I thought you were the Cadet that was bringing me some ale from the galley. Did McDougal change his mind and decide to let me work with you first?"

"Not exactly, I just got tired of the Council's boring deliberations, so I absorbed the information they wanted me to know. That took a lot less time, so we finished a few months early."

"I see, then I guess I'm still angry with McDougal," he said while frowning slightly.

Doug laughed at the doctor's flippant remark. Even when he was upset, McIntyre was delightful and entertaining.

"I'm sorry," the doctor apologized, "That did sound a little trite, didn't it? Well, I have a few things I want to discuss with you regardless of how upset I am about the Admiral being so stubborn."

"Let me hear the questions, then I'll tell you the ideas I have on improving the soldier training."

"All right, let's see...First I wanted to ask some questions about your adventures during the battle, and what side effects you encountered. Maybe the process can be duplicated by machine if not by another soldier with empathic power."

"Let me try to answer your question by offering a question in return. Do you have any empathic capabilities? I've noticed you have an unusually effective calming power with anyone who has empathic or telepathic power."

"Most observant of you, Doug. I do indeed have a little ability in that area, but unfortunately, I've never gotten very far with it. I seem to do all of the necessary work subconsciously. What does that have to do with what we were talking about? Have you discovered something?" the excited old man asked.

"I have two theories I'd like to try out, but I need a test subject with empathic ability, preferably one who has potential, but doesn't actualize the power to its full use."

"Don't stop, it's just getting to the interesting part. I'd be more than happy to participate, but tell me more."

"The first part has to do with absorbing knowledge. I can get information by looking into someone else's mind, so the question is: Can I place information into the minds of others? If it's successful, and the procedure can be recorded with the brain activity monitors, it can be duplicated by a machine in order to train Cadets faster and more efficiently."

"That sounds marvelous! It would also improve retention of the material learned. Please, go on."

"OK, secondly, I think that it's possible to open the potential of anyone with latent ability, to give them more efficient use of their power. I'm afraid that might not be able to be done by a machine though. Everyone I've encountered has unique patterns that a computer would have a hard time deciphering."

"That is wonderful, Doug! We must proceed with this, the potential for advancement is far too great. Let me calm down first. We'll wait for my ale and then continue. Oh, this is extraordinary!"

Doug liked being around McIntyre. He was always open to new ideas, and had such a childlike wonder about the undiscovered that he hardly seemed like a serious and seasoned scientist. The ale arrived via a shy Cadet, who was expecting a grumpy and agitated old man to yell at him for taking so long. To Doug's surprise, Dr. McIntyre had ordered, not just a glass of ale, but a large pitcher. Apparently the good doctor had intended to drown his disappointment with beer. Now however, he had more entertaining things to do than to get drunk. He offered Doug a glass and poured some ale for them both.

"Aren't you a little worried that I might make a mistake while I'm poking around in your head, if I'm less than sober?" Doug asked with amusement.

"Doug, with your healing ability and new metabolism, or catabolism, I should say, you could drink a fifth of Irish whiskey and still be sober. I, on the other hand, should be easier to deal with while I'm operating at less than full capacity," thus saying, he noisily slurped down the contents of his glass. "Whenever you're ready, my friend."

Doug set down his glass and entered McIntyre's mind. Instead of looking for memories, he looked for a certain neural pathway that he had noticed was extremely more developed in advanced telepaths and empaths, such as his own mind and Moira's, and still present, although to a lesser degree, with anyone who had potential, but not necessarily ability.

The majority of the Council had the specific neural pathways he was looking for, but less developed than McIntyre's, and even less than McDougal's. McIntyre's empathic neural pathway was there, although in an odd position. He guessed that McIntyre had developed his empathic talents out of a conscious effort, even if it had never surfaced consciously in use.

Doug widened the sub-pathways that already existed, and added length to a few that were developing, but not at a very fast rate. Once the modifications were complete, he showed McIntyre's subconscious the new routes he had added and then withdrew from the doctor's mind.

"I'm all finished, Patrick. How do you feel?"

"There's no need to worry about me, I'm not as old and frail as you think,...Did I just,...That's what you were feeling towards me wasn't it!"

"As a matter of fact it was. You seem to have done quite well," Doug grinned.

"This is extraordinary! I can actually sense emotions! Boy, this place sure is depressing."

"I never thought about that," Doug mused.

"How could you miss it? It's everywhere."

"No, that's not what I meant. I never thought about the training needed to block outside emotions from influencing you. That's something I'll have to modify in my technique. For now, we'll have to settle for another lesson. We can try my second idea of transferring some of my knowledge to you."

"That would be wonderful. I can hardly stand all of this excitement," McIntyre added enthusiastically.

Doug connected with McIntyre's mind and told his subconscious about mental shielding and blocking outside influences, then added all of the ideas he had on the advanced training, which included his experience with the enemy controllers. The process only took a few moments, and afterward Doug asked McIntyre if he got any of the information sent.

"I seem to know how to block outside influences, now maybe you could,...oh my!"

"What? Are you alright, doctor? What's wrong?"

"Nothing Doug, I'm fine, it's just that I suddenly knew the answer to my question before I even asked, and in more detail than I thought possible."

"Oh, that's one of the peculiarities about absorbing knowledge like that. You won't even know it's there until you think about a related topic, and then it hits you like a head rush. That might be something to note in your mind while you're developing this new method. Make sure that the student is given a visual prompt after each segment has been transmitted; otherwise, when he or she gets done, and thinks about a related topic, they'll be hit with a tidal wave of information. It could be dangerous if too much information is received at one time."

"I agree, and now that I can visualize your ideas, I can get to work developing this new method. That was most efficient. Once other scientists develop their mental processes this way, I can get so much more work done, by showing them what I'm thinking. Wonderful, simply wonderful."

"Well, I hope you don't mind, but I think I'll leave you to your work. I have a beautiful young lady waiting for me, whom I most eagerly want to get back to."

"You and Moira seem very happy with one another. I'm very happy for you both. Now you go have a wonderful day."

"Thank you, doctor; I will."

Chapter 23

Doug spent the rest of the day with his beloved, knowing that he wouldn't have such leisure for awhile. The following day they reached their destination. The new base was located in a small desolate solar system at the edge of the milky way galaxy. There were five planets revolving around its sun, one of which had a breathable, yet frigid atmosphere. The native flora was small and squat looking, but the central regions around the median of the globe had lush and beautiful forests. They named their new base New Haven, and all hoped it would indeed be a haven from the enemy.

The base site was in a spacious cavern system in the largest mountain range. Tunneling had already been done when the area was recommended for a base site, but there was still a lot of work to be done. The star cruisers landed on a plateau that was roughly adjacent to the site. They were then covered with dirt and vegetation until a more suitable camouflage could be constructed. The initial covering of the hulking monsters took almost an entire day because of their immensity.

Doug and Moira were married the first night after the landing. The only religious figure residing with the militia was an old rabbi. Since neither of them were Jewish, they decided to offer the privilege of marrying them to McDougal. Paul, of course, was the best man and witness. Both Doug and Moira had wanted a small, utilitarian type of wedding to avoid any preparations or delays. Doug whispered to his beloved, while they were standing before the Admiral, that once the war was over, they would have a proper wedding. She smiled at him sweetly for his thoughtfulness, and gave his hand a gentle squeeze.

The small group of friends sat in metal chairs from the cruisers that had been modified for the wedding. An isle was made between the rows of chairs, and native flowers were arranged all around in deep blues and dark emerald greens. Despite the rush and simplicity of the arrangements, the young couple was surrounded by a pure beauty that couldn't be duplicated or matched with any amount of planning.

McDougal read the ceremony out of an old tannish colored book, but Doug didn't hear any of the great Admiral's words. His eyes were fixed on Moira. The mental voice and images of her mind was the only thing he was aware of. Likewise, Moira was unaware of anything except Doug's thoughts and mental images of his love for her.

The ceremony continued until a potential disaster nearly ruined the entire wedding. McDougal turned his face toward Doug, and asked him for the ring. Doug blushed as he shamefully realized that he hadn't remembered the most important symbol in the wedding. There were no rings to exchange.

Fortunately, McIntyre was standing amongst the groomsmen, and stepped forward when McDougal had mentioned the rings.

"Doug, I know you had forgotten the rings in the rush. I have already decided that I want you and Moira to have the rings my wife and I used when we were married. She is no longer with us, and I know that she would want our loving marriage of twenty two years to continue with you," he said in a choked voice.

Doug began to cry as he felt the loss the old scientist felt. The groom awkwardly accepted the offer with a slightly rigid shake of his head; his eyes brimming with sympathy. Wordlessly, he placed one ring on Moira. She looked lovingly at her soon to be husband, her eyes also filled to the brim, and took the other ring from his hand and placed it on his finger. Everyone present cheered loudly. The happy couple kissed and embraced each other fiercely.

Sleeping arrangements for the first few nights were awkward to say the least. Since there were no quarters or residences yet, your bed was wherever there was room to lay down. Many people slept on the cots in the star cruisers, even though the space was limited. While traveling, cots had been shared between different crew shifts. Doug and Moira decided to reside in their starship room as well; the alternative meant sleeping on the cold hard ground, and no wedding night bliss.

That night, Doug and Moira truly became one. The bond they had thought to be more intense than any other form of expression could ever be, paled in comparison to what they felt after they had consummated their marriage. They became one with one another in mind, body, and soul. Every sensation one of them experienced was shared by the other. The overall experience was so intense that at times, Doug couldn't tell where he ended and Moira began. Every moment after that they were unseperable in more ways than could ever be explained.

Temporary showering and bathroom facilities were the first projects to go into effect, and the few facilities on the star cruiser were also used to lessen the waiting time for personal hygiene attention. The construction process was tedious, but the announcements of how well they had done overall in their battle to escape gave everyone hope that this base would be more permanent. Special care was taken with each and every detail of the making of their new home.

After three weeks, all of the rooms and quarters had been partitioned off, and then the personal touches began. Doug had been promoted to the rank of Commander by McDougal when they had first landed. He had told Doug that the resistance needed more good leaders, and he appreciated how well Doug had performed as well as the advancements being made with Doug's assistance. Doug felt unworthy of the jump in rank, but didn't argue when the time came for assigning quarters.

His new rank, combined with Moira's, allotted them a spacious little apartment with three separate rooms, including a den and a small kitchenette, in addition to the bedroom and bath combination.

Since there were so many modifications to be made, each soldier or resident either learned how to install the necessary conveniences, such as indoor plumbing, or waited for the technicians to get around to them. Doug talked to a few technicians, and absorbed all of the modern techniques for installing shower units and toilets, then promptly got to work on their new home. Moira took control of modifying the apartment with the proper decorations and aesthetics.

A full two months after landing, the newlywed's apartment was suitable to both their wants and needs. McDougal had told Doug that they were all going to take a week's vacation before resuming their planning for a counterattack, so Doug decided to explore the forest with Moira as a type of short honeymoon. She eagerly agreed, with a sensual little smile, as she thought of the potential for mischief in the large forest.

Moira prepared for a picnic, and they went on a hike through the vast forest. Even if the plants were strange looking, it was nice to be out in a forest with fresh air again. Moira had spent a longer time in the bunker-like base than Doug had, and the fresh air definitely made her giddy. She acted like a school girl out on a flower raiding expedition. She inhaled fragrances, ran through the woods, rolled in the grass and small flowers, and Doug was almost positive he saw her skipping through the trees on one occasion.

Moira chose a clearing that was beside a small stream for their picnic. Doug glanced around at the surrounding flora as they ate, and noted the extremely dark colors of the leaves and bark, most of them were a purplish black. He guessed that they had evolved that way to absorb more heat from the sun. It was mid summer and the average temperature was around seventy degrees Fahrenheit here at the meridian of the planet. He didn't want to even think of what winters must be like farther to the north.

He couldn't help but think about the war and what they were going to do. What would be the next logical step in the situation the resistance was in? Doug caught Moira staring at him and noticed the scowl imposed upon the delicate features of her face as she munched on her sandwich. She bit savagely into her sandwich, still glaring at him, and he wondered what he had done wrong.

"I was wiwing to enyoy the thenery wiff you while you were thinning about the trees, but I wone olerate you thinning bout wort while we're on ower honyman," she said around a mouthful of bread and turkey.

Doug tried his best not to laugh, since she was trying hard to appear upset, but lost all composure as he looked at her engaging scowl and listened to her food filled complaint. Moira wasn't amused at not being taken seriously.

"Just what is all that laughing about?" she choked out, then took another savage bite out of the innocent sandwich.

"I'm sorry, love, but you are just too adorable when you're upset," he answered her, still laughing.

"Welw, tha's alrigh then," she choked out, "but I'm still na lettin you off the hoot. Not unwess you come here and kith me," she mumbled around the food in her mouth.

"Not until you finish your sandwich; I already have one," he said pointing at her mouth, which was still full of turkey sandwich.

She blushed coyly as she realized she had her mouth stuffed full of food. Doug couldn't resist her whenever she blushed, so he leaned across the picnic blanket and passionately kissed her regardless of the overflowing food in her mouth. The kiss was good, but the half-chewed sandwich wasn't, and he promptly rejected the remnants of the innocent but mangled sandwich onto the ground. The young couple looked at each other for a brief moment, then burst out with laughter.

The rest of the day was spent exploring the forest. Moira finally couldn't resist the temptation and pushed him into the stream. He couldn't let her get away with such a blatant act of disregard for his welfare. Trying to think of a way to fool her into reaching out to him, so he could pull her in, he suddenly felt a surge coming from him and she toppled forward into the stream with a startled scream.

She stood up in the stream and stared at him in wide eyed wonder. Doug knew he had knocked her into the stream telekinetically, but had no idea how he had done it. Moira's stare turned to a look of fascination and pride as she slowly realized what he had done.

"Did you just do what I think you did?" she asked with a look of astonishment.

"I think so, love, but I don't know how I did it."

"This is wonderful, I've never heard of anyone having that much power telekinetically! The most I've ever heard of was confined to simple tricks and moving pencils! The most powerful telekinetic and he's MY husband!"

"I just thought of something. McIntyre and I discovered a way to release the potential of mental power in latent and poor telepaths and empaths. What if we released your power to it's utmost potential? You already have highly developed mental abilities."

"Then maybe I would have telekinetic abilities as well? That's really interesting. Then I could push you into streams all the time," she teased.

"Would you like to try? There's no harm in trying."

"I just thought of something, too. If my abilities were increased, wouldn't that improve those extra special sensations we seem to get when we make love?" she said seductively.

"Is that all you ever think about?" he teased.

"Only with you, dear heart, only with you," she said condescendingly while patting his cheek.

"Well there's only one way to find out."

He reached out and held her head gently in his hands. Closing his eyes and sending out his thoughts into her mind, he looked for the neural pathways that controlled her empathic and telepathic powers. It wasn't hard to find it, because of her well developed mind. Her pathways were far more complex than McIntyre's had been. He expanded and widened them as much as he could, then he opened his eyes and looked at her.

The beauty of the astonished bafflement on her face was enchanting. All he could do was gaze at her in adoration, while her mind slowly absorbed its new processes. Once the shock of having a more intimate view of her surroundings had worn off, she blinked, and looked into Doug's eyes.

"This is incredible! I can sense the soldiers all the way back at the base!" she stammered.

"Are you all right, love?"

"Yes, I'm fine. It's just that I've never had so many thoughts open to me at once, it's a little overwhelming."

"I know the feeling. You're the one who taught me how to deal with it, remember?"

She looked at him regaining her composure. Slowly a smile formed on her face, as she looked at her husband as if he were no more than a piece of food that was ripe and ready to eat.

"Why don't we test out that theory I had about what will happen? Now that my empathy has been increased to it's fullest potential I think a little fooling around is in order. It is our honeymoon, after all."

Still standing waste deep in the stream, Doug blushed as Moira waded toward him. She put her arms around his neck and drew him toward her. With one kiss she dissolved any resistance he had left in him, and he returned her passion with all of his heart.

Lounging on the bank of the stream, Moira and Doug held each other and discussed what had happened. Doug tried to duplicate his demonstration of telekinesis, but wasn't getting very far. The most he could manage was to move a twig on the ground a few centimeters. There was something he was missing about how he had used telekinesis before, but couldn't quite place it.

He knew he was capable of much greater and significant applications of telekinesis; it would just take some time to develop it properly. Part of the problem was that Moira was as distracting as she was encouraging. Her naked body wrapped in a blanket, counteracted any encouraging words that she said. The other problem was that they were both still dripping wet and shivering from their adventures in the cold stream.

Doug suggested that they head back to their quarters, before it got dark, and to avoid hypothermia. Moira smiled at him, and with one last kiss, agreed to go back.

Once they had reached their quarters, they shed their drenched clothing and put on fresh, dry uniforms. Moira suggested they snuggle under a blanket with a cup of hot cocoa. Doug thought her idea was marvelous, and promptly sat down on their couch as she got a blanket and curled up next to him. It was nice to feel her warm body next to him, and he was surprised to note that she still had the flowery scent in her hair that he so loved, even after their enchanting swim in the stream. He didn't want to spoil the moment, but couldn't resist rubbing in that she had forgotten something.

"Uh, you forgot the cocoa, love," he said sweetly.

"No dear, I didn't. You're going to get it," she said in just as sweet a tone.

He sighed and started to get up, but she held on to his shoulders and pulled him back.

"No fair cheating," she scolded sweetly. "You have to get it the other way. You can see the kitchen from here, and it's not that far away."

"It may be awhile before we have any cocoa then. I'm not even sure I can do it."

"Well, it's still early, only seven o'clock. As extra incentive for you, I'll tell you that I REALLY want a cup of hot cocoa. I'll do anything for you, if you can get me a nice mug of hot cocoa. Until I get a cup of cocoa, you're not getting anything."

Slightly injured by her ultimatum, Doug sulked as he began his attempt at retrieving some cocoa telekinetically. He felt it was entirely unfair to be denied his sexual privileges by his wife, unless he could do something that he might not even be able to do. As he sulked, she gently turned his head toward her and looked into his eyes.

"I didn't mean to upset you, my love; it's just a game. You ought to know by now that I wouldn't be able to go more than a few days without you," she said sincerely, and then kissed him and gave him a gentle mental touch that said in a second all that he meant to her. "But if you don't get me a cup of cocoa, I'll be very disappointed," she warned with the adorable little scowl that she knew he loved.

His disenchantment was instantly gone, and he laughed in spite of himself. He knew that because of their incredible bond, their love was amplified to the limit of human ability. He took one last look at the beautiful face he loved so much, then focused his attention on fulfilling her needs for hot cocoa.

Focusing on the cupboard where the coffee making utensils were, he tried to open the cupboard. The metallic door to the cupboard rattled, opened partially than snapped shut from the force of its magnetic closer. He tried again, but without success. Agitated from his failures he finally sent out with all of his mind and with as much energy as he could muster. The door vibrated angrily, then popped off of it's hinges and hurled through the air directly at the two lovers.

Doug covered Moira with his body, and the cupboard door hit him in the back full force. As he turned back toward the kitchen, in a slight daze from the assault, he looked down at the now motionless door. Even though the cupboard door was slightly less than an eighth of an inch thick, he was still amazed that his shoulder had left a large dent in it and that he was relatively unharmed. Moira wasn't overly enthusiastic about continuing with the odd cocoa retrieval system, but he smiled and sent a soothing thought that at least calmed her fear that he had been hurt.

Now that the cupboard was permanently open, he saw the container containing the artificial cocoa they were going to drink. He reached for it with a mental hand, and because of his increased confidence he lifted it easily. With the container still hovering in the air, he drew Moira close to him, just in case the container decided to come soaring their way. He pulled gently and the container moved toward them slightly, then he let it fall slowly to the table.

The next step was far more difficult. He reached above the island separating the kitchen and den, and reached for the tea pot on the pot rack. Then, while holding the pot under the faucet, he simultaneously turned on the water and let the pot fill up at least half way. It was difficult to manipulate the pot while it had water in it. The water would move in correlation to the pots relationship with the ground and changed the pot's center of gravity as the water swished back and forth.

He tried to keep it from wobbling as he set it on the stove, but still managed to spill water all over the floor. Then, he finally turned on the stove to heat the water.

He let out the breath he had been holding while he was concentrating. His forehead was beaded with sweat, but before he could clear his brow from perspiration, Moira reached up and wiped his forehead gently with the corner of the blanket. She smiled at him in a way that meant he was in for a wonderful night, if he could succeed in the lover's quest she had assigned to him. He brushed back the strand of her hair that seemed to always fall out of place, and desperately wished that the kettle on the stove would whistle soon.

In a matter of moments, the kettle whistled out that it had completed its task of heating, and Doug turned off the stove. After getting two mugs from the cupboard he had opened, he worked on dispensing the cocoa mix. Dishing out the cocoa was fun, because he didn't need a measuring cup, he simply formed a mental spoon, and used that to distribute the mix. He stuck a mental finger in the mugs and stirred, as he finally added the boiling water, then set the kettle back down.

Triumphantly, he levitated the two mugs of hot cocoa toward them, set one down on the end table beside himself and sent the other to hover in front of Moira. She reached out, took hold of her mug, and took a sip. Smiling in satisfaction, she reached past him and set the mug beside his on the end table.

"It's a little hot, why don't we let it cool a little," she said.

"But I thought that was the whole idea? We're supposed to drink the cocoa while it's hot, to warm up."

She gave him a sensuous smile and said, "Don't worry, dear; I have a better idea on how to get warm."

She slid her hands across his chest, leaned forward, then kissed him seriously. He suddenly felt very warm indeed. Still pressed close to him, she began to unbutton both of their clothes very slowly, caressing and kissing his body as she did. She touched his mind gently, giving him a sense of love more profound than anything he could ever hope to describe. He trembled as she did her best to completely satisfy him, and his mind and body quivered with ecstasy.

Suddenly the kettle on the stove began to scream and shake with it's violent whistling. They both sat up in wonder as they saw the kettle's antics. They dashed over to the kitchen as the kettle full of boiling water performed one final jump, leapt off the stove, and crashed to the floor. Steaming hot water and steam gushed out of the tea pot. Doug leapt away to safety, and swept Moira of her feet with one arm and held her up to protect her from the boiling water. In seconds, the heated water evaporated until there was only a small hissing puddle on the floor.

Moira and Doug looked at each other in amazement. Pyrokinesis was the only explanation for what had happened. Doug set Moira down gently, and gave her a look of disappointment.

"I think I better visit McIntyre, I have to be sure what's going on."

"Do you have to go now?"

"I better go as soon as possible. It's not safe for me to get excited, I might burn you or maybe even start a fire somewhere. I want to know how to control this as soon as possible."

"Believe me, I want you to learn how to control it, too," she said with chagrin.

CHAPTER 24

oira accompanied Doug to McIntyre's quarters. She had told him that she wanted to be with him when McIntyre gave his opinion on Doug's new ability. It was comforting to have Moira with him. He was, in fact, a little scared of his new found power. It frightened him to think of what would happen if he got angry with an opponent and accidentally used his power to burn them alive. The thought of another person's flesh burning reminded him of the room at the end of the hall he had dreamt about.

Moira sensed his anxiety, and slipping her tiny hand into his, gave him a squeeze of reassurance. Doug turned to her and smiled. McIntyre had eagerly run off to get his equipment as soon as Doug mentioned that he wanted McIntyre to run a few tests on him. The eccentric little man hadn't even waited to find out why. Doug thought it was odd that a scientist, who was used to solving long and tedious logical problems, could be so flighty.

They both could feel McIntyre's presence coming down the hall. Moira gave him a quick kiss as McIntyre entered the room. The old man was straining under the weight of a large metal box, which Doug assumed was the equivalent of a medical bag. Doug helped him with the box, lifting it effortlessly with one hand.

"Oh, thank you Doug, that box has gotten quite heavy over the years. I keep adding to it, you never know what you might need in a medical emergency."

"No problem, Doctor; I'm always happy to help."

"Now, what was it you wanted me to test for? Are you feeling ill, or does it have to do with something extra sensory?"

"The latter of the two, Doctor."

"All right then, I brought the brain scanner just in case. What exactly is the problem?"

"You might want to sit down, Patrick. This is going to be another one of those surprises that takes your breath away."

"Oh my! Wonderful! Superb! I'm always delighted to hear of your new discoveries. Hurry and tell me, I can't stand the suspense!" he cried happily.

"Well, it seems I'm developing pyrokinesis. What can I do to control it?"

"Astounding; absolutely fantastic! This is indeed the highest order of cranial development. Have you been able to ignite a significant flame and sustain it for at least a few seconds? Do you know how hot of a temperature you can generate? What is the maximum length of time that you can keep the temperature above the normal parameters of the room? Please tell me all that you know."

"Doctor, all I want to know is what theories you have on controlling the phenomenon. Has anyone ever had a well developed pyrokinetic ability before?"

"There have been isolated reports of incidents that involved spontaneous temperature changes that ranged from a few degrees to fifty. Once, I heard of a man who could start fires in thin air with his mind, but it only lasted for a few minutes at best."

"Well, I've only had one experience with it, and Moira and I are a little worried I might hurt someone if I suddenly start using this power subconsciously."

"I understand, Doug. Coming from anyone else, I wouldn't believe it possible to cause something like that subconsciously, but you have greater ability than anyone else I've ever heard of."

"Do you think you can help him, doctor?" Moira asked, her tender face full of concern.

"Don't worry Moira, I will do all I can for you and Doug. We'll find out how he generates the ability, then I'll have a better idea of how to help him."

McIntyre opened his large container, and began to haul out equipment. The metallic ring that Doug had originally thought to resemble an electrocution device when he had first arrived, was placed upon the young man's head. Wires connected to the metallic ring were plugged into the cranial interaction scanning system, or CISS. The CISS monitored specific brain wave activities, such as telepathy, empathy, and other related phenomenon.

"Now, Doug. I'm going to monitor your passive brain waves and the normal brain waves you create in everyday living. That may help me to form a better hypothesis. Try to relax, and carry on a normal conversation with Moira."

Doug and Moira tried their best to comply with McIntyre's requests. It was difficult at first to talk about anything that wasn't related to pyrokinesis, but eventually, they managed to settle down into their usual casualness. Doug had always loved to daydream with Moira about where they would live once the war was over. Moira had shown him pictures of the best cites of several different planets.

McIntyre interrupted them with a frown on his face.

"I don't mean to be rude, Doug, but look at this. The CISS is registering rapid fluctuations of your thought patterns. It's almost as if you were being sent new thoughts to think from an outside source, which then replace whatever you were thinking about previously."

Doug smiled, he turned to look at the face of the woman he loved as he explained the reason to McIntyre.

"I'll wager that if you hooked the CISS to Moira, you'd see the exact same thing. We have a very special bond. We're so in tune to each others minds that we change our own line of thinking in accordance to one another. In a way, it's exactly as you described it."

"You mean that you two tell each other what to think?! That's dreadful!" McIntyre said sounding very upset.

"No, doctor, that's not what I mean," Doug explained. "It's like having a companion with you all of the time. When she's sad or upset, my mind feels her pain, and adjusts my thinking to help her out of that sadness. Likewise, when I'm sad she does the same for me. We both change our thinking to satisfy each others' needs. It's the most wonderful sensation in the world to have a companion like that, a true soul mate."

"It truly sounds incredible. When did this happen? Has it always been like this?"

"No, it started the first time we,...ahem, had sexual relations," Doug choked out with embarrassment.

McIntyre knitted his brows in thought, completely unaware of his patient's discomfort with the subject.

"Hmmm, Did it first occur just before lovemaking, during, or was it closer to the time of climax?" McIntyre asked bluntly.

"I,...I'm not sure. Moira, do you remember?" Doug asked his mate, trying to shift the conversation over to her.

She looked at him with amusement at his discomfort with the subject, but decided to take over the explanations when she felt his distress. She touched his arm affectionately then turned to the doctor who was still reviewing the CISS data.

"If I remember correctly, doctor, the bond was there before we had sex, but it got significantly stronger, for me at least, after I had an orgasm" she said without a hint of discomfort.

"Hmmm, I would have thought it would have started later than that, but I suppose that the exploration of each others' bodies during foreplay would be sufficient for oxytosin levels to effect your bond. This is quite profound."

"Yes, it was," Moira said lewdly, and flashed a wicked grin toward Doug, causing him to blush deeply.

McIntyre raised his head from the statistics chart and arched one of his eyebrows with an amused grin.

"The bond affected the overall lovemaking experience, I presume?"

The furiously blushing Doug, and the satisfied smirk on Moira's face, were all the answer McIntyre needed.

"I see. Well, tell me exactly what type of demonstration this act of pyrokinesis was displayed as. Was it an open fire, or just a temperature change large enough to notice?"

"It was a kettle of water on the stove. The stove was off, but the water got so hot that the kettle bounced off of the stove," Doug replied, relieved that the subject of his sex life had been dropped.

McIntyre looked back at the chart, then began to pace around the room. Doug sensed that the doctor's mind was working rapidly, but didn't push to see what he was thinking.

"I think I understand the problem. You were both relaxing, and Moira asked you to fix her some kind of hot drink. Sometime shortly after the drink had been prepared, extensive foreplay occurred, and you became extremely aroused. Because of your bond, which was still partly dedicated to her need for the hot drink, your mind transferred the heated passion you felt for her toward the kettle in an attempt to satisfy Moira's need, which you subconsciously still thought present. That's when the kettle started to whistle loudly then jump off the stove and onto the floor. Am I right?"

Both Moira and Doug looked at the old doctor in amazement. Aside from the fact that Doug was using telekinesis to perform the feat of preparing the cocoa, McIntyre had hit every detail right on the head.

"That's amazing doctor, you got almost every detail. How did you know? Were you using your telepathic capabilities?" Moira asked still in shock.

"No, I didn't need to. The evidence from the CISS and what you told me was all I needed to formulate a decent hypothesis."

"There was one detail you did miss, doctor. One that you couldn't have guessed from the CISS data," Doug said. "I was using telekinesis to prepare the hot cocoa."

"Phenomenal; absolutely wondrous! You never cease to amaze me Doug. The control it must have took to manipulate objects in such a manner must have been incredible! Of course, this only expands my theory; it makes so much more sense now."

"Doctor, if my subconscious can do that sort of thing, how can I get control of it to prevent my hurting someone?"

"Not to worry, lad. You can learn to control both of your new abilities with practice and learn how not to use them, in the same way you learned to block out the thoughts of others. I see no reason why the scenario would occur again, now that you are aware of your abilities. Just to be on the safe side, don't use your power to do anything for Moira right before you make love to her," McIntyre chuckled.

Doug blushed slightly, but felt much better. He would learn to control himself as best as he could. His power frightened him, and he wasn't going to allow anyone to suffer because of his lack of education in his abilities. No one would be hurt by his abilities, with the exception of Shaleese.

CHAPTER 25

The young couple spent the rest of their vacation alone together. Doug spent a little time developing his telekinetic ability, but preferred to leave his pyrokinetic training until later. The idea of using pyrokinesis scared him, and he hoped he wouldn't ever need it. Even with Moira's consistent reassurance, he felt nervous when he was with her. The thought of even accidentally hurting her chilled him to the bone.

Moira, on the other hand, was extremely agitated every time he would avoid contact with her. By the end of the week, she had completely convinced him that regardless of his fears, she needed his attention, and in the end would succeed in getting what she wanted anyway.

Aside from his fears, everything was going well. The base combat chambers had been installed, and Doug was amazed to discover that his petite wife, despite her size, was a master of martial arts. She had far more training than he did, so sparring sessions with her were not only fun for them as a couple, but a more entertaining form of learning for Doug.

He particularly liked the apologies, which consisted of kissing and holding, when she would knock him off balance or hit him upside his head with one of the fighting rods. The slight pain he received was worth the pampering he got in return.

His wife was also an incredible cook, which he found out when she made him a fancy dinner the night after she had delivered him a smashingly painful blow to the head. The rest of her apology was reserved for when they went to bed, after which, Doug made a mental note to let her hurt him more often. Moira was utterly delightful even when she hadn't hurt him, so her excess of affection when she did was staggering, to say the least.

Once the vacation week had expired, Doug and Moira attended strategy meetings to discuss the direction that the war should take. Plans had to be made that would ensure victories. Most of the attending fleet commanders and field generals were tired of running, so there was no need to waste time trying to persuade anyone that action was necessary.

It was unanimously agreed that hit and run tactics were the only option available since the resistance was outnumbered. A few wanted to recruit the Ryeesian resistance into their plan, but most still held a grudge against the invaders. Working out the details was left to later discussions, so only broad themes and ideas were raised at the meetings.

Shaleese held several colonies captive by brute force, and several more by forced submission. The Council decided that they would begin liberating the captive colonies in order to weaken his forces in the voluntarily surrendered areas. They hoped that he would try to recapture the bases he lost with men from the surrounding colonies and bases. The hope was that this strategy would in turn weaken his control over the colonies who still attempted to resist. In effect, they could help to liberate colonies that they couldn't free otherwise due to lack of manpower or no strategic ground gained.

Doug wasn't very surprised when he was asked to lead the first assault. The enemy had several, very powerful, telepaths that he would need to overcome if success was to be insured. Aside from the loyal subjects, whom Shaleese had appointed to rule the different colonies, there were no independent thoughts from the soldiers. It was unknown how the zombie soldiers were controlled on the ground. There didn't seem to be any control bunkers or signals, radio or otherwise, being sent to the cybernetic soldiers.

Doug's mission objective was to destroy the enemy forces of the New Verdian colony and, more importantly, to try and discover how the enemy soldiers were being controlled. Doug would be given command of two hundred soldiers, which was equivalent to the number of estimated enemy defenders. They would proceed in a ground assault attack on the base and then withdraw after their mission objectives were accomplished.

For now, a destructor class star cruiser would be the designated transport for the blitzkrieg attacks, but a new vessel was being constructed that would be more efficient. Once in orbit, the destructor class star cruiser would release twelve heavily armored assault shuttles that would carry the troops to the planet surface. A small detachment of delta fighters would fly in to provide air support and soften the base's defense. The troops would advance on the base once their air cover had begun strafing the enemy base's perimeter.

Doug felt confident that he could handle any problems that would arise. He was only slightly apprehensive when Moira firmly told him she was going to accompany him. He knew she could handle herself well in combat, and it was pointless to tell her that she couldn't go with him. He loved her far too much to deny her the chance to prove that she was fit to be a soldier, so instead of protesting, he accepted her demand and appointed her his second in command. The shock on her face was quickly replaced by a profound look of appreciation and love.

A full six months after their landing at New Haven, the resistance was ready for their first strike. The troops to accompany Doug were all fitted with the ground assault body armor and ready to go. McIntyre had stopped by to offer Doug a farewell present. Doug wasn't sure what to think when the old doctor handed him a fair sized box with a large grin on his wrinkled face.

"Thank you, doctor," Doug replied as he began opening the box.

"I thought this might come in handy since you haven't been fitted with a suit of body armor yet. Besides, you might need some help when you get to New Verdia," the doctor explained with a chuckle.

Doug opened the container to find a body armor helmet with teleprompter, commonly referred to as a BAHT. Doug had sour thoughts as he looked at the BAHT in his hands.

"Go ahead, try it on," McIntyre urged.

Reluctantly Doug placed the BAHT on his head, and slid the visor into place.

"*So, they saddled me with the brain dead bohemian again. What did I do to deserve such a punishment!?*" a familiar sarcastic voice blurted.

Doug looked at McIntyre with a disgusted expression,

"You fixed it, didn't you!?" he said accusingly

"Yes indeed, the chip itself wasn't even damaged. They're difficult to construct, so I placed the chip into one of the new, modified helmet units."

"Maybe I'll get another helmet. Are the new models as annoying as the old ones are? I'd kind of like a more annoying companion," Doug remarked sarcastically.

"I thought you would appreciate an old friend to accompany you," McIntyre chuckled.

"*I hardly consider you a friend, you great pile of gruntbug dung. Furthermore, I'll have you know that malicious destruction of resistance property is considered a crime. I'm surprised they didn't put you away for your violations against a poor, defenseless, BAHT,*" the unit scolded.

Doug took off the helmet as it continued to rant and rave about the injustices a BAHT went through. Doug resisted the urge to destroy the offensive little helmet again. Looking at McIntyre with a look of disdain, he added,

"Thank you doctor, I always enjoy sarcastic and offensive companions."

"I knew you'd like it," McIntyre said as he continued to laugh.

Moira had just finished her preparations as McIntyre left, and came out of the bedroom to see what McIntyre had wanted.

"What's that dear, a BAHT?"

"Unfortunately," he grumbled.

"What do you mean by that? BAHT's are extremely helpful in any type of ground assault operation."

"Not mine. This is the same helmet I smashed when I first got here. It told me that I was an intruder and then sounded the silent alarm, so I hit it with an energy staff and destroyed it. At least I thought I had. McIntyre fixed it, and gave it to me as a going away gift. This BAHT hates me as much as I hate it," Doug complained, throwing the BAHT onto the couch like a child disappointed with a new toy.

Moira looked at him seriously for a second, then, no longer able to contain herself, burst out laughing. After taking a moment to look at the irony of the situation, Doug joined his mate in laughter. The sarcastic BAHT was unable to voice its complaints about being tossed around so roughly. Since no one was wearing it or close enough to hear its complaints it shut down in frustration. The sound of its computer shutting down made Doug laugh even harder.

After all preparations had been made, the troops boarded the large star cruiser, and the launching sequence began. The trip would last a full day, so everyone prepared for the coming battle in their own way. Some slept, some prayed, some meditated, and some even went so far as to consume as much food as they could, in order to store energy for the up coming battle.

Doug's relaxation technique was simple and effective. He dismissed himself from the bridge, went to his quarters with Moira, and they laid on their bed listening to a selection of soothing classical music while they talked. The music helped Doug to focus, and Moira helped him to relax. He was a little worried that he would fail as a Commander and lead his troops to a disastrous defeat, but most of his concern was for Moira's safety. If she stayed by his side, he knew he could look after her, so he made her promise to do so several times during their voyage. It was possible that his enhanced body and armor were enough to withstand a direct hit from a particle rifle, but definitely fatal for her.

When the time came to commit their forces to battle, Doug was feeling every bit of the leader everyone expected him to be. After addressing ground assault troops, he gave the flight group last minute instructions, and then boarded the assault shuttle with Moira. He could feel the overwhelming sensations of his troops. They wanted to fight.

The assault shuttles roared to life and disembarked from the launching bays at incredible velocity. Once clear of the hulking Leviathan that had transported them, the shuttles split into two separate factions. Gold team would come from the south, and Doug's Gray team would assault from the north. Roughly seventy five troops were allocated to each team to form less than two platoons for each side. The remainder of Doug's company was divided between the assault fighters and staff on the Destructor class cruiser.

The shuttles descended into the atmosphere of the target planet, New Verdia. Doug donned his helmet and armed the charging unit of his particle emitting rifle. Perhaps because of the situation, or perhaps because it had no energy left for insults, the BAHT unit remained silent, and Doug gave a prayer of thankfulness for the absence of the BAHT's sarcastic remarks. Doug glanced at Moira as she bent to grab her rifle under the seat, and noted with an amused thought that she even looked sexy in a combat suit.

Laughing out loud as the shuttle landed, Doug gave the order to deplane. He stepped off the shuttle, with Moira right behind him. They had landed a good two hundred yards from the colony base. Doug grunted in satisfaction at the distance. They would have enough time for the air cover to arrive, even if they started out now. Once everyone had disembarked from the shuttles, he shouted the order to move out and signaled Johann, who was commanding the gold team, to begin his advance.

Marching across the rocky ground, Doug felt the rage boiling inside of him. He suppressed it, controlling it as he had done during the space battle. Moira looked at him, wondering why he was suddenly so angry. He did his best to smile reassuringly to her, but instead his smile resembled more of a wolfish grin than anything else. She assumed an equally vicious mentality and tread forward in a crouch, ready for battle.

Doug saw the enemy fighters heading toward them in the distance. Then he looked up to see twenty delta fighters rocket overhead toward the enemy vessels. The deltas were slightly outnumbered but, because of superior ability, easily had the advantage. Doug tensed, waiting for the enemy soldiers to make their presence known. He barked a command for everyone to keep their eyes open.

The colony base was not more than a hundred yards away when the enemy soldiers started their preemptive strike. A zombie-like soldier leapt out from behind a boulder. As the enemy rushed in a hastened shamble towards the young Commander, Doug smashed his fist into the side of the zombie's head. The enemy soldier fell limp into a lifeless pile. Doug looked down at the dead body in grim satisfaction, then ordered one of his troops to carry the cyborg back to the shuttle. Maybe they could get a deeper understanding of how these zombies were controlled now that they had one to study.

Surveying his surroundings, Doug noted that the enemy foot soldiers were even more dangerous once they had been shot down. Unless terminally hit, the cyborgs would continue to fight in a mindless dedication to the wishes of their masters. Doug sent out a telepathic message to his team warning them to be wary of the fallen enemy, but was a moment too late. A young soldier was walking over a fallen cyborg when it suddenly re-animated. The young woman was tripped by the enemy's searching arm, and skewered, as she fell, by a sword appendage that the cyborg had instead of an arm.

Doug felt a deep pang as he watched the young woman die, and amended his warning by telling his troops to fire a shot through the head of any enemy they passed. Their losses were minimal, but the young Commander knew the current attacks were only a delaying action until a more organized assault could be made. The real threat would arise when the two teams attempted to overtake the base. The grim advance to the base was filled with the disgusting sight of heads blowing open like rotted melons, as gray team methodically blasted every enemy they encountered into oblivion.

Gray team, now caked with blood and quivering pieces of half dried flesh, came to a halt twenty yards away from the base's outer perimeter at Doug's command. Doug glanced to the sky seeing the delta fighters picking off the last few enemy craft. He knew their only advantage would be air superiority. He surveyed the base and saw the enemy soldiers amassing in a defensive position. There were over five hundred enemy soldiers visible, far more than had been expected. An entire battalion. The delta fighters needed to be protected from the base's anti aircraft weaponry, and Doug knew what had to be done.

Reaching outwardly with his mind, the Commander searched for the base's control room. He quickly found the few enemy soldiers that had active thought patterns in a bunker system below the base. A small group of men were starting up the defense sequence to activate the semi-automated ATR defense systems of the base. As far as he could tell, they weren't controlling the foot soldiers from that room. Seeing nothing else of interest, the powerful telepath delivered his mental onslaught on the minds of the controllers, completely annihilating the few dozen minds in room.

The delta fighters would now be safe from any form of counter attack. Doug gave himself liberty to examine the bunker complex more thoroughly. It wasn't very large, and there didn't seem to be any other control areas. There were a few soldiers, but they weren't thinking, so Doug assumed that they must be cyborg guards. Satisfied that there was nothing else there, he let his mind flow back to his body.

Moira was standing directly in front of him, Doug sensed her wariness from his mental searching. He knew she had been standing guard while his thoughts were elsewhere, and smiled as he thought of how lucky he was to have her. She turned as she sensed his mind's return, and smiled. The base was ripe and ready to be seized, so Doug sent out his mental command to begin the invasion as he radioed the Deltas to make a straffing run.

The cyborg soldiers were easy targets from gray team's place of concealment on the outer perimeter. There was an entire outer wall that had been partially destroyed during Shaleese's take over. New Verdia didn't have enough cyborgs to defend the broken perimeter defense wall, and thus the cyborg slaughter began. The delta fighters performed a few bombing runs to thin out the enemy defenses. The modified AS 15TT air to surface missiles the deltas carried were old, but reliable. Most of the resitance's efforts went into space warfare, but the modified atmospheric missiles could still get the job done.

The invasion was going well. Doug was blasting through the enemy soldiers, when he felt an overpowering sense of anger. He looked up sharply as one of his veteran soldiers screamed out while clutching his head. The graying soldier fell to the ground as his mouth began to froth. His eyes rolled back into his head and quickly died as his body gave one final spasm of pain.

The telepath Commander wasted no time in finding the source of the attack and did his best to simultaneously shield his team from the raging enemy mind. He found the source in a tower on the western face of the base. Doug could see and sense his opponent's frustration. He was a middle aged man with thinning grayish white hair. The balding man was loosing the battle and he knew it. Doug allowed a malicious grin to form on his face as he struck at the telepathic adversary with a mental force bolt.

To his surprise the bald man deflected the majority of the blow, but still reeled back in painful astonishment. Doug prepared for the bald man's counter attack. He knew he might be able to defeat the rival telepath before he could retaliate but wanted to see what kind of opposition he would face if he was the one to be attacked first in the next battle.

The balding foe summoned all of his energy and fury, and concentrated the energy toward Doug. Doug smiled as he felt the effects of the attack deflected with a marginal amount of effort. It reminded him of a small guy getting in the first punch on a much larger opponent, only to discover that he hadn't even stunned his foe. Doug could visualize the bald man dropping his mouth in awe. The astonished old man stood in the tower with his mouth agape, not knowing what to do next.

Doug pulled together all the energy he could muster, and retaliated with a tightly controlled psychic beam. The enemy telepath cried out in pain and begged for mercy as his mental shield began to weaken. Doug felt his opponents' pain and increased the intensity of the attack in elation. The young leader's excitement quickly turned to revulsion as he envisioned his screaming opponent's head explode, sending chunks of bloody skull and brain in every direction.

Moira turned to look at her lover sharply when she felt his distress. As he turned to face her, he gave her a haunted look that explained the outcome of the gruesome encounter in more than words or telepathy could ever relate. She responded quickly, and comforted her husband as best she could. Clinging tightly to the woman he loved he felt unworthy to even look at her, much less hold or love her.

For the most part, the battle was over, the frightened colony refugees would be protected, and transported to the star cruiser. The remains of New Verida's people would be given a place to live at the base. Hopefully, a few would even decide to join in the fight.

Moira knelt down to hold her husband, as he began to weep for the man he had brutally slain without mercy. The death of the rival telepath had been unavoidable, but Doug was upset from the enjoyment he had taken in his opponent's pain. He knew he couldn't be capable of such a nauseating and sickening pleasure; it had to come from something else. As he held the woman he loved, he prayed that the sadistic sensations he had felt toward the enemy telepath had not been his own.

CHAPTER 26

D oug sat in a sullen mood aboard the assault shuttle. He wanted to shed the bloody body armor as soon as he could. The sight of it only reminded him of the terrible screaming and cries for mercy from the telepath he had slain. Moira tried to console him, but she couldn't seem to snap the love of her life back to reality. Just as Doug was about to take off his helmet, the BAHT unit began to speak.

"You know, it most likely wasn't you that exploded that guy's head."

Doug's sudden interest in what the BAHT had said, snapped him back to reality, as he sat upright in wonder.

"What did you just say?!"

The BAHT voiced the micro sonic equivalent of a sigh.

"I see that your brain has finally shrunk back to Cro Magnon proportions. You aren't sophisticated enough to hear me anymore."

"Listen up, you useless piece of malfunctioning crap! Unless you want to have a repeat of our last hostile encounter,

I suggest you knock off the sarcasm and get to the point! What did you mean by your initial statement?"

The BAHT unit was silent for a few seconds and then calmly began to relate its meaning to its, seemingly unstable, master.

"I'm only trying to help, so please try to refrain from any hostile actions towards me. I said that you probably weren't responsible for exploding that telepath's head."

"If it wasn't me, then who exploded it? Did he just spontaneously combust?" Doug asked with contemptuous sarcasm.

"Look who's being verbally offensive now. If you look at the records in the resistance computer, you'll see that Shaleese has, in the past, implanted explosive devices inside the heads of his followers. The telepath you fought probably had an explosive in his head that was triggered to go off the moment his mental defenses were breached. Most likely, anyone who has information that would be helpful to use against the Overlord will have such a device in his or her head."

Doug let the significance of the BAHT's statement sink in. It did fit with Shaleese's profile and desire for secrecy about his identity. Any information that someone tried to pluck from the mind of one of his followers, would result in instant death for the source of information. Doug felt a little better, and he hoped that the sadistic sensations he had felt were somehow Shaleese's and not his own.

"Thank you," he said before taking off the BAHT unit.

He looked at Moira, who was sitting next to him and holding him comfortingly. She returned his glance with a look of relief on her beautiful face. He smiled warmly and sent a brief mental touch of the profound love he had for her. She returned the smile and love touch, and everything was alright again.

The shuttle docked with the star cruiser, and the two lovers disembarked from the cramped assault vehicle. Doug ordered for the captured cyborg body to be placed in the freezer so that McIntyre could examine it later. After all of the assault shuttles and rescue shuttles had docked, Doug gave the word to the star cruiser's captain to enter the hyper travel sequence as soon as possible. The hulking star cruiser was already rumbling as it accelerated away from the planet, and soon it would be a safe distance away from both the system's sun and the colony planet in order to enter the hyper travel sequence.

After a brief consultation with Johann about casualties and overall battle scenarios, Doug headed for his room with Moira. All either of them wanted was a nice hot shower and clean clothing. They both dispensed with their body armor, slightly revolted by the caked blood on the suits. Doug admired the view provided by Moira's revealing undergarments, as she shed the battle armor. He always enjoyed looking at his ravishing wife. With a sly grin, he suggested to the beautifully clad woman that they could save time by showering together. Returning his licentious grin, she heartily agreed.

⁜ ⁜ ⁜ ⁜ ⁜

Upon their arrival at New Haven McDougal greeted them, and congratulated Doug on his success. McIntyre was elated when he heard that a cyborg had been brought back for him to study. Doug informed McDougal of the tactical experiences the two groups had encountered, and also stressed the importance of confirming the death of a cyborg and eliminating the semi-automated base defenses. McDougal noted the advice but was far too preoccupied with visions of winning a war he had previously thought to be hopeless.

In his absence, the Council had decided to strike as many cargo space freighters and small military bases as possible, pending the success of Doug's mission on New Verdia. The hope was to whittle Shaleese's empire down to more manageable proportions. The most dangerous mission, the destruction of Shaleese's cyborg factory, would be saved until further successes were made.

Doug looked at the battle plans the Council had laid out for him. Assuming that he went from one site to the next, with no breaks or sleep, it would take him the better part of a year to complete the list. He decided to pay McIntyre a visit; it was time to augment more of the soldiers, so the more advanced telepaths could take care of a few sites without him. He needed to find out more about the capabilities of the cyborgs before he spent time augmenting anymore soldiers. If he had enough successes with the augmentations, he could convince the Council that he wasn't needed for every mission, only the worst and most dangerous.

As Doug considered all that the resistance expected from him, he felt like a secret military weapon. A biological freak that the Council only wanted for its use against Shaleese. He knew he was merely feeling sorry for himself, but couldn't help seeing the irony of the probe's mission. It had indeed succeeded in finding a weapon to use against Shaleese, even though it was a weapon with a will of its own.

McIntyre had wasted no time with the study of the cyborg corpse Doug had delivered him. In less than a week, he had a good idea of how the cyborgs operated. Doug attentively listened to the excited doctor explain how the cyborgs functioned.

"Well, as you can see on the monitor, this particular cyborg has had his personal thoughts and memories completely erased. The machinery that did this was most likely of Ryeesian origin and is highly sophisticated. Even by Ryeesian standards. Only the neural connections in the frontal lobe that form personality have been removed. The long term learning and memory of the hippocampus is undamaged, but the short term to long term transfer of information executed by the hippocampus is no longer functional.

Any fighting ability this man had, or spacecraft ability for that matter, is still in existence. He could even learn more technical knowledge, but because of the lack of frontal lobe synapses, he would need to be constantly directed. There simple is no evidence of decision making capabilities.

Their understanding of language is also present in the temporal lobes, but they are incapable of doing more than one thing at a time. In other words, once a trainer tells a cyborg to attack, that's all it does, attack. It will use any means necessary to accomplish whatever its been told to do, but limited to direct methods. This cyborg would be incapable of subterfuge, for example.

A pilot cyborg must have a different chip, because it takes more thought to control any craft, let alone combat with another craft effectively. I suspect that the ordinary ground soldiers aren't controlled like the pilots. They are simply told to fight, stand, or guard."

Doug thought of two problems with that explanation and wondered if McIntyre had thought of the obvious complications himself.

"Two questions. One, what would happen if one of our soldiers told a cyborg to do something other than fight, would that be sufficient to make them turn around? Two, how do they sustain themselves? In other words, are they told to eat, sleep, and defecate too?"

"Excellent questions. As for the second question, the cyborgs require no sleep, the hypothalamus and thalamus of this cyborg indicate no activity for at least three years. Somehow, Shaleese has bypassed the necessity of sleep. I assume that they are feed intravenously because of this IV attachment in the left arm, and they don't have feces of any form. They only urinate, which they apparently do whenever they have to. This one was rather ripe when you brought him back. There are several antibiotics that could be added to their food source to prevent infections. But overall, I wouldn't give one of these cyborgs a lifespan of more than five years.

As for the first question, I really have no clue. I'm sure Shaleese and his officials have some means of identifying themselves to the cyborgs. It would be rather stupid of him to allow such a large Achilles heel in his empire. All I know is that the occipital lobe does show use of several synapses relating to what's left of the frontal lobe. It is possible that they have a visual recognition of their masters.

There's one other interesting thing about this cyborg soldier. His body has been infused with metallic microchip fibers that appear to augment not only muscular strength, but also the tenacity of the ligaments and tendons. It almost mimics the biological enhancements you have, except that it would be extremely painful and permanently damaging over an extended period of time. They don't feel the pain, of course, and their life span is to short to worry about long term damage."

"That would explain why they can take a hit in the chest from a particle rifle, and still keep going for awhile," Doug mused. "Thank you, doctor. I've got enough information for now."

"Stop by anytime, Doug. I've been conducting some more research on the time differential during dimensional jaunts. I haven't quite figured out all of the equations. There seems to be some sort of problem with the equations for different dimensional frequencies and the time factor, but it shouldn't be long before I figure it out."

"I'm sorry you've spent so much time on that, doctor. I should have told you that I'm not going back."

"What?! Why would you not go back? I'm sure I can find a way to balance the equations."

"Well, I can't ask Moira to go with me, and I won't be separated from her, ever."

"She must really be wonderful in the bedroom if you would give up going home for her," McIntyre chuckled, and Doug smiled at the doctors rare display of humorous perversion.

"She means more to me than anything," Doug explained. "You can't imagine what it's like to not only be with a woman that is everything you ever dreamed of, but to be able to share all that you think and feel with her."

McIntyre looked at Doug seriously.

"Doug, I would give anything just to even experience the kind of relationship you and Moira have. I've never seen a couple that loved each other more than you two do. I thought I loved my wife as deeply as was possible even up to the time when she died of cancer, but I've found that I didn't know how powerful love could be."

"You're never too old to love, doctor. You're not that old and, with the empathic power I helped you to develop, you might be able to have the same kind of love Moira and I have."

"I really haven't considered it, Doug. I'm almost sixty; I don't know where I would even begin to look for someone."

"Well, start with the people you work with, then work your way outward from there. You never know. If you examine the emotions directed to you, you might just find that some lovely lady is already interested in you."

"I doubt that, Doug; I'm not much to look at," the doctor laughed. "But thank you, Doug; you've given me something to think about other than work."

Doug had returned home to be with Moira, since he had decided to hold off suggesting his plan to augment current telepaths to Admiral McDougal until the morning. When he got home, he realized Moira wasn't there, then remembered that she was still in a training session with some of the newest Cadets recruited from New Verdian. She was still the best teacher on the base.

Doug intended to surprise his wife with a nice home cooked meal when she returned. He started to get the cooking utensils ready, while he thought about how he would go about suggesting the augmenting of other soldiers to McDougal. They had to be certain that an augmented telepath would be capable of defeating a powerful enemy. It would be easy enough for Doug to test them by allowing them to strike at him. He could gauge how powerful they were by how much difficulty he had in defending himself.

Grabbing two Venilusian steaks from the freezer, he wondered if any augmented telepaths would be strong enough to overcome him. After his encounter with the supposedly powerful telepath on New Verdian, he doubted it. The attack of the bald man wasn't even a challenge. Maybe Moira would be up to a little sparring game when she got home. She had been the most powerful telepath before he arrived and augmented her abilities. If she couldn't defeat him, then it was unlikely that anyone on the base could.

Moira returned home after her training classes, and was very happy that Doug had made her dinner. She inhaled the aroma of Venilusian steak, fresh vegetables, and baked potatoes, then advanced to her husband's side and kissed him tenderly. They ate the well prepared meal, and then relaxed in their den.

Doug had convinced Moira to grapple with him in a mental sparring session, but she insisted that it wait until morning. They sat on the couch holding each other in contentment, and Moira slowly drifted into a peaceful sleep. Doug didn't need much sleep anymore, but he could sense Moira's fatigue. He held her gently while he ran his fingers through her hair and made sure that nothing interrupted his wife's rest.

CHAPTER 27

Doug had finally become too restless to sit, and carried Moira to their bedroom. After undressing his wife and tucking her in bed with a kiss on her cheek, he left his room and went to the computer center to read. His night hours were usually spent in the computer center. Since he had nothing better to do, he would read about history or study the advanced technologies of this dimension. Roughly six hours of his night were completely open for study, the rest was spent watching his beautiful wife sleep, and trying to fall asleep so he would wake at the same time she did.

Doug reviewed the computer files on the Ryeesian invasion, and the rise of Shaleese. The Ryeesians had quickly defeated Earth's primary defenses in a few months. The aid of technology, given to Earth by the Venilusians, allowed Earth to regain its freedom from the Ryeesians in another seven months. Shaleese took advantage of the weakened forces of Earth and Ryeesus to seize control roughly two and a half years after the initial invasion of the Ryeesians.

No one knew where Shaleese had come from, or where he had gained his large army of troops and resources, but the primary ships he originally used were stolen Ryeesian and Venilusian craft. Earth's population was thinned even more when survivors used the Venilusian technology to travel to distant planets for colonization, since Earth had been ravaged so badly in the war with Ryeesus. Ryeesus itself wasn't conquered until Shaleese had wrested control of Earth and Venilusia, thus expanding his cybornetic armada via the prisoners he captured.

The remaining militia of Earth fled from Shaleese, and they colonized several bases that sheltered them from the enemy until they could find enough resources to fight back. Doug was startled to see that his name had already been inserted into the computer's history files. He read about his arrival, his amazing abilities, and finally, in the latest entry, his victorious battle on New Verdia. He felt a little unworthy of being a historical figure but couldn't help feeling proud at the same time.

Doug was feeling a little tired, so he headed back to his room and to his lovely wife. He looked at the wall clock as he entered his home, and noticed that it was almost time to get up. There would be time for a short nap later, so he entered his bedroom, kissed his wife lovingly on her forehead, then went to the kitchen to fix her some breakfast. With a little food, he knew he wouldn't feel as tired, and his wife would appreciate his gesture of breakfast in bed.

Doug knew her favorite breakfast dish was Venilusian eggs over toast, with a side of sausage. He made sure to keep her mind asleep as he fixed the meal, he didn't want any of the noise he made to wake her prematurely. Fixing her a cup of coffee as well, he entered the bedroom once again, and set the breakfast cart with their two plates of food onto the end table. Sending out a love touch, he gently woke her.

Arching her back sensuously, she sat up and blinked at him with a small smile.

"Good morning, dear. I see you've finally served me breakfast in bed. It's about time," she said in a sweet tone to dampen the effect of her scolding.

"We've been a little busy lately, love. I hope I haven't disappointed you."

"Not at all, my love. I kind of like waking up with you beside me," she smiled, "I know you don't sleep much, and that you sneak away once I've fallen asleep, but do you have to read about history all the time? I'm tired of dreaming about historical genres and hearing it dictated by a computerized voice."

Doug smiled, "From now on, I'll try to read some trashy romance novels at night. Would that be better?"

"Anything's better than history," she yawned daintily.

After eating breakfast, Doug persuaded Moira to try a mental blast on him. The first couple of attempts were pathetic, and he had to continually reassure her that a more powerful blast wouldn't hurt him. Reluctantly, she focused her attack, and delivered a more formidable assault. Doug was nearly hurled across the room by her half-hearted attack. If he hadn't braced himself for the blast, he would have been knocked over. It was very impressive, even though it wasn't sufficient to break his mental shield.

Seeing him sway from her blast, Moira ran to his side and held him, as she asked if he was okay in a panicked voice. Doug looked at his stunning wife with a smile that said he was fine.

"If all of my opponents are this nice to me after they attack, I could beat Shaleese's entire army single handed," he mocked in a playful tone.

"You scare me like that again, and you won't need to worry about Shaleese, because I'll be the one kicking your butt!" she scolded while gently caressing his face.

"You didn't hurt me, love, I promise. The force of the blast just knocked me off balance, that's all," he reassured her. "It was quite impressive though. I think you're far stronger than one of Shaleese's telepaths."

"Is that what this was all about? Why would you need to know that?" she asked, with her eyes narrowing suspiciously.

"Well, if you're this powerful after I augmented you, then other telepaths will be too. I can augment the strongest telepaths here. They can go on some of the assaults, so I don't have to be present at each mission to defend our troops from enemy telepaths. Maybe with enough augmentations, we can strike several sites at once and get this war over with."

"Oh. I thought you might be planning to leave me behind next time and wanted to make sure I could protect myself while you were away," she said with a sound of disgust.

"First of all, I would never leave you behind, or let you go on another mission without me. Secondly, I know you are quite capable of taking care of yourself," he said in a serious voice.

Her eyes softened, and she embraced him as if to keep him close to her heart forever. He sent out a love touch to reassure her that he was totally hers forever, and she responded with an emotional kiss.

✠ ✠ ✠ ✠ ✠

Admiral McDougal was in his office reviewing the statistics of different enemy outposts and bases. Doug was immediately admitted to see the Admiral when he stopped by. Doug wanted to get his plan approved as soon as possible, so further victories could be achieved.

After relating his plan to McDougal, the Admiral furrowed his brows in thought.

"Do you really think it will work? I don't want to waste lives on a maybe."

"To be perfectly honest, sir, I feel completely confident that my plan will work. I've augmented McIntyre and my wife. McIntyre now has adequate ability, but Moira was already proficient with her powers even before I enhanced them. She's at least five times as powerful as the enemy telepath I encountered. He couldn't even begin to penetrate my shield; Moira at least knocked me off balance."

"So she's still not as powerful as you?"

"I don't think so, but it's hard to be certain. She wouldn't use her full force on me. She was definitely holding back in fear of hurting me. If other telepaths could be enhanced as she was, then I'm certain we could take out several enemy bases simultaneously."

"Go ahead and do it. The risk of a few losses is acceptable if we can even take out half of the bases we strike at. Can you be certain which of our soldiers will be strong enough to overcome one of the enemy telepaths?"

"I'll test each soldier that I augment personally, and only recommend the most able. If we can get even a dozen others, we'll be doing well." Doug noted, "Oh, and just so you understand, Moira and I won't be going on separate missions. She and I are a team, where she goes, I go."

"I hate it when you see what I'm thinking even with my shield up. You knew that I was wondering if you two would be opposed to the idea of separate missions, weren't you?"

Doug grinned at the Admiral as he turned to leave. Doug knew that the bond between his mate and himself was strong, and didn't want to know what it was like not to be able to sense her presence. As long as they were in the same general area, maybe even the same planet, he could feel her mind and know that she was alright. Being separated from her would be like leaving a part of his soul behind, a very important part of his soul.

Doug's plan to modify telepathic soldiers worked better than he had expected. Moira learned quickly, and helped her husband to augment the soldiers as soon as she had ascertained how the procedure was accomplished. After three days, Doug and Moira had successfully recruited twenty three telepaths that had the potential to overcome the enemy commanders. A few additional militia members were augmented at their own request, even though there was little chance they would be strong enough to effectively combat enemy telepaths. Admiral

Angus McDougal was the final addition to the optional enhanced crew.

The change that occurred when Admiral McDougal underwent the mental expansion was quite profound. Not only was he less rigid, but seemed more vivacious in all of the social engagements he participated in. The suspicion that had clouded the Admiral's decisions and friendships had been completely dissolved. Doug noticed the change when had addressed the Admiral, and was reprimanded politely, to use the familiar form of address, Angus. McIntyre told Doug that the Admiral hadn't requested anyone, friend or advisor, to use his first name in at least five years.

Doug sat on his couch with a mug of coffee, and reviewed the portable log book McIntyre had given him. It could access any computer on base but was only as big as a notepad. Doug was extremely grateful since he would no longer need to leave Moira. Now he could just read in bed. The notepad also came in useful for studying reports at home. Doug was currently going over the statistics of the telepathic soldiers he had improved.

McIntyre had insisted on documenting the differences in extra sensory magnitudes. Thus, Doug was given charts that graphed the changes of each individual soldier. The young Commander was then informed by the Council that he should go over them to see if there was anything that might help to decipher between soldiers that were worth augmenting or not. Doug didn't bother to tell the old men on the Council that he already knew there was no correlation between the before and after charts. Everyone had a different neural net, so the degree of ability would be a variable that was completely random. Two individuals who had experienced the same thing would still have different memories.

Memories and latent telepathic abilities were directly related. Mental synapses operated in a fashion similar to a computer, except that the human mind didn't store information in clusters or specific areas. A complete memory was located in several different parts of the brain. Part of the memory would consist of the sights and visual images, other parts would contain the smells, and still other parts would contain the sounds. Extra sensory abilities involved utilizing all of those different parts of the brain at the same time, and linking them to the cerebral hemispheres.

The logs were at least helpful to study the overall power of the new telepaths. Doug was still a little worried that some of the soldiers selected would be inadequate against the enemy. Training on how to search for the enemy mentally would take two weeks, and then the strike would begin. With twenty three telepaths, each taking out two bases, the resistance could crush the majority of Shaleese's outposts within a few weeks. After a few hours of reviewing, Doug decided to pair the least powerful soldiers with more formidable telepaths. A failure of a lesser telepath wouldn't necessarily be fatal if there was a back up involved.

Doug wasn't surprised when Paul asked to be augmented, and although not extremely proficient in telepathy, Paul proved to be highly above average in empathy. Paul had always been aware of other people's moods and dispositions, but hadn't learned to consciously control or focus it. Rick wanted to be enhanced, and wasn't the least bit disappointed when his augmentation revealed a general, but still below standard proficiency, in both telepathy and empathic extra sensory perception.

The biggest surprise was Joseph. Doug wasn't sure there would be even a marginal increase in Joseph's abilities, but the fun and lovable soldier stunned them all by exhibiting the highest levels of all extra sensory applications, aside from Moira and Doug. Joseph was excited about his new power, but looked equally upset when he was promoted to the rank of Commander. Joseph had an extreme prejudice toward command, especially the idea of himself commanding. He knew the necessity for powerful telepaths, but didn't feel that he needed to be the leader in any battles.

Moira was training the newly enhanced recruits in basic mental assault tactics, and wasn't due home for another few hours. Even though he had time to take a nap, since he had once again abstained from sleep the night before, Doug felt restless. He shifted the notepad to the plans for the upcoming battles. There were a total of twenty seven sites to hit in the initial strike, and a follow up strike on the cyborg facility. Doug's team would take out two of the most heavily guarded outposts near the center of Shaleese's empire.

The resistance was also sending out a few enhanced telepaths to aid in the destruction of space cargo and enemy warships. Doug knew that an assault this heavy was likely to have direct repercussions, possibly a direct retaliation by Shaleese himself. If that was the case, Doug would be more than willing to meet the enemy leader and kill him. He smiled as he thought about killing the man he had so easily had learned to hate. The resistance was taking a great risk, but the alternative was to live in fear of annihilation from a tyrant who delighted in brutally sacrificing people under his rule.

Doug was determined to defeat his opponent and vowed to give his best to all of the newly enhanced recruits he would train in the next few weeks. With a little luck, the war would be over in less than a year, and he could live a normal life with Moira. The risks being taken were well worth even the remotest possibility of success.

While deciding on various approaches to the battles, Doug started to get sleepy. He pushed away the fatigue, and continued to go over his strategy for taking the outpost Uri prime, and the follow up base, on the planet Gemini four. Both targets were similar in structure, and the key to victory on either would be troop placement. Finally, the Commander drifted off into slumber, still clutching his treasured logbook in one hand.

Moira came home, shortly after her husband had fallen asleep. She gave Doug one loving glance, then with a sleepy yawn, she curled up on the couch next to her husband and instantly fell asleep. The happy couple enjoyed their nap and shared their usual joint dream of living together on a no longer existent planet.

CHAPTER 28

The training was going well, and the time for their major offensive strike was rapidly approaching. The new telepaths had completed the basic training for mental assaults under the guidance of Moira and Doug. As expected, the newest additions to the psychic team learned very quickly, so the lessons didn't need to be repeated in great detail. After another few classes, they would be ready for combat.

Doug had spent a great deal of his time trying to put together a class for "searching for someone mentally over long distances", and finally decided that trial by test was the best approach. It was too difficult to try explaining the procedure in words, so each student was given a telepathic explanation with words and pictures. Then they were instructed to find, visualize, and describe someone at another part of the base. Even with very little instruction the students performed extremely well.

Doug regretted that he had little time to spend with Moira. With both of their schedules almost completely full, they were lucky to share an evening meal together. Doug considered foregoing sleep so he could use the extra hours to spend with his wife, but she reacted badly to his fatigue. When he was very tired, she would start to yawn and feel equally tired. He gave up trying when she fell asleep one evening on her dinner plate.

The approximated attack date was in less than a few days, so each new telepathic Commander had to be ready. Angus was pushing them hard but promised at least a few days of rest before the initial strike began. Angus himself was overly excited with the upcoming attack and intended to directly coordinate all the space assaults personally. The Council wasn't pleased with McDougal's decision to lead the space battles but said nothing to prevent his going.

The space travel scientists were rushing production of the new star cruiser that would be more efficient for the raids. The new star ship was only half the size of a destructor class vessel but was designed to hold more space for crew and engines, and less for gunnery and defense. So far only a half dozen were completed and ready. Several more were needed to commence with the strike. The destructor class ships would be needed for the space assaults, so all of the cruisers for the planetary raids had to be of the new blitzkrieg class.

Since the blitzkrieg class cruisers would be utilizing Venilusian technologies, it would operate in a fashion similar to the other resistance flag ships. All space travel involved one of two processes. The first was the folding of space, which was accomplished via small engines that were spread throughout the spacecraft. These engines enveloped the ship in an energy field which in turn pulled two edges of space together with a wormhole effect. The other method of travel, which was only used in a solar system, involved the alteration of planetary and solar gravity to repel an individual object in a specific direction.

Doug had wondered since his arrival where the Venilusians had thought up such bizarre possibilities, let alone developed them. He understood the mechanics behind the theories and technology, but doubted human thinking would have come up with anything quite as advanced even by the end of the twenty first century.

Doug had finished teaching his class on mental searching, so he was free to loaf and go over unimportant documents. Moira still had some classes to teach, so they still had little time together, but at least they had the evenings and early mornings. Doug usually spent his time reviewing his plans for the attacks on Uri prime and Gemini four. Doug was leading the assault on both targets, and wanted a good picture of the outpost and base layout.

Outpost Uri prime was the easier of the two targets. Not heavily manned and in a remote sector, the outpost was a sitting duck for a well planned ground assault. Its primary advantage was the semi-automated weaponry, which could defend it for days from a large assault team, ground, air, or both. Doug intended to nullify that advantage immediately upon his arrival. If all went well, the base would be taken and neutralized in less than half a day.

The base on Gemini four was equally equipped with semi-automated firepower but also had several brigades of troops to back up the computerized guns. Doug's entire force was just under three thousand, roughly two regiments, so Gemini four could prove to be difficult. The resistance's only advantage there would be heavy air cover, combined with Doug's ability to deprive the enemy of semi-automated defenses with relative ease.

Then, after he had lead the raid on his two targets, he would join with three other units in an attempt to destroy Shaleese's cyborg factory. If no soldiers were lost in the initial strikes, the total complement of attackers would be close to ten thousand. Doug shuddered as the thought of how much damage ten thousand soldiers could do passed through his mind. If the cyborg facility could be taken and held, Shaleese wouldn't be able to replace his losses in a short amount of time. Doug hoped that the overlord would try to take back the facility, so when he arrived, he could kill him.

Doug was going over the Gemini four base layout when Moira returned home. She wearily sat down next to him on the couch, and threw him a disgruntled look. He smiled soothingly at his fatigued wife, but the expression of annoyance remained plastered to her face.

"Why do you feel completely fine when I'm exhausted, but when you're tired, I feel like I haven't slept for days?" she asked in annoyance

"I don't know, love. Maybe I'm just more resistant to outside influences."

The wave of discontent he felt, compounded with the agitated expression on her face, told Doug that his answer had been less than satisfactory.

"Or maybe you're just more sensitive to my needs than I am to yours. I should try to be more thoughtful," he quickly amended.

Her scowl softened slightly, but he could still sense a little resistance to such immediate compliance. She seemed to be looking for something wrong with his statement that she could throw back at him. Finally giving in, she smiled and added one last jest, daring him to say anything to the contrary,

"I guess I just love you more, that's all."

Doug looked at his wife slightly puzzled. Something was bothering her, and he couldn't tell what it was. On the surface of her mind she was perfectly happy, so it had to be a deeper concern that she wasn't consciously thinking about. He thought that she might just need a break from the stress, so he decided not to pursue the problem and potentially make it worse.

"Why don't you sit in front of me on the floor, love? You look a little tense, and I think you need a back massage. Then you can tell me about your day," he offered.

She happily agreed, but he briefly felt an odd conflict of emotion emanating from her when he had first offered the back rub. She began her account of the day's events as he gently rubbed her shoulders. Doug carefully shielded his thoughts of worry and confusion at his wife's strange behavior. He hoped she wasn't sick, and that her unusual behavior was simply stress.

❖ ❖ ❖ ❖ ❖

All preparations had been made, and Doug's blitzkrieg cruiser was heading for the outpost Uri prime. Several of the other teams had left several days earlier in order to synchronize the actual assaults. The schedule was designed to calculate the distance of each target and set departure times accordingly to compensate for different traveling times. The massive attacks were scheduled to take place with only a few hours difference, and would hopefully delay any retaliation forces until all teams had withdrawn from their respective targets.

Doug was pleased that Paul and Johann were with him on the ground assault teams and likewise that Rick would be leading the air assault team. Having his friends with him helped to qualm his fears of failure. Paul and Johann were good soldiers, with far more field experience in battle than Doug had. They would help him to make good decisions that would ensure victory.

The uneasy Commander was standing on the bridge of his blitzkrieg cruiser, staring off into the pseudo-space that was produced during a folding of space fabric. Moira had continued to act oddly, and he was concerned something was wrong. She was currently in the galley searching for something to eat. Moira had been edgy for weeks, and Doug wondered if he could persuade his wife to remain on the cruiser during the attack. He dismissed the idea almost as soon as he thought it. She would never stay behind, and he knew it.

Paul and Johann had joined him on the bridge; Paul glanced at his friend when he felt the wave of frustration coming from Doug. The Commander looked at his friend and smiled reassuringly, but Paul wasn't convinced. Paul didn't even need empathy to sense what Doug was feeling. They had known each other too long for Doug to hide what he felt.

"What's wrong, Doug? Are you worried about the battle?" He asked.

"No, my diminutive friend, I'm perfectly fine," Doug jested.

"If you wanted to keep secrets, you shouldn't have agreed to augment me. I can feel your agitation as if it were my own. Now what is it?"

"Don't worry, Paul. I'm just a little worried about Moira. She's been acting strange lately, that's all," Doug answered seriously.

"Women always act strange from time to time," Paul laughed. "Don't worry about her, she'll be fine with the three of us protecting her."

"I wouldn't tell her that your watching out for her. She's been real edgy lately, and I'm sure she'll take it the wrong way."

"Oh, well, I won't say anything then."

"Wise decision, young one, wise decision," Doug said with mock portentousness.

The journey was scheduled to take five days to Uri prime, then another day to Gemini four. Doug wanted to use every possible moment to go over his plans for attack, even though he had memorized the layouts of both targets the first time he had glanced at the specs. However, the young Commander couldn't focus on anything until he had solved the mystery of his wife's peculiar ailment.

She had been extremely short with him for days and had mood swings that would shift from adoration to irritation. He had avoided her the entire first day of travel but felt that the situation had to be dealt with before the attack. Doug decided that he would pull rank on her, if all else failed. He knew it would be better in the long run to force her to stay on board the cruiser than to lose her forever, but it didn't make the idea of hurting her feelings any easier to deal with.

Doug could feel her presence in their quarters, so he headed there. He arrived in time to find his wife lounging on the bed half asleep. He was glad to see that she was in a good mood and decided to try talking out the problem before getting drastic.

"You're looking particularly gorgeous today, love. Do you mind if I join you?"

"Not at all; in fact, I was just getting ready to call you. I was getting lonely."

Doug laid down beside her and, with a sudden impulse, began to run his fingers through her lustrous jet black hair. She tried to explain her behavior to her husband, as she looked at him apologetically,

"Doug, I'm really sorry for acting so badly these past few days. I know you've been worried, but I just don't know what came over me. It's been really stressful trying to teach the new telepaths, but that's no excuse for being mean to you. I feel a lot better now. I slept almost all day yesterday."

"You have no idea how relieved I am to hear you say that. I thought you might have been sick. I was right on the verge of ordering you to stay on board, so you wouldn't get hurt during the attack. You've seemed distracted for the past few days, and that can kill in battle."

She looked at him with sincere compassion and regret for what she had caused him to feel, then kissed him lightly on the cheek.

"I'm sorry, my love. I'll try to make up for it, I promise."

"I'd settle for you not scaring me like that again."

She laughed sweetly, then kissed him again; only this time it was a much more serious kiss. The kissing lasted for quite awhile. Doug smiled inwardly with sheer joy as he held his wife tenderly. Everything was back to normal again. His wife was once again as fitting to him as she was beautiful. Her health and support strengthened him beyond measure, just as her ailment had made him feel sick as well. Now the Commander could face battle with his wife; together they were an unbeatable team.

Staring into each others' eyes, and communicating with emotion and thought instead of words, Doug sent out the familiar mental touch of love to his wife. She responded with a similar mental touch, but it was slightly different than he remembered. It had a peculiar peak to it, as if she were a different person now. Doug felt a wave of concern building in him but quickly dismissed it. Moira was fine, and tomorrow they would win the first part of a war together.

⁂ ⁂ ⁂ ⁂ ⁂

Doug was standing on the bridge again, but felt more confident than he had before. It was nearing what would be their nighttime, on the day before the assault was to take place. Moira had said she would fix a nice dinner from the galley rations, and they could "prepare" for the upcoming battle.

Doug smiled as he remembered the last battle they "prepared" for and knew she was going to add some special touches to this preparation.

The Commander of the assault regiment had practiced all the war stratagems that he possibly could, and now spent the tedious hours before battle waiting in morbid anticipation. Paul had joined him on the bridge and was standing silently next to his friend, staring out into pseudo-space. Paul was thinking hard about something, but Doug didn't want to intrude on Paul's thoughts, so he resorted to the old fashioned method of asking.

"OK, Shorty, you bugged me about my problem; now it's your turn to spill it. What's eating you?"

Paul turned to gaze at his life long friend, and leveled Doug with a thought-filled look. Taking a deep sigh, he confessed his problem to his friend.

"Doug, I know I always seem content with the cards dealt to me, but I can't help envy you."

"Why? What have I got that you don't?"

"Moira, well, not her specifically. You two have the kind of love written in the story books. How did you know she was the one when you first met her?"

"It's a long story. I can tell you that I loved everything about her. The way she looked, walked, spoke, everything. I think it was more in the mannerisms than anything else. Almost as if I knew her before I even met her, well, I did know her counterpart, but that's not what I mean. Even with Michelle it was as if I knew who she was before I even met her."

"But when did that intense bond form. I mean, you guys don't seem to have any problems expressing what you feel or need to hear. It's like you know exactly what to say as soon as Moira wants you to say something. I've never known anyone to have a relationship so great that there wasn't any friction from a misunderstanding."

Doug resisted his urge to laugh out loud over his friends massive oversight. His efforts were thwarted when the slight grin on his face contorted into an open mouthed smile, and then a snorting expulsion of air flared his nostrils as he choked back the fast building chortle. Seeing the hurt look on Paul's face, Doug suppressed his mirth and tried to appear serious.

"I'm sorry, Paul, but it is pretty funny. You of all people should know why Moira and I have that kind of relationship. You're one of the resistance's most powerful empaths now, don't you even have a guess?"

"You mean it's because you're both telepathic?"

"It has more to do with the emotional side, but yes."

"Oh, I do feel kind of dense. I just never used my empathic powers aside from the training room. I shield my mind pretty well. I don't think I really want to know how people really feel about me I guess," Paul replied a little sheepishly.

"Well, It's hard to miss when someone directs a strong emotion toward you. Even when you're shielding."

"I know. I have felt a strong emotion from someone, and I was wondering what to do about it."

"You've found a woman who's in love with you, haven't you?" Doug grinned.

"Yes. She likes me very much, and I feel the same way, but I thought I should watch how you and Moira act to see if it could be similar to the bond you guys have. I don't know how it works, but it doesn't seem to be the same; maybe it's because she isn't an empath."

"You're looking at the man who gave you your empathic power, stupid. I can augment her just as easily as I did you. Is that all that's been bothering you? You've been worried that you haven't found the right woman?"

"You make it sound so trite," Paul accused.

"From my perspective, it is. There's no way to be sure if you've found the right person for you, Paul. You have to give it a try, and go on from there. I felt strongly attracted to Moira before any type of bond had ever formed. The bond only reinforced what was already there. It's not some kind of magical bonding that forms when the planets align correctly."

"I guess you're right. I'm just unsure of how my power will affect things, and I don't want to make a mistake."

"That's the first intelligent thing you've said all day," Doug teased. "So who's the lucky girl? Anyone I know?"

"I first met her a few months ago. She was in your original unit, when you first went into battle as a Commander. Her name is Jenny."

"Oh yes, I remember her. She's quite attractive, and she did perform quite well in that fight. It's always a good thing when your woman can perform well," Doug teased. "Is she here now?"

"Yes. We were going to have dinner later tonight. Maybe you and Moira would like to join us?"

"I don't think so. Moira has something special planned. I wouldn't want to disappoint her."

"Don't you two ever quit? Sometimes I think that's all you two think about!" he teased.

"Introduce me to your prospective love, and then I can tell you if an augmentation will work."

"Let me ask her about it first, then I'll come and get you. I don't know if she even wants to be enhanced."

"Alright, I'll be on the bridge for a few more hours, so you'll know where to find me."

Paul left excitedly, and Doug watched his friend make his exit. Doug had never expected that Paul could be so deep. He had known Paul all of his life, and never once thought his friend would ever have difficulty with women. It had always been the other way around. Doug usually had the questions, and Paul the answers.

Doug realized that he had changed in more ways than he had at first considered. Everything had changed since his dimensional jaunt. Looking in retrospect, the young Commander couldn't think of any change, aside from the current war, that hadn't turned out to be wonderful. If he could make this dimension a better place by eliminating Shaleese from the picture, his life would be completely perfect.

Thinking about Shaleese and the war, Doug returned to his speculation on the upcoming battle on Uri prime. If the massive counter strike the resistance had planned came to fruition, Shaleese would be dead, and humanity would be free. Doug prayed that his new found home could pull off the rebellion it had planned.

CHAPTER 29

The blitzkrieg class cruiser Odysseus circled the small outpost moon Uri prime. Its Commander and Captain had given the order to disembark from the cruiser and to begin the assault on the small outpost. The skeleton crew that remained on the cruiser would stand watch for any potential counter attacks, although the possibility was slim. The only other soldiers to remain on the cruiser were pilots that would cover the ground troops, once the outpost's semi-automated defenses had been compromised.

Watching as the assault shuttles descended toward the base, the cameras, viewers, and sensors all centered on one cluster of shuttles. The pilots could begin their attack once the Commander had destroyed the anti-aircraft defenses of the outpost, and all eyes were poised on monitors to give the confirmation that their Commander had succeeded.

A young officer on the bridge watched in awe as the first wave of shuttles landed. The young Lieutenant Commander was disappointed that he had been assigned to bridge duty on his first mission, but there was a shortage of officers in the resistance and someone had to stay behind to keep watch. He felt proud that Commander Taylor had personally asked him to look after the bridge while the battle was in progress, and had added that if all went well, he would recruit him to the elite Wolf ground assault team.

"Lieutenant Commander Thompson, elite Wolf team," he thought to himself. It sounded good, and he hoped that Commander Taylor wasn't displeased with his performance during the operation. He didn't have much to do, other than signal to the pilots when the Commander had taken out the defenses. The chances of an enemy warship entering the sector were slim, but surveillance had to be maintained anyway.

Commander Taylor's assault shuttle landed, and the Wolf unit disembarked from the craft. The Lieutenant Commander could see all of the team as clearly as if they were in the same room with him. He noticed with amusement that Mrs. Taylor was never more than a few feet away from her husband. The two seemed to be joined with a tether that wouldn't break under any strain. Thompson hoped that he could one day find a wife as beautiful as the Commander had.

Forcing himself to pay attention to his duties, the Lieutenant Commander panned out to view the entire team. They moved with crisp, decisive movements that had developed from years of training. He studied their movements and tried to mentally emulate them, so when it was his turn he would move just as neatly.

Commander Taylor was surveying the outpost perimeter, and Thompson knew that he was searching for the enemy controllers of the semi-automated defenses. He eagerly watched the display of the Wolf team sensors, waiting for the mental energy scanners to jump with activity. His anticipation was rewarded when he saw both Mr. and Mrs. Taylor's energy levels go straight off the scale. The mental onslaught was phenomenal, it registered far past the known limit for the human species. Thompson was struck with awe as he watched the fluctuating scale bar, which indicated over two or three dozen mental blasts being delivered.

He responded to the signal given by the Commander, and ordered the launch of three squads of delta fighters. He planned to save the last squad for an emergency, although it would probably be unnecessary. The young Lieutenant Commander wanted to prove that he was cautious and thought ahead. The ground team wouldn't need three squads for bombing or strafing runs, and the reserve squad would act as a safeguard for the blitzkrieg cruiser.

Having nothing better to do, he switched his monitor to focus on the wolf unit. They would soon be engaging the enemy in combat. Even now the front line soldiers were encountering a few cyborgs that were popping out from hiding. Thompson felt nauseous as he watched the carnage of battle. Exploding heads, flying chunks of bloody flesh, and graphic mutilations flashed before the young Lieutenant Commander's eyes. He refused to give in to the desire of averting his eyes from the nauseating rampage. He was a soldier now, and had to get used to the sight of the unpleasantness that came with war.

Once the initial nausea had passed, Thompson watched his Commander with more attention to detail. The finesse with which Commander Taylor put down the enemy cyborgs was fantastic. It didn't matter whether there was one opponent or there were twenty, they all fell before Commander Taylor. Thompson remembered hearing that the Commander was an expert in seven different styles of martial arts, and had likewise mastered several types of weaponry. Pride in his Commander swelled up in him, as he watched hundreds of cyborgs fall victim to Taylor's fury.

Caught up in the excitement, Thompson was startled to realize that the proximity alarms were going off. He quickly glanced at the large tactical monitor overhead and saw two enemy warships approaching rapidly. They were smaller scouting frigates, but still had the advantage of more fire power. After a few seconds of stunned disbelief in what was happening, Thompson ordered the final squad to launch. Thompson knew he only had seconds before the enemy attacked, so with skill earned by hours of practice, he quickly assisted the skeleton bridge crew in arming the shipboard defenses and weaponry.

Looking at the frigates heading straight for them, Thompson wished that he had been better prepared to engage the enemy during his first real fight. The frigates were probably unaware of the blitzkrieg's abilities, so he hoped that if he put on a good show, they would retreat. Gathering up all the courage he could, Thompson warily ordered the configuration switched to seventy five percent of power into the weapons, and only twenty five into the shields. Thompson then ordered half of the life support and all auxiliary power to be re-routed to the weapons as well.

The crew on the bridge looked at him in fear, thinking that perhaps their young stand in Captain was grasping at straws and would get them all killed. Another order, this time crisp and firm from Thompson, quelled their fears, and the order was executed. Setting his jaw in determination, Thompson ordered a full open fire on one of the two frigates. The added power to the weapons allowed for almost all of the guns to be fired in unison, masking the fact that the blitzkrieg cruiser wasn't heavily armed. But if the scouting frigates got lucky, they could cripple the cruiser with a few well placed shots.

Thompson watched the monitor carefully and signaled the delta squad to move in position for attack runs on the flanks of both the frigates. With a scrutinizing gaze out of the viewer, he silently offered up a prayer that the enemy would be deceived.

⁂ ⁂ ⁂ ⁂ ⁂

Doug surveyed the area in front of him with grim satisfaction. The delta's bombardment of the base with modified AS-30s, AGM-135 Tacit Rainbows, and assorted Aerospatiales had thinned out the enemy foot soldiers to just under a few hundred. His two thousand troops mopped up the remaining cyborgs with ease. So far only a few casualties had been reported, and most of them were injuries. If the progress of the rest of the mission went as well as Uri Prime had so far, the wolf team would take minimal casualties.

The cyborgs weren't very difficult to beat individually; it was the overwhelming numbers combined with enemy telepaths that were the threat. So far, no one had determined how to turn them off or send them new instructions. If there was a way, it would probably be found in the main cyborg manufacturing facility that was the final target. The Commander watched in disinterest as his troops mopped up the last resistance of the outpost.

Doug was about to signal the cruiser when he felt something out of place. Moira looked at him strangely as she felt the vibration of discord as well. They looked up to the sky in unison, and Doug's enhanced eyes could just make out what appeared to be particle fire. The startled Commander sent out his mind to Lieutenant Commander Thompson to see what was going on through the youth's mind and eyes.

Doug's fears were confirmed, their cruiser was under attack. Even though the frigates were half their cruisers size, the Odysseus was still out gunned due to it's hit and run design. There was no way to get back to the cruiser while the fighting was going on, so Doug searched the recent memory of Thompson to see what actions were being taken. He allowed a brief smile to cross his face when he saw the clever maneuver Thompson had initiated. It was risky but had the best chance of working.

Doug let his mind float around the bridge to check the stats and tactical screen, and saw that one of the frigate scouts was indeed retreating. The other vessel, however, was moving into position to attack. The decreased shields of the Odysseus would only hold for a short while under heavy fire, so Doug used his power to let his mind travel to the bridge of the enemy ship.

He could see the control panel of the frigate, but couldn't understand how it worked. He scanned the mind of the nearest enemy officer, and found a rough idea of which devices controlled the weaponry and shields. Moira had told him that it was possible to control someone with a weak shield or lack of telepathic ability, so he tried to control the officer on board the enemy bridge.

He succeeded in subverting the enemy officer, and forced the struggling man to raise his sidearm. Pushing the enemy harder, Doug made the resisting man fire repeatedly at the control center of the weapons and shields. The wolf Commander smiled as the screaming captain realized his ship had been crippled and was defenseless. Doug let his mind drift back as he heard the enemy captain shouting the order to retreat.

Turning toward his wife, he smiled and explained what had went on aboard the Odysseus and enemy frigate. She grinned as he described in detail his entire mini-adventure. His enthusiasm prevented her from telling him that she was with him the whole time, and had seen first hand what he had done. With a loving stare, Moira let her husband ramble on about the mental dueling since he was enjoying his story so much.

⁜ ⁜ ⁜ ⁜ ⁜

Thompson let out his breath explosively as the second enemy frigate turned in retreat. He ordered the deltas to return to the launch bay, and thanked God that he was still alive. His plan had worked better than he had expected, minimal damages and no casualties. When the second ship had come about in preparation to attack, Thompson had feared that the smaller ship might have gotten lucky, and destroyed their cruiser.

The Lieutenant Commander looked at the wolf team monitor, and saw the Commander staring up toward the sky smiling. Thompson felt proud and hoped that the Commander would be pleased with his actions. Turning to face the enthusiastic and relieved crew of the Odysseus, the Lieutenant Commander congratulated his bridge crew with a hearty "Well done!"

CHAPTER 30

After congratulating the young Lieutenant Commander Thompson, Doug left him in charge of the bridge, and retired to his quarters to clean up. There was a full day until their arrival at Gemini four, so Doug intended to rest as much as possible. Moira had cleaned up beforehand and invited him, with a mischievous smile, to clean up, then join her in the bedroom. Doug smiled as he thought of how wonderful his life had become and eagerly anticipated the rendezvous with his wife.

The Commander groaned as he stepped out of the shower and heard the intercom paging him to the bridge. He looked longingly at his sensual wife, and giving her an apologetic look, dressed, then headed for the bridge. Moira asked him to hurry back in a seductive voice, and the Commander grimaced with a sudden dislike for whoever had called him to the bridge.

Thompson apologized for disturbing him, then got to the point of the summons.

"Commander Taylor, we've just received a deep space encrypted message from the Council," Thompson said formally.

"Let me see it, Thompson," he answered with minimal agitation.

Thompson activated the projecting screen, and Doug watched as McDougal's face came on to the screen.

"Attention all cruisers. Due to recent information, provided by Dr. McIntyre, the attack on the cyborg facility has been aborted. After all other strikes have been completed, return to base immediately. After we have discussed the repercussions of this new information, we will continue our raids accordingly. That is all."

Doug frowned in concentration. What could possibly be so important that the Council would decide to abort the final strike? The Commander and Captain of the Odysseus tried to think of an explanation for the sudden change of plans as he returned to his quarters. Doug's pondering instantly vanished as he opened the door to his quarters, and saw his wife sprawled seductively across their bed in her nightgown.

"Aren't you going to tell me what they wanted you for?" she asked sweetly.

"Maybe later, love. I thought we had some unfinished business to attend to, before we were interrupted?"

"Whatever could that have been?" she said with feigned innocence.

"Let me see if I can remind you," Doug said as he kneeled beside the bed and kissed her. As they kissed, Doug wrapped his arms around his wife's slender shoulders, embracing her tenderly. Impulsively, he sent out his, now familiar, mental love touch. She responded, by sending out a similar mental embrace, but with an odd mixture of emotion and the strange peak he had felt before. Doug pulled away from her abruptly, as he felt the strangely dual mental touch she emitted.

Moira looked at him slightly hurt at his sudden resistance to her affection. Doug looked at his wife in bewilderment, then resolved to scan her mind to find the source of the duality in her mental touch. After a brief mind link, Doug smiled as he discovered the simple answer to his wife's recently odd behavior.

Still not understanding her husband's apparent revulsion to her, and further upset by the moments of silence that followed, Moira returned a half hearted smile, her eyes moistening from the injury she felt. Doug tenderly wiped the slowly forming tear from her delicate face and sent out an apologetic thought.

"I'm sorry, love. For a moment, I didn't know what was going on, but now I think I understand why you've been acting out of sorts lately. It's quite simple really."

Moira, on the verge of breaking into tears with concern, looked into her husband's eyes, "What's wrong with me?"

"Nothing's wrong, love. You're pregnant. I felt our son's mind just a few seconds ago. He sent his father a love touch of his own," Doug smiled proudly.

Moira looked at him in bewilderment, then burst into tears of joy as she sensed the child within her. Embracing her husband fiercely, Moira pulled him onto the bed.

"I wonder how I could have missed sensing my own child's thoughts," she cried in disbelief.

"He isn't very old yet, love; at most only three months. And I'll bet you've been having unconscious reactions to his presence for nearly a month now."

Moira's eyes gleamed with maternal pride as she touched the mind of her unborn son gently. Doug was equally proud, and he embraced his family in his arms, as they joined in a mental embrace. The unborn child was enthusiastically responsive to emotions that were directed toward it, but hadn't formed much else in the area of cognitive thought.

Doug guessed that his wife had been pregnant for around three months, since there was little sign of pregnancy showing on her slim figure and that his son was developed enough to form some kind of cognitive emotional responses. Because of her extremely intense military exercise, Moira's monthly cycle was slowed down to at most four periods a year, as was the case with most of the women in the resistance. All of the commotion on base had added to the confusion, and having children seemed more of a dream than potential for either of them.

As Moira crooned softly to the happy child growing within her, Doug tried to think of a way to convince his stubborn wife to refrain from joining him in combat. The thought of losing her was bad enough, but with the safety of his son to think of, it was infinitely worse. Moira's face turned toward him as she sensed his desire for her to stay onboard during the next raid. The look of flinty steel in her blue eyed gaze completely crushed any hope Doug had of her abstaining from the upcoming battle.

Silently cursing the carelessness of his inadequate shielding, Doug gave in to the now unanimous mother and son decision to stay with him. The fact that his son didn't want to be away from him either was at least a small comfort to the frustrated Commander. Pushing aside his worries, Doug focused his attention on his family and let them persuade him into a more cheerful mood.

Moira and Doug rested peacefully for most of the afternoon. They had planned to dine in the galley with Paul and his new found soulmate, Jenny, but the new couple canceled their dinner plans in favor of a quiet night alone together. Doug understood all too well and took profound delight in tormenting his best friend. The two friends both knew the real reason why the dinner had been canceled, but Paul refused to admit it openly. As Paul fumbled to come up with more pseudo excuses, Doug would find a reason why the excuse wouldn't be a problem for each case scenario.

The Commander finally let Paul off the hook with a mischievous grin and told his friend to have fun. Paul quickly retreated with Jenny from the embarrassing fencing match that threatened to start again, if higher ground wasn't reached in haste. Doug laughed as the door closed behind him and returned to the bedroom to see how Moira was doing.

Moira told him quietly that the baby was sleeping. Doug knew that the baby was almost always sleeping at this stage, but didn't say anything. Moira was laying on the bed, still in her nightgown, so Doug offered to bring back some food from the galley. Moira smiled at him tenderly, and asked her husband to hurry back, so they could eat and then work on finding some desert. Shivering with excitement from the tone in which the erotic proposal had been offered, the Commander of the blitzkrieg class star cruiser Odysseus, ran down the corridors of his ship with open childlike enthusiasm.

[HAPTER 3I

The Odysseus arrived at Gemini Four early in the morning, by resistance time, even though the base on Gemini four was just reaching its midnight. Doug prepared the Wolf ground assault team for battle, with special care given to the newest recruit, Thompson. Doug gave his wife the duty of making sure Thompson didn't get hurt during his first mission. Doug knew that the Lieutenant Commander was still young and wouldn't want someone watching over him like a boy, so he told Moira to be discrete. She smiled at her husband with the look of "I know how to handle this" written all over her face.

Even though the delta fighters would be needed badly for the ground assault, Doug was reluctant to leave the star cruiser defenseless. The Commander reasoned that the cruiser needed the fourth squad of fighters more than he did, and gave the order for one squad to remain. Doug frowned in concentration as he looked at the base layout from the viewer in front of him. It was larger than the specs he had studied. There were at least three additional buildings on the base, and possibly more troops.

Gritting his teeth in annoyance, he barked out the command for all soldiers to board their designated craft. Doug sat in the assault shuttle brooding over the discrepancies and potential increase in resistance. Reaching beneath his seat, he grabbed his BAHT unit, and put it on. Instantly the little helmet voice embarked on a fresh tirade of commentaries, mostly directed towards Doug's lack of consideration for its well being.

"Shut up and do your job!" Doug barked in a level but dangerous tone.

"My, aren't we snippy today? What's wrong now?"

"We're heading into battle on Gemini Four, I've already downloaded the schematics I wanted you to be aware of, but the viewer onboard the Odysseus tells me that the base is larger than indicated by the charts. There are several bunker-like buildings on the south side, and that means more cyborgs. We're most likely out numbered by at least double of our own force complement. Any tactical suggestions?"

"Aside from praying, I don't know. I'll be able to evaluate further once we reach the surface and I can reduce some of the variables."

"We're landing the shuttles a hundred meters farther out than originally planned."

"That should give me enough time to come up with something. I'm sure the added troops will be of little help against our air strikes."

"Not if they've anticipated our attack and set aside extra cyborgs to man the anti-aircraft weaponry. I can take out the automated defenses and defeat any telepathic soldiers, but the sheer number of cyborgs might become overwhelming if they're positioned well."

"Don't worry, Commander, good guys always win, right?"

Doug laughed despite himself, and was actually thankful he had confided in the BAHT. Against his better judgment, Doug realized he was starting to like the BAHT unit. There was still a little friction, whenever the conversation had to do with past events, or Doug's cranial capacities. Surprisingly, the BAHT continually complimented Moira, as much as it complained about Doug. Doug wondered just how far the programming of a BAHT unit went, his seemed to be slightly overzealous when it came to Moira.

The shuttle landed, giving its passengers a jolt as the craft wobbled slightly in settling. Wolf unit disembarked, while Doug surveyed the surrounding area with his BAHT unit's binoculars. As usual, no activity was coming from the base. It seemed to be abandoned, but the wolf unit Commander knew that behind the outer fortifications the enemy telepaths were busy erecting their defenses. Switching to infrared scanning, Doug saw a force of nearly five thousand soldiers, mostly cyborg. There were probably more cyborgs in hiding among the rocks where the infra red scanners were useless.

Wasting no time, the Commander started his mental onslaught that would deprive the enemy of their lesser telepaths and semi automated equipment operators. Doug started with the defenses, telling Thompson and Moira to cover him. Moira moved in between the base and her husband, determined to shield him with her life if necessary. As Doug knocked out the operators of the defenses, his BAHT unit made churning noises as it assimilated information, and tried to draw up the most plausible method of attack.

Finishing his cascade of mental blasts on the operators, he ordered a full air strike on the base, hoping to knock out as many of the cyborgs as possible, before they could be dispersed. The BAHT made one final churning sound, then began the delivery of its results.

"I've detected the signatures of several fully automated anti-aircraft weapons. Hopefully, our delta fighters will annihilate a few thousand troops before the gunners force them to withdraw. If the cyborg soldiers can't be thinned out significantly, we may have to retreat. So far, they're clustered together, but it won't take long for the enemy to order them to spread out to different posts, making the air assaults even less effective and more costly."

"Well, let's hope our fighters can thin them out. We'll be in the middle of all the action soon, and air strikes won't be effective if we get hit, too. I'm not going to withdraw unless I absolutely have to; this is my job, I don't want someone else to have to come finish it for me. I'll take out the major telepaths now, so we can begin the assault. Thompson!"

"Yessir!"

"Organize the set up of blast cannons, and temporary fortifications along this ridge. If we have to fall back, we might need some heavy cover fire. Then send Company green to the western edge of the base, and Company blue to the western edge. Moira?"

"Yessir!" she mocked Thompson.

"Would you be a dear, and summon all the other Company leaders while I take care of the enemy telepaths?"

"Of course, dear."

Doug smiled, and sent out his mind in search of any powerful enemy minds. His mind drifted toward the base, encountered a few resisters to his search, but easily vanquished them. Probing on, he discovered the primary defender of the base. The enemy was exerting a large amount of effort to shield his identity, and Doug wondered why it was so important. Maybe Shaleese's paranoia had worn off on some of his subordinates.

Doug found that this enemy's mind was the most powerful he had encountered so far. The initial blast he sent was deflected by his foe's shield, with only marginal amounts of straining. Not wanting to disappoint his enemy, Doug waited for a counter attack.

As the blow was delivered, Doug drew back in astonishment. The force of the blow had been stronger than anything he had felt before, but there was also a haunting familiarity in the person who had delivered the mental blast. Doug had to be certain who he was dealing with, so he carefully probed into his opponent's mind. The enemy telepath strained to maintain his shield under the pressure of the powerful probing.

Screaming in pain, the enemy was knocked unconscious as Doug's mind penetrated the man's shield. The shroud that had blurred Doug's mental vision was lifted, and the startled Commander saw the face of his old friend. Although scarred severely, the face was unmistakably Al's. Doug's mind rushed back to his body as the startling discovery sunk in. Moira shared his sense of surprise, even though she didn't know what was so startling.

Sending out a condensed mental explanation to his wife, along with a visual picture of Al's face, he waited to see his wife's response. Doug wasn't even sure she had known Al. The wave of sorrow and nostalgia that emanated from her answered his unspoken question. She sent him a compacted account of what had happened to Al. Doug learned that all of Al's family and friends had thought he died during the Ryeese invasion, from an explosion that occurred on the college campus.

Doug's mind reached out to his fallen friend once again, this time with a resolve to find out why he was fighting for Shaleese. A wave of sympathy swept over him when he saw that the majority of Al's memories had been erased. All that remained was so warped and twisted, that by all rights, Al no longer existed. His memories contained only the brutal and sickening murders that he committed, all of which were overshadowed with the perverse pleasure that he got out of his victim's agony.

Doug couldn't bring himself to killing his one time friend, even if he had been turned into a distorted and evil being. Al was unconscious, and would stay that way for hours. The mop up unit of soldiers would take care of him when the base was infiltrated. He knew that there wasn't a way to reverse the effect, and bring back lost memories; his friend's entire mind had been written over.

Doug allowed his mind to drift back to his body, and gave his wife a look of profound loss. Moira gave him a mental love touch, with an added sense of condolence and sympathy. Their private mental embrace was interrupted by the arrival of the squad leaders Moira had summoned. Doug forced his grief aside in order to concentrate on the more urgent battle plans he needed to adjust.

Six of the eight Company leaders advanced to form a huddled group around their Commander. Blue and Green Company were already on their way to the destination Doug had given them. Each Company contained three platoons. Each Platoon contained around forty eight soldiers, which totaled to a combined ground brigade of two thousand five hundred when added to Paul's eight Companies.

Doug lead the Wolf Platoon, in addition to leading the northern regiment and overall brigade when including the southern regiment. Paul was likewise in charge of his own Platoon, as well as the southern regiment, which had landed on the opposite side of the base from Doug. All Company leaders present turned their eyes to Doug for their orders.

Doug felt out of place among the Company leaders, most of whom outranked him in the standard military scale. Because of the changes in warfare, modern military ranking had taken on a dual system scale. On one side was the old method of ranking, with experience, accomplishment and leadership at the front for promotion, and on the other side was the individual's ability to utilize extra sensory ability. The result was a split in rank. Doug and the other telepath Commanders were given higher rank due to their abilities, although the full title of Extra Sensory Commander was rarely used. He wondered ironically why he had such a high rank and yet was continually given the dirtiest of duties.

Doug looked at the Captains and Commodores around him and was thankful for their humility in accepting the questionable authority of an Extra Sensory Commander. He had never felt any resentment from any of his subordinates, and was silently thankful every time he gave a command and it was accepted with out hesitation. Doug's guilt of jumping in line had no foundation, but he would never know how widely he was respected by his subordinates.

The Commander pushed aside the last vestiges of guilt, and prepared to address the Company leaders before him.

"OK, we're out numbered by far more than was first anticipated, so we need to make a few changes. I've already signaled for the deltas, but they may not be very effective if the enemy has some of their cyborgs operating anti-fighter guns in addition to the fully automated anti aircraft guns that have been detected. As soon as the deltas break off, we'll head in as usual, but with a more tightly controlled spacing between the squads.

"I want each Company to spread out, but have the platoons in tight formation. We all know how dangerous the cyborgs are. They have no fear and will sometimes continue to advance after a fatal hit. They're more dangerous when they're spread out because they're unpredictable.

"Make sure all of your soldiers have their fighting rods ready. It won't be long before each squad is overwhelmed by cyborgs, and we'll need to be ready for hand to hand combat. Someone remind me to ask McDougal why these damn particle guns have such a lousy recharge rate when we get back."

The Company commanders laughed tensely.

"I also want one Company to remain here," Doug added seriously.

Doug looked at the Company leaders, and selected a younger officer who was capable, but not yet seasoned.

"Flaherty, I want your Company to hold this position, and fire the blast cannons over us and at the rear ranks of cyborg soldiers. If they cluster together like usual, the targeting shouldn't be too hard. The rest of us will try to plow through the enemy in tight units, so feel free to loosen up the enemy ranks in between our soldiers with the blast cannon. Oh, and try not to hit us," Doug grinned.

The Company commanders returned to their respective troops to prepare for the gruesome attack ahead of them. Moira gave her husband a worried look, which he subdued with a reassuring smile. Doug knew that he could very well lose a third of his forces, but the Gemini base was a crucial opportunity for victory that wouldn't be abandoned unless it was absolutely necessary.

Wolf Platoon was in the direct middle of the projected enemy resistance. Doug called his troops together and ordered the rest of his Company to flank his platoon in a wedge formation, as the delta fighters roared overhead. The first explosions shook the planet, as Doug's combined ground forces advanced toward the base. All soldiers gripped their weapons tightly knowing fully well the danger of annihilation they faced. Doug sent out an overpowering sense of determination and resolve from his tremendous mind to strengthen his troops. A growing sense of invincibility surmounted the resistance soldiers as their leader poured his resoluteness into them.

Fully geared and ready for battle, the ground regiments on both sides embarked on their quest to overpower the Gemini base. Doug viewed the surrounding terrain with his infrared scanners, hoping to get an advanced warning of a potential ambush. Glancing toward the base, he could make out the vastly depleted number of cyborgs, scurrying around in circles from the contradictory orders they were receiving. Grinning openly, the Wolf Platoon Commander congratulated himself for his good planning. The anti-aircraft weapons were now being utilized at their fullest, but the deltas had already done their damage.

Doug had a sudden insight to the enemy's methods. There was never anything new. They relied on the sheer numbers of brainless cyborgs at their disposal. The enemy always tried an ambush, then fell back on sheer numbers to overwhelm their opponents. With the defense telepaths and semi automated systems out of the way, they were sitting ducks for a blitzkrieg strike. An ordinary soldier could easily handle four of the less responsive cyborgs single handed.

As usual, cyborg soldiers attempted an ambush about fifty yards from the base perimeter. Doug was ready for the attack, as were the rest of Wolf Platoon. Medium sized groups of cyborgs popped out of crevasses and from behind rocks, trying in vain to weaken the squads of soldiers attacking their base. Doug's wolf team mowed through the enemy, and the mindless cyborgs fell like a stalks of wheat cut by a farmer's sickle.

All was proceeding as planned, until the assault on the base's perimeter wall began. Paul had reached the far side of the base with little casualties, and Doug ordered the simultaneous barrage of the gates with plasma battering rams. The two regiments of resistance ground forces breached the outer defense wall at approximately the same time, and cautiously began the slow process of infiltration.

Aside from slain cyborgs and a small handful of actively opposing soldiers, the base was empty. Doug looked around the base with his infrared visor, failing to pick up any humanoid heat signatures. He immediately ordered Companies Red and Black to neutralize the anti-aircraft weaponry on the northern side. Paul sent out two Companies as well to take care of the southern end. No one else was to proceed deeper into the base core until further scanning confirmed the base was in fact deserted.

The vile smelling Gemini base was a grotesque collage of rusty squat buildings and stinking ovoid barracks, with a few taller rust covered buildings thrown in for good measure. No one in either of the two assault regiments was upset that they were forced to wait at the edge of the foul and rank base camp. At least on the perimeter there was a slim chance for a semi-fresh breeze to blow by. Doug and Wolf Platoon, on the other hand, were knee deep in the pig sty that some referred to as a military installation.

Doug feared that he had missed an enemy telepath, and wanted to keep the majority of his regiment in reserve until he could confirm that there was no telepathic threat. If a telepath had indeed survived, Doug and Moira were the best equipped to counter his attack. Doug set up a link with Paul to advise him to join with Johann in setting up a mental shield case his regiment was the first to uncover the trap.

Ignoring the foul reek, the Wolf Platoon cautiously skirted the edges of the Gemini four base, searching for any sign of a trap. Doug felt uneasy about the current situation, and unfortunately, he subconsciously emitted that fear to his unit. Thus everyone was edgy from their leader's unconscious emanations. Doug would always wonder in retrospect, if that edginess was the cause for wolf team's fatal oversight and responsible for the greatest loss he would ever experience.

The elite team of soldiers failed to notice the activity coming from directly beneath them until it was too late. A full battalion of Ryeesian cyborgs collapsed the ground underneath them and surrounded the startled Wolf Platoon. The army of eight foot tall inscetoids vastly outnumbered the small Platoon of resistance soldiers and picked off the unaware fringes of scout soldiers in mere seconds. Doug could only stare, with his mouth gaping at the sight of Lieutenant Commander Thompson's entrails spilling out onto the ground as the young man cried out desperately for help.

The Commander snapped into action in a desperate attempt to save the young man's life, knowing fully well that his efforts were a waste. He could already feel the life draining out of the pain stricken Lieutenant Commander. With a surging anger, the Commander leapt at the responsible Ryeesian cyborg for revenge. The helpless Ryeesian easily fell when Doug ripped off its head with a single crushing blow from his energy staff.

Rapidly losing his contact with reality, and letting the anger erupt, Doug embarked on a rampage of carnage through the enemy cyborgs. Even though he was surrounded, the Ryeesian cyborgs couldn't land a significant blow on the berzerk warrior. Doug used every ounce of training he had been given to ward off each enemy cyborg long enough to kill it. His defenses were aided by his telekinetic ability to shield himself from a blow that his body wasn't quick enough to block. The remainder of Wolf wasn't as fortunate. They shared their Commander's anger, but lacked his animalistic prowess and abilities.

Moira was more in touch with reality than her husband and tried in vain to assist the remainder of wolf team with her own enhanced abilities, while simultaneously fighting off the cyborgs attacking her. Knowing that she wasn't going to succeed, she called out to Doug both verbally and mentally, to try and reach the oblivious warrior and gain his assistance in protecting the decimated Platoon. The troubled wife wasn't able to succeed until Doug had run out of enemies in his immediate vicinity and was forced to consciously think of how he could find more cyborgs to kill.

Doug turned just in time to see his beloved wife scream out in pain as a Ryeesian claw skewered through her backside and emerged from her breast. She managed to get free from the enemy cyborg, but not before the claw had fatally injured her. Doug stared at his wife helplessly, as she collapsed in front of the brainless Ryeesian. He rushed to her side, ignoring the small battle around him as tears streamed down his face.

The responsible Ryeesian staggered backwards as its body parts simultaneously burst into flame and flew apart from the force of Doug's unconscious power. Doug allowed himself a brief moment of grief as his wife's and unborn child's life forces drifted into the uncaring arms of death. In her last few moments Moira gazed lovingly at her husband and sent a final reassuring mental touch of her profound love and cherished the memory of the happiness that he had given to her.

As Doug stared at his wife's beautiful face, he pleaded with her to stay with him as her eyes slowly lost their focus. The next few moments were filled with limitless pain, as a vital part of him was wrenched out and swept away with his dying family. The pain of the deep void that had been torn into him remained equally strong even after his family had passed on, and he knew it would last forever.

An unfortunate band of Ryeesian cyborgs were advancing on the grief stricken man and met their fiery death as he glanced upward at them with absolute fury. The rage soared into a boiling crescendo, and the furious Commander welcomed it with open arms. His sanity began to waver as he delved deep into an animalistic trance. The Ryeesian cyborg slaughter began, and didn't stop until the last Ryeesian corpse had fully ceased all of its involuntary twitching.

Doug couldn't remember how long he sat next to his dead wife in a tear-filled agony. Nor could he recall how he got back to his room on the blitzkrieg cruiser. He awoke from the daze laying on his bed, with heavy chains restraining him. Still feeling the remnants of the animal like rage, he howled as he again felt the lonely pain inside him; the painful absence of his wife's mind being with him. With an inhuman fury, he broke free of the restricting bonds that held him captive, and got out of bed.

Trying to maintain at least a semblance of humanity, he staggered to his bathroom. The scruffy looking man he saw in the mirror was revolting, and the overpowering stench that suddenly filled his nostrils was even worse. Reaching the sink just in time, he began vomiting profusely. The awful stench of caked Ryeesian blood and his own urine, combined with the fresh smell of vomit, was more than he could stand. Having nothing left in his stomach to expel, he continued to dry heave as he got into the shower unit to wash off the revolting odor.

The pain was always present, and it was nearly more than he could bear. He knew the emptiness would be with him forever, and wanted more than anything to make it stop. The only thought that gave him comfort, and a reason to live, was the thought of finding Shaleese, and killing him. He knew it wouldn't make his life any better, but couldn't help thinking that it would at least make him feel better. The thought itself helped to bring him back from the edge of irrationality that he had been experiencing, and reluctantly, the Commander allowed himself a wicked smile.

CHAPTER 32

oug sat on his bed in misery. The pain would come and go, but he knew that as long as he stayed in his room, he would continually be reminded of his missing family. He wasn't sure that he was ready to talk to anyone yet, but needed to distract himself from the pain. Summoning up his will, the Commander dressed in his uniform and headed for his bridge. Anger welled up inside of him as he continually encountered frightened crew members that looked upon him with absolute terror.

Heading down the hall, the frustrated Commander finally encountered a soldier that was sending out an emotion other than fear. It was Paul, and he emitted vast amounts of pity and sorrow. Doug resented the pity more than he had the fear, and the resulting anger made him want to smash his fist into Paul's head. He quickly dismissed the anger, trying to focus on his friendship with Paul, while simultaneously sending out warning signals to alert his friend of the instability that was plaguing him.

Paul caught the signal immediately, and quickly chose to ignore the fact that Moira was gone. Instead, Paul gave his friend the distraction he needed by focusing his mind on military business. Doug breathed heavily in relief as the rage subsided and gave his best friend an apologetic glance.

"Paul, I need to know what happened on Gemini Four. I seem to have a loss of memory between the end of the battle and today," he managed to choke out.

"We did manage to neutralize the base despite the surprise attack of Ryeesian cyborgs. We retrieved you, then headed back to the resistance base. We should arrive at New Haven later today."

"The base is over four days away from Gemini four! I've been out of it that long?!"

"You were berserk when we found you. You severely injured five of our soldiers before we could get you under control. I took command and ordered you chained to your bed. I couldn't stop the rumors that you had completely lost your mind, so you might have to reassure everyone that you still have control over all of your faculties. Since you're walking around without your bed dragging behind you, I assume you broke free from the chains?"

"Yes, earlier this morning. So that's why everyone is looking at me like I'm some kind of demon. What were our casualties?"

"We lost all of Wolf Platoon, aside from you, and overall, several hundred soldiers from both sides of our ground forces. Mostly from my side. I didn't have a super soldier to wipe out all of the Ryeesian cyborgs on my end of the Gemini base."

"I see," Doug responded grimly. "I will be taking back command now, but I'll need your support. I'll address the ship personally to qualm any fears of some type of relapse. I need something to do anyway, I might as well study the statistics of the battle."

"Call me if you need anything, Doug. I'll be in my quarters."

"Thank you Paul."

Doug watched his friend depart, realizing that friends like Paul were rare, and he was lucky to have such a good friend to turn to in his times of need. Trying to focus past the emptiness he felt, the Commander continued toward the bridge. A few soldiers he passed still betrayed their fearful thoughts with looks of abject terror. Trying to counter the damage that had been done, he emitted a large bubble of calming thoughts in order to subdue the irrational fears directed toward him. Nevertheless, he hurried to the bridge to issue his reinstatement order, along with a heart felt apology for those he injured.

The Commander's presence on the bridge was awkward, not only for him, but for the crew members as well. Doug tried to remain calm, suppressing the urge to scream at the top of his lungs from the combined frustrations of his crews' behavior, and the loss that he felt. Looking around the familiar bridge, he forced himself to smile as he sat down in his command chair. The crew returned to their duties, with less apprehension to Doug's presence, but still harboring the remote fear that he would suddenly explode upon them with mindless fury.

Taking a few moments to collect his tormented thoughts into a more coherent state, Doug prepared for the unavoidable task of addressing his ship. It had to be done, if only to subdue the conscious worries of his crew. They deserved at least that much after their valiant efforts in the last two battles. The weary Commander took a deep breath, then hit the comm button to deliver his speech.

"Crew of the Odysseus. This is Commander Taylor. I know of the rumors circulating concerning my irrational behavior, and I want to assure you that I am in complete control of my faculties. I would also like to offer my sincere apology to any soldier I may have hurt during the episode on Gemini Four. I wasn't able to cope with the losses I suffered in the attack, and I temporarily lost my ability to think clearly. I hope that you can feel secure in the knowledge that I am once again myself, and won't let any danger befall any of you while under my command. That is all."

Doug felt a little better, but still agonized over the barren space that was in his heart. There would be time for grieving later, and the resistance needed him now. Wanting nothing more than to join his wife, he immersed himself in the statistics of the Gemini Four encounter, hoping to push aside the vacancy inside of him with work. Doug knew that denial was a dangerous, and only temporary, solution to the loss of a loved one, but he wished it was a possible for him to deny Moira's death nonetheless.

Hours had passed and the end of the Odysseus's journey was near. Doug had retired to his quarters in hopes of avoiding any victory congratulations upon landing. The loss of his family was enough to make him openly hostile to the elation of everyone else. The Commander knew that if he sensed one more joyful thought, he might end up seriously maiming someone. There was simply too much pain for him to handle all at once.

Doug desperately wanted someone to talk to that he knew would understand. With an unusual clarity he knew exactly who could help him: the eccentric little scientist who, at times, was the epitome of wisdom seemed to be the best choice. With a grim resolve, Doug decided to seek out McIntyre upon their arrival and face his profound loss, for better or worse.

His pondering of fate's hateful turn of events was interrupted by Paul's arrival. The grief stricken Commander called for his friend to enter and forced himself to smile as Paul walked in to visit.

"We land in less than an hour, Doug. Is there anything you want me to do when we disembark?" Paul offered.

"Not really, I need to face this sooner or later. I would like you to sneak me off this ship, though. I don't think I'm ready to answer questions yet, and I want to outrun any greeting parties or press interviews."

"I'll see what I can do, but you're going to have to be debriefed sometime soon. Admiral McDougal won't wait long before he comes looking for you."

"You might want to warn him to stay away for awhile. I want to talk with McIntyre when we touch down. I think he might be able to help me straighten things out. Contact him personally and send him to the lab. I'll wait for him there. There's one other question I need to ask."

"Anything I can do for you I will. What is it?"

"Where's Moira's body, you didn't leave her on Gemini Four did you?" Doug managed to choke out.

"No, I had her put in one of the ship's storage freezers that we converted into a temporary morgue. I'll make sure she's taken to the base morgue once we land."

"Thank you. I want her to have a good resting place. New Haven's a better place than anything else available."

"I figured you would. Stop by my place tonight for dinner."

"Thanks, I could use some good company," he said with a forced grin.

❋ ❋ ❋ ❋ ❋

Doug managed to avoid the expectant crowd with minimal difficulty and had reached McIntyre's lab. He hoped McIntyre could at least help him through the worst of his grieving. He knew that the pain would always be with him. McIntyre had lost his wife, and might be able to give some advice on how to cope with the unbearable agony of Moira's absence.

McIntyre entered the lab with a sad but resolute expression on his wrinkled face. Giving Doug a consoling glance he lowered his head and walk toward the young Commander.

"Thank you for coming, Patrick; I really need someone to talk too."

"You can't imagine how badly I feel Doug. Anything I can do will be done as soon as you ask."

"How did you deal with your wife's passing if you don't mind my asking?"

"Not at all. I had more time to prepare for her death since I knew she was terminally ill. But the pain is still the same. What I can tell you for certain is that you must never try to forget. It hurts to think of Moira's death, but trying to think of something else only makes it worse. Try to remember how wonderful she was, and treasure the love you were able to share with her."

"It's hard to think of anything but the fact that she's not with me. I can't sense her mind anymore, and it's almost like a part of me died with her."

"Her death must be infinitely worse for you than any other person who has lost someone. The more you love and depend on someone, the harder it is to deal with their absence. You see, we were made in a unique fashion. We are able to experience pleasure and love in equal measure to our ability to experience pain and loss. Without the loneliness and pain we feel when we are without a companion, we wouldn't be able to cherish and love the companions we have. Sometimes we don't realize how much our loved ones fill all that's missing in our lives until they are gone."

"So how do we deal with that missing part of my life now that it's gone?"

"You can't ever replace that missing part, but you can try to remember how you got along before you met Moira, then work your way from there. First you need to let her go. Take your time, and say good-bye in your own way. Don't ever let her memory be too painful to remember how wonderful she was."

"I'll try, but I don't think it's going to be that easy."

"I never said it would be," McIntyre chuckled. "I make it sound easy, but it took me years to finally get past my wife's death, but that was partly because I felt responsible for letting her die. I was a doctor then and still couldn't help her."

"I should have stayed next to her, or at least taken more precautions in that assault. I not only lost Moira and my son, but also all of Wolf Platoon. I should have seen it coming, or at least sent someone else instead. I wish I could go back and start over with that whole day."

Doug continued to explain the fateful battle to McIntyre in more detail, letting the old doctor hear all of the guilt he felt. Venting all of his guilt to the old man in front of him, he started to ramble about everything he should have done better for Moira while they were together. After several minutes of rambling, Doug realized that McIntyre had been sending him empathic gestures to make him let out all of his pain. He stopped mid-sentence and stared accusingly at the old man in front of him.

McIntyre smiled as Doug tried to get control of his thoughts and mixed emotions about being manipulated. Then turning to the cupboard behind him, he pulled out two bottles of bourbon. Setting the bottle down on the table, he reached for a glass and a large mug and handed the larger container to Doug.

"I hope you're not too upset with my method of helping you. I could feel that you were holding in a lot of guilt. I thought you needed to vent some of that guilt before we got to my favorite way of dealing with pain. You can handle far more alcohol than I can, so you get a mug instead of a glass."

Doug did indeed feel much better. The pain was still there, but it was at least more bearable. As he looked at the large pitcher McIntyre had given him, he managed a small but genuine smile in spite of everything. Patrick was truly a wise man and a good friend.

CHAPTER 33

Moira's funeral took place the day after the Odysseus had returned. Doug managed to keep his grief under control until he saw her face one last time, before the casket was forever closed. The small group of close friends that had attended were nearly blown away as Doug burst into tears and emitted an empathic agony so great that even the most shielded mind was hit tremendously with the unbearable suffering that Doug felt.

The moment passed, but everyone present was visibly shaken by the powerful emotions they had witnessed. Doug felt better after the funeral had ended and Moira's body had been committed to the ground. He knew he had to move on but didn't know which way to go. Spending the day alone, he grieved for his beloved wife and son in private. Paul had invited him to dinner that evening, and Doug accepted in hopes of filling some of the emptiness he felt with companionship.

The resistance still had a war to fight, and Doug was determined to see Shaleese dead. The Council was meeting in a few weeks to discuss the new discoveries McIntyre had made. Paul told him that they both were asked to attend the meeting, so there wouldn't be a long delay in continuing the discussions of the war. Doug preferred it that way and was glad he would have a chance to suggest an all out battle against Shaleese's fortress.

The following weeks were agonizing, but helpful. Sitting in his empty apartment, Doug tried to remember all of the happiness he had shared with Moira. It was painful at first, but McIntyre proved to be right when he had said that it helped to remember the joy they shared, instead of trying to forget that she was gone. The emptiness was still there, but it fluctuated from a dull ache to a piercing pain. As long as he didn't dwell on the fact that she was gone for too long, Doug didn't feel the grief as badly.

Thinking about his own dimension caused him to wonder why he even had a reason to stay here, if a way could be found for him to go back. Aside from destroying Shaleese, he couldn't think of any good reasons why he should stay or go. Doug decided to talk to McIntyre about the possibilities of returning to his own dimension after the war was over. At least he could have the chance to protect his world from the Ryeese, and a chance to kill Shaleese again.

Patrick was in his science lab as usual. Doug entered the lab to see what the old scientist was up to. McIntyre greeted him as he entered, and offered Doug a seat next to him at the computer terminal that he was using. Doug watched in amusement as Patrick furrowed his brows in thought and tried to find a suitable stopping point in his work.

"There," Patrick said with satisfaction as he looked up from his computer terminal. "Now, what can I do for you, Doug?"

"I hope I'm not interrupting anything Patrick. I could come back later if you like," Doug smiled

"No, no, I always seem busier than I really am. I need a break anyway. Would you like some ale?" Patrick offered as he got out of his seat and headed for his hidden liquor cache.

"Yes, thank you. The reason I'm here concerns my going back to my own dimension once the war's over. Do you think you could work on that for me?"

McIntyre turned to look at him, and gave Doug a bewildered look. Doug felt the emotions coming from Patrick and realized that something was wrong with him getting back home.

"Angus hasn't told you yet?" the old scientist asked grimly.

"Told me what?" Doug asked as the agitation of being left out of something crucial welled up inside of him.

"I'm sorry Doug, but travel to alternate dimensions doesn't exist. I noticed that something was wrong when I was working out the equations for you to get home. That's what the Council meeting is about."

"Then where did I come from?" Doug asked as his agitation was slowly turning to anger.

"It's quite complex, and I don't have all of the answers yet, but I'll do my best to give a possible explanation. It seems that the computer and probes we were sending out were altering the flow of time and the fabric of space, thus *creating* new dimensions, not discovering them."

Doug's anger subsided as the significance of Patrick's statement sunk in. Suddenly, he felt very insignificant as the enormity of what had happened became clear to him.

"That is quite amazing doctor. So what do we do now?"

"That's what the Council is going to decide. Should we try to collapse the dimensions we've created back into one, or quit messing around with it and hope it doesn't unravel further. You see, the fabric of space has been ruptured, and my bumbling with all this dimensional theory could potentially cause the entire universe to collapse in another twenty or thirty years."

"In that case, how can we be sure of which dimensional events are the real ones?"

"That's easy, this one. We started the fluctuations, so this is the correct turn of events."

"Time is a factor as well. You could have changed something crucial in your own dimension's past that caused it to be the way it is."

"I never thought of that. Dear God! Could it be possible that we are the cause of all our own problems?"

"Yes, but that doesn't matter. For whatever reason, some scientist began experimentation with what he thought was a dimensional transfer device, and wound up creating a big mess. It may not have even been you that assisted in the original experimentation."

"Well, at least I can be thankful that I might not have been the original man responsible for the end of the universe."

Doug laughed in spite of the dreadful news, and gave McIntyre a comforting pat on the back.

"We'll straighten it out. Do you have any ideas on how to fix it?"

"I'm almost positive that we can collapse the pseudo dimensions back into a singular dimension, but I don't know what effect that will have. We could all be living in a completely different world because of the independent changes that have been occurring in each pseudo dimension."

"Will anyone remember what happened, or will we all be unaware that any changes took place?" Doug asked hopefully.

"That's a good question. I have absolutely no idea. But I do have a theory."

"I thought you might," Doug smiled.

"You could be the only one who remembers what happened, since you are currently out of your own place of dimensional change."

"Well, there goes that idea. I was hoping I would forget the pain I feel."

"But then you would forget Moira, too," Patrick warned.

"Yes, I suppose it's better to remember how much I was able to have, even if it does hurt."

"I do think that you will be sent to the same time you left when we collapse the pseudo dimensions. The time flow is the one thing I can't even begin to figure out, but everyone has their own time signature, regardless of what dimensional fluctuations took place."

"So when will we begin all of the collapsing?"

"That's what the Council is going to decide."

⊕ ⊕ ⊕ ⊕ ⊕

Doug sat next to Paul and Angus during the Council meeting. The major problem was keeping the members of the Council in order. No one wanted the dimensional tear to cause further damage, but the division among the Council members was far worse than the fabric of space. Roughly half were for the collapsing of the alternate dimensions, another handful wanted to leave well enough alone, and the rest were swayed back and forth between the other two factions.

Angus tried to quiet the openly arguing mob, but without much success. Motioning to Doug, Angus sent a mental signal for him to try a more direct method of control. Doug was frustrated with the delay already, so he was glad for the opportunity to vent some frustration toward the stuffy old men.

Using his mental power to cause the Council members to hear his voice amplified, he stood and shouted,

"Enough! Stop your mindless bickering. Angus is still head of the Council; show him the courtesy of listening to him when he calls you to order!"

The startled Council members instantly fell silent and stared in disbelief at the towering figure standing before them.

"Thank you," Angus said calmly. "I think we can agree that the problem we now face is more urgent than the current war with the Overlord. Since none of you on the Council are qualified to give any scientific data to support your arguments, I think we should hear McIntyre's views first."

"He's the one who got us into this in the first place!" a greasy haired general snapped. He stood partially as if to say more, but slowly slunk back into his seat when he saw Doug glaring at him, daring him to say another word.

"Any other objections?" Angus asked in a level tone.

The Council members simultaneously gave a fearful glance toward the agitated Commander standing next to Angus. No one else dared to make any objections, as McIntyre stood.

"Ladies and gentlemen of the Council, I would like to start off by assuring you that Commander Taylor and I have went through the possibilities available to us, and have come up with only one option. We must collapse the pseudo dimensions back into one, or the universe will be destroyed in less than fifty years. If we delay too long, even collapsing the other dimensions may not help to mend the fabric of space.

Furthermore, our universe will drastically change when the merging takes place. We may have even been responsible for the creation of all our own problems. Our own timeline was affected during the experiments, so there's no way to be sure why the dimensional transfer processes were first attempted. A merging of the pseudo dimensions may very well erase the effects of the Ryeesian war, or erase Shaleese's domination."

"Are you saying that Shaleese will just disappear?" General Richards asked skeptically.

"That is a distinct possibility, General. Most likely, none of us will remember any change taking place, except for

Commander Taylor. He might remember since he currently is out of his own dimension of change."

"This is a fine mess you've gotten us into, McIntyre!" Kaufman, the greasy General burst out.

Doug was unable to control his blatant dislike of the slimy General any longer.

"There's no way of knowing whether McIntyre had anything to do with the original dimensional jaunting, since the time stream has been altered," Doug informed Kaufman in a low but deadly voice. "If any malice was involved with the original experiments, it would probably have been a worm like you who was responsible."

"That's enough Commander Taylor," Angus reprimanded calmly. "Kaufman may very well be a sniveling little worm, but he's still your superior officer, in title, anyway," he said with a small smile.

The expression on Kaufman's face showed that he was greatly offended by their comments, but he kept silent for fear of upsetting the living weapon that stood in front of him.

"All I want to know is when we're going to take care of Shaleese? I, for one, am ready to get him out of the picture permanently," Doug added.

"I'm sorry Commander, but I see no reason to risk lives on a mission that may be unnecessary after the dimensional collapse." Angus told him.

"No problem, give me a ship and I'll go by myself."

"I won't let you throw your life away."

"I'm not going back to my own time just to wait for this madman to pop up again! What happens if I lose the augmentations I've gained when we merge the dimensions together? Who's going to stop Shaleese then?" Doug asked with growing anger. "I won't let Moira's death be for nothing. I have to end it now."

"Alright, Doug, I'll take it under advisement."

"I know that you have all the authority on battle tactics, but the Council still has a say in which battles we fight," General Richards added as he worked his vast weight out of his chair to stand. "I say we let Doug lead a small force to attack Shaleese as an added precaution. If no one else will volunteer to go with him, I will. I may just be a fat old man, but I've still got a little fighting spirit left in me."

Several other Council members stood and acknowledged their desire to fight as well. Angus finally consented to help in the attack when nearly all of the Council was standing. Paul patted Doug on the back in congratulations, as the now eager Council began to animatedly discuss what plans to make for the all out attack on Shaleese. Looking at his best friend, he sent a mental picture to Paul of a tall glass of ale. Paul smiled, and the two friends headed for the door, leaving the strategy discussions to the Council.

Before they could reach the door, McIntyre walked in front of them, blocking their path.

"You're not going to get drunk without me are you?" the old doctor asked with a large smile on his wrinkled face.

CHAPTER 34

The upcoming battle would consist of nearly all the capital ships available. The eleven destructor class starships on New Haven would be joined by a total of six other destructors from the other bases, and one, slightly smaller, annihilator class cruiser. In addition to the heavy battle cruisers, ten of the light blitzkrieg class star cruisers would be aiding in the awesome onslaught, as well as several smaller frigates and destroyers.

The entire space assault would be a diversion for Doug and a small group of the more powerful telepaths. Doug was to infiltrate the fortress of Shaleese on Earth and try to kill him. The estimated ground force consisted of an entire Division of cyborgs, so Doug's new Wolf Platoon would wait for the massive warships to bombard the outer perimeter before attempting to infiltrate the fortress.

A direct space attack on the fortress would be a waste of time because of the immense armor plating and shielding. The cyborgs on the outer perimeter were set to guard the few entrances through the fortress' shield. Doug had been given a layout of Shaleese's stronghold from spy satellites and decided that Wolf platoon would advance through the old sewer system beneath the heavily armored citadel. The newly appointed Wolf Platoon wasn't delighted with their leaders' first tactical decision, but kept their remarks to themselves.

Doug was aboard the Gladiator along with Paul, Johann, Joseph, and Rick. Johann was the only one out of Doug's group of friends who wouldn't be accompanying the new Wolf Platoon, which contained almost all telepaths of some significance, to the surface of Earth. Rick had volunteered to be in the Wolf Platoon with Doug, and even though his mental ability wasn't as strong as the others, Doug was glad to have him along. The total complement of the Wolf Platoon was forty eight, so their was more than enough room for some of the lesser telepaths.

The journey to Earth would take over three days, so Doug decided to try relaxing. He wasn't sure how he was going to wind down, but slowly began to think of recreational activities he could draft his fellow wolf unit members into. General Richards had volunteered to man the bridge of the Gladiator, so Doug was free of any obligations during the journey. The Commander decided a few long games of poker were in order.

Doug went in search of poker players, only to run into two potential victims to his superior poker talent. Paul and his new fiancée Jenny were heading down the main corridor toward the galley. Doug could sense the intense bond between Paul and Jenny as they approached. He quickly suppressed his grief, as he was reminded of what he had shared with Moira. The irrational anger surged up in him as the young lovers approached, and he hastily erected a mental shield before Paul or Jenny could sense the growing envy welling up inside of him.

Paul saw Doug and headed toward his best friend. Doug felt the waves of affection emanating toward him, and the rage began to subside. The peculiar and irrational jealousy he felt for his best friend frightened him, but Doug was determined to overcome the rage, before a barrier could come between him and his friend. Pushing all the negativity away, he invited his friends to a poker game later in the evening.

Doug returned to his quarters to calm his emotions before they got out of control. He knew that lately his emotions had been fluctuating, but he had never in his life been so uncertain of whether or not he could retain control of his actions. The boiling hostility he periodically felt toward other people was so extreme that at times he was afraid of losing his sanity, as he had done on New Verdia. The battle with his inner demon had become more intense the harder he fought against it. If he couldn't find a way to nullify his wrath, he knew he would eventually succumb to the violent urges within him.

✤ ✤ ✤ ✤ ✤

Footsteps echoed on the floor, reverberating off the walls of the corridor. The long hallway was filled with the familiar objects that pulled at his vision, begging to be remembered. He glanced at some of the items around him, but failed to understand what meanings they held for him. He knew the objects were familiar items that he should recognize, but couldn't focus on the objects enough to discern their meaning.

As always, the corridor ended at the partially ajar doorway. Red smoke had replaced the orange and green mist that was usually there. He failed to make any connection to the significance of the color changes. He knew what awaited beyond the distant portal, and felt no urging to search the misty room again. Instead, he stopped to examine the corridor more closely than he had before. To his surprise, the corridor was far wider than it appeared. He walked to the wall on his right and discovered a row of five doors that he didn't remember from before.

Forcing his way through the middle door, he saw a large room with a table in the center as its sole adornment. To his astonishment, a cruel-looking version of himself was seated at the table and gestured for him to sit. A chess set was sitting on the table in front of him, and all of the pieces were of his friends and fellow soldiers. The opposing side consisted of friends as well. The king piece of each side was of himself, but they were different. His was a clear and well defined figure, and his opponent's was shadowy and distorted.

Looking up at his opponent in bafflement, he asked what he was supposed to do. His opponents voice cracked out the response in a hollow and lifeless voice,

"I can't tell you what to do, it's your move. Which piece do you wish to move?"

Doug awoke in a cold sweat as the vivid dream lingered in his mind. The dream seemed significant to his irrational surges of animosity toward friends and sheer bloodlust toward enemies. Doug got out of bed and paced the room in thought. He was determined to defeat the boiling rages once and for all. The answers were in his dreams, which meant that he subconsciously knew the answer already.

Doug looked at the embedded wall clock and noticed that his nap had only lasted a few minutes. The poker game he had set up with his friends wasn't going to take place for another few hours. He stepped into his showering unit to wash off the sweat that covered his body, and tried to think of what his dream meant. Thinking about his dream didn't help much, but he was certain the answers were all there.

Determined to find the answers he sought, Doug decided to force a longer sleep at night to have more chance of dreaming about his problem. Maybe the desire itself was enough to induce one of the strange dreams. One way or the other, he would find out what caused the anger, and how to stop it, or at the very least, how to control it.

The poker game was held at Doug's quarters. Even though Doug had called the players together, he felt despondent and wasn't in the mood to play the game. His friends were having a good time, so Doug was careful to shield his agitation from his friends. Paul and Jenny's bond wasn't as painful to witness, since it had been decided early on to make mental shielding a rule. It wasn't very fair to let the more powerful telepaths take advantage of their powers in the game. The odd combination of poker and telepathy gave new meaning to the term "poker face".

Doug began to loosen up after a few hands had been played. Focusing on the game helped to clear his thoughts from the problems that normally plagued his days. It was also amusing to play referee to the various forms of cheating that were available. Most of the telepathic cheating was accidental, but a few hands had to be thrown because the impulse to cheat was too tempting to resist.

Doug was the best at shielding his emotions, so he naturally won the majority of the hands dealt. No one could sense whether he had a good hand or not, and he could sense even the slightest twinges of elation or disappointment emanating from his opponents. Eventually, the other players realized that Doug would be able to catch any hints of emotion from them, and began to feel sour about the whole game. The fact that they knew their Commander also had a significantly higher level of intelligence didn't help matters either.

"This really sucks!" Paul finally stated. "You can sense every time I have a good hand or not, then you either call my bluff or fold!"

"I can't help it if you've got a pathetic shield, shorty," Doug said with open amusement. "I'm shielding my emotions, but I can't help picking up random slips from you and the others."

"That's not even the worst part," Joseph complained. "You also throw out false signals every now and then. One time, I know I had you beat, but you sent out an emotion of certain victory even though I'm sure you didn't have anything; then, the next time you did it, I thought I was calling your bluff, but it was genuine! You had three aces!"

"I was wondering if that had worked," Doug laughed. "It was very subtle, and I wasn't sure if you'd sense it."

"Well, I don't care how badly I got my ass kicked. It's good to see you smile again, Commander," Jenny added.

"You can call me Doug when we're not on duty, I'm not all that formal anyway," he grinned.

Doug felt the satisfied and happy emotions coming from his friends, and couldn't help but feel better than he had in a long time.

"Well, since I seem to have caused a slight ruffle in our game, I promise I'll work on a new type of game that's telepath proof," Doug said.

"Don't forget empath proof!" Joseph added in a slightly sullen tone.

The group of friends decided to quit their game since cheating was unavoidable and lounged in Doug's quarters to talk. Doug made coffee, and enjoyed Paul's surprise gift of a box of cigars. Rick abstained from the offer of joining in the smoking of a cigar but gladly accepted a mug of whiskey laced coffee. The rest of the group indulged in the rare treat of tobacco and soon had filled the room with a thick cloud of smoke.

The ship's automated ventilation system kicked on and attempted to purify the air as the room continually clogged with a fresh layer of smoke. The party-like atmosphere helped to calm Doug's fear that the happiness of others would trigger his irrational anger. Paul and Jenny's bond didn't seem to upset him either, and Doug was convinced that the rages he experienced weren't just a result of Moira's death, but from something else as well.

Doug felt relieved that his friendship with Paul was no longer threatened, but couldn't help wondering why he felt the overpowering anger. He was reminded of something McIntyre had said about pain and pleasure. Maybe his ability to love more deeply, as he had with Moira, had allowed him to hate more intensely. Doug thought briefly about the possibility, then dismissed it. There was nothing normal about his rages, and the love he had felt for Moira was too wonderful and pure to taint with such a vile notion.

Doug forced his problematic thoughts aside, and tried to enjoy the companionship of his friends. The coffee drinking had been abandoned, and had been replaced with the consumption of large quantities of the brown ale in Doug's cooler. Smiling, the stalwart Commander opened a case of bourbon and joined his friends in their drinking. Pushing all worries aside until later, he did his best to relax. He would find the reason for his irrational hate from his dreams, even if it meant he would have to sleep for a month.

Eventually the carousal died down, and the participants slowly but surely began to part. Doug was feeling very good about the evening in general as the last guests, Paul and Jenny, stood to leave. After thanking Doug for the evening's entertainment, they left. The evening had gone well, better than he had expected. During the first few hands of the poker game, the Commander had feared he might once again experience the extreme hostility toward his friends, or worse, suffer a relapse into the bestial rage that had overcome him on New Verdia. Despite his fears, the anger didn't surface. In fact, he couldn't even recall being even mildly agitated for the majority of the evening.

Doug sat by himself for a few moments, wondering if he had overreacted to the immediate seriousness of his previous "anger" episodes. He hadn't had difficulty the whole evening with his rages, so his friends hadn't been in any danger. He was still determined to find out where the anger came from, but felt a little more comfortable around his friends, secure in the knowledge that he could control any malice that issued forth from his sub conscious.

CHAPTER 35

The dream state began as soon as he drifted into sleep. The familiar hallway was before him, and the door he had entered last was glowing. He headed for the door, determined to overcome whatever challenges he faced. Reaching the door, he opened it and proceeded into to large room. His adversary looked up with a wicked grin as he entered and gestured for him to sit.

The chess set was the same, except that his opponent's figurines weren't defined in any detail, only in vague shapes. Doug was suddenly curious about his opponent's pieces, and began comparing them to his own. The pieces weren't the same. Some of his rival's figures were of similar shape and size to Doug's, but a few were different. He had a figure of Moira, his enemy didn't. Likewise, his enemy had pieces he didn't.

The game began, and Doug tried his best to win, but he didn't know any of the rules to the bizarre chess game. He began to get frustrated as he lost more and more of his pieces, until all of his original Wolf Platoon had been lost, save for himself and Moira. It wasn't his turn, and he knew Moira would be lost to him again, so he snatched the figurine of Moira, and held it protectively.

"You can't do that, old chap, that's cheating," his counterpart stated with a distorted and perverse grin.

"No! You can't take her! Any piece but this one!" he pleaded with tears filling his eyes.

"How do you expect to beat me, if you don't sacrifice a few pieces? That's how the game's played."

"I'll kill you before I let you take her from me!" Doug snarled as he leapt across the table at his adversary.

Doug was startled to discover that he had grasped at empty air, and looked up to see his opponent on the other side of the room.

"I win!" the hideously contorted face of his opponent shouted triumphantly.

Doug looked down at the figurine cradled gentle in his hands and saw that the face on the figure of Moira was screaming silently, and now had a Ryeesian claw emerging from her breast. The small figurine captured every detail of the agony she felt at that moment. Howling in fury, the grief stricken man fell to his knees as the memory of his wife's final moments flooded back to the surface of his mind, and the playing piece that represented his wife slowly crumbled to dust.

⁜ ⁜ ⁜ ⁜ ⁜

Doug awoke from his restless sleep with tears of pain running down his face. The violent craze started to boil inside him, but was quickly subdued by the agonizing grief he felt. He didn't want to get out of bed, but knew it was the best thing for him. The attack on Shaleese would take place the next day, and he knew he would have a life time to grieve afterward.

Not even bothering to shower, he headed for the ship's galley to get some breakfast and sort out the troubling images of his dream. It was still early, so the hallways of the ship were virtually unoccupied. He was at least thankful for that. Other people's hopeful and optimistic thoughts made him feel violent when he was depressed, so he wanted to avoid contact with anyone for as long as was possible.

The few occupants of the galley were still groggy, so their minds weren't very focused. Doug enjoyed the "mental silence" as he got a large mug of coffee to brood over. His dream still plagued him, and he wondered if it was possible to find a way to beat the adversary of his nightmares. Was he destined to have a reoccurring nightmare that would always end in agony? No, he knew that destiny was only a figment of a lesser mind's imagination. No one had a predetermined life; choices were always available. One merely had to accept the choices they had made, for good or bad.

Perhaps the nightmares could be willed dormant, so he would never again suffer during sleep. Doug continued to consider possible methods of approach to his dream problems but couldn't come up with a viable solution. Eventually he decided to leave it alone and hope his problem fixed itself. The resistance was counting on him to perform at his best during the upcoming battle with Shaleese. Doug was determined to make the universe a better place for the innocent people, even if he had failed to do the same for his own family.

Feeling slightly better about his most recent trauma, the stalwart Commander drained the last vestiges of coffee from his mug and headed for the bridge. Richards usually stood station on the bridge from early morning until late in the day, even during hyper travel. Doug hoped the General wouldn't mind company, because he was eager to talk with Richards about potential tactics of the soon to be present battle.

Doug arrived at the bridge and saw General Richard's rotund body cramped into the command chair. Richards was obviously too vast to fit properly in the average sized seat, but there was no where else to sit. Despite his enormous figure, Richards was one of the finest military men Doug had ever met. In a space battle, Richards lack of mobility wouldn't be an inconvenience, and with a ship at his command, his tactical genius was truly a dangerous weapon.

Richards sensed Doug's presence and swiveled the squeakily protesting chair towards the new arrival. He leveled a curious stare toward Doug as his keen observations of both mental and physical states, informed him that Doug was disturbed about something.

"What can I help you with, Doug? You seem upset," Richards deep voice rumbled.

"I just had a bad dream, it's nothing. I was wondering if you would be up to going over some of the battle plans with me. I may have your tactical knowledge, but not your experience."

"I thought you absorbed my experiences as well as the knowledge?"

"No two people think the same way. I have your memories and knowledge of tactical advantages in battle, but you may have a different approach to a ground assault due to the way your mind works."

"I think I understand. I would be delighted."

Discussing potential battle scenarios with Richards was exactly what Doug needed to subdue the pain he was feeling. Doug suddenly became cognizant of the simple answer to the success of taming his pain. He was experiencing extreme emotional loss, and logic was the opposite of emotion. The more he thought of the logical methods of attack, the less emotional pain he felt. As long as he could subjugate the excruciating agony from the loss of Moira's mental presence, he could deal with the rest of his pain. With chagrin he saw himself fifty years later, still consumed with working in order to hide from his pain.

Using logic to overcome Moira's death was a temporary solution, but at least he could use logic to focus his mind on defeating his enemy. The encounter with Shaleese demanded complete attention. Doug didn't want any distractions to enter into his private retribution on the Overlord. If he could maintain a logical approach, then he would be free of the overwhelming hate as well. Doug suddenly realized the true danger of his anger. Shaleese was filled with rage, and was thus consumed by insanity. If Doug gave in to his wrath completely, he would risk going insane as well. Perhaps it had to do with the corruptions of having too much power. Doug wondered if he had somehow gained more power than any human was ever meant to have and would have to fight the urges of abusing that power his whole life. Sickeningly, Doug realized that Shaleese was most likely a lot like himself, only too weak to contain the greater power and avoid corruption from it.

Richards had given him a few new ideas to mull over, so the Commander left the bridge to formulate his plan of attack. Doug knew that even with the entire resistance space force, they would only be able to hold off the enemy ships for a short time. The added might of telepathic assailants would help, but not enough for the resistance to hold their ground indefinitely. The strike had to be well planned and quick, a true blitzkrieg.

The fortress of Shaleese was situated on an open plain, so sneaking through the front door was nearly impossible. The best approach would be through the sewer system that was once used in New York city, and now directly under Shaleese's fortress. It was used by Shaleese for massive cyborg bunkers. At least the setting would be appropriate for the acrid cyborg reek that would invariably fill the enclosed tunnels. A connecting sewer entrance was located behind a pile of debris on the perimeter of the clearing around the fortress. Doug thought it ironic that one who claimed to be so powerful, would still feel insecure enough to have several tons of city debris cleared from his fortress' perimeter.

The remains of the vast city had been pushed outwardly from the fortress. The result was a large ring of city building debris that skirted the edges of Shaleese's grounds and formed a chaotic wall of defense. Fortunately, the debris was perfect cover for their landing craft, and for the entrance into the sewer access tunnels.

Time would be the crucial factor to their success. Shaleese had to be reached as quickly as possible and dealt with, before the resistance warships were overwhelmed. If he could not be reached in time, the Wolf Platoon would lose their ride home. The major time delay, aside from the trip to the surface of the planet, would be sneaking past the enemy bunkers. Doug was hoping that the majority of the cyborg troops, along with their operators, would be headed to the surface by the time Wolf Platoon reached the bunkers. Sneaking past telepathic enemies wasn't easily done.

The tunnel maps weren't absolutely accurate, so Doug made several plotted courses to prepare for collapsed caverns and memorized his back up plans in the event that certain passages were too heavily guarded. If all went well, they would reach the underside of Shaleese's fortress in thirty minutes. Angus had guaranteed a window of one hour, and potentially, could hold off the enemy warships for two hours. After the time allotted had expired, wolf team was on its own.

Doug felt ashamed as he reviewed the fortress statistics. The entire upcoming battle may never have been planned if he hadn't insisted on finishing off Shaleese. Many soldiers would lose their lives because of his petty need for revenge. He tried to convince himself that the battle was indeed necessary but continually reverted to his feelings of selfish guilt. The fact that Shaleese would cause no more harm to anyone after the fortress had been overrun was at least a small comfort. His own lust for Shaleese's death was still present, but he wished he didn't have to sacrifice any more soldiers in order to defeat his foe.

The young Commander's thoughts were interrupted by Paul's beckon at his door. His stocky friend entered the room with his face as dark as a thunder cloud. Still fuming as he paced around Doug's room, Paul seemed unable to voice the protest he had intended to register with his friend and superior officer. Doug could easily sense that the problem wasn't with him, but someone else that Paul was close to. Doug didn't need enhanced intelligence to discern that Paul's dilemma had to do with Jenny.

After pacing around the room for several minutes, Paul began to speak. "I won't let her, Doug. I want you to tell her she can't go. You out rank her. She won't have a choice if you order her to stay on the ship."

"I know how you feel, Paul, all too well. Have you tried reasoning with her?" Doug said calmly.

"She won't listen to me. She says she's going whether I like it or not."

"Then I guess she's going. I can't do anything to stop her."

"Order her to stay on the ship!" Paul fumed.

"I can't do that Paul. It would only cause resentment toward us both. She needs to be with you. I'm not going to let anything happen to either of you; and if I fail, you two would probably go with me. Would it be fair for her to live in pain without you? If you want to stay behind with her, I understand, but you either both go or both stay, no arguments and that's an order."

Paul glared at his friend for a few moments then forced himself to smile when he saw the set and determined expression on Doug's face.

"You always were a stubborn bastard. If anything happens to her I'm holding you responsible."

"The only way she's going to get hurt is if I'm dead, and the same goes for you. I've lost Moira because of my own deficiencies as a leader and husband; I can't afford to lose anyone else I care about. It wouldn't hurt the resistance too much to lose Kaufman though. Maybe we could bring him with us and put him in front?" Doug added wistfully.

Paul laughed and the two friends headed for the lounge in an attempt to relax before the up coming trial. The pressures of war seemed to be getting to everyone, and especially to those who were more sensitive to the emotional fluctuations of others. The irony of the problem was that almost all of the higher ranking officers were adepts at telepathy or empathy, and tended to take out their growing unease on their subordinates. That made the subordinates, who were unknowingly the cause of their officers' agitation to begin with, even more upset, thus making the problem worse.

Doug did his best to block out all of the negativity and focus on the now inevitable battle. He sincerely hoped it would be the last battle he would have to participate in, and hoped even more that it would be the last battle he had to lead. For the sake of any who had suffered under the tyrant, he also hoped they would succeed in issuing out some long overdue justice.

CHAPTER 36

eneral Richards surveyed the view screens in front of him. His vast bulk was wedged between the reinforced arms of his command chair. His face was dripping with sweat which he had tried more than once to wipe away without much success. The screens flashed with activity as the resistance's armada was battered by Earth's planetary defense's.

The rotund General knew that he was part of a delaying tactic to give Doug's unit time to take out the primary target, Shaleese. The only problem was getting the strike unit's ship to the surface before it was destroyed by the enemy. Even as he watched Doug's brilliant maneuvers on the screen, he was doubtful of success. The plan was for the small assault ship to pretend it was simply one of the many defending fighter craft, then simulate their destruction when close enough to make a run for the Earth's atmosphere.

Richards wondered if such an elaborate and monumental plan was attainable, even for Doug. So much was riding on that one young man. It was all well and good to think grandly in the Council room, and quite another to be present at the execution of those plans. The obese general laughed to himself with the thought of ALL generals and tacticians being placed in the most dangerous positions. Perhaps that would insure a good deal of conservative thinking in the planning rooms.

His retrospective thinking gave him a new found respect for the young Commander who was putting his life on the line in this full scale attack. Grasping tightly on the already askew arm rests, Richards watched as Doug narrowly escaped another onslaught from the enemy fighters.

"Send out the final detachment of fighters and send them to protect assault shuttle Omega five."

"But sir!" stammered a young bridge officer. "That will leave us defenseless to enemy fighter assaults!"

"I don't recall *asking* you if it was a good idea, Lieutenant. Do it now, or get off my bridge and send me someone who is capable of following simple orders!" Richards snapped.

He knew that all it would have taken was to mention that Doug was piloting Omega five, and everyone on the ship would have offered to sacrifice themselves to protect it. But only Wolf Platoon and upper staff that had the ability to shield their minds were privy to such knowledge. In fact, the majority of the resistance didn't even know Doug had left the flagship. The Lieutenant was stung by the sharp reprimand, but would eventually get over it.

The General's short temper was a direct result of his recent feeling of being small and insignificant, which was ironic considering his vast weight. He knew that even if every battle cruiser went down, it would be well worth the knowledge that Shaleese was also destroyed. Richards knew what had to be done at all costs, and that was provide time for the strike team to reach and neutralize the target. His secondary objective was simple, "try to stay alive while accomplishing the primary objective."

He watched as the reserve fighters rocketed toward the assault shuttle. Doug had already succeeded in evading and destroying half of the fighters that were dogging the assault shuttle. The few enemy fighters that remained were easily engaged and destroyed by the reserve fighters sent by Richards. The command crew of the flagship watched as the shuttle rocketed away from the mop up battle, and touched upon the fringes of Earth's atmosphere. The command crew had lost interest in the small shuttle and shifted their attention to the more ominous threat of nearby enemy warships, but Richards continued to watch the shuttle intently.

When the shuttle seemed to be well out of any danger, a shot flared out from one of the enemy craft that had broken through the resistance fighter defenses. Fumes began to trail from the damaged shuttle as smoke and oxygen were sucked out into the void of space through the lacerated hull of the shuttle. The cloud of smoke and chunks of newly frozen fluids that trailed behind the shuttle looked genuine. So real in fact, that Richards attempted to rapidly stand up in his dismay, only to be reminded of the limits of his immense size, as his wedged posterior pulled him back down into his command chair.

The gyrating shuttle began to descend rapidly into Earth's upper atmosphere, still spewing out smoldering particles which turned to ice so rapidly that there seemed to be tiny implosions all around the tail end of the crippled ship. As it plummeted toward the surface of the Earth, the ship began to glow from the friction of reentry. Finally with one last shudder the shuttle burst into a ball of fire in a explosion that extinguished rapidly due to a lack of oxygen. Richards continued to watch the view screens incessantly until the blue dot representing the shuttle on the tactical map blinked out, to signify that the craft no longer existed.

The General wiped a fresh layer of sweat from his forehead, and wondered if Doug's ploy had really worked or if he had been destroyed. He knew that there was no way to tell until Doug's unit sent out the signal that Wolf Platoon's mission was accomplished, or they all met again in the afterlife. Determined to give his best effort toward whatever end might come, Richards summoned up all of the remaining strength in his enormous body, and worked his way out of his chair.

"Call back the reserve fighters, and instruct them to cover our flanks. Change to course heading twenty five, sixty three, minus twenty two. When we get within range of the enemy cruisers, open fire with all guns on the nearest battle cruiser. Get the other cruiser's Captains on the view screen, except for Angus and the ships under his command, of course," he amended.

The startled command crew immediately began fulfilling the crisp and clear orders of the suddenly active General. Richards remained standing despite the growing strain on his legs. One by one, the other star cruiser Captains began to report in via the view screen designated for inter ship communications. Once all of the cruisers had reported in, Richards began.

"Gentlemen, the time has come for the 'final strike'. Some of you will understand that phrase, and for the rest who don't know what I mean, all you need know is that the playing pieces have been moved into a desperate position, and now we have to try and take the enemy's king before we lose ours.

"Destructor class cruisers one through six are to fall in behind me as I come through into your sector. When I give the signal each ship will devote half of its telepaths to wiping out the weapons and defense controllers on the target ship. With a little luck we can systematically destroy several of their heavy battle cruisers before they catch on to what were doing. The rest of the cruisers, whether Destructor class or not, will continue to fight off the fighters and subsidiary cruisers in the conventional fashion, but keep an eye on our backs. Don't let any enemy warships sneak up behind us. Angus should finish with the barrage on the fortress perimeter in less than half an hour. If we can hold out that long we may have a chance. Let's do our best to win this war. Doug and Angus are doing their part so let's do ours."

The other captains acknowledged their orders and signed off. Richards remained standing and followed the strategic movements, of both friend and foe on the tactical view screen. Aside from the occasional tactical suggestion to other cruiser Captains, Richards remained silent, always glancing toward the blue and white planet that they were fighting for. He knew that unless Doug was able to defeat Shaleese and find a way to help the struggling cruisers, the resistance was doomed. There were simple not enough ships to defeat over thirty superior enemy battle cruisers.

They could hold off their defeat for a short while, but there wasn't much hope of conquering an enemy which out gunned them well over five to one. If Doug had made it to the planet's surface, and by some stroke of luck did overcome the tyrant, he would still need a ride home. Richards was determined to be there when Doug succeeded.

⁂ ⁂ ⁂ ⁂ ⁂

Wolf Platoon had left the flagship and was now heavily engaged with enemy fighters. Doug was piloting the assault shuttle and operating the forward guns, while Paul was acting as the gunner for the single turret mounted to the top of the assault craft. The assault shuttle's maneuverability was poor to say the least. Even Doug's superb piloting skills were taxed to their limit. Not only did he have to stay alive long enough to escape into Earth's atmosphere undetected, but he also had to make it look as if he was barely escaping annihilation during each encounter.

The remainder of Wolf Platoon was indeed quite nervous. The Wolf members were simply a group of ground soldiers used to being in action, not sitting ducks in a vessel they weren't in control of. When the individual soldiers weren't in control they were as vulnerable as a novice Cadet, and not one of them was happy about it. The shaking and shuddering of the small craft carrying them didn't help the situation either. Rick, Jenny, and Joseph were huddled against the bulkhead of the shuttle next to the cockpit entrance.

Jenny got continual updates from Paul whenever the situation would change, and she shared any new information with Rick and Joseph. Paul wasn't aware of the fact that Doug was consciously trying to make each encounter look like a close call, so, from his perspective, things weren't going well, and he said as much to Jenny through their bond. The result was the general dismay of all Doug's companions. Emotional fluctuations of any kind were difficult for Doug to manage, and he quickly got tired of their doubts and fears.

The comm crackled as Doug's voice snapped onto the loud speaker.

"Knock it off, Jenny! That goes double for you Paul! This isn't easy, and your continual observations are causing a lot of emotional feed back for me to deal with.

If it feels bumpy back there, I'm sorry, but I have to make it look like we're barely escaping, even though I could take out all of the enemies dogging us with ease. We're going to reach the surface on schedule, even if I have to float us down in a telekinetic bubble; so quit feeling sorry for yourselves!"

The group of friends stared sheepishly at each other feeling guilty for having doubts about their Commander. Paul and Jenny simultaneously sent out an apologetic thought to Doug, and were rewarded with a calm and gentle, *"No problem, just don't let it happen again,"* followed by the mental equivalent of a laugh. As a result of the Commander's unshakable determination and resolve, the tension level in the shuttle dropped almost immediately.

Doug continued his barrage on the enemy fighters, once again jolting his passengers with a sharp turn to avoid destruction from the enemy fighters' strafing. He knew the plan they were attempting was ludicrous, and near impossible for an ordinary pilot to endeavor, much less pull off. But he also knew he was far from ordinary. Once their shuttle had reached the Earth's uppermost atmosphere, he would combine technology developed by McIntyre and his own telepathic abilities.

Doug had discovered that the enemy telepaths were eager to sense the demise of their prey. They waited in anticipation for the mental anguish produced from the combined physical agony of death and the mental anguish that ran through the victims heads as they lost their lives in a fiery explosion. Doug was disgusted by the apparent cruelty of his foes but knew they were merely emulating their perverse master. He also knew that he would need to simulate their own death throes for the expecting enemy.

The Commander had considered the viable alternatives to actually dying in order to produce such an emission. He had considered simulating his death by emitting the pain he felt from Moira's absence, then decided he wasn't willing to give his enemy any such satisfaction. Doug finally decided that he would single out the enemy telepaths focusing on the shuttle, and implant in their minds a "pseudo" anguish, similar to one they had felt previously.

The physical evidence of the shuttle's existence would be falsified with less effort. McIntyre had devised a combination of holographic display on a grand scale and a cloaking device. As an extra added touch, Doug had suggested that the cargo area be partitioned off and the rear quarter of the shuttle be filled with a condensed smoke and lubricating fluid. The rear cargo access panel was then reconfigured to open only a small fraction, which would allow the cargo contents to leak out into space for a simulated hull breech.

With all of the elements combined, and Doug shielding the presence of himself and his team, they would hopefully reach their landing point undetected. Doug was prepared to fight his way to Shaleese if necessary, but he prayed that his team would reach the fortress unhindered. Time was the crucial factor, and the fewer the losses along the way the better.

Five enemy fighters rocketed into the sector and engaged the shuttle. The shuttle's distance to the Earth's atmosphere was less than twenty kilometers, so Doug decided to punch through the fighters and rush for the safety of Earth. Before he could succeed in breaking through, a squad of deltas roared into the fray. The help wasn't needed but it was greatly appreciated. Wolf Platoon's path was now unhindered.

In a rare display of creative style, Doug used his power to prod the telepath controller to attempt one last shot at the shuttle. The last remaining fighter under the enemy telepath's control fired a desperate shot toward the shuttle, and Doug swerved into it, allowing the assault shuttle to be hit. The small craft easily absorbed this first hit, but to onlookers, it was a crucial and final blow.

Engaging the computer sequences for the simultaneous holograph and cargo exhaust, Doug prepared to warp the minds of the inquisitive enemy. While veering erratically, Doug reached out to the minds of the telepaths. He resisted the urge to simply kill them, since it would draw attention to other telepaths, and instead altered the memories of the three expectant enemy commanders. Until their last days, those three commanders remembered with vivid detail the agony of the shuttle crew. They also never forgot how disappointing that sensation was. Instead of remembering it as one of the pleasures they had grown to anticipate and enjoy, it was forever a memory of disgust and revulsion.

Satisfied with his venture into mental tampering, Doug waited patiently as the holographic sequence began its climax, and then while engaging the cloaking device, he punched the shuttle to full throttle. By the time the illusionary explosion had died down, the shuttle was well within the Earth's atmosphere, and shielded from the naked eye by thick layers of cloud. Set with a new course heading, the shuttle deviated from its plummeting dive into a level descent, with the ending point at the perimeter of what had once been New York city.

The Shuttle landed among the wreckage of old skyscrapers and commercial buildings, which had been mercilessly shoved aside to make room for the vast fortress in the center of the city. Wolf Platoon disembarked in silence. The squeaking protest of the shuttle's bay doors swinging open, and the distant rumble of particle cannon fire hitting shielded metal were the only audible sounds. Decked in full combat armor, Wolf Platoon acknowledged their leader's hand gesture and followed him from the shuttle toward the old sewer entrance.

Paul, standing amid his future wife and his best friend, stared at the ominous fortress, and pushed all fear aside. There was no turning back. Only determination and resolve would see the Wolf members safely through the day. Resolve and an undefeatable Commander who would make sure that they all lived to see the end of the war.

CHAPTER 37

After several minutes of searching, Doug finally found a sewer access tunnel that the team could use. The Platoon of forty eight telepaths headed into the gloom behind their Commander. All soldiers had their particle rifles ready, eager for the chance to use them. The cramped tunnel soon widened into what appeared to be an old railway system, and the squad immediately formed a phalanx that allowed for flank guards on both sides, as well as a small rear guard to make sure no enemy soldiers would sneak up on them from any hidden cracks or crevices.

Doug guided his squad through endless turns through side passages and reeking sewers, both narrow and wide. There was no hesitation from the Commander in his decisions to alter their course, but the rest of the Platoon was quickly lost amid the underground labyrinth. Even though they knew it had only been little more than fifteen minutes in the reeking underground, it seemed to the Wolf team as if they had been trudging through the filth of the sewers for hours.

All of the soldiers were doing their best to shield their presence from Shaleese, but Doug took the brunt of the shielding upon himself. The closer they got to the passages under the fortress, the more difficult it was for Doug to keep his shield intact. The Commander careened as he felt for the first time the powerful mind of Shaleese. The jabbing mental probing was causing Doug to sway back and forth as they trudged along. The probing was intense and uncomfortable, but Doug's swaggering was more a result of an inner battle with his emotions, and not merely his difficulty in fending off the mind of Shaleese.

As Shaleese's mind swept over the shield Doug had raised, the Commander felt scarcely controllable urges to lash out at the hideously evil mind. His rational mind told him that it was tactically unsound to attempt any mental attack on Shaleese from a distance, but his emotional mind cried out for a raging vengeance. The logical side won the battle for once, as he told himself that he wanted to see the agony on Shaleese's face when he realized he was going to die. The inner turmoil didn't cease entirely, but it was lessened enough for Doug's staggering to stop.

After treading through the sewer system for nearly half an hour, Doug called the company to a halt. They were approaching the eastern bunkers of the cyborg soldiers, and Doug detected activity with his enhanced senses and mental powers. The team gathered into a circle as Doug spoke in a quiet but deadly voice.

"All right. We've reached the eastern bunker, and there are still some enemy troops occupying the bunker. I'm not sure how many troops there are, but we'll find out before we attack. Joseph, I need you to search for the enemy telepath controlling these troops. Read his mind and tell me how many troops there are."

"Yes sir," Joseph replied with a slightly sullen tone.

Joseph resented his telepathic powers and the new found responsibility they placed on his shoulders. He didn't like being singled out, and aside from Moira, he was the most powerful of the telepaths that Doug had enhanced. Nonetheless, he always obeyed orders without question, and when Doug issued orders, he didn't even complain about his duties even in retrospect.

Joseph sent out his thoughts toward the bunker, and easily singled out the active mind of the sole telepath. A quick scan of the enemy's mind revealed the information Joseph sought, and also caused Joseph to let out a soft chuckle. Pulling his mind back, he gave his report to Doug.

"Well I've got good news and bad news. The bad news is that there are still eighty troops in the bunker. The good news is that most of them are only half functional, and the telepath is scared shitless. She seems to feel that she doesn't deserve to be left down here with semi functional freaks, while her sick buddies are topside with the fresh freaks."

"Well, she might feel differently if she was topside getting shot at by the strike force Angus is leading," Paul added.

"Do you think we could circumvent the fighting by eliminating the telepath now? The cyborgs might not attack if they aren't told too by one of Shaleese's lackeys," Doug asked.

"I don't think that would work. I got the impression from the telepath that they will attack anything that moves except her. There seemed to be a momentary delight when the freaks were running into each other while trying to chase down a rat that had stumbled across their path. She must have already given them the order to fight," Joseph answered.

"That's an interesting solution to pest control. We have to do it the hard way. Let's take out our telepath in advance anyway. We're almost there, let's not get sloppy."

"Except for the gal's exploding head you mean?" Joseph said in angry disgust.

"I am surprised that the telepath is a woman, all the rest we've encountered have been men, but that doesn't change the fact that this is war."

"No, Doug; I said gal, not woman. This telepath is only a fourteen year old girl. If you want to kill her, go ahead; but I'm not going to kill a little girl, no matter how sick and perverse her mind has become."

"Don't kill her then, but at least knock her unconscious. You're not doing her a favor by letting her live. Shaleese corrupts anything he gains possession of."

"Damn it, Doug! Don't ask me to do this! Why don't you knock her out?" Joseph hissed.

"I'm sorry, Joseph, but I have to keep us shielded from Shaleese. You're the only one subtle enough to handle this task and you're not powerful enough to shield us from Shaleese."

"I don't like it, but I'll do it. I know it *is* the only way. I just wish it wasn't me that has to hurt the little girl."

"Don't worry; when we get to Shaleese, I'm going to take it out on his hide," Doug snarled softly with a gleam in his fierce eyes.

Joseph had reluctantly knocked the girl unconscious, and Wolf Platoon was preparing to execute their plan of attack. Doug refused to remain out of the fighting even though he was limited by his duty of maintaining their shield. Their attack plan was simple. They would rush in and mow down as many cyborgs as possible, then shift to hand to hand combat if any cyborgs charged through. The odds were less than two to one in the enemy's favor, and Cyborgs weren't very effective fighters unless their numbers were far superior.

The bunker was less than thirty yards away, and situated in an alcove of the tunnel Wolf Platoon was traveling through. Trying to sneak past was out of the question. The barracks were set up without a wall or door on the tunnel side, and every cyborg would have a clear view of the passing team. Doug felt uneasy as they approached the cyborg bunker. He knew that out of the entire mission's duties, this assault would most likely be the easiest, but he hesitated to give the order to attack.

With a sudden clarity, Doug and Joseph looked at each other in amazement as they both discovered that their inhibitions had physical merit. Doug shouted for everyone to fall back, and began to push and prod his startled troops away from the bunker. Taking a rough count of his troops, Doug realized that Joseph was missing from the huddled mob of startled soldiers.

The Commander turned toward the cyborg laden barracks even as the rest of his team fled in confusion deeper into the tunnel. He raced back for Joseph, but was thwarted in his attempt as the entire tunnel seemed to burst into flame. A deep rumble had began to oscillate into a deafening roar in the distance. Flames licked the walls of the tunnel as the pressure in the tunnel began to build. The ceiling was crumbling fast, threatening to give way entirely.

Doug stared in amazement as the catastrophe took place before his eyes. With all of his might, he erected a telekinetic barrier to keep the passage open as long as possible, and to keep the flames from coming any further down the shaft. Knowing that his continued effort was futile, he began to retreat away from the bunker in slow but steady strides. Just as the ceiling was about to give way, Joseph appeared from around the corner carrying a small girl in his arms.

Flames licked at Joseph's heels as he ran, but none of the fire seemed to harm him or the girl in any way. Doug held the passage open as Joseph ran through, then followed his friend as fast as he was able. Just as they had reached the joining railway tunnel, the entire bunker and surrounding sewer tunnel collapsed in a reverberating crash. Doug looked up to see that all of Wolf Platoon had succeeded in reaching the railway tunnel, which still remained intact for the most part.

The force of the pressure in the collapsing sewer system had knocked most of the team members unconscious, and all but Doug were, at the least, stunned. The team was in no shape to move out immediately, and they had lost ground. They couldn't proceed the way he had first intended, and would have to back track to a connecting passage that would lead to the west bunker system. Even if that passage wasn't blocked it would take at least twenty minutes to reach, which gave more time for Shaleese's armada to pick off the resistance cruisers.

Doug cursed at the misfortunes they had encountered. He had hoped to arrive at the fortress and stop Shaleese quickly to minimize the casualties, but now there was little hope for Angus and Richards. Doug looked over his crew, and noticed that the majority were beginning to stir. Expanding his shield to cover the now conscious Platoon, the Commander went to check on Joseph and his ward.

The Commander looked with disapproval at the young girl Joseph had risked his life to save. His disapproval quickly turned to remorse. The teenage girl was slender and pretty, with the face of a complete innocent. The remorse was for the grotesque features that would contort her beautiful face when she awoke. He couldn't help being reminded of Moira as he looked at her. This young girl could have been his daughter one day, if Moira had lived. Whispering quietly to the unconscious girl, he promised to avenge her.

✤ ✤ ✤ ✤ ✤

General Richards was sweating profusely as he watched the progress of the assault. He was surprised to find that the resistance was doing far better than he had ever thought possible. Five of the enemy battle cruisers had been destroyed by the combined effort of Destructors one through six, and the other cruisers had managed to take out another battle cruiser and several strike cruisers. Resistance casualties had been limited to smaller craft and fighters.

The General knew that their luck wouldn't hold for long. Even as he thought about the next possible course of action, the enemy battle cruisers were grouping together. The fact that the enemy capital ships were spread so far apart was the only reason the original strike had been effective. Even at two to one odds in their favor, a destructor class attack ship couldn't hope to overcome the superior fire power of the enemy capital ships, and they were still out shipped as it was.

The shortage of telepaths on board the enemy ships made their fighters virtually ineffective, while the resistance had a distinguishable over abundance of operational fighter craft, and that was an advantage Richards intended to utilize to its utmost potential. Visualizing the potential movement of the enemy cruisers, Richards decided that the Destructors were in a position to wreak havoc on the enemies smaller craft, and yet still vulnerable to the deadly fire power of the larger cruisers. He wasn't sure of how much time Doug would need to complete his mission, so he was unsure of the end result of moving into a desperate position. If Doug succeeded in less than thirty minutes, they would still have time to extract Wolf Platoon and withdraw before they were overrun by the enemy.

The rotund General shifted his weight as his right leg began to grow numb. He decided to make the bold maneuver and risk the loses. If the enemy cruisers took the bait he would succeed in crippling the smaller vessels and to potentially damage some of the capital ships heavily.

"Get the other captains on the comm," Richards barked.

"Yessir."

The comm screen crackled, and the captains' faces rapidly appeared one by one.

"Every ship is to withdraw at once. I'm sending each ship a set of coordinates, change your courses and withdraw at full speed. Send all of your available fighters to engage the enemy battle cruisers. They won't be very effective at first, but they're too small to hit without opposing fighter craft, and they may be able to damage a few capital ships. All of the strike cruisers are to rendezvous with Angus and back him up if he needs it."

Richards bent to the control panel on the arm of his chair, rapidly punching in coordinates for the cruisers under his command. With a great effort he managed to keep from falling onto the chair. Once he had finished relaying the coordinates, he wiped the sweat from his face, and looked at the young Lieutenant.

"Don't we have air conditioning on this bridge?!" he said sarcastically.

"Begging your pardon, General, but are we retreating?" the Lieutenant asked.

"No lad, just baiting the hook."

The Destructors had seemingly withdrawn, but the vectors of their retreat converged in the distance, so that the farther they got from the enemy, the closer they were grouped into several small clusters of ships. As Richards had hoped, the enemy was deceived. In their arrogance, Shaleese's Admirals thought the resistance was retreating, and sent their smaller strike vessels into pursuit, with a detachment of capital ships not far behind.

As the destructors' vectors began to merge, the enemy strike cruiser captains began to notice the flaws in their own space command's thinking and also began to realize the danger they were in. The smaller strike cruisers were faster, but were no match for the destructors by themselves. The larger enemy cruisers were not only slower than the destructors, but were harried by the fighter squadrons and had little hope of reaching their strike cruisers in time.

Richards watched as the enemy strike cruisers began to slow down as they realized their eminent destruction, then signaled to the destructor captains for a full about face and attack. The resulting annihilation of the strike cruisers was extraordinary. Each cluster of destructors singled out a strike cruiser, destroyed it, then moved on to the next target. Within a few minutes, all of the strike cruisers chasing the destructors had been laid to ruin.

Richards let out an explosive breath as the results of his planning came to fruition. He was still sweating heavily, and now his legs were beginning to wobble from the strain of supporting his immense bulk, and his arm ached from leaning on the chair's arm rest. He stared at the tactical screen and noticed that the enemy battle cruisers were still advancing through the barrage of the delta fighters. Richards smiled as he witnessed the overpowering arrogance of his enemy. The number of Capital ships deployed by the enemy was equivalent to his own numbers, and the enemy's cruisers were still being harried by the deltas. Once the destructors engaged the battle, the enemy's cruisers wouldn't stand a chance.

Now the only concern was Angus. His armada was still in orbit around the planet and was being engaged by the remaining enemy cruisers. Angus would have to retreat and regroup with the main fleet. The dozen enemy cruisers that were assaulting the planetary cruisers could manage to take out half of Angus' strike force. Richards knew he would have to send the deltas to cover Angus' retreat, but was hesitant to leave the enemy cruisers closing on him a clear path.

His arm hurt, and his legs were straining to support him. He knew Angus needed the fighters more than he did, and was preparing to send the order when the aching in his arm began to spread to his chest. The heart attack was unavoidable, but he hoped he would at least be able to hold out for a while longer. Richards collapsed into his command chair, nearly crushing it as he fell.

"Send the deltas to help Angus," he wheezed. "Then prepare for the enemy cruisers' attack."

The startled Lieutenant looked at Richards, then called for the medical staff frantically. Richards vaguely remembered the young Lieutenant ordering the deltas to help Angus, but couldn't pry his eyes from the tactical screen, as he watch the trailing ship in Angus's fleet take heavy damage to its right flank as it veered away from the enemy cruiser attacking it. The cruiser had a large hull breech in the right bow of the ship and another in the right aft section.

The medical staff set up a quick monitoring unit on the obese General, and did their best to sustain his life. The last thing Richards saw, before he lost consciousness, was the resistance strike cruiser Ganymede plummeting toward the surface of the Earth. The General smiled. He was unconcerned with the alliance of the ship he watched the red and white glow on the screen as the Ganymede burned during its reentry to Earth. The fact that Doug could be hit by the falling ship didn't even register in the dying General's mind. Richards' vision blurred, and the beautiful blue/red color of the Ganymede superimposed onto the Earth was the last thing the General saw.

CHAPTER 38

Doug picked up the young girl into his arms and cradled her close to him, as if by simply holding her he could mend all of the damage Shaleese had done. He carefully reached out to her mind, expecting to see a shattered and fragmented memory with an immense cruelty as the only dominant thought. He was surprised to find that aside from countless memories of unspeakable acts, her mind was completely normal.

Frantically, he searched for any sign of an implanted device that would harm her if he continued to probe her mind. The Commander nearly shouted for joy as he realized there wasn't any bomb or similar contraband. With a deep sigh, he utilized the full extent of his powers and scoured her mind. After several minutes, his search revealed that the poor girl had no idea of what she had done. Somehow, her actions were a direct result of being exposed to Shaleese, and as long as she was shielded from him, she wouldn't feel compelled to commit the atrocities that Shaleese derived so much pleasure from.

Doug knew that when she awoke, she would be instantly revolted by all of the hideous acts she had taken part in. He couldn't bare the thought of the young girl being in pain, so he did the only thing that he could think of to protect her from Shaleese's perversions. He tried to convince himself that erasing the majority of her memories was a necessity, but he still felt ashamed of what he did. She wouldn't remember anything that had taken place for several years of her life good or bad, but at least she wouldn't suffer guilt and shame for acts of unspeakable perversions that had not been her fault.

After he had purged her mind of the filth that Shaleese had given her, he sent out a gentle waking signal, which roused her from her unconscious state. She opened her eyes slowly and blinked at him sleepily.

"Where am I? I,...,I don't seem to remember where I am?"

Doug gazed momentarily into the pair of blue eyes that stared at him with complete trust. In those eyes he could see his wife, and all of the sons and daughters that he would never have with his beloved Moira. Instead of grief, a paternal tenderness issued forth, and he spoke soothingly to the young girl who was still in his arms.

"It's going to be all right, Cory. You were in an accident, but you're fine now, and as long as I'm here, you won't need to worry about getting hurt again."

She smiled at him warmly, and nestling herself in his arms, fell immediately back to sleep. The Commander felt a warmth in his heart that he had never dared to hope he would ever feel again. Doug felt like he had a chance to redeem himself by caring for and protecting Cory, the way he should have been able to for his own child. Cory would need someone to take care of her during her recovery, and if she would allow it, he wanted her to be a part of his family.

His growing love for the young girl named Cory suddenly evoked a great wrath from somewhere deep inside him. His entire being cried out for the total and absolute annihilation of the man responsible for the torment Cory had been subjected to. Doug was able to partially suppress his rage, but he knew that when the time came, Shaleese would face the wrath of hundreds of thousands of tormented souls all channeled into one man. Doug could feel the rage fighting to get loose, and for once, he was glad it was there.

Doug gently laid Cory onto the ground, so she could sleep in peace. He looked up to see that the entire wolf team was staring at him, some with looks of admiration for his tenderness, and some with open amusement. The majority of the team found it hard to believe that their formerly rigid Commander had shown such compassion and warmth, but those who knew Doug best were gladdened to see him return to what they considered his normal behavior. Joseph and Paul looked at Doug with amusement, silently mocking him with their glances, for his hypocrisy.

"So what now, fearless leader?" Joseph teased.

"Now, we proceed with our mission. What are our casualties?"

"Aside from a few bruises, none," Paul answered as he got up to his feet with a subdued grimace of pain.

Jenny wasn't about to let Paul act like nothing was wrong, and told him so with a glower that contained worlds of information.

"I might have left out that my arm is broken, but it's not that bad. Just a clean break along the left ulna," Paul quickly amended after his eyes caught Jenny's gaze.

"Bad or not, a broken arm means you stay behind, shorty, and you staying behind means that Jenny and Joseph stay behind as well."

"Why do I stay behind too?" Joseph asked angrily. "I can understand keeping Paul and Jenny together, but I'm going with you!"

"No, you're not, and that's an order!" Doug replied in a cool but deadly voice. "I need you to shield the people who stay behind, including Cory. You're the only one who has enough power to block out Shaleese's probing. He isn't focusing very hard on this area because of the collapse, so you should be able to shield a non-moving party. Besides, the smaller the number I have to protect from Shaleese, the greater my chances."

Joseph remained silent, but he stared hard at the unyielding Commander in front of him. He knew that Doug was right, but he also knew that as soon as the fat was all the way in the fryer, Doug would leave behind whoever he took with him. With his closest friends out of the way there would be no one stubborn enough to object. Joseph silently cursed at the convenience of the situation, and sat down next to Cory in frustration. His suspicions were confirmed as he watched Doug select the most easily intimidated soldiers to accompany him. The end result was a nearly clean split of twenty five to accompany Doug, and the remaining twenty two standing guard over the injured.

Joseph had complete confidence in Doug's abilities, but he still didn't trust Shaleese to fight fairly. Since there was nothing else he could do, Joseph stood and wished his Commander good luck. His Commander rewarded him with a reassuring smile.

※ ※ ※ ※ ※

The Pegasus had narrowly escaped destruction, and the Admiral commanding the ship was still quivering from the resounding blows the battle cruiser had sustained. Angus forced a state of calmness over himself, and surveyed the tactical battle screen. He was satisfied with the overall outcome of the current battle. Richards had managed to eliminate several enemy battle cruisers and send aid to the planetary strike cruisers in the nick of time.

Having regained his composure, Angus ordered for a change of coordinates. The strike cruisers would be needed to reinforce the main armada, and Angus wanted to waste as little time as possible. Angus marveled at the successes the resistance was having, and hoped that Doug would do as well. The Admiral knew the resistance was depending heavily on luck, and he fervently hoped that it wouldn't run out until after the battle was won.

With chagrin, the Admiral realized that their luck had indeed run out. Three large red dots appeared on the tactical view screen just beyond firing range of the main fleet, signifying that three new enemy vessels had hyper jumped and entered into the fray. Angus felt his hopes being dashed even as he ordered the new arrivals to be displayed on the view screen. Three immense warships were displayed on the view screen, and the entire crew gasped with astonishment. Each enemy vessel was literally the size of a small city, and bristled with large guns.

Angus stared at the view screen trying his best to come up with a plan of action. He had heard the rumors from resistance spies and informants of a new type of warship being built, but had dismissed the figures of size as an exaggeration. When faced with the actual size of the warships, he couldn't help but wonder if the figures had been understated instead of embellished. They were called dreadnought class battle cruisers and had been built under contract for Shaleese. The end result of the project was a space craft that looked like a mobile fortress.

"Get me Richards on the comm," Angus ordered hastily.

After a brief interval of time, the comm officer turned to Angus with his face pale and full of dismay.

"Sir! General Richards is unconscious and in critical condition!"

"What! Did they take a hit on the bridge?"

"No, he's had a heart attack. They have him in the ships infirmary, but they don't know if he'll pull through."

"Damn that fat old fool, he was our best hope. Who's in command of the Gladiator?"

"Captain O'Donnell, sir."

"Get us back to the main fleet as soon as possible, and alert the other ships that I'm taking command of the fleet immediately."

Angus stared at the hulking ships on the view screen, knowing in his heart that unless Doug could find a way to help them soon, they would all perish. The enemy's new battle cruisers were an unknown variable. There was no telling of what they were capable of, or whether they had any discernible weaknesses. The only chance of even staying alive would be to run away while the delta fighters attempted a strafing run. If they were lucky, a weakness might be found and exploited.

"Send out the signal for all destructors and strike cruisers to pull away from those dreadnoughts as soon as possible. Once everyone is clear, we'll send in the deltas. I want all telepaths to prepare for enemy fighter assaults. We have to slow those monsters down or we'll be annihilated," Angus ordered.

After a thought filled pause, Angus decided that they also needed to know more about the dreadnought class cruisers.

"Lieutenant Zimmerman, give me an analysis of any data you can gather on those cruisers. I want you to gauge their speed, and calculate how much energy it would take to move one of them at that speed, then cross reference that with their estimated mass in a space environment and their energy signature."

"That was a mouthful," Johann said with a grin, then remembered to add, "Sir."

"I think I liked you better before Doug came and changed you," Angus said sarcastically, but with a small smile forming at the corners of his mouth.

⊕ ⊕ ⊕ ⊕ ⊕

Doug had left his friends in safety behind him, and planned to leave the rest of his unit behind at the next available opportunity. Once he was sure that he could reach Shaleese on his own, there would be no need to bring others any further. Doug knew that his conflict with Shaleese would boil down to a one on one battle; auxiliary soldiers in such a battle would be a pointless waste of life. The only obstacle he would face, was that Shaleese placed no value on any life but his own, and therefore, tried to overwhelm any opponents with sheer numbers.

Doug had deduced that Shaleese's arrogance would only permit ceremonial guards at his side since he thought himself so powerful. So the resistance Commander had decided to risk going into the final battle alone. It was the only way to ensure the safety of his troops and friends.

Doug knew the entire layout of the fortress by memory, and led his unit to an antechamber of the main compound. Once they reached the chamber, he would then head to Shaleese's throne room, which was only a few meters further to the west. He also knew that if they could reach the antechamber with a minimal amount of noise, he would be able to proceed without much hindrance. Doug was fully confident that he would be able to handle any further opposition alone.

The remainder of Wolf Platoon moved with the greatest stealth they could manage, and Doug could feel the mind of Shaleese weighing down heavily upon his mental shield. Shaleese's active mind wasn't focused on the fortress perimeter, but Doug sensed that his opponent knew a ground assault team had landed somewhere on Earth. Shaleese's arrogance dismissed the ground team as a minor threat, and he only kept a partial watch on the perimeter out of curiosity. Even with a reduced intensity, the probing mind of Shaleese was powerful enough to cause Doug a great deal of discomfort.

As the team passed through a small alcove, Doug surmised that years of paranoid delusions had sharpened Shaleese's awareness of his surroundings. There probably wasn't a single rat in the fortress that hadn't been observed by Shaleese's watchful mind. Doug began to wonder why someone who was arrogant enough to believe himself invincible would be so paranoid about a sneak attack but couldn't come up with a logical reason. Shaleese seemed to be a living oxymoron, thinking himself indestructible and yet being a coward at the same time.

The team reached the antechamber and Doug signaled for everyone to halt and secure the area. After the antechamber had been searched and perimeter guards had been established, Doug called the three remaining Lieutenant Commanders to the center of the room for a conference.

"Harris, I'm leaving you in charge. I want this room held until I get back. I'm continuing on alone."

"I can't let you do that, sir. I have specific orders from Commander Rice and Commander Baker, not to leave your side."

"What was Commander Baker's exact words, Lieutenant Commander?" Doug asked with amusement.

"To stick to you like flies on shit, sir."

Doug laughed softly then glared fiercely at the young Lieutenant Commander.

"Harris, I admire your diligence in trying to carry out orders, but on this mission, I outrank both Paul and Joseph, so their orders come second to mine, and I'm ordering you to stay behind. If I have to, I'll make sure that you *can't* follow me. Do we understand each other?"

Harris swallowed hard and nodded his head,

"I had to try, sir. They tried to convince me that since there were *two* of them, their combined rank was higher than yours," he said with a small twitter in his voice.

"I appreciate there sentiments as well as yours, but anyone that comes with me probably won't return," he said ominously, and with that final remark, he left.

CHAPTER 39

ngus glanced at the picture of the Earth that shined in front of him. With every glance came the hope that a man walking on that beautiful planet would send the signal that their mission was a success. At least then the battle could be lost knowing that they died for the greater good. The Admiral had already given up hope of ever seeing the surface of that blue planet again. He never expected to see any home he had ever known again.

Angus looked over the command crew of his ship and felt a momentary pang for the young lives that would be lost. Most of them were still hopeful of a miraculous victory, expecting Doug Taylor to pop out from behind a star and save them at the last moment as he had done so many times before. He admired their idealistic optimism but couldn't share in it. He had seen too much to believe that there was a perfect order that could be attainable in the universe. No matter how hard one tried, chaos and evil would always surge up again and again.

The view screen flashed as another Destructor class cruiser was destroyed by the awesome onslaught of the dreadnought class battle cruisers. The deltas had barely managed to slow one of the monstrosities down, and it seemed to be holding its own with smaller guns designed to protect itself from fighter craft. With the enemy vessels swarming together in a tight formation, the resistance could do little against them. Even running seemed futile since the dreadnought class cruisers were almost as fast as the destructors.

Angus looked at the surviving resistance ships, which was little more than half their starting complement, and strained to think of a way to buy more time. The battle scarred Admiral closed his eyes and prayed for the first time in over ten years. He felt guilty for neglecting all religious duties until he desperately needed a prayer answered, but prayed nonetheless, not for himself, but for the men and women under his command and especially for the one man risking his life against Shaleese on the surface of the Earth.

⊕ ⊕ ⊕ ⊕ ⊕

Despite his belief that Shaleese was overly confident In his regard for his own power, Doug couldn't help but be surprised at the lack of opposition on the way to the throne room. There were no posted sentries, no cyborg guards of any kind, and more importantly, no enemy telepaths to bar the way. The only impediment was the overpowering mind of Shaleese, which emitted intimidating waves of dread and terror. For Doug, these false projected feelings of dread were slightly intimidating at best, but for a lesser telepath it would be an overwhelming deterrent.

Doug stalked through the halls and rooms of the citadel with a growing rage inside of him, which was beginning to build into a roaring crescendo. Instead of trying to repress his anger, he slowly let it build in preparation for his forthcoming encounter with the Overlord. Acting on a sudden impulse, he began emitting a powerful sense of judgment, justice and inexorable resolve to counteract the waves of fear emitted by Shaleese. There wasn't a need for stealth any longer. Shaleese knew someone was coming, and Doug felt a little intimidation of his own was in order.

Casting his particle rifle aside, the Commander headed for the throne room, which was only a few short strides ahead of him. Reaching the throne room door, Doug stepped forward to open the huge iron door which barred the path to his enemy. Again to his surprise, it was unlocked. As Doug pulled on the door, he felt a peculiar sense of dejavous, as if he had walked down the hallway and tried to open this door before. He pushed aside the feeling, considering it a trick of Shaleese to throw him off guard, and stepped into the throne room.

The feeling of nausea he felt as he stepped into the room was overwhelming. His head spun from an uncontrollable vertigo, and he nearly collapsed onto the floor. As suddenly as it had come, the dizziness passed, and Doug stood tall and glanced around the room. At the far end of the room, a wiry man slouched in a large wooden throne raised upon a dais. Doug looked at Shaleese for the first time and was both startled and violently sick.

The man Doug looked upon was a mirror image of himself, his dimensional counterpart. After the initial shock had worn off, Doug's mind began to link together all of the pieces. Everything began to fall into place. The dreams had meaning, and all of the rages he had felt had been from his counterpart, not from the people around him. With this new revelation, Doug felt all of his irrational hatred dissipate, giving his mind a newfound clarity and direction.

Fully regaining his composure, the resistance Commander strode forward with a newfound resolve and determination. The rage toward his adversary was gone, but in its place was the desire to make amends for the evil his doppleganger had inflicted on others. He no longer sought vengeance, only justice and retribution. He no longer felt wrath toward his opponent, but a righteous anger. Shaleese stared at the Commander striding forward toward him, and slowly began to rise. He too knew that an end was coming, but instead of resolve, the Overlord felt turmoil and fear.

Doug could see that his opponent lacked the enhanced physical attributes that he had, but could sense that their minds were equally powerful. Any lack of telepathic power Shaleese had was easily compensated by his greater experience in utilizing his power. The Overlord looked at Doug with conflicting emotions, then finally broke the ominous silence.

"So, I finally meet the plague of my dreams. I should have known that only *I* could be powerful enough to invade my on dreams," he said in a snarling and coarse voice.

"Make no mistake, Shaleese, we are not the same in any way."

"On the contrary, I am what you will become. By destroying me, you destroy your future."

"That's my choice to make. If by some accident I do become as depraved as you, I hope there is another version of me out there that can put an end to me as well. I can't even bear the thought of ever becoming like you."

"It is inevitable. You will learn the value of your power in time."

"The true value of my power is to strive continually for peace and harmony."

"A fool's wish. It can never be attained. But chaos and ruin can. It's the one thing you can depend on."

"I like to think differently. Maybe with enough work the galaxy will be a more peaceful place, even if it isn't totally harmonious. With great power comes great responsibility."

"I prefer the phrase, power corrupts and absolute power corrupts absolutely," he said with a disgusting grin.

"We'll see which wins out today, peace, or chaos."

"You will lose today, as you lost Moira in the battle on New Verdia. I must admit, I felt a little badly when I sensed her death. I've lusted after her for years, but I could never find her until I felt her die."

Doug felt a sharp pang as he was reminded of Moira's death, and in that instant of hesitation, Shaleese struck at him with all the mental force he could muster. Doug raised his shield just in time, but the force of Shaleese's attack nearly broke through his hastily erected barrier. While he was still dazed by the first assault, Shaleese struck again, but this time with a telekinetic punch which threw Doug across the throne room and into the back wall. Doug was barely saved from death by his augmented body structure, but he still had to fight to remain conscious after the incredible blow.

Doug raised his head to see Shaleese pacing forward in a haughty manner, as if he had already won. Above the ringing in his ears, Doug could hear the laughter of Shaleese as the Overlord strode towards him. He had heard the same wicked laughter when he had looked into Cory's memory, the laughter of a masked Shaleese gloating over the young girl as he tormented her in every depraved way possible. Anger rose in him, not like the rages he had felt previously, but a righteous anger that cried out for justice.

Doug mustered all of his strength and struck back at Shaleese with a combined mental blast and telekinetic force that would have crushed a lesser man into a broken heap. Shaleese was prepared for the attack, and was able to deflect it, but he lost the gloating expression on his face as he staggered backwards. The expression was replaced with a look of boiling rage and fury. Doug couldn't even begin to comprehend how powerful that rage must have been. He had only experienced the side effects of what Shaleese was consumed with, not the full rage itself.

Doug staggered to his feet to meet the impending onslaught of the enraged Overlord. Both men struck simultaneously, and the invisible struggle began, but not without visible consequences. The entire throne room rumbled as the telekinetic and psychic forces collided. To an observer who was unaware of the powers at work, it would seem as if an earthquake had struck and the fortress was crumbling in the aftermath of the tremor. The battle was thus compounded by the addition of falling chunks of rock from the collapsing ceiling.

The struggle raged on, and Doug found to his dismay, that he and his opponent were too well matched for a quick and simple victory. The battle could continue for hours until one of them became too exhausted to keep going. Doug knew that his increased stamina and endurance would guarantee his victory, but the resistance wouldn't be able to hold out that long. His thoughts raced to try and find a way to defeat his opponent without sacrificing the entire resistance armada.

As he thought, he felt a presence in his mind. For an instant, he panicked, thinking Shaleese had found a way to circumvent his shield. The thought was instantly dismissed, however, as he recognized the presence. Tears streamed down his eyes as he heard Moira's voice inside his head.

"Remember the combat simulators, my love?"

Doug instantly knew what to do, and continued to weep uncontrollably as he felt the farewell touch of his wife's mind. The emptiness was awful, but the Commander straightened himself to stand tall at his full height as if he were preparing for a cataclysmic blow. Then with careful concentration, he sent out the smallest probing thought he could manage. Shaleese had been prepared for a massive blow, but missed sensing the microscopic probe as it slipped into his mind.

Just as Shaleese realized his danger and was preparing to push the presence back out of his mind, Doug expanded the tightly controlled thread into a roaring beam of force. The resulting damage was fatal for Shaleese. The Overlord screamed in agony as he felt his neural pathways being destroyed at first one by one, then by the score. Even though the Wolf Platoon members in the antechamber were the only people who heard Shaleese's cry of agony, every member of both armies felt the psychic scream of the doomed Overlord.

Doug ceased his merciless assault only when all of what could be called a thinking mind had been erased out of the Overlord's brain. All that was left of the once mighty tyrant was an empty shell that was devoid of active thought on any kind of level. Doug felt it fitting that his counterpart should spend whatever life he had left as a vegetable, similar to one of the countless zombie like cyborgs that he was responsible for creating.

Doug found that he was weaker than he ever would have thought possible. He had fallen to his knees as he was delivering the final blow to Shaleese. Forcing himself back onto his feet, he surveyed the crumbling room. Doug guessed that the throne room of the fortress would collapse soon, and he needed to evacuate the room as soon as possible. Staggering toward the exit, the Commander reached for the comm unit on his battle suit.

"This is Commander Douglas Taylor reporting to all of Wolf Platoon. The mission has been completed. Send out the signal to the armada and wait for my return for immediate extraction," he croaked in a dusty voice.

"Read you loud and clear, Doug. Good to hear your voice," Paul answered.

"Good to hear you too, midget."

※ ※ ※ ※ ※

Angus felt the mental anguish of a powerful telepath, and prayed it wasn't Doug. It felt vaguely like Doug, but he couldn't be certain. The resistance fleet couldn't afford to wait forever, and the Wolf Platoon signal was supposed to be set off once the mission was complete. Hoping against hope that Doug had won the battle, Angus watched tensely for the comm to buzz with activity from the surface of Earth.

As Angus stared at the comm unit, he was startled when the entire board lit up. They were being hailed by every enemy ship, including the dreadnought class ships. The comm officer looked up in surprise.

"Sir! All of the enemy ships are hailing us to signal their surrender!"

"What!? Put the enemy fleet commander on screen!"

"There doesn't seem to be an enemy leader; no one knows who's in charge."

Angus frowned in concentration. Glancing at the comm board once more he noticed that Wolf Platoon's signal was shining as well.

"It looks as if Wolf Platoon has completed its mission. Is it possible that once Shaleese was destroyed, the enemy commanders have lost their courage?"

Johann stood up out of his chair and turned to the admiral.

"Sir, it also might be possible that Shaleese was controlling his subordinates. I doubt his paranoid mind would be very fond of potential traitors in his ranks. I have experienced the Ryeesian version of a mind controlling device and have felt what it was like to be freed from their control. Those former enemies are feeling confused, frightened, and probably revolted at what their memories tell them they have done."

Angus considered the possibility of all of Shaleese's generals and admirals being under his control. Even if it were possible, it would be extremely inefficient to have only one view on every tactical decision, and only one line of thinking without objections. It made perfect sense that someone obsessed with power would want to share that power even for something as beneficial as a second point of view. Then he suddenly laughed out loud, startling his entire crew and distressing several others into thinking he had finally cracked under the pressures of command.

"Tell all craft to cease fire, and we'll sort this out. It makes sense, though, in an insane sort of way. And we all know that Shaleese wasn't sane. Tell Doug and the rest of Wolf Platoon to get back here as quick as possible, before our new prisoners have a sudden relapse and ruin my wonderful victory."

CHAPTER 40

Wolf Platoon had returned to the Gladiator victorious, and was welcomed by the entire crew of the enormous battle cruiser. Most of them were at a celebration on the recreation deck in honor of Wolf Platoon. Doug tried to smile as the overjoyed crew members thanked them again and again, but he couldn't get over the presence of Moira's mind that he had felt. He had tried to contact her several times on the shuttle ride back to the Gladiator, but was unsuccessful. The mere memory of her brief contact with him in the throne room caused him to start crying every time he thought about it. He was also plagued with the knowledge that Shaleese had been his counterpart. The thought that there was even the potential of becoming like Shaleese was revolting. Cory's memories may have been erased, but Doug knew what Shaleese, or rather he himself in a way, had done to the poor girl and countless others.

Joseph, Paul, and Jenny were the only people Doug had let in on the true nature of Shaleese. They had pledged their silence before he could even ask them to keep it a secret. Somehow, it no longer seemed important anyway. Doug intended to tell Angus and McIntyre as well, but he felt that could wait until the journey back to New Haven was over.

The festive moment was spoiled only by the news of General Richards' unstable condition, and Doug was saddened even more than he had originally been. The only joy Doug could find was in the knowledge that Cory was safe and happily engaged with a computer game in one of the alcoves of the recreation deck. Whenever he looked at her he felt like he had regained his family in some small way. Cory was equally glad to have Doug as her protector. Even though the memories of Shaleese's torments had been wiped from her mind, she was uneasy around anyone but Doug and some of the members of Wolf Platoon who had saved her.

The return voyage was delayed for several days since Shaleese's generals had no idea of what to do next. Most of them were too grief stricken over what they had done while under the influence of the Overlord to function. Angus spent the first two days after the victory trying to sort through all of the confusion and, with the help of Doug, erasing the memories of the generals who accepted the proposal of a fresh start.

The cyborgs were a completely different problem. No one wanted the smelly zombies, and there wasn't anyway to repair their ruined minds. The dilemma was finally solved when several of Shaleese's generals agreed to take care of all of the cyborgs as a means of restitution for their past deeds, even if they weren't considered responsible for the hideous acts.

After five days, all of the battles' aftermath had been dealt with, and the resistance headed home with the newly appropriated dreadnought class cruisers at the front of the fleet. Doug, and the rest of the command crew of Wolf Platoon, were placed on one of the dreadnoughts since Doug was needed to command one of the vast ships. Cory accompanied them because she was afraid to be separated from what she considered her family. Doug felt her particular attachment to him comforting and disturbing at the same time. She was completely helpless without someone she trusted near her, and Doug feared that the damage done to her by Shaleese might prove to be permanent. Not to mention that he was the counterpart of Shaleese, which meant she could still sub consciously think of Doug as a controling master instead of a father figure.

Doug spent most of his off duty time with Joseph, Paul, and Jenny. The four of them worked with Cory, trying to help the process of healing as best they could. Cory adored the attention, but would often burst into tears for no reason, and then tell whichever member of her adopted family that was near how much she loved them over and over again. Everyone was understanding; they knew that she simply wasn't used to affection of any sort other than the perversities of Shaleese. Eventually, Cory felt more confident around other people, and the episodes of mood swings decreased.

Doug continually thought of what would happen when the dimensional split was collapsed back into a singular dimension. No one was certain what the new dimension would be like, or even if they would exist in the new dimension. Doug's primary fear was that he would eventually become like his counterpart in this dimension. He was determined to remember the events that had taken place so that he would always know what had to be avoided at all costs. He hoped that the pain he felt for Moira's loss wouldn't be as intense as it currently was, but knew that it would be better to remember her than to forget he had ever known her.

The dimensional collapse was scheduled for one year after the fall of Shaleese. The only people who were even aware of the problem were sworn to secrecy. If it became general knowledge, it would undoubtedly cause a wide spread panic. Kaufman had proved to be a thorn in the Council's side when he continually demanded that the collapsing date be moved to a later date. He finally made the mistake of threatening to go public with the news of the collapse, and was promptly ejected from the Council and incarcerated for insubordination. The charges were weak, but no one seemed to care, except for Kaufman.

With the war against Shaleese over, the Council began to go through the motions of setting up a new government, even though they knew it wouldn't matter after the collapse. No one wanted to dwell on the dimensional collapsing date, so the political jousting involved in the governmental set up also acted as a necessary preoccupation for the Council members. New Haven was declared the capital planet in the new human government, and its lands were divided and allocated to anyone who wanted to settle there. The heroes of the war were naturally given first choice, and Doug settled on the southernmost part of the main continent of New Haven. The majority of Wolf

Platoon followed their Commander's example and settled near him, forming the oddly named Wolf City.

Paul and Jenny lived near Doug, and the three of them adopted Cory, with Doug acting as the legal guardian of Cory if anything should happen to Paul or Jenny. Doug was kept busy with the problems of the dimensional collapse, with which he collaborated continuously with McIntyre. Eventually, all was ready, and they waited only for the day to arrive when they would set their plan in motion.

When the time had come for the dimensional collapse to take place, all of Wolf Platoon, and several other close companions of Doug joined together for a farewell party. No one wanted to think of how much would change when the collapse took place, so the subject was avoided. Instead of dwelling on the fact that they might never see one another again, they spent the evening learning a new game that Doug had devised which made telepathic cheating impossible.

After the game was over, McIntyre challenge Doug to a drinking contest, with Doug drinking a highly alcoholic beverage, which tasted terrible, that McIntyre had made to compensate for his physical advantages. The contest became a high stakes gambling fest, with large sums placed on both contestants. Everyone was disappointed when the two drinkers called a mutual draw and went off singing tunes that were badly off key.

The following day dawned bright and cheery, promising a pleasant day filled with a warm sun and cool breezes. No one ever knew whether that day was pleasant or not. The collapse was scheduled to take place at ten o'clock Central New

Haven time, and most of the Council was present to watch as McIntyre activated the collapsing device. The last man to be added to the Council stood next to a young girl with bright blue eyes, and watched as the machine was activated.

For an instant, everything in the room swirled together. There seemed to be a green meadow, a barren landscape of gray stones, empty space with thousands of stars shining in the distance, and a total blackness in the room all at once. People that were in the room disappeared and others took their place, then the original people reappeared again supplanting the former ones. Finally a bright light flashed, and everything was dark and cold.

⁕ ⁕ ⁕ ⁕ ⁕

Doug awoke in a cold sweat. His head was throbbing with pain as he sat up in wonder. Everything that he remembered to have happened seemed like a dream, except for the lonely emptiness, which was still with him, but greatly diminished to a remote ache. Looking around his familiar apartment room, he noticed a few things that he didn't remember seeing before. A wrestling trophy, several Irish beer steins, and an antique dresser that seemed totally out of place in the otherwise modern style apartment.

He finally noticed that his body was as muscular as it had been on New Haven. He remembered everything that had taken place during his long adventure, and he sat back onto his bed as he realized that he might be the only person on Earth that remembered what had taken place. Getting up, he searched his entire apartment for any potential changes in scenery. The only major change he found was a painful one. He noticed a picture of Moira on one of the end tables, then realized that it couldn't be *his* Moira, but the girl of this new dimension, whatever her name might be.

He turned away from the picture as the sight of it brought back the image of his wife's death. Suddenly, he felt a peculiar twinge in his head as the pain he felt upon awakening intensified. Then like a dam bursting, he became aware of another presence that was with him, and yet was somehow a part of him as well. His heart leapt for joy. As he considered what it might mean, his phone rang. He ran to answer it, breaking through a door in the process.

"Hello?" he answer in a quavering voice.

"Doug? It,...It's Moira."

Doug felt elated beyond his wildest dreams, he knew in his heart that it was the same Moira he had lost, somehow returned to him like a miracle. He sent out the familiar mental embrace to her through the bond that had reappeared, and was rewarded with a return embrace.

"It is you. I was afraid it might have been a dream," she said with a tearful voice.

"Well, we have some catching up to do. Where are you? I'm coming to see you, and then I'm never letting you out of my sight again."

"I'm on my way to you already, I have a cell phone in my car, well, I do now. Do you still live in the same apartment?"

"Yes, well, no… I really don't know, but I can feel where you are. Turn left at the next road and follow it around the curve. It's a short cut; then look into your rearview mirror so I can see you more clearly."

Nothing could have stopped either Doug or Moira from seeing each other as soon as possible. Doug nearly pulled his apartment door off its hinges when he sensed her pull into the parking lot. Moira raced from her car even as Doug dashed into the parking lot, and they met together at the foot of the front steps. Sweeping Moira into his arms, Doug carried her to his apartment letting his mind join with hers to share all that had happened to him while they were apart.

Afraid that it was a dream, Doug held Moira close to him, inhaling the sweet fragrance of her hair deeply. Not needing speech to understand each other, they communicated with each other telepathically, caressing each other both physically and mentally. Moira had been absent from Doug's life for nearly a year, and although she had been dead in dimension Alpha one, she had never truly left her husband.

Doug felt her thoughts taking shape inside of his head. His entire being swelled with love and sheer joy. Neither of the two lovers had ever felt such completion, not even before their separation.

"I was watching over you the whole time, my love, and if it helps any, I shared your pain. I was with you, but I couldn't feel your presence."

"You were with me on Earth when I fought Shaleese, weren't you love?" He said, his mental voice thick with emotion.

"Yes dear, I was with you, and I always will be from now on. In this life and the next. If you ever lose me again, just remember that I'll be waiting for you."

"I won't ever let you leave me again. I'll die before I let you get hurt again, and then I'll wait for you."

Tears rolled down both of their faces as they kissed. Their life would be different, but as long as they were together nothing else mattered. Ryeesian's could try to attack the planet, but as long as Doug and Moira had each other the Earth would never fall to the insectoid aliens. Only time would tell if the Ryeesians would even come to the small blue planet.

THE END